TIGER SHRIMP

Tango

TIM DORSEY

TIGER SHRIMP
Jango

wm
WILLIAM MORROW
An Imprint of HarperCollins*Publishers*

TIGER SHRIMP TANGO. Copyright © 2014 by Tim Dorsey. All rights reserved. Printed in the United States of America. No part of this book may be used or reproduced in any manner whatsoever without written permission except in the case of brief quotations embodied in critical articles and reviews. For information address HarperCollins Publishers, 10 East 53rd Street, New York, NY 10022.

HarperCollins books may be purchased for educational, business, or sales promotional use. For information please e-mail the Special Markets Department at SPsales@harpercollins.com.

FIRST EDITION

Designed by Rosa Chae

Library of Congress Cataloging-in-Publication Data has been applied for.

ISBN 978-0-06-209281-6

14 15 16 17 18 OV/RRD 10 9 8 7 6 5 4 3 2 1

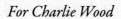

For Charlie Wood

This world is a comedy to those that think,
a tragedy to those that feel.

HORATIO WALPOLE

TIGER SHRIMP

Prologue

MIDNIGHT

The naked couple ran screaming out of the hotel, covered with fire-extinguisher foam.

Which didn't attract much attention in Fort Lauderdale.

A window on the top floor shattered. Broken glass rained down from the high-rise, followed by a toilet-tank lid that exploded in the street.

It became quiet.

The nude pair wiped chemical-retardant foam from their eyes and stared down at the broken shards scattered at their feet.

The quiet didn't last.

Another window shattered. Then another, and another. Toilet-tank lids flying everywhere and crashing in the street like a drumroll. More naked, foamy people dashed outside.

People began to notice. Police and fire trucks arrived. TV vans.

Two men nonchalantly strolled up the noisy sidewalk through ceramic chunks and suds.

"The key to my new life as a private detective is ultra-sensitive powers of observation," Serge told Coleman. "You must be able to detect the tiniest out-of-place detail . . ."

A hysterical mob ran by, scratching slippery breasts and buttocks.

"Most people walk through life without ever noticing the little clues all around that something's not right."

Another toilet lid crashed in front of them and Serge pulled a porcelain splinter from his arm. "In Florida, you just have to filter out the background weirdness."

MIAMI

The name's Mahoney. I get lied to for a living. The sign on the door says I'm a private eye, but I mainly keep bartenders and bookies in business.

My best friends—a rumpled fedora and bottle of rye—sat silently on my desk, waiting anxiously for the next case like a weasel-beater in a peep-show booth with incorrect change.

The day began like any other, except it was a Tuesday, not the other six. One of those pleasant days, real nice, right up until it kicks you in the Adam's apple like a transvestite in stilettos. The air coming through my window was heavy with heat, humidity and double crosses.

Down on the street, people's lives bounce off one another like eight balls in Frankie's billiard joint, until one of them lands in the corner pocket of my office. They pay two hundred clams up front to spill their guts about frame jobs, missing identical twins and alimony. Most of them just stink up my oxygen with alibis that are as shaky as an analogy that doesn't fit.

But this next one was a broad. She knocked on my door like knuckles hitting wood. I told her to have a seat and gave her a hankie. She blew her nose like a British ambulance, and her sob story had more twists than a dragon parade in Chinatown. But I have a soft spot for the farmer's-daughter types who take a wrong turn out of the dairy barn and end up in Palooka-ville. This dame didn't know from vice cops on the take for back-alley knobbers, which meant not having that uncomfortable conversation again, and that was jake by me.

My gut said this bird was on the level. She had no priors, skeletons or known associates. A regular Betty Crocker life in the burbs. It all started simple enough with an out-of-the-blue phone call from some mug she'd never heard of. An odd kind of threat. Clearly a wrong number. And some easy green for me. I planned on dishing it for the usual kickback to an off-duty cop named McClusky who put the arm on such jokers to knock off the funny stuff, and I'd still have time to make the eighth race at Gulfstream.

The joker had other ideas . . .

B rook Campanella strolled out the front steps of an office building on the Miami River. A ton of weight lifted from her shoulders. Brook had debated hiring a private eye, but she felt so much better now after her conversation with Mahoney.

Brook wasn't concerned about herself. It was her father. The ominous phone call had been for him, and he couldn't make sense of it either. Brook was a loving daughter with straight A's in community college. She chose to stay at home after her mother died and take care of her dad in his retirement. They couldn't have led more boring lives. Then this brief, electronic intrusion into their world changed everything. Her dad was too old for the stress, so Brook took the reins and flipped yellow pages.

Yes, it had to be some kind of mistake just like Mahoney said. And he promised to take care of it.

She smiled for the first time in an eternity and climbed into her VW Beetle.

Within days, her father would be dead, their house ransacked, and a cop involved in the case—as Mahoney phrased it—would "have caught a case of lead poisoning courtesy of Smith & Wesson."

Brook's life shattered again. Who was doing all this, and why?

She was still thinking those thoughts right up until she vanished off the face of the earth.

Not voluntarily, according to police. They found signs of a struggle and her abandoned VW.

She was in the wind.

Chapter ONE

Police stood in a solemn circle. If they'd forgotten how much blood a human body holds, they were reminded.

State Road 60 is one of those great old Florida drives. From Tampa on the west coast to Vero Beach on the east, rolling through Mulberry and Bartow and Yeehaw Junction. Phosphate mines and orange groves and cows loitering near water holes in vast open flats dotted with sabal palms, stretching for miles, making the sky big. Here and there were the kind of occasional, isolated farmhouses that made people subconsciously think: *Do they get Internet?* In the middle of one overgrown field stood a single concrete wall, several stories high, covered with grime and mildew, the ancient ruins of a drive-in theater. The top of the wall was the last thing to catch a warm glow from the setting sun.

Standing in another field were the cops, taking notes in the waning light. Forensic cameras flashed. Two detectives glanced at each other and simultaneously raised knowing eyebrows. The extremely deceased victim lay on his back. He had been sliced wide, abdomen to throat, and none too carefully. All internal organs missing. Well, not *missing,* just not where they were supposed to be. Gloved crime-scene techs reached into the surrounding grass, collecting strewn kidneys and liver and something that would be labeled "unidentified."

"If I wasn't standing here, I'd swear this was staged with fake props." The detective bent down for closer inspection. "Like a horror movie."

"One thing's for sure," said the second detective. "We've got ourselves a case of severe overkill, which means it was a crime of passion."

The first detective stood up again. "I can't even begin to think what kind of weapon did this."

"Weapon? Singular?" replied his partner. "I'd say we've got everything from a machete to spiked clubs and concrete saws."

They both looked back across several hundred yards of grazing land, toward where they had pulled off State Road 60 near the drive-in. Sparse traffic began turning on headlights. "What kind of sick—"

An out-of-breath corporal ran over. "Sir, I think we have an ID on the victim." He pointed over his shoulder. "Found his wallet behind that palm." A shaking hand held out the driver's license.

The first detective grabbed it and squinted. Then his eyes widened. "Roscoe Nash? Not from the newspaper articles."

"The same," said the corporal.

The detective made a two-fingered whistle to get everyone's attention. "Listen up. I just learned who our special guest is here. Roscoe Nash. And I've changed my assessment of the attack. The killer didn't go far enough."

They all formed a circle and looked down again, laughing heartily.

THE PREVIOUS MORNING

A jet-black 1978 Firebird Trans Am drove past the state fairgrounds east of Tampa. The original Phoenix bird design that covered the hood had been painted over with a winged skull. The wings were in the shape of Florida.

Coleman pulled deeply from a bong he'd fashioned out of colorful hamster tubes.

Serge glanced over from the driver's seat. "You realize there's a hamster out there not getting his exercise."

Coleman raised his head and exhaled. "No, he's still in there."

Serge's neck jerked back. "You left the hamster in your bong? Why on earth would you do something so disturbing?"

"So the little fella can get righteously baked!" Coleman twisted apart the tubing and tapped his furry little friend out into his lap. "Ow! He bit me!"

"Serves you right."

"Naw, he's just got a mondo case of the munchies." Coleman reached in a bag of Doritos and held out a chip. "See how fast he snatched it from my hand?"

"What next for the poor animal? LSD?"

"I considered it," said Coleman. "But he'd need to be around others of his kind who are more experienced for a soothing environment to avoid a bad trip. And of course I'd have to take the running wheel out of his cage because no good can ever come from that on acid."

"I got a crazy thought," said Serge. "How about not giving drugs to rodents in the first place?"

"Then what's the point?"

"What do you mean, what— Just forget it." Serge looked this way and that. "Where'd he go?"

"Under my seat. I set him free to explore." Coleman packed the bowl again. "If I was that small, that's where I'd like to be."

Serge momentarily closed his eyes with a deep sigh.

"Serge?"

"What!"

"Explain to me again about our new job."

"Okay, listen carefully for the fifth time." Serge took his hands off the wheel and rubbed his palms together. "I've decided to totally re-dedicate my entire life to being a private eye. Your life, too."

"Is this like all your other rededications?"

"No!" Serge pounded his fist on the dash. "Those were all spur-of-the-moment impulsive flights of silliness. Like my last idiotic idea of becoming a house hunter. Where's the challenge?"

"You don't even need a very accurate gun."

"But this is completely different. This time it's bone-deep, the whole reason I was placed on earth. I've been putting a tremendous amount of contemplation into it."

"For how long?"

"About a half hour since we finished watching that detective movie back at the motel."

"Which movie?"

"Coleman, it was the highest-grossing detective movie ever filmed in Florida."

"You mean *Ace Ventura: Pet Detective*?"

Serge winced and hit the dash again. "That's why we must become private eyes. Maybe they'll make a movie about our dashing exploits and fix that blasphemy."

"Where are we going to get our cases?"

"I'm thinking Mahoney." Serge ran a red light and waved "sorry" to honking drivers. "Now that he's opened his own detective agency in Miami, our timing couldn't be more perfect."

Coleman took the bong from his mouth. "Mahoney talks funny."

"I can't get enough of his Spillane-Mitchum-Hammett patter," said Serge. "And he's carved out a nice little niche for himself: helping the victims of scam artists. There are thousands of dupes out there who are either too embarrassed to go to the police, or if they do report the cons, they find out no laws were broken because they did something stupid and gullible."

"Gullible?"

"Coleman, did you know the word *gullible* is not in the dictionary?"

"Really?"

"Jesus, Coleman. It *is* in the dictionary, right next to your picture."

"Really?"

Serge shook his head to clear the dumbness in the car. "Anyway, word's starting to get out about Mahoney. When there's no place else for victims to go, they go to Mahoney. He's been able to make a number of impressive asset recoveries for his clients, but I'm sure I can amp that success rate by persuading the less cooperative miscreants who won't listen to reason. Because I'm a people person."

"You said thousands of victims?"

Serge nodded hard. "Florida is the scam capital of the nation, a perpetual daisy chain of old and fresh schemes that boggle the imagination. Ponzis, odometer fraud, counterfeit paintings, foreign lotteries, priceless costume jewelry, bodies stacked in single graves that are resold, repair your credit, learn to dance better, stuff envelopes at home for three hundred dollars an hour, get that new-look cosmetic surgery by a doctor who blows town when the job is only half done, leaving your face with that new 'Picasso' look. One dude mass-mailed fake dry-cleaning bills to restaurants for soup that was never spilled. But the amounts were so small, a bunch of them just paid, and the guy made a killing. Other brazen crooks waltz into low-end mortgage offices with fake ID and documents to take out equity loans on homes they don't own. Someone else sold hole-in-one insurance."

"What's that?"

"Charities are always holding fund-raisers with fantastic contests like sinking a basketball from half court for fifty thousand dollars. Of course they can't pay because they're charities and it would dampen the fund-raiser. So it's very common in the insurance industry to offer single-day policies against potential long-shot winners. In Florida, with all the golf courses, it's holes-in-one. So this grifter exclusively sold such insurance, undercutting all the legit companies, and whenever someone hit a hole-in-one, he'd dissolve the company and move on. The scams never end in this state, and that's why there's gold in them thar streets for us and Mahoney."

Coleman inspected a fingertip for something that had come out of his nose. "Does this mean you're not going to have any more Secret Master Plans?"

"Au contraire," said Serge. "This detective business is part of the biggest Secret Master Plan yet. That's why we've driven back to Tampa. We have to attend the Republican National Convention."

"Sounds boring."

"Except it's anything but," said Serge. "Especially with Tropical Storm Isaac bearing down with gale-force situation comedy. And if I'm really lucky, I might run into Sarah Palin so I can help her out."

"Why?"

"Because the woman of my dreams has fallen on hard times," said Serge. "Last time I saw her, it was at a distance on TV in a department store, and she apparently has been reduced to working behind the counter at a Chick-fil-A."

"But how does the convention fit in with your private-detective Master Plan?"

"If you're going to do something, do it big! Be the best in your field!" said Serge. "And some of the highest-paid private eyes are political investigators. They come in two types: campaign detectives that dig up dirt on candidates, and stock-market detectives who try to figure out how an upcoming congressional vote is going to swing before it's cast."

"So you're just in it for the money?"

"That's gravy," said Serge, sticking a CD in the stereo. "People in this country are at one another's throats like no time since the Vietnam War. Which brings up the main objective of my new Master Plan: to reunite the country."

The radio: *". . . O beautiful for spacious skies . . ."*

"I don't know about that." Coleman exhaled another hit. "People are getting pretty crazy out there."

"Only because they haven't heard my solutions." Serge waved his left hand around like he was writing on an invisible blackboard. "The current political climate has become psychotically polarized and nobody can figure it out . . ."

". . . God shed his grace on thee . . ."

". . . But it's as simple as choosing up teams in a school yard. You want to be on the side with your friends. It's the most basic human emotion, to be accepted and loved. I just have to convince the country we're all on the same side, then we all hug and begin spreading brotherhood..."

"And sisterhood," said Coleman.

"Right. I need to watch more *Glee*," said Serge. "And spread sisterhood..."

"*...From sea to shining sea!...*"

"But how do you plan to convince everyone we're on the same side?"

"Instead of being slaves to our toxic emotional times, we harness that outrage," said Serge. "So we just change the national slogan from 'Land of the Free' to 'Fuck Canada.'"

Coleman nodded. "I think everyone can get behind that."

"Because it's the American way."

Coleman cracked a beer, then inserted an eyedropper and drew ale up into the bulb. "What gave you this whole idea?"

"TV." The Trans Am turned sharply onto Orient Road. "I was watching the Tea Party and the Occupiers on the news and I said to myself, 'Serge, you can bring these people together, no problem.'"

Coleman held the eyedropper down toward the floor. "They hate each other's guts."

"That's just frustration talking." Serge pulled the Firebird up to a compound of buildings with vertical slit windows and spooled razor wire. "Take the Tea Party. I get it. They're a playground team with staunch work ethics and sincere values, and they're sick of watching all these lazy, political clowns throw away their hard-earned tax dollars. On the other hand are the Occupiers, the other playground team who's furious that the top one percent hire a bunch of lobbyists to bribe those same clowns and tilt the chessboard."

Coleman squeezed drops into the hamster's mouth. "Please continue."

"The two groups should be ultimate allies." Serge raised binoculars toward a back gate where an electric signal snapped a sequence of locks open. "It just gets lost in the slight nuance between how the two groups deliver their respective messages."

"How's that?"

"The Tea Party draws Hitler mustaches on pictures of the president."

"And the Occupiers?"

"They shit in public parks," said Serge. "It's such a fine line."

"I could join that last group," said Coleman.

"You're already an honorary member."

Serge continued his surveillance. A just-released prisoner signed some paperwork at the gates and began walking away from the Hillsborough Correctional Center.

Coleman leaned out the window. "Is this the county jail?"

"Yes, next question."

"Can we leave?" Coleman placed the hamster on his shoulder and glanced around. "I'm getting paranoid parked outside this place."

"Then lower the bong." Serge kept his eyes trained out the driver's side.

The former prisoner reached the end of the jail's driveway. They'd given him back his street clothes, but he still had the red plastic band around his wrist. Misdemeanors wore blue. He turned up the street, heading for the nearest bus stop, which wasn't near.

Serge rolled down his window. "Roscoe! Roscoe Nash!"

The man on the edge of the road turned around. "Who the fuck are you?"

"The person that just bailed you out. Hop in."

Roscoe was tall and lean, much like Serge, but a few years senior. Running down both arms were tattoos of defunct Roller Derby franchises. He approached the driver's side and rested folded arms on the window ledge. "Why'd you bail me out?"

"Because I have a business proposition. We run a profitable little cottage industry, except we're currently heavy on the muscle end and light on white-collar know-how."

Roscoe grinned contemptuously. "And that's where I come in?"

Serge opened his door and leaned his seat forward. "Climb in."

"Why should I?"

"Because it's hot and a long walk. I'll flesh it out as we drive. You don't like the sound of it, we shake hands and split. Worst case is you get a free ride home."

Roscoe climbed in the backseat with a condescending smirk.

Serge closed the door and patched out.

Roscoe's eye caught something. "What's with the hamster?"

"His name's Skippy," said Coleman.

"He's sliding off your shoulder."

Coleman gently boosted Skippy back onto his perch. "He's a little fucked up."

"What?" said Roscoe.

Serge snapped his fingers in the air. "Eyes over here. Pay no attention to Coleman, or we'll be talking in circles for days..." Serge drained a travel mug of coffee in one long guzzle and floored the gas. "Here's my proposition..." He popped a Neil Diamond CD in the stereo.

"... *They're coming to America!...*"

Serge turned around and smiled huge at Roscoe. "You like this country? Good! I *love* this country! And the two sides are *so* close: scribbling on the president's photo, wiping your ass with leaves, what's the difference? That's what I say. Get my drift? What's Canada's fuckin' deal?..."

Roscoe's eyes grew big as he grabbed his seat belt with white knuckles. "Jesus, you almost sideswiped that oncoming dump truck."

"I did?"

"Turn around!" yelled Roscoe. "Watch where you're going!"

"Absolutely not," said Serge. "I drive like this all the time."

Coleman exhaled a bong hit and petted the hamster. "He does."

"That's right," said Serge. "I stay in my lane by watching out the back window to gauge my deviation from the center line. And Coleman lets me know when the intersections come up."

"But—"

"Smile!" Serge snapped some photos of Roscoe, who blinked from the camera flashes.

"Intersection," said Coleman.

Serge turned around and slammed on the brakes, skidding through another red light.

"Coleman, you were late again."

"I was busy."

"Busy packing a bong." Serge shook his head. "Driving is an important responsibility. I'm becoming concerned about your recklessness."

A hand was raised in the backseat. "I'd like to get out of the car now, please."

"But you're not home yet," said Serge.

"Would you like to hold Skippy?" asked Coleman.

Roscoe bent forward. "This isn't the way to my house."

"Because I wanted to stop and show you something that will explain my proposition." Serge pulled over on the side of a remote, wooded road. "What's fair is fair: I'm giving you a lift, so you owe me a shot at my best sales pitch."

"What is it?"

"You'll find out soon enough." Serge opened his door. "Just follow me around to the back bumper."

"Uh, this wouldn't be some kind of trick, would it?"

"Trick? No, no, no, no, no!" Serge inserted the key. "It's just the trunk of a car. What could possibly go wrong?"

Chapter TWO

MEANWHILE . . .

Another typical sidewalk café in sunny Florida.

This one sat along tony Worth Avenue in Palm Beach, the non-working-capital *capital* of the United States.

A second round of mimosas arrived a few minutes before ten A.M. The bistro sat between two piano bars—and atop the world of international culinary acclaim. Although others had come close, the café had attained its rarefied reputation by pushing the edge further than anyone previously dared: a complete menu of entrées consisting entirely of a single bite of food standing upright in the middle of a large white plate. But on this particular morning, panic swept the restaurant as news reached the kitchen that two competing teams of master chefs in Paris and Berlin were secretly racing to develop the half bite of food.

Across the street, sidewalk people strolled with cashmere sweaters, purse dogs and wind-tunnel face-lifts. For the window-shopper-with-everything: perfume and crystal, Swiss watches and Persian rugs, Armani and Vuitton. Six galleries featured trending artists, two banks contained only oversize safety-deposit boxes and one place rented diamonds by the hour.

The mimosas were for a jet-setting young couple in aloof sunglasses. Actually, only he was a jet-setter, and she was just lucky. Courtney Styles had received her degree from Florida State a month earlier, and her wealthy uncle offered her use of their beach place since it was off-season. You know, to help her out while job-hunting after graduation. Except she was man-hunting. And what better place?

Courtney got her first strike within an hour. And she wasn't even trying, just standing on the corner, idly gazing at pictures in the window of a yacht brokerage.

"You like ze boats?"

"What?" She hadn't even seen him approach, but hot damn. His suit alone cost more than her car. Gold Rolex, heartthrob foreign accent and a long sexy mane like in those photos that they show you when you go to get a haircut but it never works out that way. Courtney gulped. "Why? Do you have a boat?"

"Oui." The man shrugged offhandedly. "A few."

She gulped again and offered her hand. "My name's Courtney."

He leaned and kissed it. "I'm Gustave."

She got the jelly legs, but recovered before toppling over.

"Is Courtney all right?"

She nodded with embarrassment. "Just a little hungry."

"Zat is wonderful." He placed his palms together in front of his chin like he was praying. "I know zis great little spot. Everyone is talking about their new menu."

And that's how they came to be sitting across from each other under an umbrella, plowing through mimosas in goldfish bowls. Courtney was still acclimating to Palm Beach. She looked up curiously at the royal-blue awning over the café's facade, and the name, which was simply ".".

Gustave saw the question in her look and smiled. "Ah, yes. Zee name of zee restaurant. Very hip, very now."

"It's just a period. How do you pronounce it?"

"You get ready to start a sentence. And then zee sentence is over."

"You don't say anything?" asked Courtney.

"And yet it says *everything*," replied Gustave. "All zee right people will know exactly what you mean."

Moments later, their meals arrived. Gustave placed a napkin in his lap. "What do you think?"

Courtney tilted her head at a small, vertical sprig of seared blowfish from the Azores. "They let us try a sample first?"

"No, zat is the meal."

"Seriously?"

"Zee best on zee island."

Courtney smiled with semi-acceptance and picked up a fork. "I'd love to see their appetizers."

"Oh, you absolutely must try zee shrimp cocktail. It is zee best. Tiger shrimp." Gustave turned and snapped his fingers. *"Garçon!..."*

Soon, a waiter placed an appetizer in front of Courtney. "What's this?"

"Your shrimp cocktail."

"It's a microscope," said Courtney.

"Shrimp molecules."

She sat back in puzzlement. "Is this some kind of joke?"

Gustave laughed heartily. "Yes, a joke. It is what you call . . . a gimmick. All fine restaurants must now have a delightful sense of whimsy. Not take themselves too seriously. Life is but a dream." He waved a hand dismissively toward the waiter, who briskly removed the scientific instrument.

"So he's bringing my shrimp cocktail now?"

Gustave shook his head. "There is no shrimp cocktail."

"Oh, I'm starting to get it now. When you order a shrimp cocktail, they *don't* bring you a shrimp cocktail."

"Very chic."

Courtney raised her eyebrows and grinned. *He better be loaded.* "I have much to learn about Palm Beach."

"And Gustave will show you." He picked up his fork for the first time and finished his meal. "Would you like to take a drive with me?"

Courtney finished her own meal. "You have a car nearby?"

Gustave glanced at the opposite curb.

She choked. "A Bentley."

"We will drive south along the shore, like zee Côte d'Azur."

"Uh, okay."

A cell phone rang. Gustave checked the number and stood. "Pardon me while I take zis. It is Brussels." He went inside the café to escape traffic noise.

Courtney picked up the most recent mimosa in both hands and gulped.

The bubbles started getting to her. The waiter strolled up with aplomb. "Would madam like another?"

She nodded with a crooked smile and handed him the empty glass orb.

Her next drink was half gone when she strained to peer inside the dark restaurant. *Why is that phone call taking so long?* She got up and tentatively stepped inside.

The waiter approached. "May I help you with something?"

She craned her neck to look past him into the narrow diner. "Have you seen Gustave?"

"You mean the gentleman you were dining with?"

She nodded and glanced around.

"Not since he was sitting with you out there," said the waiter. "He isn't inside the restaurant."

"What?" said Courtney. "But I saw him come in here to take a call. And there's no way he could have come out without me seeing him."

The bartender overheard. "If you're talking about the French guy with the cell phone, I saw him go in the restroom."

"How long ago?"

"Fifteen minutes, give or take."

Now the maître d' overheard. He turned to the waiter. "Jerry, go check."

"Oh, thank you," said Courtney. The maître d' smiled warmly, but she misread his intentions.

Jerry returned, shaking his head. "Empty."

"But that's not possible," said Courtney.

The bartender wiped a glass. "There's a back exit."

"But he couldn't have left," said Courtney. "His car is still out front."

"Which one?" asked the bartender.

"The Bentley."

"That's not his," said the bartender.

"How do you know?"

"Because it belongs to the von Zurenburgs." The bartender hung the dry glass in an overhead rack. "Old money. You've heard of shoelaces?"

Even the waiter was impressed. "You don't mean *the* shoelaces."

The bartender slowly picked up another wet glass and peered sideways with a glare that said, *You're starting to ask some dangerous questions.*

Courtney glanced back and forth with a near laugh. "What's going on?"

Everyone stood silent.

She turned around. "Why are you all looking at me like that?"

More quiet.

She closed her eyes a moment. *Oh, no.* Then opened them again.

"Ma'am," said the maître d'. "There is still the matter of the check."

Courtney sighed in resignation. "How much?"

It was not the Palm Beach Way to say such numbers aloud. He handed her a small leather folder and raised flared nostrils to deliberately expose unsettling dark bristles inside.

"Six hundred and ninety-three dollars!" she blurted. "For two bites of food and a few mimosas?"

"And a shrimp cocktail."

TAMPA

A vintage Firebird rolled through noon sun on Busch Boulevard, named for the famous brewery that had since been shuttered. But still operating nearby was the theme park.

Serge stopped across the street and checked his watch to see how long until Busch Gardens closed for the night.

"Serge, I think the idea about Canada is good and all, but I don't think it's enough to stop all the fighting."

"It's not." Serge stared across the street with binoculars. "The second part of my Master Plan to reinstate domestic peace is one simple word: Music!"

"Oh, yeah," said Coleman. "That's how they settle all serious shit on *Glee*."

"The Tea Party and the Occupiers are simply different twists on Parrot Heads and Dead Heads. At first impression, the Parrot Heads see a bunch of filthy people with bare feet and think, 'Get a job.' And the Dead Heads see all these wacky tropical hats and Buffett-licensed apparel and think, 'Get a life.' But the overwhelming common ground is obvious."

Coleman petted his hamster. "They both like music?"

"If we can just sit them down and listen to a mash-up of 'Margaritaville' and 'Casey Jones,' we're halfway home."

Coleman nodded. "Tequila and cocaine. I like it."

"You're missing the point. This is about uniting our fractured nation, and I've come up with a unifying theory to explain all human behavior and achieve this harmony: the Empathy Continuum."

"What's empathy?"

"The ability to feel others' vibes and follow the Golden Rule—"

Banging from the trunk.

"Son of a bitch!" Serge jumped from the car and popped the rear hood—*"Shut the fuck up!"*—viciously striking the gagged-and-hog-tied Roscoe Nash in the skull with a tire iron, returning him to unconsciousness.

Serge slid back into the driver's seat. "People who interrupt! Jesus! . . . Where was I?"

"Empathy."

"Right. In order to treat people with the utmost sensitivity, you must become acutely in tune with their every emotion: happy, sad, anxious, melancholy, introspective, that awkward sensation in the grocery store when you see someone you know really well but you're in a rush and don't have time for the kind of chitchat that nobody knows how to end gracefully, but they haven't seen you yet, so you quickly duck down an aisle."

"Especially if you owe them weed money."

"Which leads us to my Empathy Continuum," said Serge. "At one end are the totally chill cats: Mother Teresa, Gandhi, the Salvation Army, and at the opposite, Stalin, Pol Pot, Son of Sam, Ike Turner."

"But how does this unite everyone?"

"Noted psychotherapists claim empathy can't be taught, but they've never tried with the level of zeal I apply when I put my mind to something." He glanced over his seat as thumping resumed from the trunk. "And I'm going to launch my clinical trials with someone who could stand to learn empathy the most."

The hamster twitched its whiskers and strained to reach the eyedropper in Coleman's hand. "How did you find out about Roscoe in the first place?"

"It was in all the papers. Remember that rookie police officer in Manatee County who was brutally gunned down in the line of duty? Pulled over a carload of crack smugglers with UZIs on the Tamiami?"

"Sort of."

"Roscoe must read the papers, too." Serge got out of the car and walked toward the back bumper. "Because after the first of the year, Nash falsely filed the officer's tax return and had the refund check diverted to a PO box."

"How do you even figure out how to do that?" asked Coleman.

"I don't know, but Roscoe must have because it actually happened." Serge popped the trunk. "Just when you think you've seen all depravity, someone raises the bar again."

"He's another wiggler," said Coleman.

Serge rolled Roscoe over and ripped the duct tape off his mouth.

"Ow! Shit!" The captive looked up. "Who the hell *are* you?"

"Your new empathy coach, and if you pass, it could go a long way to getting you out of this jam. Believe me, you won't like my detention hall." Serge pulled a square from his back pocket and unfolded it. "For our first day of class, you're going to write a lot of apology letters. I took the liberty of composing a sample to get you started." He held the letter down to Roscoe's eyes. "I have you referring to yourself as 'the biggest prick in the world,' but if you'd like something stronger, feel free to substitute."

Roscoe spit in Serge's face.

Serge nonchalantly found a rag in the trunk and wiped it off. Then he cracked Roscoe in the head again with the iron rod and made his way back to the driver's seat. He picked up the binoculars and stared across the street.

Coleman stuck the eyedropper in a can of Bud. "What now?"

"I love Busch Gardens! Especially after it's empty at night when the staff doesn't force you to limit the park's possibilities with their rule-crazy narrowness."

"No, I mean, that guy back there."

"Roscoe?" The binoculars panned from the Montu to the Kumba roller coaster. "In his case, the psychologists were right: Empathy can't be taught."

"But you said your zeal . . . I mean, you gave up pretty quickly."

The binoculars reached the gondola over the Serengeti Plain. "I thought maybe we had environmental differences, but hocking a giant loogie in someone's face is a language that crosses cultural lines."

Chapter THREE

PALM BEACH

The drive down South Ocean Boulevard, along the sand and surf of the Atlantic, is one of the most inspiring in the country. People come away describing an almost morphine-like sense of euphoria and bliss.

"Motherfucker!" screamed Courtney Styles, punching the ceiling of her Geo Prizm that needed transmission work and non-bald tires.

She pulled up the driveway of her uncle's vacation cottage and couldn't stay mad for long. It was the cutest little bungalow, and only three doors down from the ocean, cozily tucked in a nest of traveler's palms and banana trees. Courtney especially liked the color combination of the villa's yoke-yellow Bahama shutters and a phosphorus tropical green from those giant rain-forest leaves draping over the trim.

She unlocked the front door. One step inside before her fingers went numb. Keys hit the polished, blond-pine floor. Courtney's unbelieving eyes worked their way wall to wall. "What on earth—?"

The first phone call was to the owner.

"No," said her uncle. "We'll call the cops. You go over to the neighbors where you'll be safe."

Before Courtney could ring the doorbell on the next house, nine squad cars and two vans from the Palm Beach Police Department arrived like they were paid massive bonuses for response time and overwhelming force to protect wealth, which they were. Black helmets dashed in a low crouch through the snapping foliage and took up an eight-point interlocking perimeter with laser sights and flash-bang options.

"Miss, are you okay?"

"Yes, but—"

The leader held up a hand as his walkie-talkie squawked. "Go ahead, Team Indigo? . . ." He listened, then turned to Courtney with a reassuring wink. "Indigo went in and cleared the kill box."

"Kill box?"

"Office language," said the commando commander. "Important thing is you're safe. Come with me . . ."

Courtney decided she was beginning to like the thought of going back to school for her graduate degree. They reached the front of the bungalow, and the commander introduced her to a pair of detectives with mirror sunglasses and clipboards.

"So if I understand, ma'am, a few minutes ago you returned to this unfurnished cottage when something seemed suspicious?"

"Yes, it used to be furnished."

"Of course," said the second detective. "And the previous owners took their stuff when they left."

"No, my uncle still owns it," said Courtney. "They're letting me live here this summer after graduation."

"But they stripped the place down after the season, right?" said the first detective. "Very common here. I can give you statistics."

"I'm saying it was furnished this morning." She pointed. "Seventy-inch LED flat-screen in front of that jimmied-open wall safe."

"But the safe is empty," said the second.

"That's the point," said Courtney. "They got everything. I can't believe how thorough they were."

"I see." The first wrote something on his clipboard. "When was the last time you saw this furniture?"

"About nine this morning when I left."

"And where did you go?"

"Worth Avenue."

"Did anyone see you there?"

"Wait a minute," said Courtney. "*I* didn't do it."

"We're not saying that," began the first detective. "Some homes are hit at random . . ."

". . . Others are targeted," completed the second. "We're just trying to determine if someone was watching you to establish your patterns."

"Seen anyone out of place in the neighborhood?" asked the first. "Maybe in a parked car on your street?"

"No," said Courtney. "Nobody."

"What about a suspicious truck from the power company, where a guy is up in a cherry-picker basket supposed to be working on the lines, but instead he's looking in bedroom windows with a zoom lens?"

"I would have noticed that," said Courtney.

"You'd be surprised how many don't," said the first detective.

The second detective flipped back through his notes. "You said it's your uncle's place? So you're not actually a resident of Palm Beach?"

"No, just the summer—"

The detective wrote quickly. "That changes everything."

"What's that supposed to mean?" asked Courtney.

"Nothing," chimed his partner. "So you were on Worth Avenue this morning. What did you do?"

"I met someone for lunch."

"What time?"

"Just before ten A.M."

"That's brunch."

"Okay, brunch."

"Are you changing your story?"

"No," said Courtney. "Lunch, brunch, what's the difference? I was robbed blind."

"Interesting." A pen pressed against a clipboard. "What was the name of this person you had this so-called brunch with?"

"Gustave."

"Gustave what?"

"I don't know," said Courtney.

The pen came off the clipboard. "You don't know your friend's last name?"

The second peeked over the top of his sunglasses. "Do a lot of your friends not have last names?"

"No," said Courtney. "I mean, when I say I met someone for lunch, I literally just met him."

"Where?"

"On the sidewalk. He struck up a conversation and seemed nice enough, so we went to grab something to eat."

Writing on both clipboards now. "Where did you go?"

Courtney opened her mouth, then realized she didn't know how to say the name of the restaurant, and closed her mouth.

The first detective nodded. "I know that place."

"Was it a long lunch?" asked the second.

"Pretty long."

"You probably had a few drinks," said the first. "How many?"

"Two . . . wait, three. I'm not sure."

"Hard to remember?" More clipboard writing. "And given the hour, I'm guessing Bloody Marys."

"Mimosas."

"You seem to know your way pretty well around a bottle in the morning."

"What are you implying?" said Courtney.

"Do you often discover vehicle damage you can't remember?" said the first.

"Have all your relatives stopped lending you money?" said the second.

"No!"

"So you've been borrowing large amounts of money lately?"

"No!"

"Can't keep your facts straight, can you?"

The first detective held an index finger in front of her eyes and slowly moved it side to side. "Just follow it best you can."

"I am not a drunk!"

"Tell me, how much did you have to eat today?"

"Just one bite. And a shrimp cocktail, but it was the strangest—"

"So you've been drinking all morning on an empty stomach." The first detective glanced at the second. "Gee, that fits no problem behavior model we know of."

"Look," said Courtney. "This polite guy asked me to lunch, we ordered— Can you please take your finger out of my face?"

"Is it making you dizzy?"

She just shook her head. "And when we were all finished at the restaurant, he got a phone call, and then he—"

"Stop," said the first. "He got a phone call at the end of the meal?"

"And went to take it in private?" said the second.

"But he never came back," said the first. "Sticking you with the check?"

"Probably said he had an expensive car out front?"

Courtney's head swiveled back and forth like a tennis fan's. "How'd you know?"

The detectives put their pens away.

Courtney looked from one to the other. "What's going on?"

"We'll need to get you with a sketch artist."

"What for?"

"Ma'am, I'm afraid you've fallen victim to the dating bandit."

"Dating bandit?"

"He finds his mark and follows her until he can arrange an 'accidental' meeting," said the first.

"Sometimes they go to lunch right then . . ." said the second.

". . . Sometimes he makes a date for later," said the first.

"Depending on whether his crew is in position."

"Crew?" said Courtney.

"He keeps the target occupied until getting the phone call telling him his crew is clear of the residence. Victims all over the state, from Orlando to Miami to Naples and Sarasota."

Courtney was astonished. "If he's done it so many times, how come he's never been caught?"

"The term *dating bandit* is generic," said the first.

"There are dozens of guys working separately," said the second.

"Usually it's lonely older women with a lot of jewelry."

"That's why we initially didn't suspect it in this case, because of your age."

Courtney's brain raced to process data. "I don't see any broken windows. How did they get in the house?"

"Probably a 'bump' key," said the first detective.

"What's that?"

"About twenty brands of locks cover ninety-five percent of the residential market, so they buy blanks to cover the spread . . ."

The other pulled out his own key chain. "See these ridges? They go up and down, high and low . . .

". . . But on a 'bump' key, they're all at the maximum height. Then they simply match the blank to the lock brand on your house."

Courtney checked her own keys. "That's kind of disconcerting. It just opens the door?"

"No, they have to practice," said the first.

"An accomplice grabs the doorknob and applies torque, trying to turn it . . ."

". . . And the other sticks the key in the opening of the lock and whacks it with a rubber mallet . . ."

". . . If all goes right, the internal tumblers momentarily bounce, and the knob pops open in the hand of the guy applying pressure."

Courtney leaned back against the door frame. "So what now?"

"We'll have the sketch artist call . . ."

". . . In the meantime, get your locks changed."

"I'll do it this afternoon," said Courtney. "Will that stop another bump key?"

"No."

The detectives headed out the door and down the front porch steps. The first stopped and turned. "Just one more thing, ma'am . . ."

"Yes?" said Courtney.

"How'd you like the shrimp cocktail?"

They walked away laughing.

STATE ROAD 60

High beams from a Firebird Trans Am was the only illumination for miles, splitting the thick night in that long no-man's run between Lake Wales and Yeehaw.

A hamster crawled out of a bong. "Serge, I thought you were going to take care of this guy back at Busch Gardens."

Serge slowed to let a rabbit cross the road. "I was, but realized they don't have what I need there anymore. It would have been perfect back in the seventies, except I'm guessing the safety people decided to lower the risks."

"Change of plans?"

"No, same plans. Plenty of other places have since cropped up that'll work just as well."

A few more minutes and the black Pontiac pulled up alongside a barbed-wire fence. There was a gate with a gnarled wooden sign across the top. Coleman read it and turned to Serge. "You've got to be kidding. He's going to be tickled to death?"

Serge grabbed a pair of bolt cutters. "You'd be surprised."

Soon the muscle car bounded across one of the most wide-open plains in all of Florida.

Coleman leaned toward the windshield. "Are you going to let me watch this time?"

"From a safe distance."

"Yes!"

They finally reached the approximate center of the prairie flats. Coleman started opening his door.

Serge lunged and yanked the handle shut. "Are you crazy! Want to get us killed?"

"Why are you so freaked out?" said Coleman. "There might be another bunny out there?"

"It will soon become more than evident. But whatever you do, don't get out of the car."

Serge pulled his gun and stepped out of the Firebird, pointing it into the darkness. He slowly inched his way to the back of the Firebird.

The trunk popped.

Eyes blinked like a waking child.

"Good, you're still dazed," said Serge, ripping the tape off Roscoe's mouth. "Listen, I've done some thinking and, whatever you've done, I've been displaying a complete lack of empathy. So you're free to go."

"Huh, what?"

Serge untied Nash and helped him out of the trunk.

Roscoe just stood and stared.

Serge waved with the gun. "Go on. Git!"

"Uh, okay, sure."

Roscoe took slow steps backward as Serge scrambled into the driver's seat and hit the gas like he'd just gotten the green flag at Daytona.

Coleman bounced against the ceiling as the Firebird sprang across dips and mounds. "Ow, ow, ow, what's the hurry? Ow, ow . . ."

"We need to get back outside the fence and lock the gate as soon as possible." Serge veered and barely missed a watering hole. "I didn't tell you this before because of your marijuana situation, but we're not even safe in this car."

"What!"

"It's got a tight suspension that doesn't let us go very fast in this terrain. And the windows aren't tempered to the proper strength."

Moments later, the Trans Am was back on the shoulder of State

Road 60 with the gate adequately secured. Serge and Coleman leaned against fence posts, peering into the dark expanse.

"Just remembered something," said Coleman. "You mentioned at the jail that you posted his bail?"

"What a bargain! Paid the bondsman ten cents on the buck."

"But why would you waste good money that way?"

"It's like those credit-card ads," said Serge. "Bailing a dipstick out of jail: eight hundred dollars. What happens now: priceless!"

Serge returned his gaze to the field, resting his chin on top of a post. A quarter mile away, a tiny silhouette turned in a circle and glanced around.

"Nothing's happening," said Coleman. "He's just standing in the open, looking confused."

"He will soon be accompanied by other thoughts."

"Wait, what's that?"

"Where?"

Coleman stretched out an arm. "Way over there to the right."

"Are you sure?"

Coleman looked down at his sneakers. Written across the toes in Magic Marker: *R* on one; *L* on the other.

"I mean the left," said Coleman. "Even farther away from the guy than we are. It's not moving. Just standing upright like a human, but the shape's not right."

"The guy sees it," said Serge. "He's starting to back up. The thing has spotted him and is beginning to walk in his direction."

"Where'd you get this idea anyway?"

"From a friend who worked at Busch Gardens in the seventies," said Serge. "He used to run the rib shack, and people really must have loved ribs back then because by the end of the day, they had such huge piles of ashes from the wood they'd burned that it filled several fifty-five-gallon drums. Then they loaded the drums on the back of a big Cushman golf cart, and the animal handlers would give them the all clear, open the gates and wave them through. They'd drive around the Serengeti Plain in the dark, spreading the ashes because it's a good fertilizer."

"That doesn't sound dangerous," said Coleman.

"It's not," said Serge. "Except one night when they reached their first drop point, faint yelling erupted back at the gate: *'Get out of there! Get out now!'* My friend turned and realized they hadn't secured all the wildlife. So he mashed the pedal of the golf cart all the way down, racing for the gate and praying. He'd worked at the park a long time and knew one extreme peril that the general public would never suspect."

"Peril?" Coleman looked up at the gnarled ranch sign over the gate. "I'm not buying it."

"I was skeptical, too, so I did some research on the Internet." Serge watched his former captive break into a full sprint. "Found reports of several deaths every year in South Africa and Louisiana, even videos on YouTube. One article quoted a California zookeeper saying that they'd had a couple lions escape since they opened, except they weren't worried because the big cats were old and sluggish. But there was one zoo resident whose possibility of escape freaked them out more than all the others and required the tightest security."

"It's starting to chase him," said Coleman, tracking the pursuit with a pointed finger. "Man, I had no idea they could run that fast."

"A sustained forty miles an hour, with even faster bursts." Serge raised binoculars. "That's what my friend at Busch Gardens found out."

"But, Serge, when you're waxing a dude, you usually like it to have some kind of . . ." Coleman stopped to ponder.

"Theme?" said Serge.

"That's it."

"Oh, it's got a theme all right. Some of the finest unknown Florida history around. Back in the late 1800s, they had breeding farms all over the northern half of the state, some for the meat, others for entertainment."

"Entertainment? Like this?" Coleman gestured across the field at their former hostage, who was losing ground.

"Believe it or not, they used to race these things with little jockeys on their backs. Around 1890, a farm in Jacksonville actually became one of the earliest Florida tourist attractions, with a greyhound-like track. I don't know if they placed bets. There were other races and farms, including one in St. Petersburg. EBay has some hundred-year-old sepia-tone postcards of people saddling these babies up. Then the whole thing died out until a couple decades ago when breeders started getting good money again for the drumsticks, and they began a resurgence."

Coleman looked up at the sign again: CIRCLE K OSTRICH RANCH. "So what happened to your friend?"

"The ostrich was much faster than his golf cart, so while my friend drove, the other guy from the rib shack starts pushing fifty-five-gallon drums off the back, one after another, and the ostrich just hurdles them like one of those exciting raptor chases from *Jurassic Park*. The barrels slowed the bird down just enough to let their cart shoot out the gate at the last second, and they can now laugh about it today."

Coleman's finger was still pointing. "It's almost to the guy. He's looking over his shoulder . . . But what makes an ostrich so dangerous? Their beaks don't look too scary."

"Not beaks, their feet." Serge held his hands apart like a fisherman bragging about a catch. "They're huge and powerful, and if you saw a cropped photo without the rest of the bird, you'd swear they belonged to a dinosaur, which on the evolutionary family tree is actually correct. Each foot has two toes with a giant weapon at the end that is a cross between a hoof and a talon."

"Can I borrow the binoculars?"

Serge handed them over, and Coleman followed the action with magnification. "It's just a few yards behind him now . . . How do they use those toes, anyway?"

"In the case of human attack, first they knock their prey down and pin the person on their back with one foot . . ."

Coleman tightened the focus. "Just happened."

". . . Then they start raking their victim's chest with the other foot."

A shrill, spine-tingling scream echoed across the field. "Put a check mark there," said Coleman.

"The feet are so powerful that they easily rip out all the ribs and keep going through the internal organs until the dude's on empty."

"Something went flying," said Coleman. "Definitely a rib."

"Are you enjoying yourself?"

Coleman kept his eyes pressed to the binoculars. "Ostriches are cool!"

"I'm thinking of approaching some of these farmers to start up the races again."

"What happened to your empathy thing?" asked Coleman.

"Just because I was forced to mete out justice doesn't mean I don't feel his pain."

"There goes a liver."

"Ouch."

Chapter FOUR

THE NEXT MORNING

Sunlight filtered through the leaves of a jacaranda before hitting the kitchen window.

The table had orange juice and all the sections of the newspaper spread out in reading-order preference. Toast popped.

The three-bedroom Mediterranean stucco sat on a quiet street just south of Fort Lauderdale in a town called Dania. You could tell it was an original 1925 hacienda because of the detached garage out back—not the new replicas with two or three horrendous garage doors on the front of the house that wreck the architecture. It was now worth a nice chunk of change, but a bargain back when Jim Townsend bought it in the eighties. Dania was known for having one of the last jai alai frontons that wasn't a dump.

Jim always had a knack with numbers. He was an accountant, but made more than most because he did corporate work. He could also count cards. And ex-wives, which was three.

Jim liked his toast and his jacarandas. The garage out back had recently been cleaned and emptied to make space. He was going to treat himself to something he always wanted, now made possible by the departure of his latest spouse for a defrocked priest she'd met at the holy candles.

The most important section of the paper was the classifieds. Jim found the listings for used cars. Everyone now shopped on the Internet, which meant the occasional gem could still be found in print. His finger ran down a column to the bottom, then back to the top of the next, just as it had every day for the last two weeks. But this time the finger stopped. He couldn't believe it. Jim put on glasses and read again. Right there in black and white: a 1969 Corvette Stingray convertible with four-speed manual transmission, 390 horsepower turbojet and a 427 cubic-inch V-8. A little high on miles but the right color. Lemon yellow. But best of all was the price. It definitely wouldn't last. He jumped for the phone. After eight rings:

"Hello?" Someone eating cereal on the other end.

"Yes, I'm interested in the Corvette in the paper."

Crunch, crunch. "I've been getting a few calls."

"But you haven't sold it yet?" said Jim, subconsciously thinking, *Trix are for kids.*

"No, it's still here."

"Good," said Jim. "I'd like to take a look as soon as possible."

"Where do you live?"

"Dania."

"Great. I've got to do something down there today anyway. What's your address?"

Jim told him.

"Wait, that won't work. Just remembered I got this other thing. You know that pancake house on U.S. 1 north of Hollywood?"

"Sure."

"Why don't we meet there? You can take her for a spin, and if you like it, the pancake place is there for coffee and some table space to handle the paperwork."

"Works for me," said Jim.

"But let me ask you a question: Are you familiar with Corvettes?"

"Yes."

"So you're aware the price is on the low side."

Jim clenched up. Here it comes: the catch. He played coy. "It's a *little* on the low side, but I've seen a few in that range."

"Well, I can perfectly understand if this isn't acceptable to you, but I can only do it at that price if it's a cash deal. It's a personal—"

"I'm an accountant."

"So you understand."

"Your business is your business."

"Okay, and if you have to call me again and a woman answers . . . uh, that's partly why we need to do this at a restaurant and the cash thing. We're going through a—"

"I've been divorced three times."

"So you understand."

"When would you like to meet?"

"How about tonight around seven?"

Jim was in the parking lot of the pancake house at five. Straight from the bank, no stops. The whole procedure at the bank had been a rolling anxiety attack. He'd never even seen $19,000 all in one place before, stacked high on a table. The bank had arranged a private room for security while he filled the briefcase, and even instructed an armed guard to escort him to his car and see him safely off the lot.

The sun set as Jim leaned against the trunk, daydreaming about Corvettes in 1960s beach movies. A few minutes after seven, he spotted it six blocks away. The shimmering mirage of a lifelong dream, coming toward him under streetlights that shimmered off the freshly waxed hood. It already had the top down when it pulled into the parking space. Deliberate salesmanship.

The owner wore a tropical shirt and sporty dark sunglasses that made him look cool and drive badly at night. He hopped out and shook Jim's hand. Jim was a bit wooden.

"You feeling all right?"

"Fine," said Jim. "It's . . . so beautiful."

"Good. My name's Cid. Friends call me Uncle Cid. I don't know why. Just one of those things that stuck. And I don't know why I brought it up." He tossed Jim the keys. "Let's do it."

Jim felt like a golden warrior as he sped down U.S. 1 with the wind in his hair, running that powerful stick shift through the gears as streetlights flew by.

"She's a little high on miles," said Cid, arm resting over his door. "But I'm a gearhead. Kid gloves."

Jim hit the clutch. "I can tell."

A few minutes later, they returned to the restaurant. Cid opened his door. "What do you think?"

"Sold."

"Let's wrap it up inside." Cid looked around. "I'm guessing the money's in the trunk. This is a safe area, but I'm going to stand out over here in the parking lot and keep watch until you're in the door. Don't want anybody stealing *my* money." A forced laugh.

Jim smiled and popped the trunk . . .

The waitress refilled their coffee on Cid's signal. "Here's the bill of sale and the title—just sign here and here. Maintenance records are in the glove compartment."

Jim leaned over the table with a pen. "How are you getting home?"

"Call a cab." Cid reached under the table and patted the briefcase safely tucked on the floor between his legs. "I think I can cover it."

Jim scribbled his name. "I can't believe I'm doing this. It's crazy, but ever since I was fifteen . . ."

"Don't have to explain to me. Here are the keys."

Jim stared at them in his palm like a rare creature. They even had the original checkered-flag fob.

"Hey," said Cid. "What's that guy doing?"

"What guy?"

Cid pointed out the window. "He's stealing the Corvette!"

"Holy shit!"

"Call the cops!" yelled Cid.

They both jumped up and sprinted through the restaurant, hitting the parking lot just as the thief finished spinning backward parking slot.

"Son of a bitch!" yelled Cid.

The Stingray's tires squealed and burned rubber.

Jim ran across the lot, fumbling with his cell phone to call 9-1-1. He ran along the edge of U.S. 1 so he could tell the police which way the driver turned, which was west on Hollywood Boulevard toward the interstate.

The operator came on. *"What is your emergency?"*

"I'd like to report—" He lowered the phone.

"Sir . . . Sir? . . . Hello? . . ."

"Cid?" said Jim. "Cid, where are you?"

A Dodge pickup suddenly shot out from an alley behind the restaurant.

Jim watched as the truck raced by—Cid behind the wheel—and took off south, following the Corvette.

DOWNTOWN TAMPA

Motorcycle cops directed traffic at every corner as stretch limos filled the street.

TV floodlights lit up correspondents standing in front of a cavernous building.

"Good evening and welcome to tonight's coverage . . ."

Serge and Coleman pushed their way through a mob under an overpass.

"Always wanted to attend the Republican National Convention!" Serge looked pensively at the sky. "I was afraid Tropical Storm Isaac would ruin everything, but it veered out to sea. Only some threatening feeder bands up there. If they can just hold off another hour before cutting loose . . ."

Coleman glanced around with a cupped roach. "What are you planning?"

"To unite America. Follow me . . ."

On the main street in front of the arena, police had set up rows of galvanized parade barricades on opposite edges of the road, separating rival camps of protesters.

"*Tax the rich!*" yelled one side.

"*Get off welfare!*" yelled the other.

"My people!" yelled Serge.

Security was tight, but the police had their hands more than full. Serge waited until a moment of distraction and made his move.

Before the cops could react, Serge and Coleman were in the middle of the street, walking down the center line as limos whizzed by in both directions.

Protesters paused and stared curiously at the large sign that Serge held high in the air on a long stick.

"*Hey, asshole!*" yelled a Republican from behind the barricades on Serge's right. "*What the hell's that sign supposed to mean?*"

"What do you think it means?" asked Serge.

"*I think I don't like what it means.*"

"Then that's a reflection on you."

"*Listen, mister! Don't go putting that on me!*"

"No, really," said Serge. "I'm not arguing. It's clinically a reflection on you . . ."

From the Democrats on Serge's left: "*Hey, shithead! Just who the hell do you think you are with that sign?*"

"Who do you think I am?"

"*I think you're the whole problem with this country!*"

"Then that's a reflection—"

"*He's a socialist! . . .*"

"*He's a fascist! . . .*"

Barricades began to fall. Serge grabbed Coleman by the arm. "Pick up the pace . . ."

TV correspondents looked over their shoulders. Cameras and lights swung. "*. . . There seems to be some kind of disturbance in front of the convention hall. It's centered around two men in the road with some kind of sign. I'll try to make out what it says . . .*"

Protesters began pouring into the street, tying up traffic and screaming outrage. The rest of the barricades fell as people darted between limos, running faster and faster, waving their own signs.

The first tear-gas canister flew as the two sides merged into a single, full-scale stampede, chasing Serge and Coleman past the arena.

One of the TV correspondents looked up at the amorphous, symmetrical pattern on Serge's sign as the pair ran by. He raised his microphone. *"Linda, I now know what the sign is that triggered the riot. You're not going to believe this . . ."*

Another reporter raised his mike as the two dashed behind him. *". . . It's a Rorschach pattern . . ."*

Coleman panted hard, but fear made him keep up with Serge. "Man, the country's so pissed off, they'll automatically disagree with anything." He glanced back up the street. "Sorry your plan failed."

"Just the reverse," said Serge. "It was a complete success!"

"How is this a success?" said Coleman. "Just listen to that yelling."

". . . Kill them! . . ."

". . . Get out of America! . . ."

". . . Go to Canada! . . ."

"I finally united them."

A few drops of water hit them in the face. "And just in time," said Coleman. "It starting to rain."

"Rain? It's going to be a deluge," said Serge. "The feeder bands are cutting loose."

A sudden gust of wind whipped Coleman's hair as he looked back over his shoulder. "The mob's gaining on us. There's no way we can escape."

". . . Traitors! . . ."

". . . Dead meat! . . ."

As Serge had predicted, a torrential downpour erupted. Lightning sliced the sky.

Coleman looked back again, and Serge looked at Coleman. "Why are you slowing down?"

"Because the mob is," said Coleman. "In fact, they've come to a complete stop."

The pair ceased running and turned around, watching curiously at the reason for their reprieve.

Shouting within the crowd, then fists flew. Someone got tackled; a protest sign was bashed over a head.

"What's going on?" asked Coleman.

"The rain has smeared all their signs into inkblots." Serge momentarily covered his eyes. "It's even worse than before. Democrat on Democrat, Republican on Republican."

"At least we got away," said Coleman.

Serge sighed and threw his inkblot sign in a trash can as they disappeared into the darkness under an overpass. "Crap."

Chapter FIVE

DANIA

The police expressed sympathy and thought Jim Townsend was an idiot.

Jim waved excitedly in several directions. "And then Cid took off chasing the thief."

A detective wrote in a notebook. "Didn't you wonder where he got the pickup truck?"

"He, uh, well . . ."

"It was planted ahead of time behind the restaurant, probably by the accomplice who stole the convertible."

"Cid was in on it?"

"You say you found the Corvette in a classified ad?" asked the detective.

"Yes, you can trace the phone number, right?" said Jim. "You can track down Cid?"

"We'll give it a try, but it was probably a disposable cell."

"Then what should I do?" asked Jim.

"Count your blessings."

"But I just got ripped off!"

The detective closed his notebook. "It's a common scam, but this one was more elaborate than most. I'm guessing they picked a public location so it wouldn't raise your suspicions with the amount of money involved. You're lucky."

"How is any of this lucky?"

"Usually it's an older car they're selling for three or four grand, and they give you an address that's at the end of an empty road and simply stick a gun in your face."

"This happens a lot?"

"That's why we keep telling the public never to meet a private seller with cash." The detective opened his wallet. "Here's my business card. Give me a call if you can think of anything else."

Jim now felt as stupid as the police already knew he was. He drove home in a slow funk, getting honked at when he didn't realize the light had turned green.

The accountant listlessly walked up the path to his front door and went inside. He took out the business card and walked even more slowly to the phone and dialed.

"Detective Green here."

"This is Jim Townsend. Remember? The stolen Corvette at the pancake house."

"Oh, hey. Think of anything else?"

"No."

"They why are you calling me?"

"Someone robbed my house."

MEANWHILE . . .

She was the classic Latin bombshell.

Luscious red lips, full-bodied jet-black hair, and a beauty mark to die for. Her legs were crossed sensuously in the sidewalk café. The tangerine sundress was low-cut but tasteful.

Serge easily held his own in the dating jungle. He never had the kind of striking looks that made him the first guy women noticed in the room. But he possessed what they call intangibles. Charm, manners, intelligence and a robust enthusiasm for everything. Within minutes of conversation, members of the opposite sex gave him a revised appraisal and were usually smitten by a warm, plainly handsome face. And most of all, those piercing ice-blue eyes. No need for eHarmony; if he put his mind to it, he could easily form a line in most jurisdictions.

Serge was never a cad or a deliberate user of women. He always had the sincerest feelings for his companion du jour. Plus he was one of those rare males who never felt the slightest twinge of heartache if they left him, which happened with severe frequency. The charm and other stuff could last days, even weeks, before inevitably: "This guy has serious problems—I need to leave the state." Then Serge would simply be thankful for the fun times they had shared and go whistling his separate way.

If there was any heartbreak, it fell on the women. As often as they left him, so he left them. Like a Siamese cat that inexplicably stops in the middle of a room and takes off in a totally different direction, Serge would routinely decide that he suddenly needed to be somewhere else.

Now, as he sat in a sidewalk café across from a tangerine sundress, emotions were all new and raw. He had been with her type countless times, but this one was different. She had gotten to know the real Serge and was cool with it, even amused. Serge was lost and helpless and utterly happy.

He stared like a schoolboy into her eyes as they discussed plans for a beach wedding.

Serge never heard anything as her face fell forward on the table, because the gun had a silencer. Confused, he gently put his hand on the back of her head and felt hair matted with tacky blood.

"Felicia! Felicia! Noooooooooooo!..."

Coleman waddled through the night with a crooked smile and a beer in each hand. It was a giant, wooded field. It would have been the middle of nowhere if it had been closer to other places.

After escaping the lynch mob at the Tampa convention, Serge

had plotted a long, dark drive, hopping from state highways to county roads to nameless dirt trails. They were up north of the Ocala National Forest, in a quilt of lakes where land was sparse and in anti-demand. The last stretch formed an isthmus. Just before parking, Coleman saw an owl on top of a faded sign.

HAWTHORNE.

Then they got separated and couldn't find each other for hours. There were two contributing factors: Serge's passion to explore, and Coleman's tendency to get separated.

Coleman had been wandering the woods wide-eyed all night like Hansel and Gretel. But he was properly roasted to dig the trees and crickets, and still had two beers left. He smiled and looked up at the moon through an old-growth canopy. Then a lot more trees. The first sign of anything but plants was a discarded farm contraption half buried in peat. He felt the coarse, rusted surface of a protruding wheel. It had been mule-powered. It called for a beer.

A short time later, he saw a shape in the distance with right angles. He came upon the small tilting barn and picked up a piece of brown glass from a bottle that had been drunk during Prohibition. An abrupt sound startled Coleman and turned him around. Just like the unseen frogs and birds at the beginning of his journey. But he'd gotten used to that. This noise was human.

He ventured forth and saw an even larger barn through the trees. When he drew near, a clearing opened up to reveal a farmhouse that hadn't been occupied for decades. A voice erupted again.

Coleman gulped, but he pressed on.

The voice grew louder. He reached the house and stuck his face against the porch's screen door. Empty. Except for the voice. Too weird. He was right on top of the sound, but nobody was there. He backed up. "A ghost."

The voice became even louder. Coleman got a funny look on his face, then crouched on his hands and knees and stuck his head under the farmhouse's crawl space.

The voice cried out.

"...*Felicia!...Noooo!...*"

"Serge?" said Coleman. "Is that you?"

"...*Felicia!...*"

Coleman quickly slithered on his belly until he was under the middle of the residence. Serge thrashed in the dirt.

"...*Why, oh why!...*"

Coleman shook his buddy vigorously. "Wake up! Wake up! You're having a nightmare!"

Serge flopped a last few times, then blinked his eyes. "Coleman?"

"It's cool, man. Just a bad dream."

Serge looked around. "Where are we?"

"I don't know," said Coleman. "I crawled under this old house."

"Are you still crawling under houses?"

"No, this time it was because I heard your voice and you were in trouble." Coleman rolled over to rest on his back. "All those other houses... I don't really know what that was about."

Serge rolled over on his own back next to Coleman, then snapped his fingers. "I remember now. That horrible national family spat back at the convention began giving me the shakes, and I needed to retreat to a holy place." He pointed up at the underside of the floorboards a few inches from his nose. "Marjorie Kinnan Rawlings bought this joint in 1928 and wrote *The Yearling*. But mainly she was one of those rare pioneers who preached the joy of undisturbed Florida. Today, undisturbed Florida means a place has only one titty bar."

"And the chicks try less because where are you gonna go?"

"It's a tragedy on so many levels." Serge ran a finger along one of the floor beams. "At least I'm at Marjorie's place. A Pulitzer was won right above our faces. Always feel better coming here."

"Why didn't you go inside?" asked Coleman. "The screen door was open."

"I decided to sleep under the house instead because I didn't want to trespass."

"I wouldn't really call that sleeping," said Coleman. "You were yelling loud."

"What was I saying?"

"Felicia."

Serge closed his eyes hard.

"Sorry," said Coleman. "Thought you'd gotten over her."

"You never get over something like that. You just try to keep it in a box on an out-of-the-way shelf in your brain. But then you open the closet to look for an old sousaphone—"

"I'm getting hungry."

"Thanks for listening."

Coleman poked his stomach. "But it's making the noises."

Serge turned his head sideways. "The sun's starting to come up, which is the signal to get out from under houses." He began crawling. "We'll grab breakfast at the Yearling."

"The book?"

"Just come on . . ."

The Firebird took the western bend on Alachua County Road 325, past a dark body of water, and approached a brief bridge. The sun's rise was known but not felt: A dewy fog hovered over the marsh grass, keeping the morning gray.

"That bridge sure is tiny," said Coleman.

"It's the bridge of my life." Serge pulled over on a dirt road and threw his arms out in opposite directions. "We're on a thin strip of land between two lakes, Lochloosa and Orange, and that bridge crossed the creek that connects them, Cross Creek, namesake of Rawlings's classic memoir and the Oscar-nominated movie starring Mary Steenburgen as the author."

Serge got out of the Firebird and walked toward a small wooden structure. "This is my favorite place on earth, for now. You can actually rent these little shotgun shacks right on the edge of the creek and hear the water going by. Isn't it great? Can you feel the Rawlings magic?"

Coleman rubbed his tummy. "Can we get some food now?"

"No! We must go sit in the shack and dig it!" He produced a key from his pocket.

"You rented one of these?"

"Of course." Serge stuck the key in the knob. "I first thought of lodging under Rawlings's house, but you can't open a suitcase."

"What about this Yearling place you said we could eat at?"

Serge turned around in the doorway. "See that old rustic building over there?"

"Yeah. Looks closed."

"One of the finest restaurants in Florida way out in the sticks with handed-down family-recipe cracker cuisine. There's something on the menu called cooter. Any place that serves cooter rocks my world."

"Great! Let's eat!"

"Doesn't open till lunch."

"Serge!"

Serge went inside the shotgun shack. "Gives us time to groove on the cottage. Now get in here and groove!"

It was a cozy little place with everything in one room: two classic beds with wooden posts, old table and chairs, antique cabinets that would now command top dollar as "shabby chic."

Serge sat on one of the beds and swayed with enthusiasm. "This is so perfect. Can you hear that famous water?"

Coleman moped on the other bed. "My belly."

"Maybe if you tried swaying. Just follow my example. I'm in such a happy place that I don't think I can possibly ever leave." Serge swayed some more. Then suddenly bolted upright. "I got to get out of here."

"What's the matter?" asked Coleman.

Serge ran out the door and began pacing on the dirt road. "Dammit! I came out to experience harmony and raise my empathy quotient, but then I had to go and have that nightmare. Now I can't get it out of my mind."

"Serge, it hasn't been that long yet since it happened. You need more time."

"It will always be an open wound until I find out who killed her. I didn't mention this before, but my quest to become a political version of a private detective and reunite our people isn't entirely altruistic."

"It's not?"

"I'll tell you more over lunch."

"But that's still a few hours. What will we do until then? . . ."

Time passed.

"Serge, what are you doing up in that tree?"

"Seeking the birds' perspective. Birds get stunning overhead views of both lakes, but obviously don't appreciate it like me because they're easily distracted by a mouse. Oooo, a mouse." He shimmied down . . .

More time passed.

"Serge, what are you doing in the creek wearing only your underwear?"

"Baptizing myself." Serge dunked his head in the water, then threw a fist in the air. *"Shula!"*

Coleman turned around. "I think the restaurant just opened."

"Excellent." Serge climbed out of the creek and headed for the Yearling. "I could go for some vittles."

"What about clothes?"

"Oh, right. That was almost another episode of having to talk fast on my feet."

Moments later . . .

"Whoa," said Coleman. "Look at this old place."

"Couldn't you tell that from the outside?"

"But that was like funky, broken-down old. This is . . ."

"People drive right by and never have any idea all this is inside." Serge ran a hand along a railing. "Dark varnished wood like a hunting lodge, giant library of antiquarian books, stretched-out alligator hide on the wall above the vintage Coca-Cola machine, old hotel mail slots, more country antiques in the dining room, the bare-bones stage where legendary Willie Green served up Delta blues on slide guitar and harmonica . . ."

Coleman grabbed Serge's arm. "The sign over that door: 'The Cooter Shell Lounge.' Can we go in?"

"Absolutely," said Serge. "Then I can show you all the ancient southern college football pennants, probably from 1952 when this place opened."

They grabbed stools. Double whiskey and a bottle of water arrived.

"We'd like some food," Serge told the bartender.

"I'll get you some menus."

"No need." Serge waved a hand over his head. "Already know what we want. Cooter. For both of us."

"How would you like that cooked?"

"I don't even know what it is," said Serge. "Just tell the cook that I got a fever, and the only prescription is more cooter. You may go."

Coleman looked around in the dim light at more rows of books and a movie poster. "Man, they've got stuff by that Rawlings chick all over the place."

"Because they know their history." Serge drained his water. "And few realize how Marjorie was wired into so many Florida icons like the Kevin Bacon game. They just think she was this bucolic scribe. But you know how the Ripley's Believe It or Not Museum in St. Augustine is in an old castle?"

"I liked the shrunken heads and the grandfather clock made from three thousand clothespins."

"Before it was Ripley's, it used to be a hotel run by Rawlings and her husband."

"I don't believe it," said Coleman.

Serge shrugged. "Believe it or not. They also bought a cottage on Crescent Beach, and her husband ran the nearby Dolphin Restaurant at Marineland, one of the state's earliest roadside attractions. They also managed my favorite feature of the park, a since-bulldozed-and-forgotten classic Florida watering hole called the Moby-Dick Lounge, where Hemingway once pulled a stool up to a bar shaped like a whaling ship."

Coleman chugged his bourbon. "Rawlings made Florida her bitch."

"You've broken new ground in literary criticism."

Coleman slammed his glass down hard. "So what's the deal with that nightmare about Felicia getting whacked?"

"Could you maybe ramp into the subject a little more gently?"

"But you said you'd tell me when we got in this restaurant about how the new Master Plan involves your revenge."

"That I did." Serge raised a finger to order another water. "Remember when we were back in Miami last year, and I met Felicia, who was working for the consulate of Costa Gorda?"

"Yeah, but she never did anything to anyone. Why'd they kill her?"

"Politics was involved in every level of a nefarious web that got her taken out. It became a complex espionage game of musical chairs, until there were no chairs left and she was left standing. So while I'm working on my new detective career, I've got my feelers out. Mahoney, too."

"I thought you and Mahoney were fighting scam artists."

"Correct again," said Serge. "But you hear things along the way, and I'll never rest as long as this stone is in my shoe."

"Didn't you rest after killing that big campaign organizer out in the Gulf?" asked Coleman. "The one you blamed for her death?"

"I expected the usual wave of peaceful satisfaction, but my stomach had this burning ball of acid," said Serge. "He was just a middleman; I want the hand on the gun."

"How can Mahoney help?"

"He's in the perfect position to pick up chatter since establishing his own intelligence connections. After the CIA learned he was retired law enforcement with a physical business address on the sketchy side of Miami, they started paying him a thousand dollars a week to run a dummy front corporation."

"What does he do for that?"

"Just calls the CIA number in the phone book once a month, and the people listening in think he's an actual front company, diverting attention from the real fronts."

Coleman scratched his head. "I'm confused."

"That means it's effective." Serge stared up at a vintage felt pennant for the Crimson Tide. "And Mahoney just might be loosening the jar lid."

"How's that?"

"A contact of his came up with a name, probably one of the hit man's aliases, and rumor has it that he might be heading back to Florida for another assignment. Speaking of which . . ." Serge pulled a disposable cell phone from his pocket and hit a number on speed dial.

On the other end of the line: "Name's Mahoney, flap gums."

He did. He closed the phone.

"What's going on?" asked Coleman.

"Mahoney can't tell me over the phone because he's getting paid to have it tapped. So we set a clandestine meeting for tomorrow. Clandestine meetings come in two species: secluded dark alley or extremely busy public place."

Their food arrived.

"Cooter is turtle?" said Serge.

Coleman grabbed a fork. "I'm saving the shell to clean my dope in."

Chapter SIX

THE NEXT DAY

L egos!" yelled Serge, cheerfully clapping his hands like a small child seeing clowns.

Coleman lowered his beer. "You mean like those little toy blocks we had as kids?"

"What else would they have at Legoland?" Serge swung the Firebird through the main gates of the theme park in Winter Haven.

"I don't remember any Legoland," said Coleman.

"It's new." The muscle car found a parking space. "And usually I hate new, but this used to be Cypress Gardens, the state's first theme park that opened on January second, 1936. No crazy rides or people dressed up like cartoon characters. Just hundreds of lush botanical acres showcasing the area's natural flora, plus southern belles in hoop skirts and water-ski shows that populate the reels of my View-Master collection. Not to mention the sacramental pool that was built in the shape of Florida sixty years ago by the movie people for an Esther Williams splash fest. Then horror!"

"What happened?"

Serge headed toward the ticket booth and pulled out his wallet. "Like many of Florida's majestic early attractions, it fell on hard times because people can no longer enjoy natural beauty unless they're zooming through it on a log flume or inverted roller coaster." Serge handed Coleman his ticket and unfolded a glossy park map. "This way."

"Where are we going?"

"Miniland!" Serge's finger tracked a path on the map as they made another turn. "Miniland is the best!"

"Never heard of it."

"Cypress Gardens was limping along and even closed for one terrifying year. Then the Lego people stepped in and saved us from another tragic roadside extinction. I figured, okay, sometimes you have to make a deal with the devil, and I decided to give them the benefit of the doubt, as long as they weren't going to plow under the old park and just add a few Legos to a new section. It could be a worse devil, like the Hasbro toy people."

"Fuck Easy-Bake Ovens," said Coleman.

"But instead this place turned out beyond my craziest dreams." Serge followed his map around a final corner. "There it is: Miniland! The coolest part of all is its replica of the state of Florida. And totally unexpected: I'd thought the era of high-concept attractions died with early Disney World, when they made that exhibit of robot presidents that nobody ever went to see, and I'd have the whole place to myself, but would never watch the president who had the spotlight on him for the Gettysburg Address. Instead I'd monitor the other commanders in chief in the dark, and they'd be blinking and making slight gestures. And I said to myself, 'Now this is quality. I would have come in here anyway; they didn't have to go through all the extra robot expense of Grover Cleveland removing an eye booger.' And then I went back to the attraction again right after Nixon resigned, thinking, 'Cool, the shit's really going to fly!' Other presidents ganging up: 'Yo, get the fuck out! You know what you did.'"

"What happened?" asked Coleman.

"Apparently they felt sorry for him and took the high road," said

Serge. "But you could still see Disney's trademark attention to detail in Nixon's shifty eyes that said, 'I sure hope this goes well. It's my first gig since leaving. Maybe I should open with a joke.' . . . Now Legoland is carrying the torch."

"Nixon is like Legos?"

"In more ways than one."

Coleman turned toward the elaborate panorama in front of him. "That's pretty intense. Some of those Lego buildings are twice as high as my head."

"At least." Serge trotted around the perimeter pointing. "There's the capitol in Tallahassee, the Spanish fort in St. Augustine, the Daytona 500 with little Lego people in the stands, and the massive Vehicle Assembly Building at Cape Canaveral . . ." He sprinted faster and faster past other visitors with strollers and throwaway cameras. ". . . An eight-foot-tall Bok Tower, the mind-blowing skylines of Tampa and Miami's South Beach down to intricate details like the facade of the Colony Hotel and one of the flying-saucer lifeguard stands. It even has Key West and 'Sloppy Moe's' bar instead of 'Sloppy Joe's,' which I'm thinking was the lawyers' idea."

"It's everything you say!" Coleman exclaimed. "So I need a joint to dig it completely."

"I'm onto your scheming ways," said Serge. "You're trying to play my emotions from this special moment to introduce the dope culture to this hallowed ground."

"No, I'm really down with all this. Tiny race-car fans, lifeguards," said Coleman. "Okay, you got me. Please, just one roach. I can hide between those two Miami office towers."

"I've seen this movie before," said Serge. "You'll lose your balance and it'll turn into a collision of *The Hangover* and *Gulliver's Travels,* grabbing on to the fortieth floor of that bank, taking it down with you into the Atlantic and wiping out Ocean Drive. They say there's no such thing as bad publicity, but I'm guessing that lying facedown in the water with a soggy joint under an avalanche of fifty thousand Legos won't play well if you run for office."

"That's a lot of Legos."

"Look around at the total plastic-block hegemony," said Serge. "It's like a Lego dirty bomb went off in here. You almost expect to see people start farting Legos . . . Now I'm depressed."

"Why's that?"

Serge gestured at the sprawling Florida display. "This is what I could have been doing with my life. Except back when I was working in Legos, they didn't have all the new parabolic shapes that blow wide open the possibilities for re-creating my state's history. When I was a kid, I tried to make an Apollo rocket, but it turned out square and I was still immature, so I set all my Legos on fire with gasoline, which they won't sell you if you're five, but they don't expect you to know how to siphon a lawn mower."

"I promise I'll keep my balance," said Coleman. "I can just zip in and out."

"Coleman, there are baby strollers, which makes this an official no-dope zone. Can you be dependable for once?"

"There aren't any strollers between the buildings." Coleman raised his chin toward the opening of opportunity. "And even if I get a *little* bit tippy and knock over a few blocks, there's a ton of employees here to put them back together in no time."

Serge shook his head. "Most people think the Lego corporation assembled a crack team of world-class experts to engineer Mini-Florida on a computer, but I'm not buying it."

"You aren't?" asked Coleman.

"It's way too good." Serge pointed at a two-story building in Key West. "Examine the meticulous green shutters on Hemingway's house. No, my money is on a lone-wolf manic type like the famous Latvian Edward Leedskalnin, who single-handedly built the Coral Castle back in the twenties. He operated in secret, moving multi-ton hewn boulders south of Miami, and nobody knows how he did it. Probably happened here as well: The Lego people conducting an exhaustive nationwide search among the obsessive-compulsive community. But they had to be selective and stay away from the ones whose entire houses are filled to the ceiling with garbage bags of their own hair. Then they most likely found some cult guru living in a remote Lego ashram south of Pueblo with nineteen wives, offered him unlimited plastic blocks and said, 'Knock yourself out.'"

"Why do you think that?"

"Because we can smell our own type. If *I* was offered unlimited Legos . . ."—Serge gestured with an upturned palm—". . . this is what you'd get."

A cell phone rang. Serge checked the display.

"Who was that?" asked Coleman, inching toward the bank buildings.

Serge jerked him back by his shirt collar. "Put the weed away and follow me . . ."

They strolled around Mini-Florida, past laughing children, harried parents, balloons. It was another brutally hot day, and everyone was in shorts and breezy shirts. Except the man sitting on a bench up ahead; all the other tourists had given him a wide berth. He wore a tweed jacket and rumpled fedora, and his feet were propped up on a shoeshine box made of Legos he'd just purchased from the gift shop. The reason for the wide berth was the loud conversation he was having with himself. Actually, he wasn't talking to himself but to the invisible shoeshine man buffing his hooves. "There's another fiver if you put some spit into it, Pee-Wee . . ."

"Mahoney! Over here!"

Mahoney turned to see someone coming up the path, waving. "He'd recognize Serge anywhere," Mahoney narrated. "And Mahoney could tell by the ten miles of bad road in his face that he was banjo-hitting."

"You're talking in the third person again," said Serge.

"And your sundial needs winding."

"I know I'm late," said Serge. "Got hung up on Mini-Florida, and Coleman tried to smoke dope, but the bank tower wouldn't have withstood his weight."

"Mahoney took a deep breath of stale air and queer alibis, but by *queer* he meant a husband who works on the B-and-O Railroad and gets caught by his wife with stained lace panties in the pocket of his conductor's jacket and swears it was a surprise anniversary gift."

"Look, I'm here now, okay?" said Serge. "So it's all good."

"Mahoney doubted it like a leg-breaker for a loan shark being fed a tale about suddenly having to rent a separate apartment because a conductor's jacket was left on a chair. But time was ticking like those people with involuntary facial twitches . . ."

"Let's fast-forward," said Serge. "Any word on my friend from the Costa Gorda days?"

"Forty lengths out of the money at Aqueduct."

"That bad?" said Serge.

"Chicago fire."

"Thanks for trying . . ."

"Java juice on the tube-steak fader?"

"No, I haven't found out anything yet about the dating bandit."

Mahoney smiled. "Straight flush to the paint cards."

Serge raised an eyebrow. "You have a new client and a lead on another scam artist?"

Mahoney slipped Serge a matchbook with scribbling inside.

"Okay." Serge nodded. "I'll call you as soon as I know something."

Mahoney tipped his hat—"Bizzo"—and walked away.

Chapter SEVEN

MIAMI BEACH

Unlike Serge, and almost everyone else, there was one particular man in Florida who had the kind of looks that were the first thing women noticed upon entering a room.

All women. Every time. Every room.

Smoldering Latin sexuality and charisma. And a regular clothes-horse. He consistently had them lining up in the clubs and social events and produce departments. Just one last blank to fill in. What did he do for a living? The women crossed their fingers: doctor, lawyer, banker? . . . Why, none of the above. He had a trust fund. *Ding, ding, ding*—we have a winner!

But there was this hitch. And nobody would ever believe it without witnessing it in person. And even then, they'd blame it on a trick of lighting.

It was this: Despite all outward appearances to the contrary, he was, well, to look at it from the opposite end, the luckiest man in the world at cards.

When it came to women, he could effortlessly surround himself with a harem. Closing the deal was another matter entirely. It was always something. Something Florida: category-five hurricanes, red tide blooms, Cuban unrest, election unrest, alligators, mosquitoes, Burmese pythons, brush-fire evacuations, all-purpose outbreaks of criminal weirdness and peripheral aberrant behavior.

The bottom line, the guy had never, ever scored.

He was: Johnny Vegas, the Accidental Virgin.

Johnny himself didn't understand it, but it came down to numbers. As any theoretical mathematician will tell you, it is the statistical anomaly that bears out the equation. Somehow, somewhere, in any quantified hierarchy, there is dead-last place. To put it more precisely—again in academically provable terms—if this was all mapped out on a blackboard, and in the exact center of the board was sigma designated by the hump of a bell curve, and halfway to the left side of the blackboard along the negative x axis was the beginning of the most un-laid one percent of men on earth, Johnny would approximately be across the street at Starbucks.

But to Johnny's credit, his misfortune was in proportion to his persistence. The guy never gave up. And this particular night he put on his batting helmet again and got back in the game at an ultra-hot new Washington Avenue dance club called Liquid Plasma.

Deafening rhythms throbbed out the door to those behind the velvet rope who couldn't get in because they weren't attractive, yet not ugly or self-disfigured enough to be trendy. Inside, it was dark, steamy and crammed tight with perspiring bodies hopping to the music in perfect synchronization like a North Korean military parade. The ceiling rose a full four stories over the dance floor, where crisscrossing lasers sliced the vapor of dry ice. Swooping down on the crowd were holograms of dragons, unicorns and Kardashians. The club usually reached max capacity around four A.M., but tonight even earlier because it had booked the most popular DJ on the beach, Count Dreckula. Flexible fiber-optic tubes glowed through his translucent jumpsuit as he stood in a window washer's scaffold just below the ceiling. The Count had richly earned his rabid following through years of rigorous music study, learning how to play a record on a record player.

Down in the middle of the pulsating mass was Johnny Vegas. Pressed against him was 360 degrees of willing breasts. But all that was Plan B. Because Johnny was awaiting the return of the vixen who had introduced him to the club.

Sasha.

Sasha was on the Permanent A-List with the security team at the front door because she was a consensus all-American femme fatale. First, there was her jaw-dislodging, exquisitely draped platinum-blond hair. Sure, it came out of a bottle at her hairdresser's, and she lied about it every chance. And if men ever learned that secret, their universal reaction to her black roots: "So what?" Plus that killer mane was fringed with brown lowlights an inch along the ends like some mythical jungle creature. Then her features, starting at an absolute perfect ten, but after that each of them was a notch different, not negative or positive, just . . . *off.* Her eyes more oblate and drawn to a taper, lips disproportionately fuller in the middle, nostrils with larger intake. And the total package worked, adding to the exotic allure, because that's how men work. They've all been to strip clubs. Beauty is beauty, and then there's new, like the unsymmetrical cant of Ellen Barkin's smile, or Lauren Hutton's tooth gap. Only makes them stand out more. Sasha had all that going on. It was her predatory, catlike looks and moves, but it was more. Even the way Sasha said her name. It was a laboriously drawn-out process that drew no complaints, starting with an elongated hissing sound like a vandalized tire, rising to a throaty whisper accenting the first syllable, before finally concluding with a post-coital exhale.

"*Sssssssaaa-shhhhhh . . . ahhhh.*"

She had hired a voice coach.

Women were the last thing on Johnny's mind earlier that day around noon as he enjoyed a takeout lunch of lobster salad and sparkling water from a fjord. He was sitting by himself in the sun on the grassy slopes of Dumbfounding Bay. Except it's not really a bay. Actually part of a string of lagoons just inside the barrier-island communities of Bal Harbour, North Miami Beach and Sunny Isles. It was Johnny's special place, a quick midday nature escape a convenient fifty feet south of the William Lehman Causeway and the golf course on the other side.

Johnny wiped his mouth with a napkin and began to get up when, suddenly, she was just there.

Sasha.

In all her platinum halo glory. Gently weeping, casting upon the water a dozen of the reddest roses, which were promptly ripped apart by pelicans and seagulls accustomed to human handouts from the Frito-Lay company. But the roses were quickly spit back: What is this shit?

Sasha sniffled daintily and dabbed her eyes with a monogrammed handkerchief.

J.R.

Of course Johnny was required to come to her rescue. After all, he had the same first initial as the hankie.

"Miss, are you okay?"

"What?" Sasha turned. "Oh, I didn't notice you. I, uh . . . Yes, I'm fine."

"You're crying."

She smiled and wiped mascara-smearing tears. "This is my special place. It's where J.R. and I . . ." She stopped to blow her nose with un-usual duration.

Johnny took half a step back to be safe.

She glanced at him with another embarrassed smile. "Sorry about that."

"No, just take your time."

Sasha nodded. "J.R. was a real gentleman, knew how to treat a woman." She lowered her gaze toward the water. "He's gone now . . ."

Johnny Vegas thought: *He's gone, good. Let's hear more.*

Sasha watched the remaining mangled flower petals drift south with the tide. "So you like to come out here and relax for lunch?"

"Time to time," Johnny said with underplay. He knew women loved the sensitive type. "It's so tranquil. Occasionally you need to break away from the crazy pace out there with all the calls from hedge-fund man-agers. The natural purity and solitude out here helps me meditate."

"I love the sensitive type," said Sasha. "J.R. was like that."

Johnny Vegas didn't know it, but he had inadvertently stumbled into one of Florida's most vividly historic landmarks. There were no signs. With reason. Vegas grinned. "What about you? Come here often?"

"No." A sigh. "Just once a year . . . On the day he—" The handkerchief came out again.

Uh-oh, Johnny thought, *a woman in mourning*. Grief was such a heartbreaking thing. Maybe he could use it to score. "You said this place is special?"

She nodded again. "Holds a lot of memories."

And how. Every responding police officer clearly remembers the day they got the call. The neighbors remember the fifty-five-gallon drum that had bobbed to the surface and was dragged ashore. The medical examiner remembers the ghastly contents . . .

A screech of braking tires.

Johnny and Sasha turned to see a black Firebird skid off the causeway into the grass on the opposite side of the tiny bay. The driver got out and dashed enthusiastically down the bank. The passenger tripped and rolled like a log to the water's edge.

"Coleman, stop fooling around! Stand up and get into the moment. I remember it all like it was just yesterday. They opened the steel drum and there was the legendary Johnny Roselli, who worked for Capone and Sam Giancana. Everything about his murder pointed to another legendary moment from Miami's historic nexus of organized crime and the espionage community, which began when the CIA christened Operation Mongoose during the early sixties. In 1976, Roselli was called to testify before a Senate select committee investigating Mongoose's alleged cooperation with the Mob to assassinate Cuban dictator Fidel Castro. But he never got the chance. It's long been rumored that my homey Tampa godfather, Santos Trafficante, made the call. They sawed off Roselli's legs and jammed them in the drum beside him. That's why I can't resist coming here—it's such a happy place! . . ."

Across the bay, Johnny and Sasha watched the odd couple on the other side.

"The tall one's jumping up and down." Sasha cupped a hand to her ear. "What's he saying?"

"I can't quite make it out," said Johnny. "But he sure is drinking a lot of coffee—" He cut himself off and strained for a closer look. "It couldn't possibly be them . . . Oh, no, this isn't happening."

"What isn't happening?" asked Sasha. Then she turned toward the opposite bank. "Dear Jesus, the fat one's peeing in the water. *J.R.'s water!*" This time she cupped her hands around her mouth. "You son of a bitch! . . ."

On the other side of the bay: "Serge, I think that woman is yelling at us."

"Probably one of your fans."

"Now she's throwing rocks," said Coleman. "I think they're meant for us, but her arm's way too weak."

"Do you know her?" Serge reached down and grabbed a handful of wildflowers.

"I don't think so," said Coleman. "But the guy looks familiar . . . What are you doing?"

"A historic place requires proper respect." Serge cast the flowers upon the water. "For Johnny. Let's bow our heads . . . That's enough." He sprinted up the bank to the car.

Back across the water, Sasha threw a final rock, then collapsed onto the grass in a sitting position, covered her eyes and began crying.

Johnny collapsed next to her and began crying, too.

His unlucky streak was intact.

Johnny was still covering his face when he felt something. A hand caressing his cheek.

"You're crying," said Sasha, snuggling into his shoulder. "That's *so* sensitive."

They sat still together. Eventually she raised her head. "I'm okay now."

She stuck the *J.R.* handkerchief back in her purse. Sasha never knew Roselli, or any of the others. Way before her time. But she had this quirk. Sexual. One of those rare, unhealthy paraphilias where she needed to be in danger from the man she was with. At the top of her fantasy list was mobsters. She watched the movies and read the books and visited the sites. Just standing on the edge of Dumbfounding Bay set off a joy buzzer between her legs. In another era, she'd have been a gun mol, but she was born too late. Instead she was forced to run with today's crop of low-level punks and wannabe gangsters. She was unsatisfied.

Sasha stood up and smiled.

Vegas followed suit and held out his hand. "My name's Johnny, too."

"Wow, this must be fate. Pleasure to meet you, Johnny." She shook his hand. "My name's *Ssssssssaaa-shhhhhh . . . ahhhh*."

Sasha had been able to throw a bit of ventriloquism into the delivery, and Johnny glanced behind him like her name was being announced in Dolby Surround Sound.

"Johnny," she said, putting his arm in hers. "Are you doing anything tonight?"

Inside his head: *You have no idea how much I hope so.* "Uh, let me check my planner."

"Because if you're free, I know the hottest new place on the beach . . ."

And that's how Johnny Vegas came to find himself at three A.M. on the dance floor of the club called Liquid Plasma in the middle of a breast buffet.

Soon, a ripple through the crowd as it parted for Sasha. She presented herself in front of Johnny and launched into one of the sultriest grinds anyone had ever seen outside a gentlemen's club. The performance climaxed with hands sliding down in her signature move that was almost illegal. No, it *was* illegal. Others took photos and videos with cell phones.

Sasha finished her routine and threw her arms around Johnny's neck. And her tongue inside his shirt. The crowd congealed back around them and resumed hopping again as a single organism. It went on like this for hours, Johnny and Sasha tripping the light fantastic with the aid of the new ultra-strength energy drink, Tripping the Light

Fantastic. They waved glow sticks and did cocaine bullet-snorts offered by fellow dancers, and Sasha sucked a glow-in-the-dark, amphetamine-laced baby pacifier.

Pouty lips went to Johnny's ear. "It's getting late," she said just before noon. "Let's go back to your place."

Johnny practically knocked people over dragging her by the hand for the nearest emergency exit.

After running six red lights, Johnny parked his gull-wing Porsche GT1 behind a beach house. The couple stumbled and giggled together as they struggled up the front porch steps facing the dunes and bright sun over the Atlantic. Liquor, anticipation. She embraced him hard, and they crashed against the gingerbread trim next to the front door. Her mouth went to his ear again. "I've never told anyone this before, but my secret fantasy is to . . ."

The rest was inaudible except to Johnny's eardrum. Bubbles hit his brain. Johnny fell one way, and Sasha the other, both landing on their asses. They stared at each other a second, then giggled even louder. Johnny dug in a pocket for house keys with renewed urgency. Yes! The streak is over!

Sasha got up and looked around. "Where's my shoe? I lost a shoe . . ."

Johnny's trembling hands fumbled with the keys, dropped them, and fumbled again. Sasha wandered in unsteady circles on the porch. "Where are you, shoe? . . . Come here, shoe . . ."

Keys hit the ground again. Anxious fingers snagged them but had trouble aligning the end of the key with the lock. "Let's *goooooo*, focus!"

"Here shoey-shoey . . . Where are you, shoey? . . ." Sasha staggered around the corner of the house. "Motherfuckin' shoe, where are you!"

The lock finally popped. Hooray. The door creaked ajar, but Johnny wasn't looking inside. He stared off the side of the porch. "Sasha, the house is open . . . *Sasha? . . .*"

Then he finally looked though the front door.

"What on God's earth? . . ."

In the background, squealing tires.

The cops arrived fifteen minutes later.

Johnny sat on the top porch step, face in his hands again. Shoulders shaking with sobs.

A detective approached the officer in charge of the crime scene. "Magruder, what have we got here?"

"Seems pretty open-and-shut." The sergeant closed his notebook. "Our pal Mr. Vegas here spent all night in one of the local clubs with some young thing he had a chance meeting with yesterday afternoon, and he came home this morning to find his place stripped to the walls."

"Another dating bandit?"

"Except a new wrinkle."

"How's that?"

"This one was female."

They became distracted by a louder bout of weeping from the porch steps. The detective jerked a thumb sideways. "What's his problem?"

The sergeant shrugged. "He's been crying off and on ever since we got here."

"Doesn't he know insurance covers this?"

The sergeant raised his voice in Johnny's direction. "Mr. Vegas, just call your insurance company . . . The important thing is you're safe. She didn't even touch you."

The crying became deafening wails.

"Wow." The detective turned toward the sergeant. "He must have really loved that furniture."

FORT LAUDERDALE

Fingers impatiently tapped a counter in a strip mall. Hanging from a pegboard: chew toys, catnip, fish pellets, and electronic dog collars that create an invisible fence around your yard.

An employee rushed back to the register through a vortex of animal-waste aromas that combined to smell exactly like all pet stores everywhere.

"Sorry for the delay." He wiped something green on his shirt. "How may I help you?"

"This is a rescue intervention," said Serge. "You've seen those news stories about heroin-addict mothers forgetting baby strollers on escalators while they shoplift?"

The employee scratched his head. "I'm not following."

"I need you to take in a hamster."

"We don't buy hamsters," said the clerk. "They're multiplying fast enough as it is back there. Unless you bought it here and it's sick or something, then I'll need a receipt."

"No, I didn't buy it here and I don't want to sell it." Serge reached in his hip pocket. "I want you to adopt it. His current owner needs parenting classes. He's passed out in the Firebird right now . . . Oh, and he may have a drug problem."

"Your friend in the car?"

"The hamster, too. He's being raised in a toxic environment. And when Coleman lost consciousness a few minutes ago, that was my big chance to save him, so it's not really a kidnapping, right?"

"But I don't think—"

Serge set the furry critter on the counter. "His name's Skippy."

The clerk looked down, then quickly up again with an odd expression.

"What's the matter?" asked Serge.

"That's not a hamster."

"What is it, then?"

"A mouse."

"Does that affect the adoption?"

"Well, we can always use mice."

"Good. *Great!*" Serge bent down to talk to the rodent. "Hear that? You've found a loving new home, where you can get clean and sober."

"Yeah," added the clerk. "We feed them to the snakes."

Serge's eyes flew wide. He snatched the small animal off the counter and clutched it to his chest. "Not Skippy!"

"But it's just a mouse."

Serge crashed backward into a sales display. Tiny aquarium castles plunged to the floor. "What kind of monster are you!"

"Look, they pay me shit."

Serge ran out the door to a jingle of bells.

Coleman sat up in the backseat when Serge peeled out. "What's going on?" He looked around the car. "Where's Skippy?"

"Taken into protective foster care." Serge skidded around a corner. "And we should probably change his name to Mickey."

"Why?"

They took off in the Firebird. It was noon along the countless finger canals that characterized the city.

A landscaping crew was putting in yeoman duty. Three trucks with trailers and the heavy rigs. Constant buzzing and sawing and people riding other noisy things around. A tiny one-man tractor grunted to a stop.

A '78 Firebird pulled up to the curb.

Serge approached the man climbing out of the safety cage. "What are you going to do with that?"

"Probably make mulch." The man wiped sweat and dirt off his forehead. "Why?"

"How much?" asked Serge.

"You want to buy it?"

Serge nodded.

"Okay, fifty bucks. No, a hundred."

Serge opened his wallet. "Split the difference at seventy-five, and you help me load it in the car."

"Cool."

The yardman deftly maneuvered the tractor into position behind the Firebird. He threw a black-knobbed lever, flipping down the front-loader claw and dropping the item into the trunk. The car's back end bounced on the suspension. Not a remote chance of closing the hood, so it was tied with twine.

Serge dusted dirt off the top of the fenders. "Got a business card?"

"Sure, it's somewhere in here"—going through one of those thick hoarding wallets on a chain. "There we go." He handed it to Serge. "What kind of work are you thinking of having done?"

"Stump removal."

"Huh?" The landscaper narrowed his eyes, staring at the trunk of the Trans Am and the protruding, recently purchased stump.

Serge grabbed his door handle. "Pleasure doing business." They drove away from the competing whines of small gas-powered engines.

The phone rang. Serge recognized the number in the caller ID.

"Hey, Mahoney, what's going on?"

"Mahoney mulled the lowdown he was about to lay on Serge like a dirty ward boss with a case of the crabs and a day-old racing form."

"Mahoney," said Serge. "You're doing third person again."

"Serge was a sharp cookie, like a broad in a gin joint who sees all the angles, from acute to obtuse—"

"Mahoney, look, if it's about the cases, we've been working round the clock. I just picked up a stump."

"Serge made as much sense as wearing a belt with suspenders."

"What I could use is a little help on your end," said Serge. "Call some of your old contacts and get all the police reports with similar dating-bandit MOs. As for the newest victim who hired you, I already told you I only need—"

"Mahoney was sly to Serge's jones and ready to roll Romans like loaded crap dice that always come up boxcars."

"Why didn't you say so?" Serge grabbed a pen. "I'm ready for that phone number."

Mahoney gave it.

"Thanks, I'll let you know how it works out."

". . . Like a one-legged unicycle jockey . . ."

Serge began closing the phone—". . . *Scootily-bop* . . ."—and hung up. He immediately dialed again.

"Hello?"

"Yes, I'm calling about the yellow Corvette for sale in the paper."

Chapter EIGHT

MEANWHILE . . .

Cheeto-encrusted fingers tapped a keyboard in an otherwise sterile cubicle.

A mug shot popped up on the screen.

An e-mail was forwarded.

Another file of random statistics opened.

It was an anonymous cubicle, and it could have been anywhere, but this one was in Tallahassee. The man behind the keyboard had an engraved brass nameplate on his desk: WESLEY CHAPEL. It sat on the front of his desk, which was pressed against one of the walls of the cubicle, and the nameplate could not be seen. But that was okay because Wesley wasn't a people person, which meant he was perfect for his job.

Here's what Wesley did: He made sense out of nonsense.

And he was the best the company had, sifting and crunching and correlating the white noise of meaningless numbers and GPS coordinates until patterns emerged. One entire floor of the company housed huge mainframes filled with raw, non sequitur information that had been dragnetted from every corner of the Internet. Some were free public records; others databases purchased from numerous companies who valued their customers' privacy.

His was one of a growing number of firms in a field that had endless buyers lining up for a geometric progression of knowledge. The nascent industry had plenty of niches in which companies could specialize. They variously offered millions of searchable newspaper and magazine articles, indexed scientific papers from leading research universities dating back to 1888, legal precedents and up-to-the-minute Shepard-ized case law for all fifty states and the federal districts.

Wesley's company specialized in prying, and it easily had the longest line of clients clamoring for their product: networks wanting to know the volume of cable subscribers in Michigan's Upper Peninsula, test mar-keters seeking the median age of people who bought laundry detergent with credit cards, municipal planners looking for the neighborhood that voted least so they could locate the new sewage transfer station.

They were like the business world's version of the Elias Sports Bureau. You know, those people who ESPN quote on *SportsCenter* when they want to know the last year in which the Red Sox gave up an extra-inning blown save on an inside-the-park homer against a switch-hitting platoon infielder born south of the Mason-Dixon with the nickname "Jukes."

Wesley never needed to reorder business cards, because he didn't get out much; his were still tucked neatly in a bottom drawer, embossed with the company's previous name, Event Horizon, Inc. The moniker was an astrophysics term for the point of no return where all matter and even light itself cannot escape the gravity of a black hole. It was meant as an analogy for the moment when the interstellar nebula dust of Internet gibberish is pulled together to form actionable intelligence. The name was way too highbrow for the buyers, and people kept on driving past the building, having no idea or concern about what was going on inside. So the name was changed to Big Dipper Data Man-agement. All the new clients liked the mental image of a soup ladle. The founder of the company had thought up both names, because he'd recently purchased a telescope.

Oh, and they had a new client. Law enforcement. Most of the police upper brass was old-school and couldn't grasp the utility. But the new whiz kids who retrieved deleted files from the laptops of pedophiles—they all sent word up the chain: This is the future.

It started at the beginning of the methamphetamine explosion, back before honest citizens needed a U.S. passport and long-form birth certificate to buy over-the-counter sniffle remedies. At the encouragement of police, state lawmakers hired Wesley's company and used the supporting data to show an undeniable statistical relationship between pockets of violent street crime and volumes of cold-medication sales, which led to pioneering legislation drying up the basic ingredients for drug labs.

That opened everyone's eyes. Cold remedies? What about cold *cases*? Everyone remembered all the previously unsolved murders that had been cleared at the dawn of DNA. This looked like a silicon version of genetics, and another step forward in the march of technological justice.

The theory: We've got all these electronic files of credit-card purchases, utility bills, tollbooth hits, property taxes, airline tickets, car titles, etc., etc. Obviously too circumstantial to hold up in court, but what if we mashed all those records together, filtering for time and place. In the coldest of cases, it might at least narrow the field and generate a short list of those who deserved a closer look.

For instance: a rash of mystery rapes hit the Pensacola area in the late nineties. Then nothing for years. Police figured the assailant either moved, died, went to prison, or was shipped out with the military.

Then, in 2004, Pensacola authorities noticed a bulletin out of Jacksonville. Serial rapist. As they read, chills. Almost identical details: sliding-glass-door entry, panty-hose mask, one-sided serrated knife, even the exact verbatim instructions to each victim that they had withheld from the press: counting to one hundred, then back down again, before attempting to loosen the same kind of knots.

The Pensacola police got in touch with Jacksonville, and they decided to meet halfway. Literally. Tallahassee. They hovered over Wesley in his cubicle. First, he set the parameters for Pensacola during the six-month period of the first attacks, which pretty much created a list of everyone who had produced personal ID for anything, only about 1,850,000 people. Then he percolated that list through the last month's info in Jacksonville—looking for those who had been in both places during the two time periods—which brought the number in the overlapping circle down to 2,379.

"Damn," said the lead investigator. "I though we might have had something."

"We do," said Wesley. "That's a workable number."

"Workable?" said the detective. "It's over two thousand."

"That's nothing the null sets can't neutralize."

"I have no idea what you just said."

"The null sets are the silver-bullet statistics." Wesley typed even faster as he spoke. "You say the attacks stopped in Pensacola in '98 and resumed in Jacksonville in '04? So what we do is take our list of two-thousand-some-odd suspects, flip the filter, then kick *out* all the names who had any hits in either city during the intervening six-year quiet time when the assailant was supposedly in jail or whatever..." He stopped typing for a dramatic pause, then pressed a final button.

The investigators leaned toward the screen. The number 2,379 quickly spun south. A thousand, 500, 80, 15, until it finally came to a stop: 1. And a suspect's name. The last piece of data was a video-store rental no less. Chevy Chase vacation comedy. Detectives made some calls. Unbelievable. A seaman at the Naval Air Station in Pensacola had been shipped overseas, then six years later he was transferred back to another base in Jacksonville.

A dozen police vehicles were waved through the security gate and skidded up to the barracks. Military prosecutors arrived, and in less than five minutes the joint interrogation burped up a signed confession. The state of Florida wanted to take custody, and the navy said they were always happy to assist local law enforcement, but first they'd like to hold on to him for another hundred years.

Serge strolled the aisles of the home-improvement store, sucking coffee from a tube under his shirt.

"What are we looking for?" asked Coleman, slurping from his own tube of vodka.

"I'll know when I see it. Just keep your eyes open for gigantic iron corkscrews."

"What are those?"

"They're hurricane tie-downs you twist into the ground and secure stuff when you don't want to retrieve your aluminum shed from someone's living room on the next block. That's always an awkward visit."

An employee in a yellow store vest came around the corner and smiled as he had been trained. Then the smile stopped. "Are you guys okay?"

"Great!" said Serge. *Slurp, slurp.*

"What's with the tubes?"

"We have medical conditions," said Coleman.

Serge nodded earnestly. "We're in self-help."

The employee sniffed the air. "Do I smell liquor?"

"A lot of things smell like liquor," said Serge.

"Yeah," said Coleman. "Like other liquor."

Serge pulled up his shirt. "I'm clean. This is a clear plastic bladder that sports fans strap to their bellies with Velcro to sneak alcohol into arenas and stadiums. I learned it from Coleman, but I use it for coffee strictly due to my on-the-go needs."

Coleman raised his own shirt. "This is water. You can't test it because of my rights." He lowered his shirt.

"We need your assistance," said Serge. "Usually I can immediately lay my hands on anything in this place, like garage-door openers to activate bad stuff. You're the expert: Do you think personal electronics can really bring down a 747?"

"What?"

"Of course you can't speak on the record." Serge slurped and rotated his head for answers. "Where are the hurricane tie-downs?"

"You trying to secure a shed?"

"Bigger!"

"A metal garage?"

"Needs to be bigger than that!"

"What on earth are you tying down?"

"That's classified." Serge briefly flashed a *Miami Vice* souvenir badge. "Give me the big mothers. Plus a short metal plumbing pipe like you'd use to rough in a showerhead, and your strongest plastic fasteners for electrical cables. Jigsaw, baseboard, paint, thumbtacks, balsa wood." *Slurp, slurp.* "And can you escort us through checkout? Had some recent problems there. Our pictures might be on some flyers."

Moments later, several employees whispered as Serge and Coleman walked out the door with plastic bags in their hands and four enormous iron corkscrews perched over their shoulders.

MIAMI BEACH

Neon glowed in an artistic rainbow from the landmark Art Deco hotels along internationally famous Ocean Drive. Red, pink, green, blue, orange, yellow, as if the owners had held a meeting.

Farther north on Collins Avenue were the larger, old-guard flagship resorts. The Delano, the Eden Roc, Fontainebleau, Deauville. At a newer, lesser-known resort in the middle, the clientele finally calmed down around three A.M. Some asleep, some passed out, some sitting up in bed with the TV remote, determined to squeeze out more vacation value.

By four A.M., most of the lights had gone dark up and down the hotel's thirty-story facade.

At 4:02, the first phone rang. Room 1911. A couple from Manitoba celebrating their copper anniversary, which was number seven. The wife answered from REM sleep and a dream about the national cricket team.

"Uh, mmmm, hullo? . . ."

"Ma'am, this is the front desk . . ."

Seconds later, the wife hopped onto the bed screaming in panic. "Kevin! Wake up! Wake up!"

He opened one eye on the pillow. "What is it?"

"An emergency! We have to get out of here!"

They dashed into the hallway. There was a white box on the wall and a sign: In Case of Emergency, Break Glass.

Glass broke.

In the next room, two former classmates from Syracuse on a girl-friend trip. The phone rang.

"W-what? Hello? Huh? . . ."

"This is the front desk. Please stay calm, but we have a serious emergency. There's been a highly poisonous chemical contamination to your floor from the air system. We need you to evacuate your room immediately . . ."

"But how did—?"

"Ma'am, there's no time. We have too many rooms to call. The hazardous-material teams are on the way. In the meantime, we'll need the total cooperation of our guests. Once you get to the hall, grab a fire extinguisher and spray yourselves down with the foam. That will temporarily neutralize the contaminants' effects on your skin."

"What will it do to my skin?"

"You don't want to know right now, but there's only a remote chance of amputation. And after you're covered with foam, take the stairs—not the elevator!—and hurry to street level and exit the hotel onto the sidewalk. Once there, strip off all your clothes as fast as possible. By then, the hazmat teams should be waiting with the hoses to properly complete the decontamination procedure."

The women dashed into the hall. Ten other people were already there, half covered with foam, the other half flapping their arms in whimpering panic. "Spray me next! Spray me next!"

Other doors flung open. More guests in the hall. A second extinguisher was broken out of its harness. The stampede began. No! Not the elevator! They burst into the stairwell, a race of sudsy people down landing after landing, until they reached the bottom and sprinted out onto the sidewalk.

Clothing flew with abandon into the night air.

Traffic on Collins Avenue was sparse at that hour, but even the most jaded motorist couldn't help but rubberneck at the sidewalk festivities. A silver BMW coupe rear-ended a Miata.

Finally, all clothes were off. The naked guests experienced a modicum of relief. Then they looked around. Where were the hazmat teams?

No chemical response was on the way, but multiple 9-1-1 calls brought six patrol cars screaming down the fashionable avenue with all lights flashing. The first officer got out in front of two dozen frothy, nude people. He'd seen almost everything working the South Beach beat. But . . .

"What in the hell is going on?"

Simultaneously, the staff from the hotel's front desk emerged from the lobby. "What in the hell is going on?"

What was going on:

One week earlier, somewhere in cyberspace, a chat room sat empty.

At precisely eleven P.M., members began logging in with code names. More than a hundred people from Palm Beach to Monroe County turned up the volume on their computers' speakers.

A silent, streaming feed from a telephone line. The quiet was broken by an Internet voice. "Two minutes to go . . ."

All the members opened a separate computer browser to a live webcam they had previously located on A1A.

That's how they selected their missions. When the group first began operating, it was just audio from the phones. But then someone threw out the idea that webcams were now everywhere. Listening to the action was great, but actually seeing the fruits of their work would put it over the top.

"Thirty seconds . . ."

Anticipation built. Then they heard various pulse tones of a phone number being punched in. It belonged to a national fast-food burger franchise across the street from a beach webcam in South Florida.

Someone answered.

"Hello, this is ____. How can we help you today?"

"I'm District Manager Frank Daniels from the regional office. We've received multiple alarms from your location. You have a major gas leak."

"What?"

"There's no time. Just listen: We need to vent the entire restaurant before there's an explosion. See the four giant plate-glass windows on the front of the building that look out toward the road? Break them."

"Explosion?"

"Shut up and get moving! The gas levels are rising every second!"

"What do I break them out with?"

"Use the chairs! Don't you remember anything from the safety drills?"

The restaurant employee couldn't remember anything from the safety drills about breaking windows with chairs, but he didn't want the district manager to know that. The people in the chat room heard the employee yell away from the phone: *"Guys! Grab the chairs . . ."*

The group's eyes went to the webcam feed on their monitors. The first chair crashed through the southernmost floor-to-ceiling pane. Then in quick succession, windows two, three and four. Customers and staff ran screaming out through the broken glass. Police arrived. Gas company trucks. Pandemonium.

All over the Gold Coast, fingers typed rapidly on keyboards.

"Excellent gig."

"Top-notch."

"Nice touch with the safety drill."

"I concur. Puts him on the defensive so he's not thinking straight and doesn't question authority."

And so on, through dozens of additional comment threads critiquing the mission.

Welcome to the modern Merry Pranksters. That was actually their name. They would have been anarchists and Luddites except they couldn't imagine life without the power grid and social media.

Near midnight, the cyber-posts turned to a new subject. Next mission.

"Webcam thoughts?"

"I found one with a great panning view of a thirty-story hotel on Collins Avenue."

"Perfect, but we'll need to change the hotel game plan."

Everyone knew why.

The hotel gig was otherwise excellent. It had been honed and improved through eight separate successful runs. Post-mission critiques added suggestions to make the prank calls more convincing. "Toss in a part about taking the stairs instead of the elevators. Everyone's familiar with that, so it's a legitimizing reference point."

They continued refining the script until it couldn't miss:

A hotel room phone rang on one of the upper floors.

"Hello, this is the front desk, and we have an emergency. There is a fire of unknown origin, and our sprinkler system is not responding even with manual override. We need you to evacuate immediately by the stairs. Do not take the elevators! Repeat, do not take the elevators! And on the way out, we need you to break off all the sprinkler heads in the hall with a shoe . . ."

But the hotel gig developed an obvious new problem. Since they were now using webcams, the entertainment value of the chaos in an internal hallway would be unseen. They put their heads together.

"We need to get them out of the hotel and onto the sidewalk in view of the cam."

"But how?"

"What about chemical or biological contamination?"

"That'll work."

"Okay, so people are standing on a sidewalk. What's funny about that?"

"It'll be late. They'll be drowsy in their pajamas."

"I'm still not feeling it."

"I got it. We tell them to spray one another with fire extinguishers to prevent chemical burns . . ."

That got the ideas flowing.

". . . And once they're on the sidewalk, we tell them to take off all their clothes."

Perfection.

They came up with the place, time and date, and agreed to meet back online.

They began signing off. Until only a single person was left.

The Internet has what is known as lurkers. Means just about the same in real life. They sneak into various alleys of cyberspace and never post. Simply watch and listen, and you'd never know they were there.

The last person left alone in the Merry Pranksters' chat room was one such lurker. He read down through the entire evening's activities and printed out a complete transcript.

Then he logged off.

Chapter NINE

THE NEXT DAY

Sunset. A black Firebird Trans Am pulled up to a pancake house on U.S. 1 just north of Hollywood.

A lime neon sign said the establishment also made good pies. The tables in the windows were full of customers holding the kind of laminated menus that had big pictures of food to speed the process.

Coleman crumpled a beer can against the top of his head. "Look at all those people eating breakfast at night."

"I love eating breakfast at night," said Serge. "It means you're calling the shots."

"With me it means I passed out and lost my watch."

"Coleman, you don't wear a watch."

"Right."

The pair jumped out of their car.

"Oh my God!" Serge placed a hand over his heart. "It's what I've dreamed of my whole life!"

A smiling man slapped the hood of a Corvette Stingray convertible. "You like?"

"Hell yes!" Serge ran over and extended a hand. "I'm Serge."

"I'm Cid. Friends call me Uncle Cid, but I don't know—"

"Can I drive!" Serge hopped up and down like a first grader. "Can I? Can I? Can I?"

Cid thinking, *This is too easy.* "Sure, get in." He tossed the keys.

Serge caught them on the fly and vaulted the unopened driver's door. The sports car roared to life and sped away from the restaurant, where someone else was hiding in the alley with a planted pickup truck.

"Uh, you might want to slow down a bit," said Cid.

"No, I'm fine." They screamed through a yellow light.

Cid gripped the dashboard. "Have you ever driven one of these before?"

"Oh, many, many, many— No. But I've watched other people." Serge gripped the stick shift and got both feet ready on the pedals. "Here's what's really fun about these babies. I'm skipping a gear now."

"What?"

Serge hit the clutch and jumped from second to fourth with a gnarling sound that repair shops love to hear. They were pasted back in their seats like the upper stage of a Saturn rocket igniting.

Serge tilted his head with a smile. "Ever seen *Scent of a Woman*? Al Pacino is this blind guy who doesn't give a poo and bluffs his way into taking a sports car for a test drive. I love that movie!" He punched the gas. "Bet you never guessed I was blind. What color is this car anyway?"

"You're blind!"

Serge wove back and forth over the center line.

"Ahhhhhhhhhh! Stop the car! Stop the car!"

"The car's yellow." Serge playfully punched Cid in the shoulder. "I was just joshin'. Don't you remember I caught the keys when you tossed them? You should see someone about your nerves." He floored the pedal, and they were flattened back again.

"Slow down!"

"I can't hear!"

"Slow down!"

Serge skidded to a stop at a green light. Horns blared as speeding traffic swerved around. "I couldn't hear with all the wind and the engine. What were you saying?"

"Good Lord! Do you always drive like this?"

"Of course not." Serge accelerated again. "This isn't my car, so it's only proper respect to drive extra carefully."

Cid wiped his forehead. "I'd hate to see how you drive what you own."

"What?" said Serge, pointing in the rearview. "You mean that thing?"

Cid twisted around and saw Coleman behind the wheel of the black Firebird, trailing a few lengths back. His head turned toward Serge. "What's he doing following us?"

"I don't understand," said Serge. "We always do that."

"You always have someone follow you when you're taking a test drive?"

"No, when I'm kidnapping someone." Serge conscientiously checked his side mirror and hit a signal for a lane change. "That way my car's conveniently right there to throw the hostage in the trunk, eliminating the always annoying foot chases through backyard clotheslines."

"Fuck you! Pull over right now!"

Serge drove into a boarded-up gas station on the corner that was usually occupied by someone selling velvet rugs of Elvis, Malcolm X and kittens. But the rug people had knocked off early. The Corvette parked next to rusty pumps, and Coleman stopped behind it.

Serge turned with a .45 automatic in his hand and a toothy grin. "Let's take another test drive."

Serge and Coleman sat on the ends of their motel beds, intently watching TV.

"That kid in the wheelchair is so cool," said Coleman.

"And what a voice," said Serge.

The show ended and Coleman packed a bong made from a motel room lamp. "Those *Glee* kids sure are something."

Serge grabbed the duct tape. "I already feel better as a human."

"They've taught me so much about understanding people who are different." Coleman leaned over the bong with a Bic lighter. "What's the duct tape for? There's already some on his mouth."

"Yeah, but this guy's working it loose with his tongue." Serge walked over to the chair with the tied-up Corvette owner. "A lot of them do that. Just wastes tape."

Coleman exhaled. "He's not earth-friendly."

Serge grabbed the edge of the gray strip and ripped it off.

"Ahhhhhhh!"

"I let you watch *Glee* with us, and this is how you repay me?" Serge bashed him in the head with the big roll of tape. "You're letting those kids down . . ." He tossed the tape aside and walked to the dresser.

Revvvvvvvvvvvvv . . .

Coleman pointed with a beer bottle. "What are you doing now?"

Serge ran an electric jigsaw through a piece of wood molding. "My latest project," he said from behind safety glasses. "You and our contestant will soon be amazed."

He turned off the saw and smoothed his cut with eighty-grit sandpaper. Then he grabbed a portable drill and inserted one of those massive circular-boring attachments that they use on unfinished doors to create the hole for the knob.

Revvvvvvvvvvvvv . . .

Serge bored. Coleman scratched his butt. The captive's eyes bugged out.

Then prying with a crowbar. Hammering nails. Slicing balsa wood with an X-Acto knife. Cutting string with scissors. Dipping a small brush in a bottle of model airplane paint. Opening a package of thumbtacks.

Coleman tossed the empty beer bottle toward the trash can in the corner, except it was the wrong corner.

Serge opened another package and looked up at the sound of breaking beer-bottle glass. "You're cleaning that up."

Coleman stared at Serge's hand. "A piece of cheese?"

Serge set it in place. "The final step to make my project operational."

"So now what?" asked Coleman.

"Where's Skippy?"

"In my pocket."

Serge held out a hand. "Give him to me."

Coleman clutched his own hands over his right breast. "Stay away from Skippy! I know what you did last time I passed out and you took him in the pet store. That's janitor interference."

"Custodial interference." Serge gestured with his hand for emphasis. "Now give!"

"No!"

They began wrestling. Serge got Coleman in a headlock.

"Let go of me!"

"Not until you give me Skippy!"

"Never!"

They tumbled off the bed, and Serge performed a wrestling spin maneuver, capturing Coleman in a half nelson.

"Stop it!" yelled Coleman. "My arms are breaking!"

Serge squeezed harder. "Then give me Skippy."

"Okay! Okay!"

Serge released, and Coleman handed over the rodent.

Serge petted the animal on the head, then lowered him to the floor. Skippy grabbed the piece of cheese and disappeared inside one of the motel's walls.

Coleman had a puzzled expression as he stared down at a perfectly rounded, semi-circular hole in the room's baseboard that Serge had created. Over the hole, hanging by string from a thumbtack, was a tiny balsa-wood sign: HOME SWEET HOME.

Coleman looked up at Serge. "It's like one of those mouse holes in the cartoons."

"I know," said Serge, placing the drill back in its carrying case. "Isn't it great? When I was a kid I always wondered why I never saw one in real life. So I've wanted to make my own ever since but never got the chance because there wasn't a mouse handy."

Coleman remained confused. "That was your new project? How does it help kill our hostage?"

"It doesn't." Serge beamed with pride as he gazed down upon the hole, where Skippy stuck out his head and wiggled his whiskers. Serge tossed another chunk of cheese. The mouse grabbed it and disappeared again.

"But we did all that shopping," said Coleman. "I thought you were coming up with another genius way to whack a dude."

"Killing jerks isn't the only reason for home-improvement stores."

"It's not?"

Serge resumed packing up his tools.

"So what's going to happen to Skippy now?" asked Coleman.

"I've released him back into the wild," said Serge. "He's now a free-range mouse."

Coleman pouted. "He was my pet."

"Coleman, if you love something, set it free." He turned to the captive. "You and I aren't quite there yet."

Coleman cracked another beer. "You're not going to kill this asshole after all?"

"Didn't say that." Serge punched the captive with brass knuckles. "You stole from my client in your car-sale scam. Tell me where the money is!"

The man spit out a tooth. "Eat shit and die!"

"If that's how you want to play it, Uncle Cid, if that's really your name." He wrapped his mouth in tape again.

"Serge, did you say 'Uncle Cid'?"

"Yeah, some made-up name." Another punch. "Who knows what it means?"

"I do," said Coleman.

Serge turned. "What?"

"It's code." Coleman took another hit. "Uncle Cid. Cid. A-cid. Acid."

"You're higher than a bastard."

"No really. All the heads know this." Coleman exhaled again. "When you want to have a big LSD party with a giant bowl of spiked punch, you get on the phone. But because the fuzz might be listening, you say you're having Uncle Cid over that night. And sometimes a bunch of college kids would hold an open LSD party for all who *knew*. They'd put a classified ad in the student paper with an address for Uncle Cid."

"Since when do you read college papers?"

"Just the classifieds," said Coleman. "For Cid parties."

Serge turned around. *Punch.*

"Why are you still hitting him?" asked Coleman. "His mouth is taped and he can't tell you where the money is."

"To be honest, it's now more about the hitting than the money." Serge swung hard again with a meaty thud on skull. "But I just *know* I'll get grief from Mahoney."

"Why? You cracked this case for him."

"Yeah, but in all the movies, you're supposed to get the money back." Serge rubbed his sore hand. "Except I'm fairly confident that his client will be equally satisfied with the results I have in mind..." *Punch, punch, punch.* "... But I have to at least go though the motions so next time Mahoney asks, I can honestly say I tried. You're a witness." *Punch, punch, punch.*

"Serge, his face is a bloody mess. It's making the duct tape peel off."

"He's abusing our landfills." The tape removed much easier this time, and Serge crumpled it into a ball. "You ready to listen to reason? Tell us where the money is or else!"

"Or else what?"

Serge reached in the duffel bag. "Or else *this*!" He removed a giant iron corkscrew and slowly twisted it in front of the hostage with diabolical drama. Then raised his eyebrows. "Pretty scary, eh?"

"I have no idea what the hell you're doing."

"Oh, *realllllllly*." Serge paced methodically with hands behind his back. "Then how about . . . *this*!" He swiftly whipped out a small galvanized pipe and held it to Cid's face.

"What's that?"

Serge shrugged and tossed it on the bed next to the hurricane tie-down. "I think it's used for showerheads."

"You're insane!"

"That's the last straw," said Serge. "I'm not letting you watch *Glee* anymore with us."

He roughly blotted the blood on Cid's face and wrapped more duct tape.

"Look!" said Coleman. "Skippy's back! He's running over to me and up my leg."

"That's the second half of 'If you love something, set it free.'" Serge carefully examined the corkscrew. "If it comes back, you know it's yours."

"I can keep him?" Coleman hugged the mouse to his cheek. "Skippy!"

"And for his happiness, I now have the equipment and skill set to instantly whip up a custom mouse hole in any motel room. But be prepared: The day will finally come like in all those tearjerker animal movies when he won't leave the mouse hole, and you'll just have to let go as the credits roll." Serge tucked the pipe and corkscrew back in his duffel bag. "Coleman, what do you think? Is it dark enough outside yet?"

"I'd say it's pretty dark."

Serge grabbed the bag's handle. "Let's rock."

Chapter TEN

MIAMI BEACH

All quiet on the nineteenth floor of a luxury resort hotel on Collins Avenue.

Three A.M.

People spoke in whispers and hushed tones inside suite number 1901. All eight of them. It was the gang's first team effort. Up until now, they had always worked solo, receiving assignments from their leader. Totally firewalled. Nobody knew anyone else's action, to minimize damage in the event someone was captured and flipped for the prosecution.

Sitting on the edge of one bed were Gustave and Sasha, the dating bandits, and some others we haven't met yet. Leroy and Short Leroy, who took out fraudulent mortgages; Tommy Perfecto, head of the burglary crew that struck while others kept their targets busy, Puddin'-Head Farina, the king of the obituary scam; and Pockets Malone, who sold hole-in-one insurance.

Standing before them was the brains of the operation, South Philly Sal, who was from Miami. He did financial backgrounds and surveillance on all the marks before making the final decision and dispatching his henchmen to ply their trades. He looked around.

"Where's Uncle Cid?"

"Don't know," said Tommy Perfecto.

"What do you mean you don't know?"

"I was waiting in the pickup truck behind the pancake house like we always do, but he never came back from the test drive."

"Dammit, we need all hands," said Sal. "That idiot's going to shave the size of the score."

The score.

Sal wouldn't have otherwise risked penetrating the firewalls, but this one was too tasty. He got the idea from the Internet, literally tripped over it while lurking in a chat room. He stood and faced the rest of the gang. "You've read the transcripts?"

They nodded, holding packets of stapled pages from the Merry Pranksters' last online meeting.

"Good, so you know how they work." He pointed at the room's TV, where a laptop had been wired into the auxiliary port and now displayed a webcam view that included their hotel's entrance.

"What now?" asked Short Leroy.

"We wait and watch," said Sal. "That's the beauty of this. The television gives us all the intel we need as everything unfolds, from our targets' location to police response."

Gustave raised a hand. "Are we working with the Pranksters on this?"

Sal grinned. "They don't have a clue. Which is the cherry on this sundae. Not only are they cracking the safe open for us, but once the authorities figure out what happened, they'll get the blame. Nobody will be on our trail . . ."

I f only I could pick up their trail," said Serge.

"Whose trail?" asked Coleman.

"The Corvette guy wasn't working alone. Mahoney's client said an accomplice helped steal the car, and I'm guessing the tentacles reach much farther. Possibly a large organized gang preying on the most vulnerable. That really pissed me off."

"What else pissed you off?" asked Coleman.

"When I open a website and music I didn't ask for suddenly starts playing. And now the burden is on me to remember how to mute the computer."

"Yeah, what the fuck is that about?" said Coleman.

"Someone forcing their musical taste on me, like I don't get enough of that in Florida traffic."

"It's just too much to take," said Coleman. "And then they expect you to get a job."

Serge turned. "Coleman, what does any of this have to do with not getting a job?"

"It has everything to do with it."

"No, it doesn't," said Serge. "You always try to work into our conversations why whatever we're talking about is a reason to stay unemployed."

"It's worth a shot."

The black Firebird left the city behind and rolled down an unlighted country road.

". . . And another item from the growing file of people who voluntarily wear dunce caps," said Serge. "You'll be talking cordially to someone and make an offhand reference, 'I recently read where—' and they'll cut you off and say, 'Oh, I don't *read*' . . . This is a tragedy on so many different levels. First, because they don't read, they don't know enough to keep it to themselves. Next, and this is the most amazing part, they use a demeaning tone like *I'm* the stupid one for wasting time with books."

"How can you respond to that kind of person?"

"I usually say something like, 'But you *can* read, right? Or is that name tag on your fast-food uniform just a bunch of gibberish?' And then they go in the back, and I bend down and squint at counter level and see them spit on my hamburger. I don't care much for that either."

"Want to hear what really pisses me off?" said Coleman.

"Get it of your chest, man!"

"You know what the worst customer service in the world is? I'll tell you. It's the weed guys. You just cannot depend on these people. They'll give you a time, right? And you're looking forward to it all week and get off work on Friday at five. Of course I personally wouldn't know, but I've heard of people with jobs. And the weed guy never shows up, and he doesn't answer his phone, and you drive by his house and his car's gone, and then you're totally un-stoned at midnight and accidentally bump into the guy at a party and go, 'Dude, what's the deal? We had a time,' and he says, 'I was doin' stuff,' and I say, 'Like what?' and he says, 'Listenin' to music' . . ."

"Coleman—"

"Wait, wait, wait! So then I say, 'How would you like if I wasn't there at the time?' And he says, 'But we had a time.' 'Exactly.' 'It's not the same thing.' 'Yes, it is.' 'No.' 'Yes.' 'No.' 'Yes' . . ."

"Coleman—"

"Hold on! And every weed guy is the same. A disgrace to the drug community. And I'm arguing back and forth with this guy, and it's like talking to a mirror."

"You mean 'brick wall,'" said Serge. "Correction: You do mean a mirror."

"And I say, 'You pull this same bullshit every time.' He says, 'Bullshit on you.' 'Well, fuck you.' 'Fuck you, too.' 'I hate your guts.' 'Don't talk to me for the rest of your life.' 'You're dead to me.' 'I screwed your mother last night.' 'I boned your sister up the ass.' And people separate you before the punches fly, and you walk into the next room of the party and walk back five minutes later: 'You still got that weed?' 'Yeah, man, you got the money?' 'Here it is.' 'Here's your dope.' 'Cool.' 'Thanks.' 'Same time next week?' 'We're on' . . ."

Serge stared speechless at Coleman.

"What?"

A banging sound from the trunk of the car. Coleman twisted rolling papers in his lap. "I think the hostage came to again."

"And just in time," said Serge. "I hate carrying them unconscious into a remote field."

Coleman licked a gummed edge. "Walking them at gunpoint is better."

They parked next to just such a remote field and walked the hostage out with a .45 barrel in his back. Serge forced him to the ground and bound his ankles with plastic fasteners meant for electric cables in underground conduits. He handed Coleman the gun. "Just keep your finger off the trigger."

"How am I supposed to shoot?" asked Coleman.

"You're not," said Serge. "He isn't going anywhere with those fasteners, but you never know. The threat of that gun alone should be enough."

"Where are you going?"

"Back to the car for the hurricane corkscrews and shovels."

Coleman scratched his hip with the end of the gun. "Don't tell me I have to dig again."

"We're not digging a hole. We're filling one."

Coleman stretched his neck in a straining attempt to see in the dark. "What's that big thing over there?"

"Another recent purchase that I dropped off earlier."

Serge reached the Firebird and was on his way back. Suddenly a distant flash. Followed by the delayed sound.

Bang.

Coleman slowly toppled over. Serge dropped the shovels and went running. "Coleman! . . . Coleman! . . . Please, God! No!"

He arrived and fell to his knees next to a face-in-the-dirt, motionless buddy. Tears welled in his eyes. "Coleman . . ."

Coleman turned his head. "Serge, get down. Somebody's shooting. I hit the ground when I heard the first shot."

"Coleman, what's that next to your hand?"

"Cool, a gun." He grabbed it. "We can shoot back."

"Coleman, I saw the flash from back there. You fired the shot."

"No, I didn't. I was just scratching my . . . Ohhhh, that's what happened." He stood and looked down at his right side. "The shot went through my pocket." He stuck the gun barrel through the hole. "And I liked these shorts."

Bang.

Serge swiped the gun away. "No more bullets for you."

"Good. Less to stay on top of."

"Now grab the shovels and my duffel with the hardware."

"Crap."

"Hey, I have to drag this guy by the ankles."

Coleman perched the spades on his left shoulder and grabbed a canvas strap. "Where are we going?"

"Over there."

"You mean toward that thing I saw earlier?"

"Just don't fall behind like the other times." Serge tucked the ankles under his armpit and hiked forward, dragging the scam artist across the rocky terrain like he was hauling out a bag of trash, which he was.

"Hey, Serge, now I recognize what that is. I remember when you bought it earlier."

Serge stopped and released the captive's legs. He dialed his cell phone. "Hello, I'd like to get some work done in the morning . . . Yes, I have a credit card . . ."

MIAMI BEACH

Five A.M.

Paramedics wrapped blankets around naked foamy people while police took statements.

"He said he was from the front desk . . ."

"Sounded so official . . ."

"What convinced me was the part about not taking the elevator . . ."

Other detectives confirmed the coordinated wave of incoming "front-desk" calls and traced them all to a proxy Internet server that disguised their true origin. Uniformed officers swept the nineteenth floor. They chalked up the smashed surveillance camera at the end of the hall to more mayhem from the Pranksters.

The authorities gave the okay for the guests to return to their rooms. The police left.

Thirty minutes later, they were back.

Another burst of 9-1-1 calls. They met the irate guests in the hallway of the nineteenth floor. Seems every one of the twenty-two evacuated rooms had been hit hard. Jewelry, laptops, cameras, expensive video stuff—all the things you'd expect from tourists in high-end resorts.

The police maintained poker faces, but they had to give the crooks grudging respect. They'd done their homework: It was one of those fancy hotels where the doors to the rooms don't automatically close all the way, which meant no need for forced entry. And details of the hoax, especially the fire extinguisher and nudity parts, guaranteed guests would be leaving in a hurry without wallets and purses.

The police issued an APB and canvassed all exterior security cameras for vehicles leaving the premises between four and five A.M.

What they didn't know was the most savvy touch of all. Since the gang knew the police would check surveillance tapes for departing cars, they made sure not to appear on them. Instead, they went to the very last place the police might think to look, where they would remain until checkout time when the coast was clear: in their own room on the twentieth floor, enjoying the contents of the minibar.

Chapter ELEVEN

JUST BEFORE SUNRISE

A convoy of landscaping trucks arrived before most people were out the door for work.

But those people were not near. The field was down a soothing country road west of the city. It curved through cattle land and bulldozed citrus groves awaiting rows of identical pre-fab houses with screened-in pools stacked on top of one another. Small egrets picked bugs off the backs of cows. Herons worked the standing water, and vultures worked the road.

Mini-tractors and other riding equipment were unchained and rolled backward off flatbed trailers. A lone machine began buzzing, which touched off many more, like the first cricket in a mating swarm.

Someone with a chain saw on a long pole attacked a dead limb overhead. Twin bush-hog mowers went at the field from opposite ends. Another tractor-like vehicle lowered a mechanical arm in front of the cab. At the end of the arm was a whirling vertical cutting disk with menacing carbide teeth along the circumference. The operator had a protective screen of safety glass to deflect any high-velocity debris as the disk hit the ground and swept side to side.

A giant branch snapped with a loud crack. A man in a construction helmet took off running with his chain saw before the limb landed where he'd just been standing. The bush hogs made progress to meet in the middle of the field like spike-drivers on the Transcontinental Railroad. The employee with the spinning disk had ear protection and didn't hear when he hit metal. But he wondered what had just bounced so violently off his safety glass.

Then someone else in a helmet ran at him, waving wildly. "Stop the stump grinder! Stop the stump grinder!"

The employee operating the grinder was suddenly blinded when an aggressive red spray covered his safety glass. The machine went silent. The spinning disk slowly rotated to a stop.

All the mechanical crickets in the field were quiet when police arrived. The other employees had abandoned their own equipment and were standing around the stump grinder. Then they were told to stand somewhere else. The crime-scene people initiated a grid excavation with surveying stakes and twine. The only things they could bag and tag were small fragments of possible evidence.

The detectives hated wearing suits in open fields at noon. They threw their jackets in the cars and went looking for the medical examiner.

"Where's the body?" asked the lead investigator.

"Working on it," said the coroner.

"You called us out here and we don't even know if we have a body?"

"No, we have a body all right," said the examiner. "Just can't rush and disturb the scene. This is an ugly one."

"So where is it?" said a second detective.

"Right there."

The detectives looked down at a broad circle of bloodstained wood chips. "Okay, that's the homicide scene, but where'd they move the body to?"

"They didn't."

"What?"

A forensic excavator worked tediously with an archaeologist's brush. He dusted off one of the larger roots along the edge of the stump. "Sir, I found another one."

"Another what?" asked the detective.

The coroner didn't answer as he knelt next to his assistant. "Okay, slowly cut the root, freeing the eyelet . . . Perfect. Now start twisting carefully . . ."

The detectives watched in bewilderment as an unidentified object slowly rotated up out of the ground and revealed itself.

"What's that?"

The examiner grabbed it with a latex glove and pulled it the rest of the way from the dirt. He walked back to the detectives and slipped it into one of his larger evidence bags. "Hurricane tie-down."

The investigators stared at the iron corkscrew. "Tie-down?"

"Found three so far, and I'd bet my paycheck there's another in the fourth quadrant," said the examiner. "They're screwed into the ground to firmly secure sheds and stuff from being overturned or blown away in tropical storms."

"I'm not making the connection here."

The examiner handed the bag to an assistant. "The culprit used these to hold down the stump."

"Forgive my ignorance," said the second detective. "But don't stumps do a pretty good job holding themselves down? That's why people have to pay for heavy machinery to come out and remove them."

The examiner shook his head. "Not this one. There are two ways to deal with stumps: Use a grinder to chip it down just below ground level, leaving only the roots. Or use a small front-end loader and scoop the whole thing. This one was scooped from somewhere else."

"It doesn't make any sense."

"It makes perfect sense." The examiner pointed to where his team now worked with lengthy crowbars to tip the stump. "After it was originally removed, someone sheared away the underlying root structure, leaving it with a level base to lie flat on the ground. And with the roots gone, the hurricane screws became necessary. They became the roots."

"But why did they need to do that to begin with?"

"To hold the stump in place over the victim."

"The victim's under there? Jesus, are you saying he was killed by being buried alive?"

"You're halfway there." The examiner grabbed another evidence bag from an assistant and held it up toward the detectives.

"Looks like a small plumbing pipe."

"For showerheads." The examiner handed it back. "It's how the victim was able to breathe underground. And the pipe was the first thing that bounced off the grinder's safety glass."

"You mean his face was right under—" The detective placed a palm on his stomach. "I think I may be sick."

"I told you it gets ugly. Whoever did this had a lot of rage. He left the guy overnight to think about it, and arranged for the landscaping company to come in this morning and do the dirty work. Literally."

A third detective arrived.

"Got any leads?" asked the one in charge.

The new guy shook his head and opened a notebook. "The property owner of record checks out. Clean rap sheet. Says he never ordered any work. And the landscapers say the job was requested over the phone, which turns out to be a prepaid disposable cell that's impossible to trace."

"Payment?"

"Stolen credit card."

The detective stared down again at the nasty pool of blood, then closed his eyes tight. "What kind of monster are we dealing with?"

DOWNTOWN TAMPA

Skyline. Hustle and bustle. Historic theater with balconies, the hockey arena, the landmark "beer can" building. People moving briskly to the thriving rhythms of the big city.

In one of the towering buildings, people came and went in slow motion, indicating it contained government offices.

A black Firebird pulled into a metered spot at the curb.

"Lower that joint!" Serge jerked a thumb sideways. "That's the county office."

"But we just wrapped up that Corvette case for Mahoney." Coleman cupped his hand for a quick hit. "It's our day off."

"Since when do we ever have a day off?"

"We're always just aimlessly driving around."

"*That's* our job. Everyone else is too busy." Serge grabbed a stack of papers from the glove compartment. "And since I did close that case, it'll buy me some time with Mahoney to get started on my political private-eye career. Investigate some congressmen. The American people can't wait much longer to be united."

"And Felicia's killer?"

Serge pursed his lips. "Okay, that's the primary reason."

"So how are you going to start?"

"I already did." Serge flipped through the pages in his lap. "You can find almost anything on the Internet: voting records, campaign donors, business associations, even travel. And what I couldn't find, I'm submitting Freedom of Information Act requests to be sent to Mahoney because we really don't have a mailbox."

"Who are you investigating?"

"Remember that political operative we took care of in the Gulf? He was wired into the whole conspiracy that got Felicia killed. So I figured why not start with the candidates he placed in office. It's a two-for."

Coleman stubbed out the roach. "Find anything yet?"

"Not sure." Serge held up a page and squinted. "Like I said, the whole universe runs on patterns. And all his guys have some connection to Costa Gorda: junkets, trade bills, vacation villa, but it's always something."

"So you've figured it out?"

"Not yet." Serge stuffed the papers away. "I'll know more when those document requests come in to Mahoney. Meanwhile, we need to infiltrate the political parties so we can gather intelligence on the ground."

"How do we do that?"

"The obvious first step is registering to vote." Serge got out of the car with quarters for the meter. "We should do that anyway. It's the sacred obligation of every citizen to participate in democracy and preciously preserve the integrity of the voting booth. So I got some fake IDs."

Serge led Coleman into the building and up an elevator.

"How soon till they let us vote?" asked Coleman.

"Since we haven't done it in a while, I'm hoping immediately."

The elevator dropped them in a sterile office that was cut in half by a long counter with a series of customer-service stations. Serge took a paper ticket with a number, and they grabbed two chairs against the wall.

Coleman tugged Serge's sleeve. "Are all the employees dead?"

"What?"

"They're like statues. Nobody seems to be moving."

"The human eye is inadequate. But special time-exposure scientific cameras have recently discovered they're actually living organisms. It is believed they are the building blocks that create bureaucratic reefs."

Serge raised his shirt, pulled out a clear tube attached to a plastic bladder Velcro'd to his stomach and began sucking coffee. *Slurp, slurp, slurp.* Coleman lifted his own shirt to grab a bladder tube for vodka. *Slurp, slurp, slurp.* A stranger sitting on the other side of Serge stared at them a second, then got up and moved six seats down.

Serge got up and took another chair six seats down next to the stranger. He clenched the tube in the corner of his mouth. "You got a lower number."

"What?" asked the stranger.

"You have a lower customer-service number on your ticket than I do. Good for you, fair and square. Mine's forty-three. People automatically think that the numbers are non-transferable, but they're blind to possibilities. Like sometimes I'll just go to a motor-vehicles office or a supermarket deli when I have no plans of conducting any business. Then I grab fifty numbers and wait for a whole bunch of people to arrive. And I redistribute the numbers based upon apparent need and good behavior until I've shuffled the whole social structure of the crowd." *Slurp, slurp, slurp.* "It's one of the few chances you get to play God. I know I shouldn't play God, but the temptation is too great. You into Conrad? *Heart of Darkness? Apocalypse Now?*"

The stranger got up and moved another six seats away.

Serge stood and moved six seats with him. *Suck, suck, suck.* "Because the ticket system is a micro-example of everything that's wrong with the country. We're barreling full tilt into social Darwinism. Can't thrive in the free market? Lie down in that unpatriotic ditch and die. Same thing in a supermarket deli. Low numbers often go to the pushiest people. Like I'll see some young mother trying to manage three tots in a shopping cart, and then this buttoned-down young prick intentionally rushes past her to grab a number first. But he has no idea I've got my fifty numbers. So I hand the mom my lowest number and wish her blessings. Then more people arrive, and I give numbers to other moms, old people, the poor and the handicapped. Now the prick is ten more spots back. And he glares at me and opens his mouth, and I go, 'Don't say a word. I've got forty more numbers and can do this all afternoon.' But he says something anyway—not polite to repeat it. And guess what? I did it all afternoon: Every time someone new arrived, I gave them a lower number, and the jerk could never get to the counter for his marinated mushrooms. I'm guessing about that part, but he looked the type . . . I sure would like your ticket, but I'd never ask. No, no, no, that would put you on the spot, and I'm all about not making people uncomfortable."

The stranger tossed the stub in Serge's lap—"take it"—and rushed out of the office.

Serge strolled back to Coleman, who was leaning with his head turned toward the door. "Man, that guy sure left in a hurry. Wonder what got into him."

"Probably heading to the deli to play God."

From flush-mount speakers in the ceiling: *"Number forty-two . . . Number forty-two? . . . Is forty-two here? . . ."*

"He went to the deli," yelled Serge.

Coleman tugged his sleeve again. "The guy gave you his number before he split."

"Oh, right!" Serge jumped up and waved his ticket in the air. "Me! Me! Me! I'm forty-two!"

They took a couple of seats at the counter.

"Now, how can I help you today?" asked a matronly civil servant.

"We want to vote!" said Serge.

"Good to hear. You want to register to vote."

"Right, and then we want to vote."

"When?"

Serge sucked the clenched tube. "Immediately."

"But there's no election going on."

"What?" Serge removed the tube. "Listen, is this some kind of deal where you're just trying to leave work early?"

"That's not it—"

"Because I understand the hardship with government pay and all, but it's nothing like the minimum-wage customer-care people. I won't mention names, but you know the stores . . ." The tube went back in, *slurp, slurp, slurp.* ". . . Those lard-bricks have it down to a science with a one-size-fits-all answer: 'No.' And I'm trying to return a toaster, with a receipt no less, but it's after the thirty days . . ."

"Excuse me—"

". . . And the woman says I can only exchange it for the exact same model, and only if it's defective, even though I've already told her that I want to upgrade to a better toaster and am willing to pay the difference—like she's not listening to a single word I'm saying . . ."

"Excuse me—"

"So she plugs it in and says it's not defective. And I say, 'Oh, it's defective all right. It doesn't meet my toast requirements.'" *Slurp, slurp.* "I need 'fast' toast with my coffee for today's balls-out lifestyle . . . Oh, if that last phrase was offensive, I meant like juggling a lot of balls in a hectic schedule, as opposed to, say, my balls. Darn, I'm just making it worse. Anyway, I *love* toast, especially with runny yolk, but toast is like the last food left that you can't microwave, even though I've tried with special homemade reflectors that they 'say' you're not supposed to put in the microwave, but I wasn't believing it . . ."

"Excuse me—"

". . . Now I have to return a defective microwave, and they asked, 'What the heck did you put in here?' and I said, 'Just toast and hope.' And they wouldn't give me my money back because of so-called misuse. But here's the remedy for that scenario: If you approach ten employees in these stores, you get ten different answers. So I waited until they went on break and found someone else at the counter who was busy texting and gave me my refund, which I wanted even less than to vote right now . . ."

"Excuse me—"

"So if you don't mind, I'd like to try someone else in this office for a different answer. What about that fat lady over there eating a bag of Funyuns? Maybe I'll ask her."

"Sir, I'm quite sure of this."

"What about early voting? Or absentee voting? Or one of impenetrable ten-paragraph constitutional amendments on homestead ad valorem reform. I'm ready to be counted!"

"Sir, there aren't any elections for weeks."

Serge pouted and pooched out his lower lip.

The woman smiled warmly. "Why don't you just register to vote for now, and then it's taken care of and you'll be ready to vote when the election does come?"

Serge slowly sat up straight. "*Allllll* right. I guess that will have to do."

"Good," said the clerk, getting out the forms. "Do you want to register with one of the political parties so you can vote in the primaries?"

"Definitely," said Serge.

"Which one?"

"Both."

The woman looked up. "You can't join both."

"Why not?" asked Serge.

"That's just the way it works."

"Are you sure you don't have to leave work early?"

"I'm positive you can't be in both parties."

"Can I register to vote twice?"

"No."

"I'm not getting this," said Serge. "You can have dual citizenship. Surely loyalty to a political party isn't more important than the country."

"Actually it is."

"Let's fix that." He opened a notepad and scribbled.

"Why do you want to join both parties anyway?"

"Because each has some great ideas, as well as some that are quite stinkaroo." Serge stuck the tube in his mouth again. "Why not harness the best that both have to offer so it's morning in America again? I already did the math."

"You sound like you mean well, but the parties' rules don't permit it."

Serge raised a fist over his head. "That's the whole problem! I have no issue with fellow citizens pushing opposing viewpoints as long as it doesn't involve drum circles or long-term magazine subscriptions. In fact, I've changed so much over the years that now I disagree with most of the people I used to be. And I liked those guys, who were me. Where is that tube? Oh, it's in my mouth." *Slurp, slurp, slurp.* "My beef isn't philosophical; it's strategic. The parties want half of America to hate the other half so we're distracted from their real game. 'Look! Over there! Two dudes are making out!' 'Where? I don't see anything . . . Hey, I'm upside down on my mortgage, and my retirement account just lost three fucking decimal places!' "

"Sir, your language."

"I'm on it." *Slurp, slurp.* "You do that long enough to people and there's open insurrection in the streets until we're Northern Ireland, spending entire lives cutting through fields of shamrocks so we don't pass any parked cars. I have enough on my plate already."

The county clerk saw a way out of the quicksand. "You do realize there's no rule against *volunteering* for both parties."

Serge stopped for a moment with his mouth open. Then he grabbed Coleman by the arm and ran out the door.

Chapter TWELVE

TROUBLES-VILLE

A rusty freighter sailed down the Miami River, destined for Jamaica and Hispaniola, where they delivered stolen electronics. Once empty, the freighter would buy stolen electronics and head back.

The small ship cruised under the Interstate 95 bridge. On one bank was a series of business endeavors that required barbed wire. Then a vacant lot with copulating dogs and a run-down two-store office building at 15 percent occupancy.

Five percent of that occupancy was sitting behind a second-floor window. A hat rack stood in the corner with a single rumpled fedora. On the desk was a black rotary phone, a bottle of rye and a dirty glass. The person behind the desk had his feet propped up, repeatedly shuffling a deck of cards without intention. His necktie had a pattern of dart boards. The playing cards had stag-party pictures of dames.

The phone rang.

And rang.

The feet eventually came off the desk. Cards scattered. He grabbed the receiver.

"Mahoney, mumble to me."

Former state agent Mahoney, officially retired in the greater Miami-Dade community with a private office in the shadow of a drawbridge. The frosted glass on the original 1940s door had gold letters with his name and PRIVATE INVESTIGATIONS.

The person on the other end of the phone was a recent client, the victim of a fly-by-night mortgage-loan scam. Mahoney could barely understand because the client was talking so fast, expressing profuse thanks. Once again, he'd gotten someone's money back, and word was getting around.

"Ice it, Goldilocks," said Mahoney. "Just hoofin' my beat. Two-bit shylock bent job."

More thanks in closing.

Mahoney nodded. "Shama-lama-ding-dong."

He hung up and gathered the playing cards. Before he could resume shuffling, the phone rang again. Mahoney eyed it. He never answered on the first ring. Because once he did, mundaneness set in. But until then, the possibilities were endless: a coded message from a wharf in Bangkok until the line went dead after a gunshot; someone with an eye patch wanting to arrange a border crossing in East Berlin; a dizzy broad with a mysteriously dead sister, but that turned into a case of split personality when she pulled out the meat cleaver. Or even, dare he hope . . . Hollywood.

The phone reached the tenth ring. He snatched the receiver.

"Mahoney, your dime."

It was the credit-card company.

Mahoney winced. But not because he was behind on payments. It was the inevitable march of technology. Serge had persuaded him that no matter how loathsome this intrusion of the modern world, he needed to start taking credit cards to stay in business:

"It seemed like just yesterday," Mahoney said to himself. "I was listening to a maudlin strain of jazz that mocked my run of bad luck, performed in the same schadenfreude riff as a dope-fiend trombone player who moonlights for his habit doing studio-session work that involves overdubbing Warner Brothers cartoons with a toilet-plunger *wah-wah-waaahhh* after an animated coyote suffers another setback . . ." He glared over his shoulder at the corner of his office, where Serge stood with a trombone: *Wah-wah-waaahhh.* Serge removed the toilet plunger from the end of his instrument. "What?"

"Mahoney just stared down into his empty glass of rye like a calico cat that gets its kicks watching water circle a drain."

"Maybe this will cheer you up!" Serge ran over to the desk with Christmas-morning zeal. "I just got a cool thing that plugs into the earphone jack of my new smartphone. Smartphones rock! I can check the rainfall in Tulsa, play roulette online, ask it to give me voice street directions and quiche recipes, identify constellations, track airline flights in real time, scan bar codes to see if duct tape is cheaper nearby, and watch YouTube videos of hilarious injuries involving archery equipment and trampolines. I've heard rumors it also makes phone calls but haven't had time to verify that yet."

"El gizmo?" said Mahoney.

"Oh, right." Serge twisted a tiny piece of plastic into the top of his phone. "This thing swipes credit cards! Isn't that fucked up?" He waved his free hand, magically wiggling fingers. "Then it flies through the air and ends up in your bank account."

"Skeeze rap the skag twist."

"Of course I need it," said Serge, fiddling with the top of the phone. "I have to run people's credit cards every day."

Mahoney stared.

"It's the weirdest thing," said Serge. "I don't even ask; they just offer. It started right after I got the smartphone and was so excited I couldn't help running up to people: 'Have you seen these? They're the shit! You have to get one! I'm going to show you every single app I've downloaded. Only takes a couple hours. I've almost figured out how to use it to blow things up from a distance, and this little accessory on top even swipes credit cards.' Then someone just hands me a Diners Club . . ."

It took a week. But finally, Mahoney fought every fiber in his being and decided to accept Serge's advice in the name of keeping his noir dream alive. He placed the dreaded call. Since he had a rotary phone, he couldn't navigate the automated menu options.

"Yo, chief!" said Mahoney.

"You did not enter a valid selection. Please try again . . ."

"Gaffer!"

"For business hours and mailing address . . ."

"Brass, honcho, *jefe*!"

"To return to the previous menu, press pound . . ."

Mahoney began banging the phone on the side of his desk. "No-good bottom-deck-dealing riverboat guttersnipe . . ."

"I still cannot understand your request. I will now put you through to a representative . . ."

Mahoney stopped with a curious look and silently placed the phone to his ear.

"This is Calista with National City Group Banc Corp. How may I help you today? . . ."

And that's how Mahoney got approval to take credit cards. Almost. Only one last step.

Applying *for* a card is one thing, but accepting them is an entirely different level of background vetting. Anyone can now set up shop with a phone and start churning pilfered plastic. So the companies hire outside firms who contact the applicant with a series of challenge questions that, in theory, should stump anyone who had stolen an identity. Always multiple choice, like: Have you attended any of the following schools? Which, if any, of these cars have you owned? In what state were you issued your Social Security card?

Mahoney was passing his challenges with flying colors. Until the last question. It came to a screeching halt.

"Hello?" asked the questioner. "Are you still there?"

"Yaza."

"Would you like me to repeat the question?"

No, Mahoney remembered it all right. "In which of the following towns is Blue Heron Boulevard located?" *Jesus,* Mahoney thought, *I haven't lived there in thirty years. Who the hell knows all this about me?*

"Sir," said the phone. "I'm afraid you're going to have to answer the last question or—"

"Riviera Beach."

"Excellent," said the phone. "You are now officially approved by the National City Group Banc—"

Mahoney hung up. It got him to thinking. Who was collecting all this information? Since he was a private eye, he found out. He picked up the phone again.

Another phone rang at Big Dipper Data Management.

"This is Wesley Chapel."

"Chapel-de-dapple, Mahoney here. Low-down sling on the dry-gulch dust-'n-rust."

"What?"

Mahoney worded it a different way. ". . . with the rhino spondulix."

"What?"

Still another way. ". . . on a Dutch flogger."

"I'm not understanding a word you're saying."

Mahoney sighed and took a deep breath. "I'm a private investigator, and I'd like to hire you to gather information on some people I'm tracking."

"Why didn't you say so in the first place?" said Wesley. "We do that all the time. You got a credit card?"

Chapter THIRTEEN

FORT LAUDERDALE

Two men burst into the room and slammed the door. Weapons came out.

"Cool," said Coleman, grabbing an appliance handle. "This is one of those motels that has a microwave and a mini-fridge and you didn't even expect it."

"It's always more excellent when you don't expect it." Serge unzipped his gear bag. "It's a sign that God accepts you as one of His children. And I never take it for granted because I'm otherwise perfectly content making grilled cheese sandwiches on the ironing board and filling the sink with ice for a cooler and then having to wash my hands in the shower the entire stay. But the surprise micro-fridge is God's way of saying, 'I like the cut of your jib. This one's on Me.'"

"But, Serge, why don't you just use the regular cooler we have out in the car?"

"It's just not done that way."

"I'm stoked you picked a place on A1A," said Coleman. "It's twenty-four-hour, take-no-prisoners partying!"

"Coleman, we're not here for your enjoyment." Serge continued unpacking. "It was Mahoney's idea. He wants us in position."

"For what?"

"He hired this consulting company called Big Dipper, and they've been crunching some random data on one of the scams."

"What have they found?"

"Nothing so far. But this area is the last place one of the scammers struck."

"So now what?"

"Hole up and wait for more data."

Coleman bent down and peeked inside the freezer. "It's even got ice-cube trays!"

"Gifts keep raining from heaven." Serge unrolled a thick electric cord.

Coleman went to the sink with the trays. "What's that thing?"

Serge stuck a plug in the wall. "My power strip. The key to holing up in motels is bringing your own power strip and taking control of the situation."

"But the room has plenty of electric sockets."

"Except they're strewn all over the place including behind the bed, which is fraught with the peril of forgetting the stuff you're charging: camera, cell phone, iPod, electric razor, laptop, camcorder, bullhorn, and miscellaneous flashlights including my giant search beam."

"Do you have a bullhorn and search beam?"

"Not since I forgot the last power strip and lost everything. I don't want to talk about it."

"That's how they get you."

Serge stared at the sink a moment. "Coleman, what are you doing?"

"Making ice cubes."

"But you're only filling the trays halfway. Not even."

"That's the point." He slipped the trays into the mini-fridge. "I let the first half freeze, then I'll take them back out in a few hours, add the rest of the water and let that freeze."

Serge went back to his power strip. "I guess I've been doing it wrong all these years."

"Don't be hard on yourself." Coleman closed the freezer door. "You're doing it the normal way, but I have to go half and half for this . . ." He held a tall round cylinder next to his head and smiled.

Serge rubbed his chin. "Am I missing something?"

Coleman pointed at his hand with the other hand. "It's a roll of Mentos. You haven't heard of them? They're breath fresheners for kids who want to fuck like in the commercials."

"That wasn't my question," said Serge. "I'm hip to what's going on out there with the Mentos and fucking. I'm just not getting the ice-cube connection."

"*Ohhhhh . . .*" Coleman nodded. "Okay, here's the deal. You've seen what happens when you put Mentos in soda?"

"Yeah, it shoots an unbelievable geyser of foam because of a unique and unforeseen chemical reaction from a combination of polysaccharides, glycoproteins and potassium benzoate that generates a ferociously rapid release of carbon dioxide. The record eruption from a two-liter bottle is something like twenty feet."

"How do you know all that?"

"Works much the same way when I was a kid and we'd launch toy rockets with baking soda and vinegar. And there are a bunch of viral Mentos-and-soda videos on the Internet." Serge sat on the side of a bed and folded his arms. "Please continue, Professor Putz."

"All right." Coleman set the roll of candy down. "Here's the part that's off the hook! Say you're at a bash, and some dude wants a drink, and you say, 'I'll get it. Is rum and Coke good?' He says, 'Goddamn right.' And you go in the kitchen giggling and make the drink. And you drop these ice cubes in the glass, except they're not *normal* ice cubes. They're the ones where you froze half, stuck a Mentos in the middle, then froze the other half on top of it. But the guy's not going to see the Mentos in the middle of the cubes because rum and Coke is dark, and you hand the drink to him while he's talking up some chick. And a few minutes later when the cubes melt . . ." Coleman waved both arms in the air. "*Blooooshhhhhh!* Foam exploding everywhere, all over the guy's clothes, up his nose, in his eyes, and all over the pissed-off chick, who's definitely not going to fuck him now."

"So Mentos can also be used for birth control."

"They should put that on the label," said Coleman. "The whole thing's priceless, everyone laughing their brains out. Except if it's a really expensive house with nice carpeting and sofas, and then the owners are screaming maniacs, 'What the fuck?' Either way it turns out good for me."

"Coleman, that actually took some advance thought," said Serge. "We may have discovered an undetected lobe. I'm taking you in for a PET scan—"

A cell phone rang.

"Serge here . . . That's great, I'll do it right now."

He hung up and plugged his laptop into the power strip.

Coleman lined up Mentos on the counter. "What was that about?"

"Mahoney just e-mailed me more crime data . . ."

PALM BEACH

The noon sun glinted off a hood ornament of a winged human.

Another Rolls-Royce rolled down pricey Worth Avenue. Then another.

But two Silver Clouds in a row didn't turn any heads at the sidewalk cafés, because the island boasted the highest concentration of Rolls in the world.

At one of the outdoor tables, a fashion-plate couple leaned forward for private conversation. Gustave wore his yacht-club blazer and prepared to work his magic again. But not on the woman at his table, who was his latest partner in crime.

Sasha.

The two dating bandits had created a more than respectable revenue stream for their gang, but now it was time to raise the bar. It was

South Philly Sal's idea. If they teamed up, the pair could land some really big game.

Swingers.

The couples tended to be more affluent, especially in the jewelry department. And more secretive. The Palm Beach social register was invented for gossip. And this was tawdry stuff. Sal figured that when blue-blood swingers reported the burglaries, they'd become suspiciously vague when police inquired about their day's activities. Not only would the couple provide ultra-vague descriptions of the suspects, but cops don't like it when information is withheld. Even when it's from victims. And the cases would fall to the lowest order of priority.

Another Rolls drove by the tables. Gustave suddenly noticed something over Sasha's shoulder and stood up with an engaging smile. "You must be the Kensingtons."

The couples exchanged introductions. The Kensingtons were at least fifteen years older with gray hair, and that was a critical part of the plan when Gustave had reeled them in with discreet e-mails through a special off-shore website that hooked up such like-minded adventure-some couples. Imagine the Kensingtons' luck at finding such an attractive young pair who didn't mind a little age difference. Mr. Kensington also wore a yachting jacket, but his sported an admiral's insignia, because he had bought the insignia and told the maid to sew it on. He pretended to read the menu, instead guessing which positions Sasha might be into and if she'd mind wearing the admiral's jacket to bed. He glanced up at her. "What looks good today?"

"Try the shrimp cocktail."

Microscopes arrived, then four bites of food.

An hour later, the Kensingtons stood bewildered with the check in their hand, wondering where their lunch partners had disappeared to. A half hour after that, they stood in their living room, wondering where all their valuables had gone.

The police arrived.

A detective opened a notebook. "Have you seen anyone suspicious outside your home lately? Maybe in a utility truck?"

They shook their heads.

"What did you do earlier today?"

"We had lunch with some friends," said Mrs. Kensington.

"What were their names?"

"Uh . . ." Mrs. Kensington turned to her husband.

The detective stopped writing and looked up. "You don't know the names of the friends you just had lunch with?"

"They were strangers," said Mr. Kensington.

"Strangers or friends, which is it?"

"Friendly strangers," said Mrs. Kensington.

The pair began to wilt under the detective's glare. "Look," said Mr. Kensington. "The tables were pretty full and we met this nice-enough couple who offered their two empty chairs."

"What did they look like?" asked the detective. "Start with the man."

The Kensingtons answered simultaneously.

"Tall . . ."

"Short . . ."

They glanced at each other.

"Medium."

The detective wrote *swingers* and closed his notebook. "Are you an admiral?"

"Not really."

HIALEAH

A black Firebird cruised down the Palmetto Expressway.

Serge turned toward his passenger.

"What?" said Coleman. "Why are you looking at me in that creepy way?"

"Coleman, you're a genius!"

"I am?"

Serge nodded hard. "You just gave me the perfect concept for my next science project."

Coleman smiled confidently and hit a joint. "Never really thought about it, but I guess I am a little on the brainy side." Another exhale. "So how am I smart?"

Serge waved for him to be quiet. He already had the phone to his head. "Alfonso, Serge here. I need a favor . . . What do you mean you don't want that kind of trouble? . . . When has anything ever gone wrong? . . . That was just that one time . . . Okay, twice . . . Okay, now that time I did not burn down your warehouse . . . No, it was an electrical short from shoddy contractors . . . I did not overload the circuits making a Tesla arc transmitter to create artificial bursts of indoor lightning. Nikola Tesla won the Nobel Prize, so it had to be perfectly safe . . . Listen, I hate to remind someone when they owe me big-time . . . That's better . . . Just a few things: a couple of fifty-five-gallon drums, arc-welding equipment and secure privacy. Got a pen? . . ."

Coleman noticed the Trans Am speeding up. "Where are we going?"

Serge still had the cell to his ear. ". . . And of course safety goggles." He hung up. "Did you say something?"

"Where you driving to?"

"Alfonso's Scrap Metal, Recycling and Lounge."

"Lounge?"

"It's on the edge of a weird municipal zoning thing, and Alfonso took advantage of it." Serge hit his blinker for a Hialeah exit. "But he learned that after the lounge opens at night and drinking starts, it's a good idea to turn off the hydraulic car-crusher and the big magnet that picks vehicles up. What were those people thinking?"

The Firebird rolled down an access road in an industrial district characterized by forklifts and Dobermans. They turned through a barbed-wire gate and into a cavernous sheet-metal building.

Serge zestfully jumped out of the car. "Alfonso!"

A lanky man in jeans raised the visor on his welding helmet and cut the gas to his torch. "Serge, it's been three years."

"I was in the neighborhood."

"Whatever happened to 'You wanna get some lunch'?"

"Why? You hungry?"

"No," said Alfonso. "It's just that most people don't call out of the blue and go, 'I'm five minutes away, and I need all this crazy shit, and seal the building tight so police can't get nosy. And why do you need three different types of fire extinguishers?"

"To cover all bases," said Serge. "I wouldn't want you yelling at me again: 'What's with all the fucking lightning in here?'"

"Forget it." Alfonso made a casual wave. "All your stuff is over there."

"Excellent!" Serge clasped his hands together. "First I'm going to weld—"

"Stop!" Alfonso held up a hand. "I don't want to know. I'm going to lock the place up now, and if you're interrogated, I was never here."

Coleman suddenly gasped.

"What is it?" asked Serge.

He pointed in horror at a sign on the door to the adjacent building. Lounge Closed Until Further Notice.

"Oh, that," said Alfonso. "One of the bar customers figured out how to turn the big magnet back on. Made the papers."

Serge walked over to his new toys and picked up a heavy black helmet. "I won't forget this."

"I wish you would."

Serge lowered the visor on his helmet and ignited the torch.

Chapter FOURTEEN

PALM BEACH

Police had no leads on what they referred to in-house as the "Swinger Bandits."

South Philly Sal had struck gold. And diamonds and artwork. It seemed Gustave and Sasha couldn't fail. Until they did.

The de Gaulles owned the biggest mansion yet. And the grifters didn't even have to detain them at lunch. The old farts just talked and talked. Usual stuff. Their vacation cottage on Nantucket, the chalet in Zurich, meeting the royals in Lisbon. Then, chaos. A cell phone vibrated in Mr. de Gaulle's pocket.

The burglary crew had failed to detect the secondary alarm system, and a text alert had just been sent. But since the primary system hadn't gone off, the couple figured their dog had probably gotten into mischief.

Mr. de Gaulle abruptly stood. "Sorry, but we have to go."

"They're bringing dessert!" said Gustave.

De Gaulle tossed a few hundreds on the table. "Our alarm went off. Probably nothing, but our dog is home."

His wife grabbed her purse. "We just love Poopsie."

They sped away in an Aston Martin.

Gustave fished out his own cell for the standard abort call. "Shit."

"What is it?" asked Sasha.

"Battery's dead. Give me your phone."

"I didn't bring it because you had yours. What are we going to do?"

What they did was race to the home. The Aston Martin was already in the driveway, but the couple was still on the footpath.

Gustave screeched up to the curb and yelled out the window. "Wait!"

Mr. de Gaulle's face was a swirl of questions. "What are you doing here? . . . How'd you know our address? And why are you driving that crappy Datsun?"

Gustave jumped out and ran across the lawn, followed by Sasha. "Hold up! I have something important—"

"Just a second," said de Gaulle. "Right after we check on our dog. Why isn't she barking? That's not like Poopsie."

Gustave was almost there, ready to try anything. Seize the house keys and explain later.

Too late. He was already twisting in the knob and the door opened. The couple casually blustered inside. "Here, Poopsie, Poopsie— What in the hell?"

Four men with gloves froze where they stood in the dining room, literally holding the bag. Next to a dead dog. Everyone locked eyes.

The staring contest seemed like it lasted an hour, but was less than two seconds. The de Gaulles turned to run out the door for help and crashed straight into Gustave and Sasha, who beat their skulls in respectively with a sterling candelabra and a bronze statue of a little boy peeing.

Mr. de Gaulle was pronounced DOA, but his wife lay safely in a coma. Swingers or not, police closed ranks around the town and turned up the heat. Time for South Philly Sal to move south.

THAT EVENING

Coleman contentedly burned through an ever-dwindling twelve-pack suitcase of Busch. A lawn chair in the back of the warehouse gave him a front-row seat to the fireworks show of sparks shooting toward the ceiling and bouncing benignly off Serge's thick rubber apron.

Serge turned off the torch and walked over to a drill press. Even louder noise this time. When the metalwork was finished, he gathered all the machined parts in the middle of the building and banged them together with a mallet.

Serge stood and nodded to himself in approval. He dialed his cell phone again. "Crazy Legs? This is Serge. I need a huge favor immediately . . . Has it really already been five whole years? . . . Because I was in the neighborhood . . . But— . . . I thought— . . . Why? Are you hungry? . . ."

Serge eventually negotiated an end to the conversation. Then he grabbed a crowbar and began disassembling the apparatus.

Coleman raised his hand.

"Yes, the student in the back of the class."

"Serge, you just put it together. Why are you taking it apart already?"

"You always do a test fit in the lab to avoid on-site glitches during final assembly and launch." A round disk clanged to the floor. "I should have worked on the Hubble Telescope."

Coleman cringed at the sound of heavy metal dragging on concrete.

Serge stopped and wiped his brow. "Are you going to just sit around or give me a hand?"

"I was hoping to just sit."

"Shut up and get over here."

Coleman shrugged and shuffled across the warehouse. "What are we doing?"

"Loading all this for transpo to the final destination." Serge took another deep breath. "I forgot to tell Alfonso that I also needed his van. Oh, well, he's not using it tonight . . . Grab here like I am and pull. On three . . ."

Three came and they pulled. They stopped. "This isn't working," said Serge. "Let's roll it."

They reached the rear of the van, and Serge tilted the main assembly upright. He opened the back doors. "Coleman, get inside. I'll lean it against the bumper to boost it from this end, and you pull from the other . . ."

Success. Coleman jumped down from the vehicle, and the doors slammed shut.

"Where to now?" asked Coleman.

"The biggest liquor store we can find."

"Wait." Coleman looked up into the empty sky. "Do you hear angels?"

"We're not going for that reason," said Serge. "It just happens to be the kind of place selling all the remaining requirements for my science project."

Moments later, the van sat in a crowded parking lot while the pair roamed the aisles.

Coleman walked slowly, in awe. Arms outstretched religiously. "It's as big as a department store."

Serge pushed the shopping cart. "That's why they call it Liquor Universe."

"What are you shopping for?"

"These." Serge stopped in front of a shelf and began filling the cart.

"Why do you need that stuff?"

"Of all people, I thought you'd know." He ventured to a different section of the store and filled the bottom part of the cart under the basket.

"Are we finished?" asked Coleman.

"Almost," said Serge. "I'm depending on your expertise. Find me an ice pick."

Coleman closed his eyes, in a trance. He opened them. "Aisle six, middle shelf, halfway down on the left."

Serge stared inscrutably at his colleague, then walked to the appointed spot and immediately located a broad selection of ice picks. "Coleman, have you ever been in this place before?"

"Never set foot."

"But then how—"

"It just comes to me. I can't explain it because it doesn't happen anywhere else except head shops."

"Don't turn around," said Serge. "And cover your eyes. What's directly behind you?"

"Wild Turkey, in the seven-fifty-milliliter bottle."

"What's next to it?"

"Same brand, select barrel, full liter," said Coleman. "Did I get it?"

"You are the chosen one." Serge wheeled toward the register.

From halfway back up the aisle: "Can I uncover my eyes now?"

"Yes, come on!"

They loaded up the van, and Serge began stabbing away with the ice pick.

"Just one question," said Coleman. "How did you decide on the final destination to assemble this?"

"The location picked itself. Remember I said we were waiting for data from Mahoney? He e-mailed me last night with more info from his latest clients, and I was able to make contact with prime suspects over the Internet." *Stab, stab, stab.* "Criminals tend to operate in zones of comfort, but if all goes according to my plan, this will be the opposite of comfort."

A few last stabs. "There, all done." Serge tossed the pick on the dashboard. "Coleman, pass me my bottle of drinking water. I need to fuse this internal component and let it cure."

Coleman handed it over and giggled like a five-year-old.

Serge poured water into an old rag. "You're stoned out of your freakin' mind."

"No, I'm laughing because I finally get it." More uncontrolled snickers.

"Coleman, that's a personal record. You've never figured out my projects this early."

He clutched another hit. "Definitely! I'll bet I could even put it together all by myself."

"Grasshopper, your journey is almost complete." He started up the van and reversed course on the Palmetto Expressway, heading east toward A1A. In the rearview, the sky over the Everglades glowed blood-red from a just-set sun. Ahead, over the Atlantic, deepening purple. "Excellent timing. We'll arrive under cover of darkness, which is critical because we'll be exposed."

They reached a causeway.

"Hey, Serge," said Coleman. "Weren't we just here a week ago?"

"Correct again, Mensa boy."

The van pulled off the road and into a small park where they weren't supposed to be after sunset, but bolt cutters gave them an invitation.

They stopped next to a small boat ramp, near a small vessel that was anchored out of sight around a bend in the mangroves. Serge removed his shoes and socks and began walking down the ramp's incline.

"What the heck are you doing?" yelled Coleman.

Serge entered the water and was quickly up to his knees. "Called in a favor from Crazy Legs. He lent me the boat, but couldn't leave it in a trailer in the parking lot because the county would tow at closing time . . . I'll be right back." He dove into the water and swam quickly around the bend.

Coleman sat on the back bumper and urgently burned a jay to enhance the coming attractions. "I cannot wait for this!" He peered into the darkness as the nose of an eighteen-foot fly-fishing Carolina Skiff emerged from the edge of the mangroves. Then the whole boat came into view, riding silently because Serge was using an ultra-quiet electric trolling motor that fishermen favor when they don't want to scatter their quarry on the flats.

Next, Serge and Coleman rolled a giant metal tube down the ramp and strained to hoist it over the side of the craft. After that, the rest of the loading was chump work. Serge started the trolling motor again and sailed around the bend. This time he wedged the boat deep in the mangroves to avoid daylight detection. Then he swam back to the boat ramp.

"That's it?" said Coleman. "We're not going to use it now? I hate waiting when I'm high."

"We don't have any contestants yet." Serge got out his keys. "Unless you want to volunteer."

"I'd rather wait."

THE NEXT AFTERNOON

A van from the electric company rolled slowly through the finger canals off Las Olas Boulevard. Fort Lauderdale's answer to Worth Avenue.

Since Miami-Dade was now two-thirds Hispanic, much of the wealth had migrated north over the county line into Broward. They called it Anglo flight.

The waterfront homes were getting ridiculous in scale. Thanks to building codes. Most ordinances in other cities limit the size of structures. Not here. In order to increase property values and the tax base, you could not purchase one of the older homes unless you agreed to bulldoze it and build something so big it would blot out the sun. Seriously.

Wayne Huizenga, former owner of the Miami Dolphins, Florida Marlins and Blockbuster video, has a home there. It's a short limo ride to the downtown offices, but he likes to take the chopper from his backyard helipad. Seriously.

"There's the house now." Gustave pointed out the windshield. It wasn't Huizenga's place, but South Philly Sal was still impressed. "When are you supposed to meet this couple?"

"Noon for lunch. Actually a picnic."

"What about the location?" said Sal. "That mess back in Palm Beach with the couple who came home early is still fresh. We need to watch our profile."

"Sasha personally picked the spot," said Gustave. "She's totally comfortable there."

"Okay, then." Sal turned around to the rest of the gang in the back of the truck. "Everyone, we're on at noon . . ."

At twelve on the dot:

Sasha merrily swung a wicker picnic basket as she strolled down a lush embankment of grass overlooking a mirror surface of water.

Gustave was close behind with a large checkered blanket. "What's with you and this place? I don't see how special it is."

"Dumbfounding Bay?" said Sasha. "Are you joking? The history—"

"I know, I know," said Gustave. "You have this thing for dangerous types." He spread out the blanket under a nest of palms.

"Make sure none of those coconuts are over our heads," said Sasha. "One knocked me out when I was a kid."

Gustave looked up and slid the blanket to the left.

Sasha unpacked Evian, paper plates and pickles.

"What have you got in there?" asked Gustave.

The deli sandwiches came out next. "Wasn't sure what they'd like, so I got a little of everything. Egg, tuna and chicken salad."

Gustave checked his watch and looked around. A few cubicle people were enjoying lunch away from the office, but no couples. "Where are they? It's already five past."

Sasha opened the coleslaw. "They'll be here."

Two men walked up. "Are you Gustave and Sasha?"

The question caught them off guard.

"Why? Who are you?"

"We're the people you're supposed to meet. You know, the e-mails."

"But . . . you're two *guys*."

"Is that a problem?" asked the man. "Because I can perfectly understand. It's just that it's usually cool in the swinging community."

"No, we're fine," said Gustave. "It's just that when you said your names were Nathan and Jamie, I naturally assumed—"

"Is that tuna salad? I love tuna salad."

They all sat down for lunch and small talk.

"This place sure is beautiful," said Nathan.

"Sasha picked it out," said Gustave.

"She must have a thing for Mob types."

"Why yes," said Gustave. "But . . . I mean . . . How did you know?"

"You kidding?" said Nathan. "The history of this place. They found Johnny Roselli bobbing in a drum right over there with his legs sawed off. That gives me an appetite." He took a big bite of his tuna sandwich.

Gustave and Sasha glanced warily at each other. "Uh, what exactly do you do for a living?"

Nathan noshed another bite. "Consulting work mainly. Right now I'm getting a lot of action from a private investigator. He was just hired by the family of this couple that was attacked in Palm Beach . . ."

A cell phone vibrated. Gustave flipped it open. Sal screamed so loud on the other end that everyone could hear: *"Abort! Abort! The house is occupied! The people you're meeting aren't who they say they are—"*

The phone was snatched from Gustave's hand and flung in the water. Then a gun barrel pressed between his eyes. "My name's actually Serge. I thought you should know that since we'll be spending some quality time together."

Chapter FIFTEEN

MIDNIGHT

Watch your footing," said Serge, helping Sasha out of the trunk. "There's a lot of algae on these ramps. Wouldn't want you to slip and hurt yourself . . . Coleman, stop fooling around and assist that gentleman."

Coleman pushed himself up from the ground. "I slipped."

Serge had previously retrieved the hidden skiff from the mangroves, and it sat anchored in shallow water.

"All aboard!"

It took the persuasion of a pistol, but Gustave and Sasha settled in nicely. Serge worked the till of the trolling motor, backing the skiff away from the ramp.

Coleman sat up on the bow with a joint for a running light. "So this really is where they found that chopped-up mobster?"

"That's right, Dumbfounding Bay." Serge cut the rudder hard to starboard and switched the motor out of reverse. "They found Roselli right over there."

"But if you're going to do what I think you are, we can't be out in the water."

"We can if it's a falling tide and there's a shallow shoal that I personally know about."

Serge expertly navigated the channel, slipping clandestinely under the lights of waterfront homes backed up against their seawalls. One family was eating dinner, another watched a Harry Potter movie on a big screen. Someone else paced feverishly with a telephone, cigar and bitterness. Nobody was visible in the next house, but Serge recognized an oil painting in the living room from one of the founding Highwaymen.

The skiff was almost there. Serge gently ran it aground on the submerged sandbar. He slipped over the side, which gave the craft more buoyancy, and pulled it farther onto the shoal. The only tricky part was getting the fifty-five-gallon drums over the side and wedged into the bottom muck without raising a ruckus. Especially since the barrels were welded together, end to end. Serge had cut the bottom out of the top barrel, creating one tall cylinder. It rested sideways on the edge of the skiff. "Ease it in gently."

"I'm losing my grip," said Coleman.

"Don't drop it!"

He dropped it.

Splash.

Serge and Coleman ducked in the boat and stared up at the mansions along the seawall. The man with the phone and cigar came to the window and glanced around, then went back to chewing someone out.

"That was close," said Serge.

"Look, the barrels landed upright," said Coleman. "Can I put the next part together?"

"The floor is yours."

Coleman reached down into the bilge as Serge aimed his .45 back at the tied-up couple. He motioned for the woman to scoot away from her companion.

"Okay, Sasha, here's the deal: Your pal is going in that big tube I made—"

Panicked screaming from under the man's duct tape.

"Shut the fuck up!" Serge cracked him in the forehead with the pistol's butt. Then he scratched his own temple with the gun barrel. "Where was I? Oh, yeah, he's going in the tube, and I'll take your duct tape off, but if you make one peep or otherwise try to get the attention of the residents up along that seawall, then you're the one who goes in the tube. Do we understand each other?"

She nodded eagerly.

"Good," said Serge. "Coleman, give me a hand with Gustave."

Coleman grabbed the man's bound feet. "He doesn't look too happy."

"Don't know why not," said Serge, grabbing him under the arms. "I welded two barrels together instead of using just one and having to saw his legs off."

"You're always courteous like that," said Coleman.

"And yet so few say thank you."

Coleman got Gustave's feet through the opening of the tube, and the rest was only a matter of letting gravity slide him down. His feet touched bottom and his eyes barely peeked over the edge of the top barrel. He made whiny sounds under the tape.

"I smell something," said Coleman. "I think he just shit his pants something horrible."

"In the world of poker, that is what's known as 'a tell.'" Serge reached over with his right hand and knocked on the top of Gustave's head. "Eyes up here. I'm the Man with the Plan, and I know what you're thinking: 'He's going to put the lid on and I'll suffocate.' But that's not how I roll, so you can relax." He held up the lid and pointed at where he'd used the drill press to created a dozen half-dollar-size holes. "See? You can breathe. But the big question remains: What does ol' Serge have in store for me?"

"And Coleman," added Coleman. "I thought of it."

"That's right," said Serge. "He did have this idea. And they don't come around often, so you should savor it like a passing comet." He reached down in the boat and held up another round piece of metal the same diameter as the lid. Except this one was made of steel mesh like the part of a barbecue that lets charcoal drop its ashes. "I machined this so it seats three inches below the lip of the top barrel, keeping your head pushed down slightly away from the lid, because you strike me as the kind of person who would cheat by putting his mouth right up to one of the air holes, and that would be such a disappointment for me." Serge placed the mesh disk over Gustave's head. "Okay, crouch down some more so I can wedge this into place."

Serge positioned the mesh, but Gustave fiercely resisted. "I said to crouch down. There's not enough room with you standing up."

Serge pressed hard on the mesh, and Gustave strained to stand as tall as possible.

Coleman tossed a roach over the side of the boat. "I don't think he's listening."

"That's what the rubber mallet is for. I call it The Cooperator."

Wham, wham, wham, wham, wham . . .

"His head doesn't like the mallet," said Coleman. "He's crouching."

"And now I'll use the mallet to give the mesh a snug fit . . ." *Wham, wham, wham, wham.* ". . . And next the lid." Just before setting it in on top, Serge stuck his face over the barrels. "You're about to become a science pioneer, and that's something nobody can ever take away from you." He gave Gustave a cheerful wave. "Well, toodles!" The lid went on.

Wham, wham, wham, wham . . .

Coleman reached into one of the liquor-store bags. "Is it time?"

"Right-o. Uncap that sucker." Serge stuck his hand in another shopping bag.

The pair met at the side of the boat and began pouring the bottles of alcohol through the air holes. Then they tossed the empties in the bilge and reached into the bags again. More pouring. "Repeat as needed . . ." They made several more short trips until the bags were empty and the bilge was full of garbage.

"Coleman, get the anchor." Serge flicked on the electric motor and silently backed away from the shoal. He reached a range of a hundred yards and dropped anchor again.

"Okay," Serge told Coleman. "You're on."

"Huh? What do you mean I'm on?"

Serge aimed his thumb sideways. "Sasha. Check the expression on her face. I'm sure she's dying to know."

"You want me to explain the experiment?"

"It was your idea," said Serge. He took a seat next to her. "Rock this joint."

"Wow, you've always been the one to explain before." Coleman stopped and placed his palms on the sides of his face. "Okay, this is my big break. I don't want to mess it up. I'll tell that part, and that part, and, no, that other part comes first . . ."

"Any day now," said Serge.

"Okay." Coleman cleared his throat. "I'm a little nervous, so I'm probably not going to get any laughs. Here goes: It all started when me and the Buzzard were getting royally baked. We had this giant glass bong shaped like a T. Rex, and I mean we were just totally splattered, so freakin' high that we spent an hour hung up on heavy philosophical *Seinfeld* questions like, What on earth are they planting to grow seedless dope? And then you wake up the next morning and swear someone must have broken in while you were asleep because all the furniture is rearranged and your shoes are in the microwave. You know what I mean? Those really great nights? And then the next morning me and Buzzard. Hold on, it wasn't Buzzard. It was Taco Tommy. Was Buzzard there? That's right, they were both there because we had this windowpane acid that we broke into four doses and there was one left over, so that's how I remember, and we all dropped LSD for breakfast. And you know at the veterinary office how they sometimes have to put those plastic cones around a dog's head so it won't bite stitches or whatever? About halfway through the trip, Buzzard and Taco made me put on a plastic cone 'for my own good,' and I spent the rest of the trip wandering around the house wearing this cone like I'm a lamp, and only being able to see the top halves of the rooms . . ."

"Ahem," said Serge.

"What?"

Serge made a twirling motion with his left hand. "You can fast-forward."

"It's my story."

"It's offtrack."

"You get offtrack with your history."

"But history is a key element of the death monologue."

"Partying is just as important to me."

Serge turned and smiled at Sasha. "Will you excuse me a moment?"

She watched Serge walk over to Coleman, and the two began arguing in brusque whispers that she couldn't make out. They both stopped and smiled back at her like everything was cool, then more harsh whispering.

They began wrestling, mildly at first, then rolling violently on the deck. Serge's legs got Coleman's head in a scissor lock.

"Serge, stop. I can smell your butt."

"Stick to the story. We have a guest."

"I'll grab your nuts."

"You better not . . . *Ahhh,* let go!"

"You let go!"

"Okay, at the same time . . . Ready? Let go . . ."

They did. The pair stood and smiled at Sasha again. Except she couldn't see Coleman's smile because his T-shirt was pulled up over his face. "Everything's cool."

"Yeah, we're good."

Serge returned to his seat, and Coleman pulled his shirt back down. "So right now your friend Gustave is standing on a block of ice inside the barrels. Yesterday, Serge used a sharp pick to carve out a cavity in a block, which we got at the liquor store. Then he rubbed a wet rag over the top of the ice to get it slick and melty so it would fuse together with a second block that he placed on top of it and stored in a freezer back at the warehouse. Finally, after Gustave was sealed in the tube, Serge and I poured in a bunch of mixers that we also got at the liquor store."

Serge looked at Sasha. "I see you have a question. You can go ahead and speak."

"I don't get it. What's going on? What are we doing now?"

"Waiting for the ice to melt," said Serge.

"Because the mixers were Coke," said Coleman. "And inside the ice-block cavity are twenty rolls of Mentos."

"Look," said Serge. "The ice just melted."

A dozen jets of soda foam shot high into the night.

"That's got to be a record," said Coleman.

"And it's not stopping."

"Must be hitting other rolls deeper in the ice," said Coleman.

"Excuse me," said Sasha. "So he's going to drown?"

"No," said Serge. "That's why I drilled all those air holes. Otherwise the thing wouldn't be safe."

She watched the relentless fountain of suds form a pretty pattern over the water. "Then what will happen to him?"

"The real tragedy is that the carbon dioxide from the soda evacuates all the oxygen in the barrels, and of course you can't breathe carbon dioxide because you'll suffocate. It's like committing suicide by putting a plastic bag over your head, except this . . ."—Serge looked toward the tube, where the fountains were subsiding and foam sheeted down over the sides.—". . . is more like assisted suicide."

Sasha began absorbing the full scope of Serge's mental condition. Normally, one in her position would be shaking uncontrollably and stuttering: "W-w-w-what are you going to d-d-d-d-do to me?"

Instead, Sasha took measured breaths. "What are you going to do to me?"

"I'm not going to do anything to you," said Serge. "In fact, I'm letting you go. It's part of my plan . . ."

A deeper voice: "I said, 'What are you going to do to me?'"

"I just told you—"

Coleman elbowed him. "Her hand is rubbing the side of her breast."

"Oh, so that's what it is?"

"Is what?"

"She's into bad boys. It's a sexual paraphilia." Serge stood and began unhitching his shorts. "Would you like to see what I'm going to do to you?"

Coleman raised his hand. "I would."

Without looking back, Serge put a foot in the middle of Coleman's chest and shoved him backward into the water.

Coleman bobbed to the surface, "Serge!"

"Stay, Fido." Serge dropped his pants to the deck and charged.

Sasha came at him with equal velocity. They crashed together in the middle of the boat and hit the hull hard. They smacked and kicked each other. Arousing profanity. Bruises, bloody lips. Their naked bodies slammed one side of the boat and then the other, over and over, fighting for the top position and making a racket like a flopping, just-caught marlin trying to get back in the sea.

It became so loud that lights came on in all the seawall mansions. But instead of grabbing the phone for the police, they grabbed binoculars and video equipment. The predatory lovers finally reached a quivering, simultaneous conclusion. Serge jumped up, grabbed his shorts and casually flicked a wrist as he walked away. "That's what I'll do to you."

The still-nude Sasha sat up panting. "Will you call me?"

"Who knows?" Serge pulled Coleman aboard. "I got a nutty, nutty schedule."

"But I'm a witness. You can't just let me go."

"That's precisely what I'm going to do." He steered the skiff back toward the boat ramp.

"No, you're supposed to take me hostage and tie me up again," said Sasha. "And stick a gag ball in my mouth, and do other unspeakable acts with the devices in my purse. I promise I won't scream."

"Jesus," said Serge. "Okay, okay, *maybe* I'll give you a call and we can go get some ice cream, but no promises."

"Yes, ice cream. And then you'll force me at gunpoint to lick it off your—"

"Enough!" Serge held his hands to the sky. "Out of the boat or I swear I won't call."

She reluctantly climbed over the side into three feet of water. "I'll do anything for you."

Serge threw her clothes in her face. "Now that has possibilities."

Sasha slipped into her top. "Name it."

"I've been hired to help some scam victims. And even though I'm starting to crack cases left and right, my boss has been getting on me just because I keep forgetting to retrieve the money." He pointed back at a large metal tube standing on a shoal in the bay. "I'm easily distracted."

"What do you want me to do?"

"Go back to the streets, and if I get a case I'm having trouble with, I might give you a call to see if you know anything."

"So that's the reason you're deliberately freeing me?"

"No, that idea just popped in my head when we were cumming. I do some of my best thinking then."

"So what's the real reason?"

"To tell all the other scam artists working this state that there's a new sheriff in town."

Coleman raised a beer. "And I'm the deputy."

Chapter SIXTEEN

SOUTH AMERICA

Toucans and parrots squawked from the edge of the jungle.

The mountains fell steeply before gently sloping into an apron of dense green foliage that ended in the sandy coastline along the unpatrolled border of Chile and Peru.

Surf rolled in from the Pacific, before an explosion of mist on the rocks. There was a piece of driftwood here and there, crabs darting out of holes, and a tiny beach villa pressed back against the jungle. It was the only sign of a human hand.

Curtains billowed out the living room window.

Inside the sparsely furnished bungalow, a tall, wiry man sat shirtless in dry swim trunks. He had ultra-short blond hair, a week's growth after shaving his head. He was wearing the trunks because he was going for another mile swim in the ocean. That accounted for the muscular shoulders and pecs that were disproportionately developed for the rest of his torso. The swim, though, would have to wait.

The man's job was to wait. Just live in the villa. The only task: Check in once a day on the Internet at precisely 2:35 P.M., like a nuclear submarine coming up to periscope depth and raising its antenna to get instructions from satellites. And like those subs, the vast majority of the time there were no instructions. The important thing was 2:35.

Because if a message did come, it would be dropped seconds before, to be read as quickly as possible and immediately deleted. Employing another espionage trick, the messages were never sent, so they could never be intercepted. Instead they were saved as drafts in an e-mail account, and the villa's occupant had the password.

The villa's previous occupant also had the password, and liked to take those ocean swims. But he was gone, at the hands of the current resident. Nothing personal. Orders. The earlier resident had received a message at 2:35 and went to Miami to handle a situation. But he got sloppy and became compromised. The person now at the villa's computer had also been in Miami as backup, prepared to sanitize any mess that might develop, and there had been a big one. That's how he inherited the bungalow.

It was a strange juxtaposition, the occupation and the house. The remote spot on the beach lent itself to decompression. Just the waves and the birds and your thoughts. It reminded the man of the assassin played by Max von Sydow in *Three Days of the Condor,* who found tranquillity by meticulously painting tiny cast-iron soldiers from forgotten wars.

2:34.

Fingers tapped the keyboard. An Internet account opened. Moments later, an e-mail popped up in the draft folder. He read it quickly. This time there was also a photo of the target, but he didn't need to save it because he would be receiving a hard copy later that day in a briefcase exchange. He hit delete. The swim trunks would stay dry. Something had come up. Florida again. The flight left in two hours.

He went to a louvered closet. At the bottom was an already-packed carry-on of essentials for just such an occasion. Then he opened a round wall safe and thumbed through passports of various nationalities and names. He decided on Bolivia.

Dark clouds rolled in from the ocean, and wind carried the salt mist. He shuttered up the beach house and climbed into his Jeep, holding a mental image of the face he'd seen on the computer.

MEANWHILE . . .

"And here's another thing about the people who don't read." Serge hit the gas when the light turned green. "They're the same ones who think you're a moron if you don't text. I don't text because of a philosophical code against the growing depersonalization predicted by Alvin Toffler and George Orwell."

"I don't text because my thumbs are too big," said Coleman.

"But the non-readers are texting away like it's the war effort," said Serge. "They'd eliminate the debt if we could convert that energy to durable goods and stick it on cargo ships. It's half the gross national product."

"What's the other half?"

"Car insurance," said Serge. "Watch any channel on TV for any length of time, and every other commercial is a British lizard, an upwardly mobile caveman, a calcified chick named Flo, the anthropomorphic jerk named Mayhem who tricks you into accidents, the guy in a hard hat who hits cars with sledgehammers, the character who played the president in the show *24* saying, 'That's Allstate's stand,' 'Nationwide is on your side,' 'Fifteen minutes could save you some shit.'"

"I like Mayhem," said Coleman. "He makes me not feel so bad about breaking stuff."

"And yet we're still not manufacturing anything you can hold in your hands," said Serge. "There's your downfall of a global superpower. When space aliens visit centuries from now, they'll whisk the dust away and conclude that America was dominated by a race of tiny-thumbed people who drove badly."

"We're not?"

"You may have a point," said Serge. "And think about this: the simultaneous rise of texting and car insurance. Coincidence?"

"Last night's episode of *Glee* warned about texting and driving," said Coleman.

"Those *Glee* kids just keep on caring," said Serge. "But the nation's plight is now bigger than any teenage chorus line can handle. Technology has just passed our survival instinct, and the country is spinning on a stationary existential axis of make-believe importance: We text about a Tweet of a YouTube video posted on Facebook with a clip of *Glee* about not texting that we just texted about. Instead of actual life, we're now living an air-guitar version of life."

"Yow! Watch out!" Coleman lunged and grabbed Serge's arms in an attempt to take over the steering wheel. The Firebird swerved across the lane. "Don't you see it!"

"Coleman, get your fucking hands off me!" Serge swatted the arms away. "You almost made us crash. What's gotten into you?"

He grabbed his chest. "You almost hit that weird beast in the road!"

"Coleman, it was a hooker." Serge looked sideways with an odd expression. "And she'd already made it through the crosswalk."

"You sure it was a hooker?"

"No question," said Serge. "We've lived in Florida long enough that you should be able to identify them now without flash cards."

"It must have been the snakes coming out of her head," said Coleman. "That means it's kicking in."

"Why? What did you take?"

"I don't remember," said Coleman. "But it must have been good shit. That's a sign of good shit: You don't remember taking it and then see monsters and almost crash."

Serge stared at him with scorn, then faced forward. "We need to buy insurance."

"More head-snakes," said Coleman, face pasted to his passenger window. "Where are we?"

The Trans Am raced due south on a major artery. They passed an open-air drug supermarket with handshake exchanges of bindles and cash, then pawn and beauty-product shops with door buzzers and baseball bats under the counters, a run-down motel full of police cars responding to aggravated domestic violence and an escaped monkey that had been in the news. More prostitutes, guys drinking from brown bags, shopping-cart pushers, slumped-over bus bench urchins, and run-on-sentence conspiracy preachers. The intersection people beckoned drivers at red lights to roll down windows for one-dollar flowers, bottled water and an underground newspaper written by hand. The area had become so notoriously sketchy that civic leaders snapped into action and fixed everything by installing new rows of expensive, decorative light posts.

"I absolutely love Orange Blossom Trail," said Serge. "Also known as OBT and south Orlando's red-light district, but that's a bit judgmental."

"Two dudes are having a sword fight with broken-off car antennas."

"Ooo! Look, look!" yelled Serge. "They put up those supercool new light poles that tell people they're in the wrong part of town."

"The poles are bending toward the car and growling." Coleman nodded. "Good shit."

"I always seek out those poles," said Serge. "They steer you to interesting new friends . . . Like this guy."

A light turned red. The Firebird stopped. A bearded man on the curb made a rolling-down motion with his hand. Serge cranked the glass open. "What's the good word, my fine fellow statesman?"

"Can I have a dollar?"

"Sure thing." Serge uncrinkled a George Washington from his wallet and passed it out the window.

"Appreciate it."

"Hey, wait," said Serge. "Where's my underground newspaper? I saw you give one to that other driver."

"It was my last. Actually my only. Handwritten. That way no stray copies can fall into the wrong laps. That's how they got Charlie."

"Serge," said Coleman. "The light turned green . . . I think."

"Let 'em go around." Serge hit his blinking hazards and turned back to the man. "Then what else do you have?"

"Let's see." The man reached in his back pocket with a quizzical expression. He removed a wad of paper. "Oh, yeah. I drew this last night."

Serge took it through the window. Coleman looked at the page, then screamed and flattened himself against the passenger door. "Swarms of locusts with scorpion tails, people's intestines sliced out, nuns with wooden rulers . . ." Quietly weeping in his hands now. "Serge, please make this stuff wear off."

"It's not the drug you took," said Serge. "He really did draw this . . ." Then at the man: "And not too bad, if I do say so. What's it represent? The Apocalypse from Revelation?"

"No, I was just doodling in the hardware store up the street." The man wiped his brow. "They have air-conditioning. I get some of my best inspiration in there."

"I know exactly what you mean." Serge tucked the picture in his pocket and handed the man another dollar. "What's the word on the street?"

"They just caught another monkey."

"It's getting embarrassing."

"No kidding." The man stuck the dollar in his pocket. "Busting up mailboxes and lawn statues all the way to Altamonte Springs. It just wasn't right."

"Like the famous Tampa Bay monkey," said Serge. "He was becoming a regular D. B. Cooper."

"I read about him," said the bum. "Sightings all the way west to the St. Petersburg exercise trail, but police think that was just a copycat in a monkey costume, jumping out and dancing in front of Rollerbladers before darting back into the woods."

Serge stared at the ceiling and scratched his chin.

"Serge." Coleman peeked out one half-open eye. "Is that why you made me wear that outfit?"

"It was you guys?" said the bearded man.

"Why text when you have imagination?" said Serge. "What about Casey Anthony?"

"Just scraps of rumors and dubious innuendo. Harder to find than the monkey." He pointed north. "She's been reported everywhere from a Magic basketball game to a Ruby Tuesday's . . ." His arm swung south. "And someone swears they spotted her at the Tupperware Museum."

"Wait a sec," said Coleman. "You're pulling my leg. There's no such thing as a Tupperware Museum."

"Oh, but there most certainly is," said Serge. "From the old days. Roadside-attraction gold."

"You're really serious?" said Coleman. "Tupperware?"

"Not only that, but the histories of Orlando and Tupperware are intertwined farther back than Disney." Serge turned to the homeless man. "What was Casey supposedly doing there?"

"In the gift shop buying a gelatin mold."

"Must be a false sighting," said Serge. "From all reports, Tupperware isn't how she likes to get her freak on."

"My thinking, too," said the man. "Unless she's into something so twisted we have yet to fathom."

Serge began rolling up the window. "Still, all leads must be followed." The light turned green again. He switched off his emergency flashers and sped south.

Coleman sagged in his passenger seat with his head lying atop the window frame. "I don't see hookers anymore."

"Because we crossed the skank equator back into family land," said Serge.

"The places with baby strollers where you don't let me smoke dope?"

"Until I say otherwise."

"This sucks." Coleman idly flicked his lighter. "Let's go somewhere else."

"Can't," said Serge. "Mahoney's idea. Wants us in position again. He's trying to track another scammer with that Big Dipper company. Credit-card receipts, turnpike cameras, crime reports. Then they did a geographical probability cone like a hurricane chart pointed at Orlando. But like a hurricane, it's a cone of uncertainty."

"What are we supposed to do in the meantime?"

"Sit on standby and wait for his call like a nuclear submarine."

Coleman flicked the lighter again and waved it in front of his eyes. "So what's all that jazz about Florida and Tupperware?"

"Some of our richest heritage unknown to the general public."

Serge grabbed the coffee tube under his shirt. "Remember the home parties when you were a kid?"

"Those seriously rocked!" said Coleman. "Outrageously huge celebrations . . ."

". . . Neighbors descended from all over in reverent awe like someone had discovered a glowing meteorite in their backyard," said Serge. "But what got lost in that Tupperware gold rush were some of the earliest shots in a watershed social movement."

"I crawled under a table and stole all the deviled eggs . . ."

"Women's lib!" said Serge. "Except they didn't realize it at the time, so they still wore long, elegant white gloves."

". . . Got a tummy ache."

"Who were these pioneers? you ask. Why, Brownie Wise and her troops," said Serge. "Earl Tupper invented the product but had trouble moving it in department stores. Then he noticed all these huge sales orders coming in from a single person in Florida, and he's, like, what incredible store is this? And Brownie says, 'No store. I hold parties in homes.' What? Just one woman roaming the Orlando area and chatting in living rooms? That's impossible. But then all the top executives triple-checked her sales figures, which surpassed some of the largest department stores in the country, and they practically shit in every piece of Tupperware in the office."

Coleman giggled. "The gelatin mold."

"Let's not push the metaphor too far," said Serge. "Anyway, here's the key part: Back then, a lot of men would condescend to women and say, 'Don't hurt your pretty little heads thinking about business stuff. That's our work.' But Brownie had already recruited a multi-tiered marketing force of latter-day Rosie the Riveters. They went wildcat around the male world, creating their own business model, ordering the product under the radar, and just did it. By the time everyone noticed, it was a stunning success that couldn't be denied."

"Serge, you don't mean to say . . ."

"That's right, the Tupperware party was invented in Florida!" said Serge. "And not more than a stone's throw from right here."

"Tupperware's got my respect," said Coleman. "And all the stoners, too. Plastic burp lids may not be our bag, but stoners *know* from parties, and we have to give a major nod to their munchy spreads. My old group had a couple heads who knew how to cook—not too many, because the rest of us compared notes and found products in the supermarket where you could open the package, stick your hand in, then stick your hand in your mouth. That was our version of cooking. But a few of the guys actually did all that unnecessary stuff and whipped up some boss nibbles for after the weed guy finally arrived except the weed guy was always late, and everything got too cold or warm and started drying and looking funky, and you called the weed guy and said, 'You've fucked up the burritos again, dude'..."

"Coleman—"

"But the best stoner munchie layout isn't in the ballpark of even the weakest Tupperware party. Deviled eggs were just the beginning: You had your celery with cream cheese, tomatoes stuffed with tuna salad, olives with toothpicks, Ritz crackers and Velveeta. That's real food."

"It was a magic time," said Serge. "They made me go to bed, which just made me want to stay up. So I snuck down the hall and watched my mom preparing with the local rep, stacking lettuce tubs in perfect pyramids on top of a card table in front of the Magnavox. And I couldn't believe my eyes: I'd never seen the tube off in the evening. Tupperware was even bigger than TV!"

"Like the Beatles and Jesus..."

"And later the party got so effective that it spilled into our backyard with mosquito torches and Harvey Wallbangers, and I spied on the adults by sticking my head through my bedroom curtains and watching the rest of the night as they continued drinking, buying more and more Tupperware and lighting the wrong ends of cigarettes. Except back then, God knows why, they made some bedroom curtains with tiny pieces of fiberglass in the fabric, and all the next day my neck itched like a bastard. Same as now whenever I go to the barber and they put on that whole bullshit charade of wrapping the paper strip around my neck and sprinkling talcum powder and finishing off with that home-plate-umpire brush, and I say, 'Let's dispense with this Cecil B. De Mille production once and for all. We both know a bunch of little hair pieces will get down in my neck no matter what you do, and it'll itch like crazy. So the sooner I pay, the sooner I can go jump in the ocean like I always do.' And the whole time I'm thinking of Tupperware."

"You're a complex person," said Coleman.

"And yet I'm content with the simplest things." Serge reached in a pocket and smiled as he unfolded the one-dollar drawing from a bearded guy.

A cell phone rang. Serge checked the display and sighed.

Mahoney.

Chapter SEVENTEEN

DOWNTOWN ORLANDO

The hallway ran past offices with giant windows and massive banks of TV monitors.

The rooms were dim; colored lights blinked on vast control panels that looked like they belonged in launch control at Canaveral. Red digital numbers flickered to measure whatever they were measuring in thousandths of a second.

The hallway continued past the offices until its carpeting abruptly ended in dust at the entrance of a dingy corridor with a plain concrete wall. Across from the wall was a barrier of unpainted plywood held up with two-by-fours. It was the framework of an illusion. Backstage.

On the other side of the plywood: the cheerfully bright television studio of Live Action Eyewitness Orlando News 12. But it was just after ten A.M., so there wasn't any action or news, just the local mid-morning feel-good show, *Feel Good Orlando!* A lone anchorwoman sat behind a clear acrylic anchor desk that was internally illuminated with fiber optics. It was specially designed for high-def, because good feelings were better in digital. She read introductions off the teleprompter before tossing the show around to a series of mini-sets located throughout the studio's plywood maze, where the various segments featured a middle school math team, a doctor who used lasers on unsightly veins, someone demonstrating how to get your neighbor's dog to stop barking with an ultra-sonic transmitter disguised as a birdhouse, and a trainer from the local zoo with a misbehaving hedgehog that got loose and ended up in the fake kitchen where viewers would soon discover guilt-free cheese cake.

Past the studio, the illusion faded into conventional administrative offices.

A phone rang.

The person who answered it was unimpressed at first, but then began taking copious notes.

He hung up and went to another office, where an assignment editor dispatched a video crew to a run-down motel near the Orange County line.

It was about telegenics. The footage would lead the next day's show.

The next day's show:

The entire half hour was dedicated to a pair of guests who had phoned the station in desperation the day before. They didn't know where else to turn. They called Orlando News 12 because of the station's consumer hotline motto: "When you don't know where else to turn!" The station hung up on most of the callers.

A tearful father was led onto the set and took a seat in front of the cameras. Next to him sat his son. The small boy had no hair. As they often say, *pediatric* and *cancer* are two words that should never go together. But this case went far beyond the expected heartrending narrative.

The father had spent so much time taking care of his son that he'd lost his job. Which meant the family lost their insurance for the boy's care. So he paid out of pocket, letting all other bills slide until they were evicted from their home. The father had thought that since their house was all paid up, state homestead laws protected it from being seized for other debts, and he was right. Except for one exception. Property taxes.

Their asses were on the street, where they now lived in a series of roach motels when they weren't living in their car. Oh, and the mother was killed last year by a drunk driver.

It couldn't possibly get any worse, right? Just watch Channel 12: The father sold his car to afford a "desperate" program of treatment for his son. The program was designed to help people precisely in his situation. If the family qualified, the father would pay what he could—a tiny fraction of the cost—and a network of foundations would pick up the rest of the tab. He found the program on the Internet.

The son never got treatment. The program was all a scam, devised to prey on the parents of terminally ill children.

The TV station had never seen such an extreme combination of sympathetic victims, hateful villains and great video. It was the perfect storm of tragedy for *Feel Good Orlando!*

By the end of the show, the station's switchboard lit up until it crashed. The community was coming through. They wanted to do whatever they could for the family—and kill the people behind the scam.

A bank account was set up in their name. Donations flooded in.

So did ratings. The show's producers had the family back the second day, when the interviewer got their names wrong. "Paul, I mean Phil. Sorry . . . So, Paul, how has the generosity of our station changed your life, because we're here *when you don't know where else to turn!*"

The father dabbed his eyes. "I can't thank you enough . . ."

A week passed. The station's editors held a meeting to determine upcoming programming. One item was a no-brainer: Get that father and son back again. Their previous two segments had garnered the largest viewerships in months. And get some more footage from that depressing motel to juice the ratings. A TV van was sent out. It had a giant eyeball on the side.

The crew arrived at the dump. A hooker propositioned the camera-man as he strapped on the battery packs, but he said he was working. The reporter slipped into a bright blue jacket and grabbed a microphone.

"How do I look?"

The cameraman gave a thumbs-up.

"Good morning, Orlando. This is where the desperate father and ter-minally ill son have been forced to live . . ."

They went to the door and knocked.

And knocked. And knocked.

It finally opened. The father looked like he'd been dead asleep. Except not. The cameraman caught a startling glimpse and forced the door open. The video was beyond the wildest dreams of the *Feel Good* executives: openly scattered bottles of booze, drug paraphernalia and cash. The cancer-stricken child covered his face from the camera lights. He was wearing a bra.

What the hell?

The initial shock wore off quickly as reality quickly revealed itself: The boy was actually a petite twenty-six-year-old woman who had shaved her head. It was all a sickening, elaborate scam. The commu-nity had been ripped off for thousands of dollars. One of the saddest plights on earth exploited by sociopathic crooks and non-verifying journalists.

The TV reporter was giddy with elation. He had an excellent scan-dal to report, and he hammered away with hardball questions as the couple scrambled to gather up cocaine and cash.

"Are you the worst people to ever live? . . ."

The TV people ran outside as the grifters jumped into a red Camaro.

"Do you think you'll burn in hell? . . ."

Six hours later, on the station's main anchor set:

"Good evening, our top story tonight: a shocking scandal that is still unfolding in an exclusive report that you will only see on Live Action Or-lando Eyewitness News 12. An unidentified couple has perpetrated one of the most heinous scams . . ."

The broadcast highlighted footage of earlier interviews and repeatedly expressed outrage that its viewers had been duped out of large sums of money because the TV station hadn't checked any facts. Except they left out that fact.

What the station did learn was that the bank account had been systematically emptied in $9,500 increments—deliberately under the $10,000 trip wire for IRS reporting—until there was nothing left.

The switchboard lit up again. Where had these assholes fled? Would they be arrested? How were the viewers going to get their money back?

One group of viewers intently watched the report on a flat-screen TV in a luxury high-rise hotel overlooking the Intracoastal Waterway. The report ended, and the celebration began. A cork flew from a bottle of bubbly. South Philly Sal raised a glass to toast the newest members of their team.

"To Omar and Piper, who brought in one of our biggest hauls ever."

Indeed, $36,000. And as they said in *Goodfellas*, they did the right thing. They shared it with Sal, because he had recruited them and concocted the scheme down to the last detail, including monitoring local TV coverage for the station with the least accurate reporting.

They partied into the evening. Except for Sal, who had stopped drinking after his first, nominal glass of champagne. He sat alone on the far end of the suite, writing at a desk. Addresses, names, known routines of targets broken down into twenty-minute blocks. Sheets of paper were folded and slipped into separate envelopes. Each of the party's guests would be given their next assignment upon departure. Fun was fun, but there was more work to do.

ORANGE BLOSSOM TRAIL

A black '78 Firebird peeled away from another budget motel and raced south. The trailing remnants of a metropolis gave way to open pastures, which in turn became bulldozed acres of upstart suburbia. Then more fields and an expressway overpass.

Serge hit a blinker for the left lane. "You know the difference between Floridians and everyone else in the world?"

"We drive around all day and get totally baked?"

"Alligators," said Serge. "We're so used to them we don't even notice anymore. And TV drops our guard even further. Local news can't grasp economic stories any more complex than the price of gas, and an 'in-depth' investigative report means chasing the owner of a pet-grooming salon across a strip-mall parking lot, demanding to know why all the poodles went bald. So in Florida we're left with perpetual loops of the same cheap video: aerial footage of anything on fire, legs of surfers with shark-teeth marks, ground-level footage of anything on fire, anything weird that beaches itself, a retiree with a jumbo American flag fighting the homeowners' association . . ."

"And alligators?" asked Coleman.

"Any alligator not in a swamp, because all of this *was* their swamp, and now they're living alongside us, using our swimming pools and golf courses and shopping-mall fountains until both sides have grown accustomed to the arrangement."

"You mentioned the rest of the world?"

"At the mere sight of these modern dinosaurs, foreign tourists spaz out with disposable cameras. Especially the British. I love watching the British go gaga over gators. Last year, I was driving across the glades on the Tamiami Trail and saw all these cars pulled over and people gaping at the roadside canal, and I thought that maybe another sightseeing van had rolled into the water. So I stopped and noticed a single gator had crawled up on the opposite bank, and dozens of people in shorts and dark socks were snapping a million pictures. Their reaction was priceless, like a small boy finding his penis for the first time."

"Ahhhhhhhh!"

"Did I bring back a bad memory?"

"No!" Coleman pointed. "I'm getting a second rush wave! Those gigantic alligator jaws coming toward us. Please tell me it's a hallucination!"

"Sorry to disappoint you, but it's definitely real, like ten or twelve feet high." Serge pulled into the parking lot. "But luckily it's historic

Gatorland, with the huge landmark fake jaws at the entrance to lure tourists off Orange Blossom Trail and into the venerable 1949 roadside attraction. The fantastic part is they dropped anchor just south of Orlando long before Disney ever saw the possibilities. But Gatorland did!"

"The jaws are snapping," said Coleman. "Concrete can snap, right?"

"No, that's a hallucination."

"Mescaline."

"What?"

"I finally remembered what I took . . . Or was that another time, or another person?" Coleman leaned toward the windshield and the snapping jaws. "Whew! Definitely mescaline!"

"How can you tell?"

Coleman urgently opened the passenger door and doubled over on the ground. Serge heard the ever-familiar sound of his pal sending a high-pressure spray of stomach contents onto pavement. Coleman climbed back into the car. "Excellent stuff!"

Serge just stared.

"What?" Coleman wiped the back of his mouth with his hand. "Why are you looking at me like that?"

"Puking is excellent?" said Serge.

"I keep telling you it's the best, man. Always look forward to it." Coleman picked a couple things off his T-shirt that made Serge wince, then flicked them out the window. Except the window was closed, and they stuck to it.

"Got it under control," said Coleman, wiping the window with his forearm but just making it smear.

Serge grabbed his own stomach and covered his eyes. "Please fucking stop it. I have to eat again this century."

"I'm surprised," said Coleman. "You usually want me to keep your vehicle clean."

"Just tell me when you're done so I can open my eyes."

Coleman continued rubbing. "Don't be a buzzkill. I told you I always look forward to throwing up. All the heads understand this."

"You enjoy getting sick?"

"It's like that Carly Simon ketchup song about anticipation. After taking a dose, the first half of the trip is a lot of work, getting yourself situated to the effects, and that can be some serious heavy lifting if you're in unfamiliar surroundings: distinguishing what's moving and what's stationary, the difference between solids, liquids and gases. See, the whole key to a mellow and enlightening mescaline trip is not to ram your head through something solid like a TV set, just because you wanted to meet the people inside. That takes a lot of responsibility . . ."

Serge tentatively opened one eye at Coleman as he continued to work on the window.

". . . But once you get sick, it's clear sailing." Coleman illustrated by moving a level palm through the air and whistling. "All the great organic psychedelics are like that. If it doesn't involve a little tummy unrest, keep shopping."

Serge opened the other eye. "Enough of this dumb show. I'm going in the park . . ."

"Wait for me!"

They arrived at the entrance and stared up at concrete teeth.

"Coleman, remember we're in a family setting, so don't attract any unnecessary attention." Then Serge clenched the coffee tube in his teeth and sprinted into the jaws.

Chapter EIGHTEEN

FORT LAUDERDALE

Earth-friendly canvas grocery bags sat on a kitchen counter. Out came split-pea soup, rigatoni and five plum tomatoes that had been scrutinized back at the produce section.

A female voice called into another room. "Dad, it looks like you have a message on the answering machine."

"A what?"

"Answering machine!"

"Okay."

Ronald Campanella had retired from the New York City Fire Department two years before with prestigious honors and lingering joint problems from falling through the floor of a burning housing project. That was back in the early nineties. Both knees had scars from multiple surgeries. He didn't like to wear shorts.

The woman unloading canned vegetables and Benefiber was Brook Campanella. Brook, for Brooklyn. That kind of family. Four generations from the borough across the East River from the Manhattan skyline. Ebbets Field still choked him up. So the idea of Ronald spending his golden years in Florida held no allure, but he made the retirement move anyway, because he was supposed to.

Brook was the caboose. With three adult offspring already in college, Muriel Campanella had come home from a routine doctor's visit with an unroutine announcement. Surprise! They did the math. Ronald and Muriel would be raising a teenager in their sixties.

The answering machine rested on a small antique end table in the living room. The eighth-floor condo had an open floor plan from kitchen to balcony. Next to the answering machine sat a yellowed firehouse group photo from 1987, a King James Bible with family records, and a young portrait of Muriel, who had recently passed from a family history of heart disease. That's when Brook decided to follow her father south and help around the place. Florida needed paralegals as much as New York.

That hadn't been her plan. The whole family always said a law degree was in the cards for their National Merit Scholar. They scrimped and saved for tuition. Brook flew through her first year with straight A's. Then a conspiracy of interruptions. Always family. Crisis after crisis, and it usually involved money. She began a cycle of repeatedly dropping out and re-enrolling, until the financial woes forced her into night school. Then there wasn't money for that. Then her mother's health . . . and now her father. Family always came first.

"Oh, and the mail came," Brook told her dad as she opened a large brown envelope containing the kind of application forms that never provide enough space for address and Social Security. The top of the documents had the name of a local college whose campus sat between a pain clinic and a liquor store in a nearby strip mall. The two businesses next to the college had an unusually high overlap in clientele. Oh, well, at least the move to Florida and her mom's modest life insurance policy would allow her to resume classes. Brook was a ferocious student. Under the best of circumstances, there was at least a year left of credits toward a degree, which meant Brook would be taking her bar exam in six months.

She opened another envelope and called to her dad again. "Looks like you got your replacement credit card."

Ronald walked into the kitchen and grabbed a banana. "You mean for the one someone used to buy ten plasma TVs in San Diego?"

"At least the card company's fraud-alert system caught it. You're not responsible for a penny."

"But how is that even possible when the card was still in my wallet in Florida."

"They steal the digital data and replicate the magnetic strips."

"What?"

"It's computers, Dad."

He shrugged and headed into the other room to check the phone message.

A wrinkled, almost pink index finger pressed a button. The message began to play.

Brook was making neat rows of Jell-O boxes in the cupboard when her father returned. She looked over at him with a smile. "Hey, Dad—" Her smile vanished. "Dad, what's the matter? You're white as a ghost!"

A half-eaten banana hit the floor. Ronald's legs began to betray him. He pulled out a chair and grabbed the edge of the kitchen table as he eased himself down.

Brook ran over and sat next to him. She leaned in with a hand on his shoulder. "Dad, what is it? What's going on?"

Speechless. He just pointed into the other room.

Brook dashed over to the answering machine. She pressed the button to replay the last message.

"*This is Special Agent Rick Maddox with the DEA in Washington, D.C., and I am calling concerning prescription medication that you illegally purchased and took possession of during the last two years. Please call me back immediately to schedule a mutually agreeable arrangement in order to avoid the undue embarrassment of an arrest at your residence.*"

Brook spun around at the message's conclusion. "Dad, there has to be some kind of mistake."

He tried to stand. "I need some water."

"I'll get it." She raced to the sink.

Ronald's hands shook as he took a few timid sips.

Her hand on his shoulder again. "Don't worry. They've gotten something wrong somewhere."

"But I've had a lot of prescriptions over that time. My knees, a colonoscopy, root canal. It was all legitimate."

"Except these are from new doctors," said Brook. "Not like the ones back in New York that you'd been going to for years. I can't tell you how much I've learned about medical corruption in South Florida."

"What are you saying?" asked Ronald.

"That you didn't do anything wrong," said Brook. "It must have been a doctor. Maybe his license lapsed. Or maybe your prescriptions were on the level, but he was over-prescribing for other patients and your name accidentally got lumped in."

He began standing again. "Then I'll call the agent back and straighten this whole thing out."

Her hand tightened on his shoulder. "Don't."

"Why not?"

"I only work for tax attorneys, but if there's one thing I know, it's that you never respond to this kind of inquiry without counsel."

"But I don't have a lawyer."

She pulled a cell from her purse. "You'll soon have one of the best."

For the next half hour, she paced and burned through Verizon minutes, working her way down a list of referrals until she had one of the most expensive criminal defense firms on the line . . .

ORANGE BLOSSOM TRAIL

"I absolutely love Gatorland! But what to do first?" Serge ran back and forth over the same five feet of pavement. "A hundred and ten family-owned acres of real Florida nature exhibits, not the bogus indoor air-conditioned ones where they lure gators out of the water with heat lamps from gas-station fried-chicken counters." His head jerked back and forth. "There's so much true wildness I'm suffocating from selection shock. What's the most natural thing here? . . . Ooo, over there!"

Coleman followed Serge as he dashed across a boardwalk and skidded to a stop. They peered down inside a glass dome.

"What is it?" asked Coleman.

"The Dome of Dreams." Serge knelt to see through the front of the glass. "It's a classic pneumatic injection-molding machine that lets you watch while it makes a tiny wax alligator, then uses a hamburger flipper to scoop it into the chute for your recovery."

"Looks futuristic," said Coleman.

"And it's the best kind of futurism—old!" Serge extracted bills from his wallet as fast as possible. "This primitive souvenir machine was considered space-age back in the sixties." *Slurp, slurp, slurp.* "I remember as a kid watching the intricate hydraulics pump out my little wax dolphins and Weeki Wachee mermaids, thinking: 'We can't let the Soviets get hold of these.'"

The machine sucked Serge's currency into the slot. Steel rods began pushing together the halves of the mold. "It's working! It's working!" Serge hopped up and down and turned to passersby. "It's working!" He completed a pirouette. "Coleman! What are you doing! You're going to crack the dome!"

Coleman was pressing his forehead hard against the middle of the glass. Serge grabbed him from behind. "It's solid! You can't put your head through it!"

"Good call." Coleman stood up straight. "Dodged another close one."

"People are staring," said Serge. "I told you, it's baby-stroller zone: absolutely no unnecessary attention . . . Holy cow! The mold is opening! The mold is opening!" He turned to the crowd on the boardwalk. "The mold is opening! Come see, it's a miracle! . . . No, don't stare at me. Look in the dome. And why isn't there a line forming like the old days? Wait, I know how to start a line. Look! On the side of the alligator, it's the Virgin Mary!"

More people stopped to stare.

"I thought we weren't supposed to attract attention."

"Not to ourselves," said Serge. "To the dome."

"The burger flipper's coming," said Coleman.

"And the cool thing about the machine is it's similar to those carnival cranes that fish for prizes, except with the domes you win every time, guaranteed!"

"The flipper stopped."

"What the— Oh God, no! My alligator is stuck at the end of the injection platform and won't fall into the chute! It's like those satanic vending machines with bags of Skittles hung up on the corkscrews, but this time I can't pound the crap out of the sacred dome." He covered his eyes. "Why! Why! Why!" He opened them with a smile: "I know! These are old machines before they invented those little security doors preventing you from sticking your arm up inside through the chute to steal stuff." Serge dropped to the ground. "I think I can reach."

"I'm not so sure," said Coleman. "It's pretty far up there."

"Look down in the dome and be my navigator," said Serge. "I'm up to my elbow now. How far is it?"

"Not even close."

Serge twisted on the ground and grunted as he strenuously pushed his arm. "I'm all the way in as far as I can go. Tell me what's going on."

"You got your wish," said Coleman. "A line's forming."

"No, I mean inside the machine."

"Oh, that—you're *so* close. Fingertips almost there."

"I can't reach any farther. My arm is completely inside the chute."

"But, man, if you could see how close you are."

"Okay, fuck it," said Serge. "I'm getting that alligator, but I'll need your help. Lift my torso and when I give the word, jerk me hard to the right."

"What for?"

"To dislocate my shoulder. It should give me an extra inch."

Coleman bent down and grabbed him around the chest. "Tell me when."

"Now! . . . *Ahhhh! Ahhhhh!* The pain! . . ."

"You got the alligator!"

"I know! I can feel it in my hand! Now pull me out . . . Coleman, pull me out . . . Coleman!"

"I am pulling, but you won't budge."

"Coleman, I'm seriously stuck and my shoulder's out. I can't do this myself."

"I don't know what to say. I'm pulling as hard as I can." Coleman reached for a tighter grip around his chest. "Serge, you should see the size of the crowd now. I think they all want to be like us."

"I can't see them," said Serge. "My face is pressed to the ground and wedged against the bottom of this thing."

"I know," said Coleman. "Your voice is going under the small space beneath the machine and echoing out the back."

"Put some elbow grease into it!"

Coleman pulled harder and began giggling.

"It's not funny," echoed Serge's voice. "I can't live like this."

"I'm sorry," said Coleman, stifling more laughter. "It's just the way your face is crammed down there with your arm all the way inside, and your hand is raised up in a glass bubble holding a wax alligator like some holy object. I mean this mescaline is good, but damn."

"Wait, I felt something move. Okay, I'm going to twist my arm and you pull as hard as you can. Ready? Now! . . . *Ahhhhhhh!*"

The arm came free and they tumbled backward on the boardwalk. Serge stood and dusted himself off, grinning mildly at the agape crowd. He gestured at the machine with the gator in his hand. "I'm finished with it now. You can go ahead and use it. I just left a little skin in the chute."

Coleman tugged his sleeve. "Security's probably coming."

"I don't see anyone, but let's move along anyway because there's so much to experience here." Serge looked around the other boardwalks, the covered verandas and gator-filled ponds. "Where's the next most natural setting? . . . Ooo, a penny-flattening machine . . ."

Coleman found himself in a chase again. He arrived out of breath. Serge was already sorting through pocket change in his hand. "The penny machines are even better than the domes. But you need the shiniest penny. Then you just stick it in this slot here and start cranking the big wheel . . ."

"It fell in the chute," said Coleman. "We didn't have to get limbs inside this one."

"We're on a roll now!" *Slurp, slurp.* "Where's more nature? . . . Over there! The souvenir shop!"

Serge left the gift store with a topped-off shopping bag. "It's weird. Souvenirs and coffee turn me into Ivana Trump."

"Next nature stop?" asked Coleman.

"Up there!" Serge shielded his eyes. "They put in a zip line for my convenience . . ."

. . . Ten minutes later and fifty feet above the ground: "Serge, I don't want to ride a zip line over the lake of a thousand alligators. I'm on mescaline."

"Off you go!"

Push.

"Waaaaaaaaaaaaaaaaaaaa . . ."

Back in the Firebird: "Serge, isn't Mahoney going to be mad? He called this morning and wanted us to check out a lead at that motel. But instead we just wasted a bunch of time back there."

"And that's what everyone thinks: If you're a private eye, you're supposed to follow the plot, but I say fuck that linear bullshit." Serge slurped coffee from the tube while wearing children's Gatorland sunglasses with cartoon characters on the corners. "Real life rarely stays on point like in the movies . . . These sunglasses are too tight for my head. It hurts . . . Ninety percent of our existence is tangents. So tangents are actually the real plot. But even more importantly, if you avoid a tangent you normally would have taken, you could create a rip in the quantum fabric of the universe."

"What's that mean?"

"It's like a *Twilight Zone* episode where the future is forever altered because some time traveler goes back to 1899 and saves an Albanian woman from getting creamed by a streetcar in Syracuse, and then President Johnson is never born."

"So what you're saying is if we didn't screw around back there at Gatorland . . ."

Serge nodded. "We could have been spun off into the galaxy."

Coleman fired up a joint. "Then we should probably stop again."

"Good thinking." Serge hit his blinker and sucked the coffee bladder dry.

A cell phone rang. Serge checked the display.

Mahoney.

"Serge here. And before you say anything, I can explain: We had to make sure everyone was born."

Chapter NINETEEN

FORT LAUDERDALE

A cell phone sat upright against a bowl of fruit on the kitchen table. It was the eighth-floor condo of a retired firefighter from New York. Brook Campanella pressed a button.

It was one of those calls with speakerphones on both ends.

A disembodied voice came from the middle of the table. "This is Ken Shapiro, and I have one of my partners, Linda Tataglia, in the office with me. Miss Campanella, I understand your father is with you?"

"He's right here."

"Good. First thing, another colleague of ours is calling the Washington DEA office right now to say we represent you, so that shuts them down there. They'll have to go through us from now on and cannot legally contact you directly. And if for some reason, they *do* call, tell them you've retained counsel, give them our phone number and say good-bye . . . Excuse me, Linda has something she'd like to say . . ."

"Mr. Campanella, this is Linda Tataglia. I also need to advise you that if they come to your door and ask you to step outside for a private conversation, don't do it. That's a common ruse. They can't arrest you inside your home without a warrant. Outside, they can."

"But what if they have a warrant?"

"If they did, they wouldn't ask you to step outside. They'd just show it to you."

Ronald began shaking again. "But I didn't do anything!"

"That's irrelevant. Right now what you need to do is let the law play out. From what you've told us, it doesn't sound like you're who they're really after. We'll take care of this as quickly as we can."

"Excuse me," said Brook. "You're making this sound a lot more serious than it actually is."

"It's not more serious, just more complex," said Ken. "When you have an entity the size of the DEA, and the proverbial train has already left the station, it can entail a bit of red tape. The important thing is not to worry."

Ronald scoffed. "Easier said than done."

"There is some good news," said Ken.

"How's that?"

"They contacted you by phone. If you were a serious target, they would have tried to catch you off guard, like in a parking garage. People are more talkative under such duress."

"So what does a phone call mean?" asked Ronald.

"I'd bet almost anything that, like your daughter suspects, their real target is a doctor. I think they're fishing for witnesses and got your name from a patient list. But here's where you have to be careful and let us handle it. Sometimes, instead of asking for a witness's help, they prefer to go through the witness."

"Through?" asked Brook.

"Indict as a co-conspirator, then deal down with a plea bargain in exchange for testimony."

"But he didn't do anything," said the daughter.

"Doesn't matter. It's simply a game of leverage. I know a lot of people over at the agency, and every one of them is a total professional. But occasionally you'll get someone who's played the game so long that they've lost empathy and don't realize the havoc it plays on people who aren't part of their world."

Ronald took a deep breath. "I don't feel so good."

"Hold on," said Ken. "Our colleague just returned to the conference room and said he couldn't reach the agent. But he left a message, so we're covered on that front. Just relax and let us run it from here. We'll call as soon as we hear something."

"Thank you for helping us so quickly," said Brook.

"Take care," said Ken.

ORLANDO

A black Firebird sat on the corner of a motel parking lot with the radio on.

"... *Happiness is a warm gun ...*"

"Cool," said Coleman. "*The White Album.*"

They were on stakeout, which meant coffee and bottled water on the driver's side; joints and Jäger shots for the passenger.

"... *Bang, bang, shoot, shoot ...*"

Serge grooved to the classic Beatles cut. "I just realized something about the sixties. Because dope came along, comic books went out, so there were never any hippie superheroes."

"Yes, there were," said Coleman. "The Fabulous Furry Freak Brothers. They had their own underground comic books."

"But they weren't superheroes." Serge raised his binoculars toward a particular motel room. "They didn't have any superpowers."

"Yes, they did," said Coleman. "They had the power to score weed under any circumstance."

"That's not a superpower."

Coleman raised an eyebrow at Serge. "My friends would beg to differ."

"... *Happiness ...*"

"The motel room door's opening." Serge tossed the binoculars in the backseat. "We're on."

The Trans Am raced across the parking lot and screeched up in front of a tall man and a petite woman.

The surprised couple jumped back. "Watch where you're going! You almost hit us!"

Serge jumped out. "Everything's under control. I'm a political detective, and this is my associate, Coleman. He has superpowers."

"I can score dope at will."

The man glanced toward his female companion—"street loons"—and began walking around the pair. Serge sidestepped to block their path.

"Is there a problem?" the man said menacingly.

"I was hoping we could get together and form a flash mob. Check out our moves."

Serge and Coleman began doing the robot.

"Get the fuck out of our way!" The man started pushing past.

Serge blocked him again and squinted at the pair. "Do I know you from somewhere?"

"Move or get hurt."

"No, I definitely remember you but can't put my finger on it." Serge looked closer, then raised a finger in epiphany. "I got it now! You're the people from the TV shows! You're famous . . . Hey, Coleman, we have a couple of celebrities here."

"I can make a bong from the contents of any kitchen."

"Man, I can't believe the things they're reporting about you," said Serge. "Faking that whole terminal-disease thing and ripping off the compassionate. How does it feel to be the most hated people in South Florida? At least for this week?"

"Okay, fella, I warned you!"

Then the guy felt the gun in his ribs.

"Why walk?" said Serge. "When there's plenty of room in my trunk?"

A nother dingy motel room.

Serge marched them inside at gunpoint.

"Okay, you sit here, and you sit here . . . and it's pointless to resist.

I don't know why I always say that, but I hear it on TV and wouldn't want to disappoint."

Soon they were both tied up with sailor knots.

The couple's eyes weren't blinking.

Serge tugged the ropes behind their chairs to make sure they were snug, then circled back around.

"W-w-what are you going to do to us?"

"You tell me," said Serge. "What *should* I do to you? I mean, how does someone get their head around such a disgraceful level of predation? There's low and then there's sick. On the other hand, up to two percent of the population are psychopaths, so you can't help it if you have no empathy for others. They say empathy can't be taught, but I don't buy that for a minute! I've got a great lesson planned for you, and then we can have recess and milk."

He tore off two sections of duct tape and roughly strapped them around their heads. Then he flicked open a switchblade and held it to the man's mouth.

Curiously, eyes went wide again. "Hold still," said Serge. "I wouldn't want to cut your lips . . ."

Then he was done. The couple didn't know what to make of it.

"It's a little different than the gag I usually use," said Serge. "I cut a small hole in the middle of the tape to fit those plastic tubes that are now sticking into your mouths. And the tubes are connected to these things. Depending on your culture, you might not recognize them, but they're a couple of flexible plastic bladders that people use to sneak alcohol into places."

Serge reached for the dresser and uncapped a two-liter bottle of soda. But instead of brown cola, it contained chalky-white fluid. "Just a little something I brewed up. Don't worry, it actually doesn't taste half bad . . . Coleman, we need theme music!"

Coleman set a bong down and walked to their boom box. "What do you want to hear?"

"The Doors should be appropriate."

"You got it." A chubby finger pressed a button.

Serge smiled and slapped Omar on the shoulder. "Now we're cooking." He raised the first bladder high in the air and began pouring from the soda bottle. "Coleman, stand here and hold this." Then he repeated with the second bladder.

"*. . . No one here gets out alive . . .*"

"That should about do it." Serge set the bottle down. "And as I anticipated, you're blocking the end of the tube with your tongue, so here's the deal: I'm going to pinch your nose shut. That way you won't be able to breathe unless you drink what's in the bladders, then I'll reward you by releasing. Ready? I'm pinching . . ."

The man held out as long as he could, then chugged rapidly and panted through flared nostrils.

"Now your turn, miss." She held out even longer than the man, but there never was any other result. The elixir slid down.

Serge plopped himself on the end of a bed and clapped with excess enthusiasm. "Don't you just love a good mystery? And here's the part I know you're just dying to find out. Just what the hell was that stuff he made me drink? Even though you have to admit it did taste pretty good." *Wink.* "I'll tell you! You know how there are all these medical labs where dedicated professionals work tirelessly to cure diseases? But in order to come up with cures, they have to *create* diseases, so they've developed serums that induce tumors in mice. Then they go to work on the rodents with scalpels and shit . . ."

Movement below distracted the couple. They looked down as something small and furry grabbed a piece of cheese and darted back through a semi-circular hole at the base of the motel wall. HOME SWEET HOME.

"That's just Skippy," said Serge. "He's like family, so no medical experiments on him. Anyway, when I heard about the tumor-inducing serum, I just had to get my hands on some. Which is pretty difficult, but not because of security at the labs—who wants to take that stuff? The real hurdle is there's no black market. Actually now there's a black market of one: me. So you have to go to the source. I can't believe how easy it was to break into the place last night, and the cabinet wasn't even locked. Guess you were just lucky . . ."

The couple began thrashing against their rope bindings.

"Whoa! Hold on! You're going to hurt yourselves," said Serge. "And right now you need to keep your heads because good ol' Serge always leaves his students a way out. If you listen carefully and follow my instructions, you just might emerge unscathed from this little adventure. Do I have your attention?"

They nodded.

"Good. And here's the important part. I don't really know the dosage translation between mice and people, which is great news for you! It could take hours or even a day before the tumors start to grow. So if you can catch it in time before it reaches a certain level of cellular formation and goes malignant, you're home free. I guess you'll need to find a treatment center and get radiation or something. I'm fuzzy on that, but the people there will know . . . Would you like a lift? It's up to you." He tapped his wristwatch. "Tick-tock, tick-tock . . ."

This time even more emphatic nodding.

"Coleman, looks like another road trip." He stood and grabbed his gear bag. "You can turn off that boom box."

"... *This is the end ... my only friend ...*"

Chapter TWENTY

ORLANDO

A '78 Firebird rolled through downtown at lunch hour.

Serge glanced in the rearview at the couple in the backseat. "The hospital's coming up, so look sharp. I'm sure you understand that I can't be seen near the hospital or get caught on their security cameras. We'll just drop you a few blocks away, but you'll be able to see it."

A minute later, a red light stopped the Trans Am at a bright intersection with a concrete bus bench advertising affordable cremation.

Serge turned around and reached toward the pair. "This is as good a place as any." He slashed their wrist straps with a box cutter. Coleman opened the passenger door and leaned his seat forward. They took off running.

Horns honked.

"The light's green," said Coleman.

"Everyone's in a rush." Serge rolled forward another half block and pulled up to a car wash.

"Why are we stopping?"

Serge raised binoculars. "Because I want to see the rest of my plan unfold."

"Did you really give them tumors?"

"No. That would be mean."

"Then what was that stuff you made them drink?"

The binoculars followed the couple as they raced across the street. "Ipecac and magnesium citrate. Both are available over the counter."

"What are they?"

"The first is an agent to induce vomiting in case you ingested something you shouldn't have . . ."

"Like the time I ate all those mothballs?"

". . . And the other stuff is what you take the night before surgery to completely evacuate your bowels. Both are highly aggressive and render the user quite helpless to control the effects. You essentially have to camp out in the bathroom. It's like the old Robin Williams joke: two exits, no waiting."

"I've been there," said Coleman. "And that makes more sense because the tumor thing doesn't sound like it would work."

"Oh, not only will it work, but it *has* worked."

"You've done it?"

Serge shook his head. "Little-known police case. This dude in perfect health suddenly died, and they couldn't figure it out—got classified as unknown natural causes. And it would have ended there, except a second person in the family died. So now there's an urgent investigation because they think they got a food-contamination epidemic like salmonella and they'll have to yank chicken wings off grocery shelves, or maybe it's the beginning of a chemical cluster like Love Canal, where some factory has to buy up all the houses."

"Which was it?" asked Coleman.

"Neither," said Serge. "Authorities discovered organ damage in the two victims but couldn't figure out what was ingested to cause it, so they sent tissue samples away to a lab, and they had no answers either. Then by sheer luck they gave the evidence to another scientist to double-check, and she looked up from her microscope and said, 'This was no accident. This was murder!' "

"How'd she figure that?" asked Coleman.

"Turns out the scientist previously worked at a pharmaceutical company and said she had seen these types of cells before—in deliberately triggered mice tumors. But they never happen in humans. She told the cops to find a connection between a family member and someone who works with lab mice, and they'd have their killer. Sure enough, one of the sisters had just broken up with some asshole who worked in medical research, and he'd snuck in the house while they were away to poison something in the fridge."

"Far out." Coleman looked back up the street. "But what about that couple? How is the stuff you gave them instead supposed to teach them a lesson?"

"I've set up a behavior model of distilled irony." Serge watched as the couple slowed down on the sidewalk and grabbed their abdomens. "The first step was to firmly plant the seed in their brains that they're doomed without immediate medical care. Then the effects of my yummy concoction will fool them into thinking the serum was real."

"When will it start working?" asked Coleman.

"I think it just kicked in."

"Let me see!"

Serge handed him the binoculars. "Oooooo, gross. Look at all the people scattering away from them on the sidewalk. Cool."

"It's only another block to the hospital, but it will be a very long block," said Serge. "On the bright side, it won't be difficult to track them."

Serge started up the car and began following in the slow lane.

"So what's the irony part of your lesson?"

"That will unfold when they get in the hospital . . ."

MIAMI

A porkpie hat Frisbee'd through the air, missed the hat rack and sailed out an open window of a two-story office building overlooking the Miami River.

The man who had just thrown it talked to himself in the third person: "Mahoney glared at the empty hat rack like a pile of torn-up betting tickets at the track . . ."

He grabbed a stale cup of coffee and an even staler glazed doughnut.

A rotary phone rang. He swallowed a rock-hard bite and chased it with a swig of cold joe.

"Mahoney, start jawing . . ."

The phone had been ringing a lot lately. Mahoney was cultivating a nice little reputation for rescuing scam victims. The word of mouth was just a trickle, but multiplied by the exponential volume of fraud in South Florida, it amounted to a respectable jingle of pocket change. Calls were coming from as far away as Orlando. He already represented three victims who had been swindled out of donations by the father with the sick boy on Channel 12.

He held the heavy black receiver to his head as he accepted another client. "Mahoney told the dame on the blower that he was all over the case like big hats on the pope, and she could chill like an underboss with a no-show job at the railroad, which doesn't require a conductor's jacket and all that it leads to . . ."

He hung up.

The phone rang again. Mahoney usually let the phone ring, but he was thinking about his hat down in the parking lot.

"Mahoney, rattle your molars."

"Yes, Mr. Mahoney, this is Wesley Chapel from Big Dipper Data Management, and I've just detected a statistical trend that I thought you'd want to know about right away . . ."

Wesley began a careful explanation of what he had learned. "And Mahoney listened like a dope fiend watching the Big H start to bubble in a spoon he stole from Mooky's Diner because he doesn't have any spoons left in his flophouse, and the neighbors no longer believe he needs to borrow some to play spoons in a jug band . . ."

"What? . . ."

"Lay it on me."

"It seems that some of the scam artists you're having me investigate are painting an unusually large radar signature with their data. Statistically impossible."

"Like the queen yodels."

"What?"

"Give it to me in English."

"The only explanation is that they're all working as part of a larger, organized gang of grifters who travel together. That means if you get another client who might have been taken in by one of the gang, they'll be much easier to trace. On the other hand, it also means increased danger for any of your men in the field. I'll keep you up to date as more comes in."

"Bingle-schnapps."

Mahoney hung up again. But didn't take his hand off the receiver. He quickly dialed. Someone answered.

"Hello?"

"Get me Serge, toot-sweet!"

"Mahoney," said Serge. "Don't you recognize my voice?"

"Mahoney cogitated on what he was about to reveal, like a pimp deciding how to tell a hooker she's been sent down the minors to work on her skin flute."

"Who are you talking to? . . ."

DOWNTOWN ORLANDO

Serge closed his cell phone.

"Who was that?" asked Coleman.

"Mahoney thinks some of our targets are part of a larger, organized gang—specifically the dating bandits and that couple up ahead running for the hospital."

"Speaking of which . . ." Coleman bent toward the windshield.

The couple reached the ambulance drive-up and made a slippery turn toward the building.

They sprinted into the emergency room, the place where people with urgent needs go to wait. It was packed with rows of un-cheerful people in molded plastic chairs, sitting for hours. A variety of injuries and malaises, but the most common threat was dying of old age.

Omar and Piper practically crashed into the admittance desk. "We need help!"

The nurse looked them over and didn't see any bones sticking through skin. She pointed at the clipboard on the counter. "Sign in and have a seat."

Piper leaned forward as far as she could. "You don't understand!"

"Wait a second," said the nurse. "I recognize you now. From the TV news."

"I need cancer treatment!" said Piper.

"Sure you do," said the nurse.

"I'm serious this time!"

"Just like last time?"

"I'm so sorry. I need help!"

The nurse yelled to get the attention of everyone in the room. "Look who just popped in to grace us with their presence: the scam artists from television. They'd like to get some medical care."

A drone of murmurs rolled around the room. People began pointing. Mumbles rose to outraged voices. *"Those are the assholes who stole all those donations!"*

"We hate you!"

"You're lower than worms!"

"Please die!

"One more thing," yelled the nurse. "They also want to cut in front of you."

To this audience, that played worse than the original scam.

"Son of a bitch!"

"I've been waiting since dawn!"

"My gout!"

A few began standing. Someone called the television station on from a cell.

Omar and Piper pleaded desperately with the nurse. "We'll do any-thing! You have to help us!"

The nurse had already picked up her own phone. "I'm calling secu-rity. The TV said there are fraud warrants out on you."

"Wait! Don't! We'll give you all the money!"

The nurse hung up. "Security is on the way." Then she sniffed the air. "Jesus! What is that god-awful smell?" She leaned over the desk and looked down at the floor. "That's disgusting!"

"I told you we were sick," said Piper. "This guy made us drink some stuff . . ."

Three security guards ran down a disinfected hallway.

But other things first:

The couple felt a presence from behind. More and more patients surrounding them. *"You're the devil!"*

"My grandmother gave you money!"

"What's that smell?"

Someone shoved Omar into the desk, and another pushed Piper. The rest joined in. *"Let me get my hands on them! . . ."*

Security guards burst through double swinging doors on the side of the emergency room. They immediately spotted the couple but couldn't reach them because of the growing mob.

"Kill them!"

"You suck elephant dicks!"

"What he just said!"

Omar noticed the guards working their way through. "We have to get out of here!" He grabbed Piper by the arm and charged into the crowd. People grabbed and ripped their clothes. They each lost sleeves but pushed on.

The mob wanted to stop the couple, but everyone was now skating around on diarrhea. Omar and Piper made it through the pack with shredded shirts. They dashed back out the emergency room doors and onto the sidewalk.

The crowd paused, looking at one another, thinking about losing their spots in the emergency room. Then: *"Get 'em!"*

The room emptied in a hurry. Patients made a hard left turn outside and ran up the street. The security guards stopped at the doors, because they weren't paid much.

Omar and Piper only had a half block lead, but all the people chasing them were sick and injured.

A cameraman pointed through a windshield. "There they are! At the front of that crowd!" The Live Action Eyewitness Orlando 12 News mobile unit had arrived.

The TV van quickly passed the crowd and slowed so they could roll alongside the couple as they ran. The satellite dish on its roof began beaming the video feed back to the station. Regular programming was interrupted for breaking news, as it had been every time a live chase came through the greater Orlando area. Except this was the first one on foot.

Viewers at home began texting in votes to a poll that just went up on their screens. Others recognized the street on TV as the same one just outside where they were sitting. They angrily poured out of shops, restaurants and Transcendental Meditation classes, joining the pursuing mob. Still others lined the sidewalk ahead, spitting on the couple and splattering them with rotten food.

Two blocks north, a black Firebird sat on the side of the road. Serge lowered his binoculars. "Here they come now. The plan is unfolding beyond expectation."

"That one guy just hocked a big snot-rocket right in her face." Coleman chased pork rinds with Pabst Blue Ribbon. "This is better than pay-per-view."

Serge raised the binoculars again. "I should be in charge of programming somewhere."

Back up the street, a reporter with a microphone hung out the passenger window of the TV van. "Our live poll shows that ninety-six percent of viewers believe you should be tossed in a blast furnace. Your thoughts?"

More people streamed from sports bars and convenience stores until the mob was five times its original size.

The couple rapidly approached a busy intersection where heavy traffic blocked their escape. They made a left at the corner and hit the brakes. More TV viewers had emptied into the street and charged from that direction. The pair looked back at the gaining crowd, then up at the green light over the road. "Come on, turn red!"

It didn't turn red. Lynch mobs converging from two pincer directions would be on them in seconds. They glanced at each other and nodded. The traffic wasn't *that* bad. And a break between buses was coming up. They could easily get across if they timed it just right . . .

Serge handed the binoculars to Coleman. "They're going for it, but it'll be close. That second crowd will get there almost simultaneously."

"I say they'll make it."

"Me, too."

The TV van pulled up next to the anxious couple. A microphone out the window: "Are you going for it? It's going to be close . . ."

Those at the front of the mob reached them and went to grab what was left of their shirts, but the couple was too fast. The break in traffic came and they bolted . . . In the clear!

Coleman pointed with a pork rind. "I don't think they see that bus."

"Which bus?" asked Serge.

"The big one with the ad on the side for the children's hospital . . . Ooo! God!" Coleman covered his eyes.

Serge threw the Firebird in gear. "That's ironic."

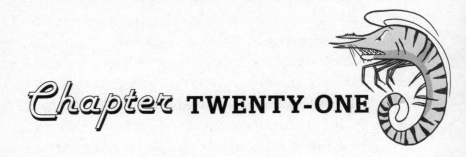

Chapter TWENTY-ONE

FORT LAUDERDALE

A blue glow filled an eighth-floor condo unit.

"I'll take 'Rectangular U.S. States' for two hundred, Alex."

Ronald Campanella turned the volume down with the remote control. "I don't want to watch *Jeopardy!* anymore."

"Come on, we always used to play," said Brook. "You need to keep your mind occupied."

"But what if the lawyers are wrong? What if I have to go to trial?"

"That's nonsense," said his daughter. "We just need to wait it out and let them fix the misunderstanding."

"I can't take this not-knowing business." Ronald began breathing rapidly again.

Brook got up from the sofa. "You need a drink. I'll get you one."

"I don't want a drink."

"I didn't say you wanted one. I said you need one." She went to the cabinet for a bottle of Scotch. Her cell phone rang. Brook made a detour for her purse.

"Hello?"

"This is Ken Shapiro, from Shapiro, Heathcote-Mendacious and Blatt. Sorry for calling so late, but we have some preliminary good news that I thought you'd like to hear."

"What is it?"

"Nothing confirmed, but based on our experience, we don't think your father is a very high-value target."

"Why do you say that?"

"The number you were given to call back turns out to be the main DEA line in Washington, which indicates a certain lack of urgency. After some more calls, we learned there is no agent by the name of Rick Maddox in that office, but there is one in Miami. And he's a polygraph examiner."

"That's weird," said Brook.

"That's what we thought. It's not the kind of position dealing with heavy trafficking enforcement, so that should lower your stress level."

"Really appreciate you calling."

She hung up and headed back to the living room. "Dad, I have some good news."

Ronald stood up, grabbed the center of his chest and, without a word, toppled forward on his face.

"Dad! No!"

ORANGE BLOSSOM TRAIL

A cell phone rang. And rang.

Serge checked the display. It kept ringing.

"Aren't you going to answer it?" asked Coleman.

"Mahoney again, probably ungrateful that we didn't get the money back from those scam artists with the medical donations."

"Bus accidents rule."

"Or he wants us to jump right on another case," said Serge. "But you have to pace yourself. If we actually are dealing with an organized gang, that means recharging my idea reservoir for unique ways to dispatch them."

"Why?"

"To maintain a quality standard. Unlike you, I have a reputation to uphold." Serge sucked the coffee tube but only got air. "You start phoning in your murders and people talk."

"Where are you going to get new ideas?"

"A special place of inspiration." Serge handed his bladder tube to Coleman. "Coffee me."

Coleman grabbed a thermos and watched as the Firebird turned onto a long, stately-looking road with sprawling, professionally maintained lawns on both sides. They drove toward a massive, low-slung building in the distance. Straight ahead at the end of the road—in the building's courtyard—stood a giant metal sculpture that looked like a dandelion. It sprayed water from the ends of hundreds of prongs into a fountain pool.

Coleman stuck his head out the window and gazed up at rows of countless flags on each side of the building. "What is this place? It looks like the United Nations."

"It sort of is," said Serge. "Florida-style."

They parked and climbed the steps to the courtyard, heading for the main entrance, but Serge had to go back and retrieve Coleman, who was trying to climb into the fountain and stick his head in the giant dandelion. "No more hallucinogens for you."

"Serge, the building says 'Tupperware.'"

"Correct again." He pulled the tube from his mouth. "World headquarters built on the site selected by Brownie Wise, who envisioned a utopian Shangri-la of togetherness and keeping food fresh. She was a pioneer, way before any of the theme-park honchos saw the potential of all the available sun-blessed land south of Orlando. I'm guessing the Disney advance scout team flew in from Los Angeles, took a drive down Orange Blossom Trail, then immediately rushed back with wax alligators and burp lids and said, 'Look no further.'"

They entered the building and approached the front desk. Serge stopped to stare down the hallways running off the sides of the lobby toward the management offices. It was pretty far away, but he could make out extensive displays of plaques with photos and more international flags.

Serge gave a slight elbow jab and whispered: "Coleman, I need to check out something. And take photos. Those plaques are calling me. But it's another one of those employees-only areas where they unfairly don't want strangers popping in off the street and wandering the halls of private offices, just because it's their building and they're trying to run a business."

"Stop the oppression."

"They force you to be sneaky when you want to burrow deep inside corporate sanctums and take candid pictures. Sure, they claim that capitalism is opportunity for all, but how else can you learn to join the club if they don't let you watch how they do it? And then some guy blocks my path and asks, 'Can I help you?' which really means, 'What's your fucking problem?' Another nuance game. But the first time it happened, I thought they were sincere and responded, 'Yes, you can help me. I want to join the club. And you're the company to watch! Outsourced boiler rooms, raided pensions, securities violations. What's the secret handshake?' And then I thought they were taking me to the clubhouse, but it was just an exit door to the street, and they threw me really hard against the mailbox on the corner . . . Spin it any way you want, but that's not help."

"I remember that mailbox," said Coleman. "I was tripping on 'shrooms and accidentally got away from you and used the Xerox machine to make five hundred copies of my nipples."

"So now when they ask if they can help, I hold up an official-looking blue document with notary stamps and say, 'I'm here to serve a subpoena but can't tell you who because I have to physically hand it to the person, and if they get advance notice, the guy usually ducks out a fire door or sits on a toilet and pulls his feet up.' Then I flash the document again, prominently showing the word *fraud*—which covers everyone in the building on the DNA level—and the guy bugging me usually says he has to use the restroom, and I follow him in a minute later and bend down, but I can't see feet . . ."

A voice from behind: "Those are the walls of fame."

"What?" Serge turned.

The receptionist smiled. "They honor the top representatives from each country." A bigger smile. "Please take a look."

Serge did look. At Coleman. "Sounds like a trick."

"She seems nice enough."

"Until I ask to join the club. Then it's mailbox time again." Serge checked his camera settings. "But I have to see those plaques. Cover my flank and stand back to back against me as we walk down the hall so you can see if anything is coming up on us from the rear."

"Is this some kind of sobriety test?"

"Just do it!" The pair crept down the hall, *flash, flash, flash* . . .

They returned to the desk.

"Serge, nothing happened."

"Something's definitely fishy. Let me see if I'm right—"

"Welcome to Tupperware!" said the receptionist.

"We just popped in off the street and wanted to wander around."

"That's great . . ." said their greeter.

Serge raised an eyebrow at Coleman.

". . . Have you ever been here before?" continued the receptionist.

"Driven by hundreds of times and wanted to stop, but it was always something, and it was usually banging in the trunk . . ."

Her smile remained.

"I remember my mom having Tupperware parties as a kid." Serge's hands swiftly sliced the air, stacking invisible objects. "I *loved* those parties, the whole neighborhood hanging out in our backyard by the mosquito torches in an iconic sixties experience."

"Cream cheese and celery," said Coleman.

"The curtains had fiberglass," said Serge.

"Deviled eggs," said Coleman.

Serge frantically scratched his neck.

Coleman slowly moved his hands in front of his face. "Whoa!"

Her smile never wavered.

Serge uneasily grinned back.

Coleman tugged his sleeve. "Isn't this the part where they usually ask if they can help you?"

"That's the problem," Serge said out the side of his mouth. "Her game is to deliberately throw me off-balance."

"How's she doing that?"

"By *tolerating* me." He pulled Coleman aside a step. "This has never happened before. I know I'm a little exhausting to be around, but I'm also a pretty good student of body language: People usually try to break free by the time I get to the Pavlovian itch-response to curtains."

"Serge, I don't find you exhausting. But I self-medicate."

"And that's the dynamic of our special friendship. But the receptionist is totally lucid. Not only is she tolerating my high-octane quirks, but she's actually encouraging them."

"How is that a problem?"

"Because this is a business negotiation," said Serge. "And in every hardball negotiation, there's a point where you shut up, and the next person who talks loses. Except I've never gotten to that point before because people always jump in and shut *me* up. But this woman's good. I've never encountered such a formidable foe who can indulge my verbal incontinence."

"The temptress."

"Time to get back to the negotiation," said Serge. "Be cool."

"It's hardball."

Both stepped back up to the desk and grinned.

The receptionist grinned back.

Serge and Coleman smiled harder.

The woman maintained even pleasantness.

Serge began to perspire.

The woman didn't.

"Okay! Okay!" said Serge. "You win! I want to see the Tupperware Museum."

"We used to have a museum, but we updated the displays and it's now called the Confidence Center."

"I'm all about positivity." Serge opened his wallet. "How much?"

"It's free." She handed them flowery visitor stickers for their shirts. "Hope you enjoy it."

A cell phone rang. Serge turned it off.

DOWNTOWN MIAMI

The lunchtime crowd strolled along Biscayne Boulevard. They passed the eternal torch at Bayfront Park, and a bench where someone was eating Cuban rice and beans out of a Styrofoam container.

The person on the bench was alone, wearing a golf shirt and aviator sunglasses on a cloudy day. He had a tightly cropped haircut. Cheekbones jutted like a cross between Nicolas Cage and a competitive bicyclist. Under his shirt was a deceptively powerful, angular frame he'd developed from ocean swimming.

He finished lunch, grabbed his briefcase and headed toward a garbage can on the corner to toss his trash.

So did someone else.

Wham. They ran into each other, and he dropped his briefcase.

The other man also dropped a briefcase. Funny, but the two cases looked striking similar. Actually identical.

"You okay?" said the second man.

"Fine."

"I'm so sorry. It was all my fault."

"No, I wasn't looking where I was going."

"Did you like the movie *Collateral*?"

"What?"

"This is just like that."

"Don't talk anymore."

They picked up each other's briefcase and left in opposite directions.

The first man waited for a red light and crossed the boulevard toward an upscale hotel, where he had received an express check-in as a platinum customer. Then he headed for the elevators and hit 10.

Once in his room, the man set his sunglasses atop the TV. He opened the briefcase on the bed, removing a rifle with a folding stock and detachable barrel. Then an Austrian nine-millimeter and silencer. Beneath the weapons was a large tan envelope sealed with red wax.

He pulled out a chair at the desk and broke the seal. Out came the dossier, complete with eight-by-ten black-and-white glossies taken at long range.

His assignment.

There was a calendar of the target's recent movements and detailed background on confirmed associates. Current status: location unknown, but believed to regularly frequent the Miami area.

He reached in the envelope again and removed a genuine Florida driver's license with his own photo and new identity for the operation.

Enzo Tweel.

If there was a single word to describe Enzo, it was *precision*. He had the closest possible shave and rigidly manicured fingernails. Each evening he used a pair of tiny travel scissors and checked his clothes for stray threads.

Right now that focus was on the contents of the briefcase, which he arranged atop the dresser with geometric tyranny. Weapons, ammunition, untraceable cell phone, cyanide capsules, badges from five law enforcement agencies, and tiny rubber fingertip cups with fake prints. Then he went to work at the desk, creating neat rows of dossier documents surrounding a stack of perfectly aligned photos.

When he was satisfied, he walked to the window and pulled open the curtains, revealing the twinkling edge of Miami overlooking Biscayne Bay. To the left, South Beach and all its urgent emptiness. To the right, the Rickenbacker Causeway and the Seaquarium. Straight ahead, cruise ships in the port. And right below, the bench at Bayfront Park where he had just been sitting.

He watched the pavilion's eternal torch flicker, and he exhaled a rare sigh. The whole vista grew painfully familiar. Had it already been two whole years? What an omni-dimensional fiasco. If only they had hired him as the primary shooter, instead of making him play backup to that incompetent amateur they had stuck in the sniper's perch. Not only had he been a bad shot, but even worse in the art of concealment.

The idiot got discovered and was forced to kill two cops, which meant that *Enzo* had to silence the sniper and sanitize the nest. That really irked him. Enzo much preferred the solitary tranquillity of adjusting a rifle scope on a distant target than a close-quarters judo fight in a hotel room.

Enzo looked around. Was it this room? Hard to be sure after two years, but it could have been. He stared out the window again at the jetties flanking the Government Cut shipping channel at the end of Miami Beach. His mind drifted back to the added inconvenience from that last nightmare of a visit: creating a dead scapegoat to take the fall for the whole scandal.

Felicia.

A cell phone began vibrating next to the silencer.

He answered. It was the counter-intelligence electronics expert on call if he ever needed anything. And now he did. With the target at large, the best lead was the closest associate identified in the dossier. Recent calls from the associate to the target had already been confirmed. He ordered up a wireless phone tap that would be routed by satellite to a message app in his smartphone.

Then he tossed a few items from the dresser into a small leather satchel and headed out the door.

Chapter TWENTY-TWO

ORANGE BLOSSOM TRAIL

Serge stuck the coffee tube back in his mouth and hustled Coleman down the hall. There was no specific beginning to the exhibit, but the building gradually changed.

"Freaky," said Coleman. "There are no straight edges in the room. Everything curves and bends and is shiny."

"And it's all covered with retro circles and swirls and starbursts in colors only found on Jefferson Airplane's tour bus." Serge marveled as he slowly snaked through the winding displays. "Check out these lighted bubbles in the walls and domed pedestals with the funkiest Tupperware I haven't seen since I was a kid. It isn't just an homage to nostalgia. We're actually *in* the sixties. This is like the last and greatest parts of the Carousel of Progress from the 1964 World's Fair that Disney disassembled and rebuilt up the road at the Magic Kingdom. Then at some point they chucked the sixties diorama and ruined everything, but who knew it landed over here."

"Trippy—" Coleman turned and rotated his head. "I hear God's voice."

Serge pointed up at flush-mounted speakers. "Piped-in narration."

"... *Every one-point-seven seconds, a Tupperware party starts somewhere in the world* ..."

"I didn't know the parties were still going on," said Coleman. "And that they're using stopwatches."

"So that's what those international plaques in the hallway were about," said Serge. "The parties may be played out a little here in the States, but the rest of the world is just discovering that hand-to-hand gelatin-mold transactions are a joyous intermission between Greek austerity riots."

They walked past a concave sequence of interlocking screens flashing historic Technicolor images, and approached a round column of pinwheel flowers.

Serge tucked the flex tube under his shirt. "I feel like I'm in one of John Lennon's dreams."

"Did his dreams have a dollar-bill slot?"

"What? ... Oh my God!" Serge ran up and placed respectful hands against the column. "A vending machine for miniature Tupperware souvenirs on key chains ..." Serge fumbled for his wallet again. "Someone must have been spying on me when they conceived this place."

Moments later, Serge's pockets bulged with key chains hanging out. He stared into the billfold. "No more singles. Just fives and tens ..." He looked up. "Where'd you come from?"

The employee smiled. "Do you need change?"

"No, I better cut myself off," said Serge. "But thanks."

The person smiled again and dematerialized behind the column.

"That was weird," said Coleman.

"I know." Serge put his wallet away. "Again, behavioral quirks that are shunned everywhere else are aggressively nurtured here ... And I think I've just received my inspiration for dealing with the next scam artist ... To the gift shop!"

They strolled the aisles with gusto. Coleman poked Serge's arm and glanced backward: "There's somebody following us."

"I'm aware. Just be cool and ignore her." Serge mentally cataloged the inventory of passing shelves. "I knew this was too good to be true. I've pushed our visit into the annoyance zone, and now the hammer is about to come down. But it's critical that I pick up a few things first before we hit the mailbox."

Coleman glimpsed back again. "What are we going to do?"

"Stall her long enough before we hear the fatal words—"

From behind: *"Can I help you?"*

Serge seized up and clenched his eyes. "Damn, so close." He turned around with a guilty heart. "Why? I wasn't doing anything."

"You looked like you could use some assistance finding something."

Serge glanced oddly at Coleman.

Coleman shrugged.

"Uh, I actually could use a tiny bit of help."

"Sure, anything..."

Seconds later, Serge led the employee briskly down another aisle: "How much is this?... How much is this?... How much is this?... Is this in a different color?... Is this in a different size?... Can this withstand radiation?... How much is this?..."

"Serge," whispered Coleman. "She's answering every question. And she's not getting pissed."

"I know," Serge whispered back, and headed for the cash register. "Now I get why they call it the Confidence Center: It's an ethereal never-land of serenity that's not as much a corporate headquarters as the meditation retreat of a controversial church. I feel such inner peace and unconditional acceptance that I never want to leave."

They left the building by the giant dandelion.

Serge turned his cell phone back on, and it rang immediately. He began opening it.

"You're actually going to answer this time?" said Coleman.

"Since I now have my inspiration, our appointment schedule just opened up." He placed it to his ear. "Hey, Mahoney, what's shaking?... I know you've been trying to call. My phone went dead and had to be recharged, and when I turned it back on I saw all the times you tried to reach me. Must be awfully important . . . Sure, we're free to come back to Miami to get in position. Be there in a few hours. Later . . ."

Serge and Coleman walked off into the sunset with brimming Tupperware shopping bags in each hand.

FORT LAUDERDALE

Floral arrangements continued arriving.

All shapes. Ovals, horseshoes, a bunch of roses supposed to look like a fireman's helmet.

They sat on easels along the front wall. The flowers kept coming because people didn't. Couldn't break away from New York or afford the trip in the economy.

Brook Campanella sat in the first row of a room full of empty folding Samsonite chairs. The casket was open for the viewing. The funeral director solemnly stood off to the left side near the door. His hands were clasped in front of him, and his face was a long, sad countenance of deepest empathy. He was thinking about an upcoming fishing trip.

Brook had set her cell phone on vibrate, but what did it matter?

It vibrated.

She flipped it open. "Hello?"

"Ms. Campanella, this is Ken Shapiro of Shapiro, Heathcote-Mendacious—"

"I know," said Brook.

"I'm calling because I have great news. Upon further inquiry, I ultimately received a press release faxed from the DEA about a fraud alert on someone impersonating one of their agents in a phone scam. If your father had been present to answer the call, he would have been told of pending charges against him that could be dropped if a civil fine was immediately paid through Western Union. It was all a hoax."

"What?"

"After getting the news release, I did an online search and found several chat rooms where all these furious people want to strangle the fake agent. Apparently the guy was good, and some victims paid up to six thousand dollars. The chat rooms tell almost identical stories of being on the phone with him, shaking uncontrollably and almost having heart attacks. One Internet bulletin board is even making progress tracking him. He's hit Maryland, Tennessee and is now believed to be in Florida."

"But—"

"I know your next question. The common denominator was that all his marks had recently had their credit-card data compromised. Did that happen to your father?"

"I . . . uh, have to go."

"Okay, but I knew you'd want to know right away. Aren't you happy?"

She hung up.

Brook sat quietly alone for the rest of the viewing.

At the end, she heard someone clear his throat. The funeral director.

"Yes."

"I'm very sorry for your loss."

Brook dabbed her eyes. "Thank you."

The director smiled with practiced sympathy. "But you'll have to move on."

She nodded—"I know. My father would want me to"—and got out another tissue.

"No, I mean you have to go." The director pointed toward the doorway and two employees standing in the hall. "They need to wheel in the next casket. The family's already starting to arrive."

Brook got up without reaction and drove home in a ten-year-old Ford Focus. If electrode pads had been attached to her head, they would have detected brain activity on the level of a major thunderstorm.

She pulled into the driveway, went up to the condo and opened the door.

Brook stopped with an open mouth.

On top of the TV stand was a lot of air. Her eyes went to an empty shelf where the stereo had been. She roamed room to room. The silverware stuck deep in the closet was gone, including the cake knife from her parents' wedding. They'd gotten Ronald's watch and favorite cuff links.

The police were exceptionally polite, taking notes and offering condolences. They had been encountering more and more burglary victims wearing black.

Brook fought tears at the kitchen table. "What are the odds my father died because of a scam . . . ?" She turned generally toward the living room. ". . . And then *this*."

"I'm afraid it probably wasn't a coincidence," said the lead detective, still jotting on a pad.

Brook looked up quickly. "What do you mean, not a coincidence? Are you saying that the person who left the phone message also robbed us?"

The detective shook his head. "What I mean is you put a funeral notice in the newspaper, right?"

"Yeah, so?"

"So you shouldn't have done that."

"What are you talking about?"

"It's a sad commentary on the direction of society," said the detective. "But we've begun distributing Crime Stopper tips to grieving relatives about what details to withhold from the newspapers."

"What for?"

"Because most of the people reading funeral notices today in South Florida are criminals looking to burglarize the homes of survivors during the viewing. You may want to have someone watch this place."

"Why?"

"Sometimes they come back during the burial."

"What the hell is wrong with these people!"

The detective solemnly bowed his head. "They have no empathy."

Soon, all the notebooks were closed. The police offered their condolences again and let themselves out.

Brook was left sitting alone in silence. The thunderstorm in her brain spun off downpours with hail.

Chapter TWENTY-THREE

Cigar smoke was thick, but an off-shore breeze quickly carried it off the patio.

Three cocky types with red ties and American-flag lapel pins puffed big Hondurans grown from Cuban seeds. A waitress came by with their drinks. The men tipped well, which entitled them to ask her to bed. The seafood restaurant was called Barnacle Buddy's.

The trio blew smoke rings and faced the ocean.

Serge faced them.

Coleman sipped a rumrunner from a glass the size of a flower vase. "Serge, what are we doing here? Don't get me wrong, I'm drinking."

"Multi-tasking," said Serge. "The Master Plan is hitting its stride and working on three different levels. First, we're in position again because Mahoney gave me the last critical details on the next targets, but it's not going down until tonight. Second, in the meantime I'm continuing to recharge my idea reservoir because it looks like there'll be a lot more jerks than I originally anticipated. And third, I'm scouring for a political infiltration point to track my elusive main quarry and achieve closure."

"Felicia?"

Serge flinched at the name. "The people at the hotel desk across the street said this is where a lot of political operatives hang out, so I'm studying them to learn how to blend in."

"They're just smoking fat cigars and trying to fuck the waitress."

"To the untrained eye it might seem boorish, but since they're always telling us how to live our lives, they must know what they're doing. That's why I need to observe their behavior in the wild. Then, after our mission tonight, we'll use what we've learned to volunteer at local party headquarters."

"I don't know," said Coleman. "I get the feeling they won't like me."

"I'm sure they won't," said Serge. "But that's not your fault. I've been studying politics my whole life, so I know exactly how to get along. Right about the time that they throw you out of the office, they'll probably be carrying me around on their shoulders and chanting my name. Just gather what intelligence you can before you're ejected . . ."

Coleman pointed. "Looks like they're getting up."

The trio of operatives finally put out their cigars and went inside. The table was quickly taken over by three more guys with flag lapel pins. They fired up stogies and ordered drinks.

Serge opened a notebook. "This should be an interesting comparison."

"But they're the same as the other guys," said Coleman.

"No, they're different," said Serge. "The first guys were Republicans; these are Democrats."

"How do you know?"

"They didn't tip as well before trying to screw the waitress." Serge stood. "Get up."

"But I haven't finished my drink."

"Bring it with you. We're switching surveillance back to the first guys before they leave."

The pair returned to air-conditioning. The restaurant was dim with dark mahogany walls covered in oars, life rings and antique harpoons.

"There they are," said Serge.

"They seem to be having fun," said Coleman. "Listen to them laugh."

"That means the country's on the right track."

The pair walked over and leaned against the wall behind the trio, who were whooping it up and egging one another on in a spirited competition.

"Those things are so cool." Coleman chugged his drink and wiped a spot on his shirt. "I used to love those crane games at carnivals where you tried to capture stuffed animals and hand grenades, but I could never win."

"And now a bunch of seafood restaurants across the country have crane games with live lobsters in a tank," said Serge. "And these guys are playing it. I think this is important."

"What does it all mean?"

"When a country begins grabbing live lobsters with carnival cranes, it means capitalism has an insurmountable lead." Serge nodded. "Forget oil pipelines and the space race. The Russians are watching this on YouTube and going, 'Just fucking great.'"

"The winners are leaving," said Coleman.

"And so are we," said Serge. "I need to buy cigars and lobsters."

"What for?"

"They just recharged my reservoir."

AFTER MIDNIGHT

It was another upscale high-rise hotel overlooking Biscayne Bay.

They paid for the view. Down below, convertibles raced along the twisting waterfront like a grand prix. Fleets of taxis whisked away people who had enjoyed themselves over the legal limit. There was a party on one of the yachts anchored off the MacArthur Causeway.

Up in the rooms, some were asleep, some watched TV, others had sex with strangers they'd just met in a cab.

In one particular suite on the seventeenth floor, a fleshy man sat on the foot of a bed, working the remote control.

"Serge, check out the movies you can get in this place: *Naughty Housewives, Naughty Housewives Volume Two, Backdoor Housewives, Kitchen Counter Housewives, Housewives and the Lawn Guy, Housewives and Rico from the Transmission Shop That Overcharges, Housewives and the Birthday Clown* . . . That one looks interesting." Coleman clicked the remote. "And it says the titles won't appear on your bill."

"What more could you ask from a classy joint?" Serge paced in front of the giant picture window.

"That's weird," said Coleman. "The clown's there, but where are all the children? . . . *Ohhhhh,* I get it now . . . Hey, Serge, you have to see this. They're playing pin the tail on the donkey, except with her snatch. Man, this really is an upscale hotel . . ."

"Coleman, just stay sharp."

"And now he's busting open the piñata with his cock." Coleman killed a tiny bottle of Jack from the minibar. "I'm starting to get the idea this guy isn't a legitimate clown."

"Coleman! Turn that off!" said Serge. "We have to stay focused on our mission."

"What's the next step?"

"I told you: We wait for the phone call." Serge glanced at a digital clock that read 1:58. "And it's almost time . . ."

Two minutes later, the phone rang.

And rang.

Coleman polished off another miniature. "Aren't you going to answer it?"

Serge continued staring out at the bay with hands on his hips. "You're closer to the phone. Why don't *you* answer it?"

"Because I don't know everything that's going on like you do."

"In this phase of the plan, it doesn't matter who answers the phone," said Serge. "Just as long as someone does."

"Cool." Coleman got up. "I've always wanted to answer a phone but you never let me." He grabbed the receiver off the nightstand. "Hello, you got the one and only Coleman . . . Yes? . . . What? . . . Oh my God! . . . Holy shit! . . . Fuck me! . . . Appreciate you calling."

Coleman hung up.

There was some background noise as Serge enjoyed the flickering lights of a cruise ship off the coast. Suddenly he noticed something alarming in the window's reflection, coming up fast from behind. He spun and tackled Coleman.

Crash.

Porcelain exploded.

"Coleman, what the hell do you think you're doing?"

"That phone call." Coleman panted and pulled a sliver out of his palm. "The guy at the front desk said there was a gas leak and I had to immediately break out the big window with the toilet-tank lid."

"That's why I told you *not* to break the window with the toilet lid."

"When?"

"When we first got in the room."

"You were talking to me?"

A calamity of sound began coming through the door. Frantic voices in the hallway. Sprinkler heads snapping off. Fire extinguishers.

"Forget it." He grabbed Coleman by his shirt. "We have to hurry!"

They ran to the front of the suite. Serge gently opened the door a foot. The crazed voices from the foam-soaked hallway were now but distant echoes as people galloped down the stairwell instead of taking the elevator. Serge left the door ajar, then hustled Coleman into the bathroom, cut the lights and hid.

The stairway echoes faded until the hallway was silent. Just Serge and Coleman breathing in the bathroom and trying to adjust their eyes to the dark.

"What are we waiting for?" whispered Coleman.

"Shhhh, I think I hear it."

The hallway silence was broken by a herd of padding footsteps. Then doors creaking.

"What's going on?" asked Coleman.

"They're hitting the other rooms," said Serge. Footsteps grew closer. "No more talking."

Coleman's heart pounded in the still bathroom. The door to their own room slowly began to creak.

"Hello? Anyone home? . . . Excellent. And they left their wallets right out on the dresser . . ."

Serge listened until he could tell by the sound that their new guest was sufficiently into the suite, then he tiptoed out of the bathroom to the room's hallway door and pushed it shut behind him without concern for noise.

The intruder spun around in surprise.

"Actually someone *is* home," Serge said with a big smile and bigger gun. "Now grab that chair and have a seat."

Coleman climbed onto one of the beds with a sigh. He was bored. Coleman generally figured out what was coming next because he'd seen that show a hundred times. He clicked the TV on with the remote and searched for something to watch. He had known Serge for almost two decades, and their traveling hotel lifestyle had become so routine it was now utterly predictable: Serge tore off a generous length of duct tape. Coleman sucked a bong rigged from the room's ice bucket. A clown put out birthday candles by beating off.

Fifteen minutes later, Serge gregariously slapped his lucky contestant on the shoulder. "That chair comfy? Didn't tie you up too tight, did I? Good!" He dragged over a table, turned his back to the hostage and reached into a duffel bag. "Today we're going to play show-and-tell. I loved show-and-tell as a kid, but I don't think my teachers were really into it. Like if you're doing the model volcano for science, and instead of following the directions with baking soda for a cute little milk shake of a volcano, you buy potassium nitrate at the drugstore and mix it with iron filings, which creates a spectacular nine-hundred-degree pyroclastic blast, which should get you to the top grade. Except they never mention that if you scorch the blackboard and melt the floor, it's an F."

He began laying out a variety of weapons on his show-and-tell table.

"Serge," said Coleman. "I'm now going to watch *Housewives and Rico*."

"You do that." Serge continued arranging a switchblade, kung fu stars, a billy club, guns, a noose, and a bottle with a skull on the warning label.

"Rico just overcharged a housewife at his transmission shop, but she can't afford the whole amount and asks if there's any way they can work it out." Coleman turned up the volume. "I wonder where they could possibly be going with this story."

Serge stepped in front of his captive and formed an enchanting smile with a tube clenched in the corner of his mouth. *Slurp, slurp, slurp.* "Here's the deal. I don't like you and have uncontrollable urges to do something ghastly with my weapons . . ."

"Now they're down in the lube bay," said Coleman.

". . . But I'm also open-minded and maybe misjudged you."

The pupils of the hostage's eyes darted back and forth between his clearly insane hosts.

Serge snapped his fingers in front of the man's face. "Don't be distracted by Coleman. He's got problems. Maybe I'll try my hat again." He reached in another duffel and donned a helmet with a red beacon on top.

"Hey, Serge, isn't that the same helmet when we were here a couple years ago, and you had that superhero costume with a cape?"

"That's correct."

"But why don't you wear the cape anymore?"

The beacon began revolving on top of Serge's head. "Because I realized I looked ridiculous."

Muted whining from under duct tape.

"Oh, sorry," said Serge. "Back to the contest and the open-minded part. That's why I always give my contestants a chance to win and go free. And here's your big chance! Sometimes I'm unable to fight my urges, so I'm going to do something to you one way or another." He shrugged. "I know, it's a hang-up. But I'm also hung up on the bonus round because I'm a silver-lining kind of cat. I've laid out a variety of weapons to choose from. You got your automatic pistol, revolver, single- and double-edged knives, poison, hatchet, hand grenade. That's just a drawing of a hand grenade, but I can lay my hands on a real one in Miami at any hour. And your ice picks, cattle prods, etcetera . . . It's your choice."

The captive looked up with a question in his eyes.

"That's the contest," said Serge. *Slurp, slurp, slurp.* "What will this maniac use on me? You make the call!"

The man's eyes couldn't have been wider.

"Don't look at me," said Serge. "The clock's running. Tick-tock, tick-tock. Actually you can't see the clock because I'm keeping time on the field. But if you haven't chosen before time's up, then I get to pick."

The man's eyes swung to the table. The item in the middle immediately jumped out. His face snapped back toward his captor.

"By that expression, I know what you're thinking," said Serge. "Is choosing my weapon a trick question? . . . Because you just noticed the cigars. And they're a real prize, three authentic Cubans, the Cohiba, Partagás and El Rey del Mundo. Not cheap."

The man nodded.

"You want the cigars?"

He nodded harder.

"The cigars it is! Excellent decision." Serge lifted another duffel bag from beside the bed. "And I definitely appreciate the selection because Florida relevance always motivates my work. With the Cuban influxes of 1960 and '80, these beauties are now ubiquitous in Miami, which has become the free-Cuba cigar capital of the world." He unzipped the bag. "And now to prepare your selection . . ."

A number of benign and confusing items came out of the bag, plus an emergency travel tool kit. Serge smiled over his shoulder at yet another bewildered expression. "What? You didn't think I was just going to let you smoke these? They're bad for your health."

He produced three small metal canisters. "Ever get a bunch of dust in your laptop's keyboard? Drives me crazy!" said Serge. "But luckily most computer stores sell these cans that contain compressed air to send those little dust bunnies scurrying."

Into the bag again. This time three plastic containers came out.

"And these are empty pump spray bottles that you can get at any drugstore. Mainly women use them to spray shit in their hair, so that's why they're foreign territory to us men. But if you're a dude, simply remember they work just like perfume bottles: When you press the little pump button on top, the liquid inside is transformed to a fine mist in accordance with the Venturi effect, named after Italian physicist Giovanni Venturi, who derived complex equations for fluid transfer in different diameter channels. Who would have thought it would lead to spray-on butter? . . ."

Serge cut and snipped and taped and twisted for half an hour. Then a last tap with the butt of a screwdriver. "There." He stood.

Coleman looked up from the moaning transmission shop. "You're done? We're leaving?"

"Yes and no," said Serge. "We *are* leaving, but I have to come back later and activate this sucker."

"I don't understand."

"We need to let it set and cure awhile until it's ready. Like letting a fine brandy breathe."

Coleman hopped off the bed. "Can we go to a bar?"

They headed down the elevators and Coleman popped a beer. "So did the guy guess right with the cigars? It's what I would have picked."

"So would most people, and that's exactly why you *don't* pick the cigars."

"But, Serge, you always give someone a way out," said Coleman. "And everything else on the table was a deadly weapon."

"The revolver was unloaded."

"Pretty clever."

"I even had it turned toward him so he could see the empty chambers, but he was too busy freaking out."

"Some people are just naturally nervous."

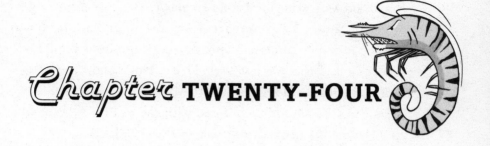

Chapter TWENTY-FOUR

FORT LAUDERDALE

The three A.M. repeat of the eleven o'clock news just closed with word of a strike by another dating bandit, this one a more mature woman going for the Hope Lange look from the sixties smash-hit television series *The Ghost and Mrs. Muir.* The news report noted that the show also starred Charles Nelson Reilly.

The kitchen was dark except for the glow of the TV and a laptop screen on the table next to a mug of coffee and a bottle of bourbon. The computer had surfed to an Internet chat room devoted to fake DEA agent Rick Maddox.

Eyes leaned close to the screen. An index finger tapped the scroll button down through recent posts.

D.L. in D.C.: "I'm killing that son of a bitch if I ever find him!"

Mango Mark in West Palm: "Not if I find him first!"

Pirate Fan in Pittsburgh: "I can't believe he actually had me shaking the whole time I was on the phone. Said importing illegal Oxy carried a ten-year sentence. I've never even seen Oxy."

Wasted in Margaritaville: "Same thing happened to me. Thought I was going to stroke out!"

Pirate Fan: "At least he didn't take you for a grand!"

Wasted in Margaritaville: "No, two grand!"

Djgherbr Smith: "Hey everyone, I was able to unblock his bogus 202 area-code number, and found he's moving south from Tennessee."

Choco-holic: "That was last week. He's in Florida now."

Shitless in Seattle: "I tracked him to Miami."

Mets Fan: "You got him confused with the real DEA agent who lives in Miami. He had his name stolen by this fuck-head."

Shitless in Seattle: "I know that. But the fake guy's going there, too."

Pirate Fan: "Did anyone see where we shut out N.Y. tonight?"

Mets Fan: "Stay on subject. Is this asshole really in Miami?"

Lucy Skrooz-Alot: "I can confirm that. Hired a private investigator. He thinks the fake agent is going to the city where the real agent works as a smoke screen to throw us off, because he must be reading our bulletin board."

The Fluffer: "Lucy, can you e-mail me your picture?"

Lucy: "Drop dead."

The Fluffer: "Check your handle, slut."

Mets Fan: "Everyone cool out. Lucy, what else did your PI say?"

Lucy: "That's all. I ran out of money to keep him on retainer."

Wasted in Margaritaville: "I'm willing to pitch in to get him back on the case. Anyone else?"

Djgherbr Smith: "Count me in."

Choco-holic: "Me, too."

Shitless in Seattle: "Make it four."

Pirate Fan: "Hell, why not?"

Mets Fan: "Let's do it! And while we're at it, what do you say we all take a relaxing warm road trip south."

Djgherbr Smith: "I'm game."

Choco-holic: "I'll go."

Shitless in Seattle: "Wouldn't miss it."

Wasted in Margaritaville: "I'm already here."

The Fluffer: "Is Lucy going?"

Lucy: "Not if Fluffer's going."

Mets Fan: "Lucy, ignore him. What's the name of your private eye? . . ."

Brook Campanella tossed back a shot of whiskey at her kitchen table, and scrolled down through the message board until finally arriving at Lucy's answer. She got out a pen and wrote a name.

DAWN

The police initially thought it was a duplicate call.

Made sense because of the record volume at the 9-1-1 center. The Merry Pranksters had struck again, this time a luxury high-rise resort on Biscayne Boulevard. And they had graduated from practical jokes to grand theft. Cleanup crews were still sweeping porcelain from the street, and insurance adjusters took photos of parked cars with toilet lids through windshields.

The cops had been back and forth to the hotel all night—from the initial naked, extinguisher-foamed chaos in the street to the later discovery of all the burglarized rooms—and now dispatch handed them another urgent request to return to the resort.

Seconds after arriving again on the seventeenth floor, it became clear the call was no duplicate.

An extremely late guest, tied and gagged in a chair, sat with his head slumped lifelessly to the side.

"Holy Mother, what happened to this poor guy?" said the first sergeant on the scene. "And what the hell are those weird things on the floor?"

The room grew in popularity. First the detectives in suits, then evidence techs, the medical examiner and finally the precinct captain, with gold braids on his visor and shoulders, to manage damage control because of all the satellite-TV trucks in the street.

"Nobody says a word of this to anyone. All statements will come from community relations at headquarters. Understood?"

Nods around the room. Then back to work.

The captain strolled over to the medical examiner. "What have we got here?"

"Cigars," said the examiner, working with tweezers and a clear bag.

"I know they're cigars," said the captain. "I meant, do you think we'll get lucky and be able to extract the killer's DNA so we can close this case fast? I hear just a little saliva on a cigar—"

"Doubt there's any DNA here." Tobacco remnants fell into a bag that was sealed and signed.

"Then why are you starting an evidence chain?" asked the captain.

"Because it's a murder weapon."

The captain did a double take. "Come again?"

"This is what the killer used."

"I don't— What?"

"That's a normal reaction." The examiner opened another bag. "It'll take a long explanation because this required a bit of technical expertise. But these definitely did the victim in."

"Wonderful," said the captain, closing his eyes and massaging the bridge of his nose. "Absolutely fantastic. The press is going to be all over this." He opened his eyes. "Please tell me those aren't Cuban cigars."

"Afraid so."

"Dammit," said the captain. "Freak murder. Killed by Cubans in Miami . . . Could this crime be any more headline-ready?"

"Not really."

The captain took off his hat and pulled up a chair. "Okay, get me up to speed so I can start piling the sandbags back at headquarters."

The medical examiner pointed to an evidence bag containing three drinking glasses with a tannic film inside. "This was the first step. He put one cigar in each glass and filled them with water. Then he let it set. After a few hours, the water turned dark brown from the cigar's ingredients—hold that thought in your mind. Now, this guy was sharp: He used Cuban cigars to ensure his plan worked."

"Why's that?" asked the police captain.

"Because of the embargo, you often see ads for cigars grown in other countries from Cuban *seeds,* but they're not the same." The examiner set a bag aside and picked up another. "It's all about Mother Earth. Most places with rich topsoil are inches deep, but because of Cuba's prehistoric volcanic activity, its richest soil often goes down seven or eight feet, which nurtures cigars that are a league apart in strength. Think of it as Bud Light versus grain alcohol."

"I still don't see how it killed him."

"Stay with me." He held up the next bag. "These are common pump bottles from a drugstore. Spray anything with them like perfume . . ." Another bag. ". . . And these are compressed air canisters from a computer store to clean keyboards. See how it has a long tube to get in tight spots between the keys?"

"Yeah, so?"

"So the killer substituted his own flexible tubes, and inserted the other ends into holes he had fashioned into the spray bottle's pump mechanism. Then he disabled the original mechanism."

"Slow down. I'm having trouble following."

"Okay, it simply accomplished this: Instead of having to pump your finger on the button every time you wanted the spray bottle to squirt something, the can of compressed-air keyboard cleaner now powered the spray bottle, creating a continuous mist."

"I'm starting to catch up," said the captain. "Now what?"

"I'd love to meet this guy and pick his brain."

"No, I mean what was the next step with these contraptions?"

"He activated all three by using heavy-duty duct tape to hold down the buttons on the air canisters."

The captain just stared.

"You don't get it?"

"Lost me again."

"These cigars obviously contain a high amount of nicotine, which is also used as a powerful pesticide. In liquid form, that is. So after soaking the cigars, he poured the fluid in the spray bottles and activated the air canisters. Then I'm guessing he left pretty quickly. See those three circular tan stains on the carpet? They're just like the marks you'd get if you didn't lay down newspaper first before using Black Flag to bug-bomb a room."

"He was bug-bombed to death with Cuban cigars?"

"I'd bet my paycheck you won't find a single roach anywhere in here."

"But why go through all that trouble?" said the captain. "Why not just use regular bug bombs?"

The examiner shook his head. "Not strong enough. The victim would get dizzy and nauseous, maybe require a brief hospitalization. The killer knew he needed maximum strength." A smile crossed his face. "This was at least a dozen times more toxic, with a pretty cool Miami angle."

The captain glared.

"Sorry, I know you're not looking forward to the headlines."

A police captain stormed out through the lobby of a luxury high-rise resort on Biscayne Boulevard.

A team of workers from a local glass company stood idle next to a man in a tuxedo playing a baby grand.

Someone called to the officer. "Excuse me?" It was the hotel manager.

The captain turned. "What!"

"When can you release those rooms? We've got a lot of customers coming in and the glass company is waiting."

"I'll release them when I feel like it!" Then he was out the door.

The manager turned and barked even louder. "What are all of you looking at? Get back to work."

The staff at the reception desk quickly stared down at their computer screens.

The day wore on.

Competition for tourist dollars was especially fierce among the downtown resorts. It was the economy, and it was Miami. The hotel manager was particularly testy because the home office had him on a brutal occupancy quota, and now twenty rooms on the seventeenth floor didn't have windows. Which meant added urgency to free up all other suites.

He stuck his head in a back room. "How are those maids coming? I want every last room ready in thirty minutes or you're fired!"

The tension spilled into the hotel lounge, where guests were stacking up and going through free liquor courtesy of the management. The three o'clock check-in time had come and gone. Now it was almost five. The manager knew the booze could hold them at bay for only so long, and then it would turn on him. The bar had a theme of eighteenth-century sailing ships, complete with masts and riggings. The manager took over one of the reservation computers himself to speed the process. He nervously glanced over at the lounge and was met with a row of icy stares coming back at him through the portholes.

Detectives and crime-scene technicians began dribbling off the elevator. *That's a good sign*, thought the manager, typing away.

The people in the lounge grew surlier as they drank. Except one person. Sitting alone at the bar. The eyes of every woman were on him. Because he was:

Johnny Vegas, the Accidental Virgin.

Johnny didn't mind the delay because he never intended to stay at the hotel—although he wouldn't mind suddenly needing a room.

A tap on his shoulder. Johnny turned around.

"Hi there." The luscious blonde swayed with an umbrella drink in her hand. Twenty-five years old, tops, with a plunging neckline and come-hither green eyes. "My name's Fawn. What's yours?"

"J-J-Johnny."

"Well, J-J-Johnny. My girlfriends and I placed a bet . . ." She looked back at a corner table, where four equally fetching gals whispered and giggled over their own drinks in pineapples and coconuts. Fawn took the stool next to Johnny, except she misjudged and Johnny had to grab her arm.

The bartender looked up with raised eyebrows, thinking, *Nice save.*

"My knight in shining armor," said Fawn, sipping her tropical drink through the stirring straw. "What was I talking about?"

"You had a bet with your girlfriends."

"We wanted to know how long your ring finger was compared to your index finger."

"Why?" He curiously held up his hand.

Fawn grabbed his wrist. "Holy shit!"

She pulled up his arm to display his hand toward the table in the corner. Four jaws fell. Then they huddled over the drinks and giggled again and something got spilled.

Johnny looked toward the circular booth and back at Fawn. "What's going on? What's with the fingers?"

"It's supposed to indicate the size of your . . . you know." She covered her mouth and chortled. "I can't believe I'm doing this. Normally I would never . . . I'm a little drunk."

Thirty seconds later, Johnny crashed into the reception desk that was staffed by the manager. "I need a room immediately! I don't care what it costs!"

"Do you have a reservation?"

"No," said Johnny.

Perfect, thought the manager. Those who already had reservations would keep; some were even non-refundable. But a walk-up was one more room in the occupied column.

The manager typed rapidly and grabbed a walkie-talkie. "How's it coming up there on seventeen?"

"The cops have only released four rooms, and the glass guys just got started."

"You have to give me something."

"Well, there's one room where they didn't break the window, and I think I see the cops leaving now."

"Excellent. I want it cleaned and ready in ten."

"It'll take a lot longer. There's quite a mess."

"Ten minutes! Just make the beds and grab the trash."

"What about everything else?"

"Trust me," said the manager, watching Fawn tonguing Johnny's neck. "They're not going to mind."

"You got it."

The manager completed the paperwork with cloned pleasantness. "Here are your room keys. Hope you enjoy your stay."

Johnny snatched the magnetic cards and dashed for the elevator, dragging a now-shoeless Fawn. They reached seventeen. The hallway was still half full of remaining investigators. Johnny swerved and dodged with Fawn in hand. Her high heels were back in the lobby under a baby grand.

"Watch it!" yelled a police photographer.

"Sorry." Johnny reached the door and led her into the suite.

The staff actually hadn't done a bad job. The only noticeable issue was three brown circles on the rug.

Fawn threw open the curtains. "Look at that great view! You can see the Pacific Ocean!" Then she threw off her top.

Johnny gulped as she turned around and he saw the kind of perfectly formed breasts usually found only in artwork. She took a running start—"Yippee!"—and jumped on the bed with a bounce.

She rolled over and squirmed out of her jeans, then twirled them on her foot before flinging them aside. Next, the black panties . . .

Johnny fell back against a wall, the only thing now holding him up.

Fawn rolled over on her stomach, idly kicking one leg up and down and tossing her blond locks in abandon. If Johnny's eyes were lasers, her ass would have burst into flames. She grabbed the remote control that was sitting in front of the alarm clock. "You like porn? I love porn! Let's watch some porn."

"Uh, okay."

She clicked on the set. "What have we got here? . . . *Naughty House-*

wives . . . Seen that, seen that, seen that twice, seen that, seen that . . . haven't seen that." She made the selection on the remote, triggering 1970s porn music with a bass guitar and moog organ.

"Cool," said Fawn. "Pin the tail on the donkey."

The quickest way for Johnny to get out of his clothes was the epileptic floor-flop method. He jumped up in his birthday suit.

"Wow!" said Fawn. "They weren't kidding about the finger-size thing. Be careful not to knock over any lamps."

"What?"

"That was a joke." She ran a hand slowly around her left breast. "I could really use another drink. And why don't you make one for yourself, too. I like a drinking man."

Johnny almost somersaulted to the minibar. He mixed up the simplest cocktails and raced back to the bed.

Fawn took the cold glass and pressed it against her cheek. "That feels sooooo good." Then she placed it farther south . . .

Johnny knocked over a lamp.

"Easy there, fella," said Fawn. "Let's watch what this clown's doing on TV. I want to be *your* piñata."

Johnny crawled into bed. Literally. His legs were shot.

Fawn took a big sip of the drink. "That doesn't taste bad, considering you weren't measuring and just splashing everything all over the table and furniture."

"Thanks."

"Ooooo, I want you so bad. I want you in me right now."

"Me, too. I mean you. I mean—"

"Wait, what's this?" asked Fawn.

"What?"

"Did you get an unwashed glass?"

"No, why?"

"It looks like there's something in the ice cubes—"

Blooooosh!

A geyser of foam gushed out of the glass. Up her nose and in her eyes.

"You son of a bitch! Is that your idea of a joke?"

"What are you talking about?"

"You put Mentos in the ice cubes and made me a rum and Coke. I know that prank."

"I swear I didn't."

Fawn was already halfway back in her clothes, sliding the top over her head. "And you wouldn't believe what I was thinking of doing to you! Now you'll just have to imagine."

"But, baby, the people who stayed here before us must have made the ice cubes . . ."

Fawn slowed on her way out of the room. She turned around. "You know, you're right. We just checked in. You wouldn't have had time."

"Exactly," said Johnny.

"Maybe I was a little hasty." A mischievous grin returned to her face.

Johnny sat up with renewed optimism.

Fawn began a slow, sexy grind dance in place where she stood. She tucked a finger in her mouth and sucked it as her hips swayed to the music in her head.

Johnny gulped: *Yes! My luck has finally changed, especially since the streak ends with one that I was sure had gotten away. The floodgates will now open and I'll probably score twenty times by Sunday.*

Fawn continued grinding as she slowly pulled the moist finger from her mouth and put it . . .

Johnny practically choked on his tongue.

"Oh, you like that?" she said with a husky bedroom voice.

Johnny concentrated to remember how to nod.

Another wicked smile crossed Fawn's face as her other hand slid lower. Her eyes and mouth formed an expression of pure lust.

Then her face changed. She felt something tickling the back of her bare feet. Whiskers.

"Eeeeeeeek!"

Fawn ran out the door.

Johnny looked down. A small mouse disappeared though a perfectly semi-circular hole in the baseboard. HOME SWEET HOME.

The weeping started as barely audible peeps, then rose up through his chest in loud, body-racking sobs as Johnny cried into his own drink.

Blooooosh!

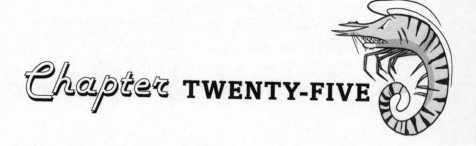

Chapter **TWENTY-FIVE**

STRANGE BEDFELLOWS

Serge sat and smiled.

The man on the other side of the desk smiled back. He wore a white dress shirt and red tie. His jacket was over the back of his chair. Twenty-nine years old, tops. He tapped the eraser end of a pencil to indicate he was a man of action.

"So you want to volunteer?"

"Absolutely," said Serge.

"That's great," said the man. "We can always use more good people."

"More is good."

"But you didn't bring a résumé?"

"Résumés can come back to bite you," said Serge. "Paper trails and all."

"Ahhh, yes." The staffer nodded with understanding. "By that comment, I see you must have had a lot of experience."

"Definitely," said Serge. "I've been an American my whole life, and I'm ready to get to it!"

"No, I mean working on political campaigns."

"I once beat up a flag burner."

"Well, we don't actually condone that, but nobody here is going to hold it against you," said the staffer. "You were provoked . . . So tell me, what makes you want to volunteer for the Miami Republican Party?"

"I'm tired of activist judges."

The staffer nodded. "Couldn't agree more. Un-elected, activist judges are always overturning the will of the people."

"Like the ones who elected George W. Bush," said Serge.

The staffer stopped and stared. "No, activism became wrong *after* that."

"It was a joke," said Serge.

"Oh." He leaned over a printed form. "So back to what you mentioned earlier. You're in favor of our proposal to ban flag burning?"

"Thousands of patriots died to defend that flag."

"Great. I'll mark the 'yes' box in the litmus test."

"No," said Serge. "The flag stands for freedom of speech."

The staffer raised his pencil in puzzlement. "Are you saying you wouldn't attack the flag burner if you had it to do over again?"

"Actually I'd probably beat the piss out of him even harder." Serge sat back and crossed his legs. "The flag also stands for my freedom of expression."

The staffer leaned back in his own chair. "I'm getting a half-and-half take from you."

"Good," said Serge. "I hate to be predictable. Next question?"

The staffer appraised Serge for a moment, then leaned over his form again. "How do you feel about guns?"

"Love 'em! Can't get enough." Serge formed his index finger and thumb into a pistol and fired at the ceiling. "It's like my hand isn't complete without a pistol in it."

"Excellent, that's an easy one." He hunched over the page. "I'll mark the box that you're against handgun control."

"No, I'm for it," said Serge, blowing invisible smoke off the end of his finger. "There's a massive handgun epidemic in America. You'd be blind not to see it."

"That's contradictory. What about *your* guns?"

"I'm part of the problem."

"So your guns should be taken away?"

"Fuck no! From my cold, dead hands! . . ."

. . . Across the street stood another office. Red-white-and-blue banners strung over the parking lot. On the reception desk were help-yourself baskets of American-flag lapel pins and candidate buttons.

Like Serge, Coleman was sitting across the desk from another partisan staffer.

A pencil tapped impatiently.

Coleman fidgeted and stared at the ceiling with his mouth open.

"Am I boring you?"

"Starting to," said Coleman.

"I thought you wanted to volunteer for the Miami Democratic Party."

"That was my friend's idea," said Coleman. "He's across the street volunteering right now."

"He's volunteering with the *Republicans* but sent you here? That makes no sense."

"Says he wants to stop all this bickering in America and unite the red and blue states so it's purple mountain majesty."

The staffer went into we'll-get-back-to-you mode and shuffled papers. "I'm not sure we have something for you today, but appreciate you dropping in."

"Great, I was afraid I'd have to do some work." Coleman glanced around. "Want to burn one?"

"Excuse me?"

"You know . . ." Coleman held a thumb and index finger to his mouth in the international toking sign.

"Well . . ." The staffer checked his watch. "It is almost lunch."

"Excellent. Let's rock."

They ended up sitting on the ground with their backs against the rear of the building just behind the Dumpsters.

Coleman passed the nub of a joint. "The Democratic Party is cool! You guys do weed!"

"Just some of us younger ones."

"So what happens after lunch?" said Coleman. "Let's get abortions and give a bunch of condoms to some kids. They'll think we're cool!"

"That's not exactly what our party—"

"Can I meet some hot chicks on the pill?"

"I don't think you understand—"

"Want to burn another?"

"Sure."

The metal loading door opened into the alley with a loud grinding noise.

Coleman and the staffer whispered back and forth to each other.

"Shhh!"

"Put it out!"

"I'm putting it out!"

A young woman stepped into the alley and sniffed the air. "I recognize that smell . . . Roger? Are you out here?"

"Oh, hey, Susan. We're behind the Dumpsters."

She walked around the bins and smiled coyly. "I know what you guys are doing."

"Hubba, hubba," said Coleman. "Are you on the pill?"

"What?"

"Coleman's a little unpolished, but he's got some killer weed. Want to join us?"

"Sure." She took a seat on the ground . . .

. . . Back across the street, the staffer named Jansen leaned over a litmus test with a freshly sharpened pencil. "Death penalty?"

"Love it in theory; hate it in practice," said Serge. "Screws the poor."

Jansen set his pencil down again for the last time. "Please don't take this the wrong way, but are you sure you have the right place?"

Serge pointed at a sign out in the hall. " 'Republican Party Headquarters'? Hell yes! You don't think I'd go across the street where I sent my friend to volunteer?"

"You sent your friend to the Democrats? Why would you do that?"

"Because he's more their flavor. And I'm more Libertarian, so I'm in line with your platform of a smaller government that needs to get its nose out of our bedrooms, except that's the opposite of what you actually do. And since I'm sure those are typographical errors, I thought I'd help proofread."

Jansen shook his head. "We always need extra hands on our campaigns, but I have no idea how to use you."

"Why?"

"We've had a lot of people volunteer over the years, but I've never met anyone quite like you. Half the time you're enthusiastically in favor of what we stand for, and half the time you're not. And often on the very same issue." Jansen crumpled the hopelessly inconclusive litmus test. "In fact, just about everything you've said contradicts itself. There's nothing consistent."

"That's no accident," said Serge. "Consistency is the natural enemy of compromise."

"Whoa, back up. Did you say 'compromise'?"

Serge smiled and unbuttoned his tropical shirt to reveal the custom-made T-shirt underneath:

I LOVE MY OPPONENTS.

Jansen's eyes bugged in alarm. "What in the hell's the meaning of that?"

"It's obvious," said Serge. "I've got lots of friends who think I'm Satan's elf and will burn in hell. In turn I make wisecracks like 'Gay marriage threatens the sanctity of Newt Gingrich divorcing his next bedridden wife,' and yet we still all get along and have lots of chuckles over Bloomin' Onions at Outback . . . See, the brilliance of my plan is its simplicity. There's only one thing holding America back from realizing her full glory. Ready? You want to write this down? No? Okay, here it is: We need to stop taking ourselves so seriously."

"Uh, why don't you leave your phone number and we'll get back to you when something comes up. My assistant will lead you out."

"Sounds great." Serge stood and shook hands and was escorted through an office floor that was a hive of industrious activity. Staffers feverishly worked the phones and computers and practically crashed into one another running to and from the copy machine.

Serge crossed the street and entered another building. He looked around the empty reception desk. "Hello? Anyone here? . . ." He banged the little bell. "Helloooooo? . . ." Leaning over the desk: "Anyone behind there . . . ?"

Serge bypassed the reception area and opened a door to the main office. He stopped and surveyed dozens of neglected phones and computers. Everyone was clustered in a circle in the center of the room. Serge approached with curiosity. There was laughter and people throwing pencils into the ceiling.

Serge drew closer, but stopped in surprise when he noticed who had their attention in the middle of the group.

"Coleman?"

"Oh, hey, Serge . . . Everybody, this is my friend Serge that I was telling you about . . . So how'd it go across the street with the other party?"

"Not so good." Serge pulled up a chair. "They said they would call me back, which means they'll never call back."

"Really?" said Coleman. "They all love me here!"

Everyone nodded with bright smiles.

"So what is this?" asked Serge. "Some kind of afternoon break?"

"No, we're working," said Roger.

"Working?" Serge looked around an office of abandoned desks and ringing phones.

"We work in theory," said another staffer. "Very high-concept stuff, such as what wind farms will look like in the twenty-third century."

"Serge, this kind of work is cool!" Coleman threw a pencil that stuck in the ceiling.

Someone else nudged Coleman. "Tell us again about the chicken bong."

"Okay, I opened the fridge . . ."

"Excuse me," said Serge, working his way into the circle and taking Coleman by the arm. "We have to be somewhere."

The disappointed staff: *"Auuuuuuuuuu . . ."*

One of them suddenly pointed at Serge's chest. *"What's that?"*

"What?" said Serge, opening his tropical shirt and looking down. "This?"

I LOVE MY OPPONENTS.

"What's that bullshit supposed to mean?"

"Are you some kind of troublemaker!"

"Nazi!"

Coleman raised his hands to the group. "Everyone mellow out. Serge is cool."

"If you say so, Coleman."

"Take care, Coleman."

"Hurry back . . ."

ACROSS TOWN

A load of untaxed cigarettes sailed up the Miami River.

A man in a porkpie hat watched from a second-story window of an all-but-abandoned office building. He tossed the hat on an antique rack in the corner and propped his feet up on the desk next to three fingers of rye in a dirty glass.

A rotary phone rang.

The man glared at it. Possibilities rattled his noggin: a busty divorcée with a framed brother in Sing Sing, another floater in the bay, or—dare he hope—a break in the 1947 Black Dahlia case?

He grabbed the receiver on the ninth ring. "Mahoney here. Gargle in the soup can."

"What?"

"Talk in the phone."

"Oh, well, Mr. Mahoney, my name is Brook Campanella, and I want to hire you to find who tried to scam my father—"

"Where'd you scarf my digits?"

"What?"

"How'd you get my number?"

"You came highly recommended from an Internet chat room," said

Brook. "Some people hired you to track down a fake DEA agent who swindled them."

"Itchin' to parlay your chips straight to the hard eight?"

"Uh . . . huh?"

Mahoney sighed. "You want to team up?"

"No, I don't want to go in with the other people," said Brook. "In fact, I'd rather they not know I'm involved at all."

"Dangle the angle."

"Whatever information you're reporting to them, I also want you to give to me," said Brook. "I'll pay double."

"Deuces wild."

HIALEAH

Tiny white rocks rumbled under the tires of a black Firebird as it drove down an industrial road next to the expressway.

"Shouldn't take it so bad," said Coleman. "At least the Democrats dug me."

"I don't want to talk about it."

Coleman looked over into the backseat. "I get what you did with the cigars, but how can that other thing you just bought possibly fit in?"

"Watch and learn." Serge cut the steering wheel.

A cell phone rang. Serge sagged. "I wish Mahoney would get off my back." He checked the display and looked at Coleman.

"What is it?"

"Not Mahoney. And I don't recognize the number." He put it to his ear. "Hello? . . . Oh, Sasha, how's it going? . . ." He rolled his eyes at Coleman. ". . . Of course I was going to call you back . . ." Coleman began giggling uncontrollably, and Serge punched him in the arm. ". . . No, that was the radio . . . Listen, I'm kind of busy right now and— . . . What? Where'd you hear this? . . . Yeah, I got a pen. Go ahead and give me the address . . . Thanks . . . I am not trying to avoid you. I haven't been answering my phone because I'm in and out of a lot of places where there's no signal . . . Of course I'll call . . . I got to run . . . I really got to run . . ."

Serge looked over at Coleman in exasperation and stuck a finger in his mouth like a gun, then pretended to blow his brains out. ". . . No, it wasn't just physical . . . Of course I'll call . . . I don't know when . . . I promise . . . I said I promised . . . Something's on fire!" He hung up.

Coleman looked around. "There's nothing burning."

"I know. It's an efficient way to end a call with a woman. Another is to yell, 'Snakes!'"

"What was her problem?" asked Coleman.

"It's a delicate battle that's going on right now all over the world," said Serge. "Women have sex control; guys have phone control."

"I never knew this."

"But there's an upside." Serge hit the gas to make a yellow light. "She just gave me a lead on the next scam. And perfect timing, too. A chance to test out my newest inspiration."

The Trans Am turned through the gate of a tall chain-link fence topped with barbed wire. It proceeded across a parking lot of disabled vehicles and stopped outside a metal warehouse with a faded wooden sign: ALFONSO'S SCRAP METAL, RECYCLING & LOUNGE.

Alfonso emerged from an aluminum door, wearing a hard hat and an incredulous expression. "You didn't even call this time!"

"Hey, Alfonso," said Serge, jumping down from the driver's seat. "What's shaking?"

"What's shaking is that I'm out of the favor business."

Serge placed a hand over his heart. "That hurts. You think the only time I want to see you is when I need a favor?"

"Yes!"

"Fine, then." Serge slid his driver's seat forward and reached in back. "I'll just set it up myself."

"Set what up?"

"No, I don't want to bother you." Serge grabbed an industrial handcart leaning against the outside of the warehouse. "Never mind me. Because friendship is my number one priority, and I'm not about to do anything that would seem presumptuous. I'll just find an empty spot in the warehouse and mind my own business."

"But it's my warehouse!"

"And a great warehouse it is. You wouldn't guess from the outside, but it's got tons of room." Serge grunted as he slid a recent purchase out the back of the Firebird and onto the handcart. "I'll just take up a little corner and be quiet as a church mouse."

Alfonso stared at the handcart as Serge wheeled it toward him. "What the hell are you going to do with that big aquarium?"

"Put water in it." Serge set the cart down horizontally and grabbed a hose off the side of the building. "I got it super cheap with all the trappings. See how it came totally ready?" He placed his thumb partially over the hose nozzle to create a high-pressure stream.

"What are you doing?" said Alfonso. "You're blasting all the gravel out of the bottom."

"It came totally ready, just not ready for my purpose." Serge tilted the tank up as he sprayed, draining the gravel-mud onto the ground at Alfonso's feet. Then he reached down into the muck and looked up. "You want the plastic treasure chest with the skeleton that pops out?"

"Not really," said Alfonso.

Serge raised one eyebrow. "You sure? It's brand-new."

"I'll take it," said Coleman.

"What are you going to use it for?"

"I can bore a hole on top for the stem and use the keyhole as a carburetor—"

"I get the picture." Serge tossed the tiny plastic chest to his buddy and began wheeling the glass tank into the building. He found a sturdy machinist table in back. "Coleman, help me."

It was touch and go at Coleman's end of the aquarium, but they eventually got it safely atop the metal platform. Serge turned around. "Ah, you startled me. What are you doing back here with us. I told you I wouldn't be a bother."

"Dammit, Serge." Alfonso took off his hard hat. "I have a million things to do, but now I've got to know."

"You positive?" Serge wiped down the inside of the glass with a rag. "There are accessory-before-and-after-the-fact laws."

"Just tell me what you're going to do."

"Suit yourself," said Serge. "It's your warehouse."

He wheeled the handcart back to the Firebird's trunk, loaded a weighty cardboard box and returned. Alfonso and Coleman watched intently as Serge removed a dozen clear cylindrical tubes from the box and set them on the table. They were filled with something gray and granular. Serge sequentially dumped the contents of each tube into the aquarium, carefully creating an even layer across the bottom.

"What's that?" asked Alfonso.

"You should know." Serge opened another tube. "It might even have come from your scrapyard before it went through a processing center."

"Iron pellets?"

"Good guess." Serge spread another layer on the bottom.

"But where do you get something like that?"

Serge used his palms to smooth out lumpy spots. "They come in a variety of sizes. Large, mixed ore balls for smelting fodder. And super-pure tiny pellets from mail-order technology wholesalers to use in semi-conductors and electron beams. These are in the middle, a uniform half millimeter sold by school-supply houses to make science projects. But not *my* science project! That's why I needed to get rid of that other gravel. Stay here . . ."

Serge took off running and came back with another box from the car. The side of the cardboard: PERISHABLE. He opened the flaps of the carton, which was lined with thick plastic designed not to leak. Serge waved urgently. "Check it out!"

Alfonso peeked over the edge before looking up. "A live lobster?"

"His name's Shelly. Can you take care of him for me?" Serge took off running. "Coleman, let's rock!"

"Where are you going?" Alfonso yelled after him.

"To fill five-gallon jugs of salt water at the ocean."

Alfonso jogged to the warehouse door. "But what am I supposed to do with a lobster?"

Serge threw the Firebird in gear. "I think he likes music."

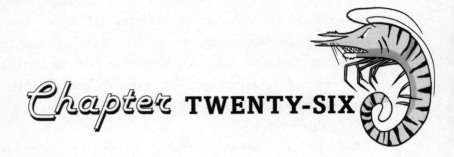

Chapter TWENTY-SIX

NIGHTFALL

A sliding metal door creaked along its track.

A Firebird skidded to a stop in a cloud of dust. "Don't lock up yet!"

Alfonso turned with a padlock in his hand. "Serge! Dinner's waiting at home!"

"I'll just be a minute."

"That means six hours."

"Three, tops." Serge popped the trunk. "Coleman, grab a handcart."

Alfonso exhaled with frustration and slid the door back open.

The pair began wheeling bluish five-gallon plastic jugs like the guys who service water coolers in office buildings.

Alfonso followed them as Serge filled the tank. He plugged in the aerator, and the bubbles started. Then Serge reached in the "perishable" box and petted the carapace. "That's a good Shelly. I've made you a nice new home." He let the lobster slip into the water and settle on the bottom. Serge pressed his face against the front glass and held up his right hand like it had a prize. "Since you like music, I also bought one of those underwater radios that can go in swimming pools or when you want to sing in the shower." He clipped it inside the tank and turned it on.

The aquarium pulsed to muted bass tones.

"... *Surfin' U.S.A.!* ..."

"You're playing him beach music?" said Alfonso.

"It's very important that a lobster's transition to a new home be as stress-free as possible," said Serge. "Or you know what could happen?"

Alfonso shook his head.

"He could get shell shock."

Alfonso just stared.

Serge smiled and slapped him on the shoulder. "That's a joke from the movie *Rocky*. It's a groaner, but a good one. I love Rocky! ..." Serge threw phantom punches in the air. Then he began absorbing a wicked series of combinations and body blows, staggering backward with each one—"*Adrian! Adrian!* ..."—before crashing into the wall and taking down a large tool rack.

They ran over and helped Serge up into a sitting position. "Are you okay?"

"*No rematch!*"

"Serge! ..."

He jumped up and ran back to the glass again. "I think he digs the Beach Boys album *Pet Sounds*."

"All right," said Alfonso. "I can't stand it any longer. I know I'm going to regret this, but what's with the aquarium full of iron pellets?"

"It's the most amazing thing." Serge affectionately tapped the glass. "You know when lobsters migrate in those cute little lines on the ocean floor in the *National Geographic* shows? They actually can sense the earth's magnetic field to chart their course. And you know how we found out? They did an experiment right here in Florida, at the Three Sisters Reef down in the Keys, where they set up underwater magnetic coils, which altered their migratory routes."

"So you're doing some sort of experiment with lobster navigation?"

"No." Serge tapped the glass again and turned around. "This is another facet of lobster magnetism. What I'm really interested in is his equilibrium. Familiar with how we humans use our inner ears? Similarly, lobsters have these little sacks of highly sensitive skin. And here's the nutty part. They eat all kinds of crap on the bottom, but during digestion they filter a single extremely tiny rock into the sack. Gravity naturally makes the rock rest on the bottom of the sack, and the soft tissue there tells the lobster which way is up and down."

"How does the aquarium come in?" said Alfonso.

"This is where science seriously kicks ass!" Serge reached in the tank and pulled out a single pellet. "Lobsters frequently excrete their 'equilibrium' rocks and replace them. So if you dump all the regular gravel out of an aquarium and refill it with iron pellets, it will eventually absorb one into the sack. Then, if you hold a powerful enough magnet over the lobster, the pellet will be pulled up against the tissue along the top of the sack, fooling the lobster into thinking he's upside down, and he'll flip over." Serge tossed the pellet back in the tank with a small splash. "It's hours of fun for the whole family."

"But why on earth would you want to flip a lobster over in the first place?" asked Alfonso.

"Why else?" said Serge. "For a trigger mechanism."

FORT LAUDERDALE

Light rain fell on U.S. 1 as evening traffic passed the strip malls just north of Dania.

Bells jingled at the front of a narrow storefront with a sign that said it was proud to have opened in 1981. The owner looked up from the counter at a petite woman coming through the glass door, which had chipped lettering in reverse: BENNY'S PAWN, GUNS & PACKAGE.

"How may I help you today?"

She pointed down inside the display case. "I want a gun."

"That was direct." The owner chuckled. "Ever shot before?"

"No."

"It's the perfect time to start." He leaned forward and reached into the case, grabbing something off a stand. He held it sideways in an open palm. "This is a twenty-five automatic. Lots of women like them because they fit easily in their purses and have a mother-of-pearl handle. In case you've heard the rumors, this is top of the line, virtually jam-free."

"Too small."

"I like your moxie." The owner grabbed another pistol. "A nickel-plated Smith & Wesson three-fifty-seven Magnum. And it's a wheel gun, so if purse size isn't an issue, you don't have to worry about it jamming."

"You said the other didn't jam."

"Except when it jams."

The woman examined the Magnum. "Still too small."

The shopkeeper raised his eyebrows without comment, and reached under the glass again.

"This is an absolute cannon." He handed her the heavy weapon. "Colt Python forty-four, the *Dirty Harry* gun."

She reached in her handbag for a credit card.

"You didn't even ask the price."

"I don't care."

"And there's a waiting period."

"How long?"

"Three days."

"Too long."

"What? 'Too long, too small.'" The owner whistled. "Jesus, someone must have really pissed you off. But hey, that's what we're here for."

"Does everything have a waiting period?"

"No," said the owner. "Just the handguns. Anything up there on the wall you can just walk out the door with."

She raised her arm. "Even that? But it looks like a pistol."

The owner glanced briefly over his shoulder, then appraised her stature a moment. "How much do you weigh?"

"That's pretty rude."

"No, I mean you're pointing at a twelve-gauge shotgun."

"Looks like a big pistol."

"Because it has a pistol grip and minimum-legal-length eighteen-and-a-half-inch barrel, so it doesn't get hung up going through door-ways. That baby's designed for urban warfare."

"Perfect. Wrap it up."

He looked her up and down. "What are you, barely a buck-ten soaking wet?"

"What's my weight got to do with anything?"

"It doesn't have a shoulder stock and kicks like a mule. Plus you've never shot before."

She simply handed him her credit card.

"I'll also need to see your driver's license."

She fished it out of her purse. The owner held it under a jeweler's lamp and jotted down the particulars. Brook Campanella, five six. The state of Florida said she was twenty-five, but the photo looked seventeen, tops. Freckles, straight brown hair, devoid of menace. Could be a kid who gets you popcorn at the movies. He finished with the license and swiped her Visa.

"Okay, everything's in order," said the owner. "Want some ammo with that?"

"I guess."

He slapped a box on the counter.

"I'll take ten," said Brook.

"What about a tactical carrying case?"

"Sure."

He gestured toward the rows of bottles in the package section. "Want anything to drink with that?"

"Not right now."

"What about a hacksaw?"

"Why would I need a hacksaw?"

Chapter TWENTY-SEVEN

THE NEXT MORNING

Two men with dirty fingernails shoveled quickly, burying the body in an eight-foot hole.

A number of people saw them but didn't pay attention because the body was in a casket, and the men wore the green work uniforms of the Fort Lauderdale cemetery.

In the background, a second casket rested on a series of straps above another hole. There was a tent and rows of folding white chairs. At one end of the casket, a preacher opened a Bible as his vestments began to blow. Black clouds rolled in from the Everglades. The tent had been meant for the sun, but now held back rain. Only three of the chairs were occupied, a young widow and her children. It was hard to hear the preacher because of the heavy traffic on the adjacent freeway. The widow had her own Bible in her lap, and restless fingers kept busy rubbing the crinkled, tearstained newspaper obituary in her hands. It mentioned her husband's five tours in Iraq and Afghanistan.

The rain chased the gravediggers away from the other plot and back to the maintenance shed. Someone else who had been laying a bouquet on a grave took shelter under a royal poinciana. He had placed the bouquet at the tombstone of someone he never knew or cared about. Now he watched the preacher in the distance and held a cell phone to his head. "Yeah, it's started. You're on."

Several miles away, a cable-TV van was parked at the curb of a residential street. It became un-parked. The truck rolled slowly and turned up the driveway at the appointed address.

The house was a turquoise bungalow with potted yellow-and-red crotons that are popular with local landscapers and as economical hospital gift plants for less serious ailments, like whooping cough. An American flag hung from the porch, and a swing set stood out back.

The cable workers exited the van and walked around to the side door for privacy. The first one glanced back a last time, then stuck a bump key in the lock. Another person twisted the knob as the rubber mallet struck. The door popped open with facility. They entered the laundry room, opened their burglary sacks and marched single file toward the kitchen. The living room was around the corner past the refrigerator, which created a blind spot. When the first in the crew reached it, the baseball bat caught him in the throat.

He promptly dropped to the tiles in writhing voicelessness. The others jolted to a surprised halt as Serge stepped out from behind the fridge with a Louisville Slugger and a .45 ACP. That was the official signal to run.

The cable van screeched out of the driveway just before Coleman screeched up in a Firebird.

Six hours later. Darkness and traffic and croaking frogs. All businesses along the industrial access road were shuttered for the night. A black Firebird sat in front of a warehouse. Serge had already slipped a damage deposit under the door of Alfonso's office for having to use the bolt cutters on the entrance gate's padlock—and a few more bucks for what would come later.

Coleman torched a fattie and smiled down at the man in the chair.

The man's eyes bulged with terror. But not from threats he understood. Because every element of his predicament was so weird and fresh that his brain hadn't caught up yet.

First there were his captors, beginning with this Belushi character in front of him. During the ride over, Coleman had continually spilled vodka on himself and puffed nonstop on a bong made from a decorative aquarium treasure chest. Then there was the driver. Where to start? . . .

How about *at* the start? . . . The Firebird pulled away from the nearly burglarized widow's house and picked up the Palmetto Expressway. Serge turned around, slurping from a tube clenched in the corner of his mouth. "How you doing back there? I'm guessing you didn't read the full obituary because it mentioned he was a war vet with a wife and kids, and even a burglar couldn't be that low. So I'll give you the benefit of the doubt. Actually there isn't any benefit coming up; sorry, didn't think that offer through. You comfy? Hope you are because we got a long wait for sunset. Personally, waiting drives me crazy, so I apologize in advance because I need the cover of darkness. You know the waiting that really drives me nuts? When you're in a convenience store, and the checkout chick has no supervisor and she's on her cell phone the whole time, ringing up my coffee and water distractedly with one hand. And I could cut her slack if it was an important call, like the lions grabbed her mother at the zoo. But surprisingly it's never *that* call, just pointless chitchat: 'I told the bitch to stay away from my Hector, and she always brings up that one little time I blew her boyfriend . . . Right, like that excuses everything.' And even worse, convenience stores have started putting in glass countertops at the checkout, which display the rolls of scratch-off lottery tickets. So now the slowest shitheads in the community are *shopping* at the cash register, the most critical bottleneck you can't shop at. The checkout is the Khyber Pass of convenience stores, and if history has taught us anything, it's to keep the Khyber Pass moving and clear of shithead clogs or it becomes the opposite of convenience." *Slurp, slurp, slurp.* "But what really burns my ass is when you're checking into a motel, and the only guy at the front desk is tied up on the phone with some Walmart-cafeteria reject who's going on and on . . ."

"Serge," said Coleman. "You might want to watch the road."

"*You* watch it. I'm talking here." He released the steering wheel and Coleman grabbed it. Serge folded his arms atop the back of the driver's seat. "I can at least cope if the guy on the phone to the motel is making a reservation. But no, I'm standing there waiting in person, and he's asking a million questions about the place to decide if it's the right fit for his lifestyle. How late is the pool open, do they have HBO, is it a hot complimentary breakfast or just those big clear dispensing vats of Froot Loops. You know what I did the last time it happened? I lunged over the counter and grabbed the phone and said, 'Listen, fuck-stick, if you check into this motel, I'll enter your room in the middle of the night and open your chest cavity with a concussion drill.' Then I handed the phone back to the desk guy: 'Funny, he hung up. I'd like a room, please . . .'"

And now, five hours later, the captive sat strapped in a chair, staring up at a comfortably numb Coleman.

A banging on the door of the warehouse. *"I'm baaaaaack!"*

Coleman smiled down at the hostage. "That's my buddy."

Serge slid the door open and led two more people inside.

"Who've you got with you?" asked Coleman.

Serge held each one around the waist as they staggered forward. "You remember Roger from the Democratic Party, and this other guy is Jansen from the Republicans."

"They look drunk."

"Naw, I just gave them a shot of Sodium Pentothol in the parking lot when they were getting off work. Grab me a couple chairs . . ."

Coleman helped Serge get them seated. "But Roger was nice to me. Why do you have to kill him?"

"What are you talking about?" said Serge. "I'm not killing any-body—I mean not these two. I just need to explore the political terrain further, because after I was shunned and they embraced you, I realize I don't know anything anymore. And since we still have a few hours until traffic clears off the industrial road, I thought I'd put it to use." He looked around at the ceiling. "This warehouse reminds me of *Reservoir Dogs*. That whole movie was a bunch of conversations in a warehouse, with some torture and death in between, just like here."

Serge tossed a wad of cloth, and Coleman caught it against his chest. "What's this?"

"Just go in the bathroom and put that on." Serge knelt in front of his two newest guests and tapped them lightly on the cheeks. "Anybody in there?"

Jansen's head wobbled on his neck. "Wha—? Where am I?"

"A warehouse."

Roger started coming around. "I feel funny."

"You'll be fine," said Serge. "That's just the truth serum I gave you."

"Why'd you do that?" Roger asked in a dull monotone.

"Because I don't know anything anymore. Our political process appears to be a toxic dance of mutually assured destruction that takes all the citizens down with you, and that can't be right. So I've prepared a little experiment."

"What kind of experiment?" slurred Roger.

"You're positively going to love this!" Serge excitedly flapped his arms. "I've got the best candidate you could ever hope to recruit. Absolutely everyone will vote for him. He's completely unselfish with a blemish-free record, and he loves all the people. But he's not sure which party to join."

Roger lolled his head. "And you want to know which one of us will pick him?"

"No," said Serge. "He's a no-brainer as the top candidate for either ticket. You'll both fight like wild dingoes over him. That's a given. But only one party can win. So here's the experiment: After the election, can the other party unite behind him for the sake of the nation?"

"Depends on the candidate," said Jansen.

"Like I told you, he's an automatic," said Serge. "It's the one and only . . . Jesus Christ!"

"Jesus Christ?" said Bradley. "But he's dead."

"Well, he came back," said Serge. "That possibility was always left open. I'm sure you heard the stories."

Roger twisted his head around. "Where is he?"

Serge called toward the bathroom: "Jesus, can you come here a second?"

No response.

"Jesus, get out here!"

Roger and Jansen leaned in the direction of Serge's gaze.

"Dang it!" Serge marched to the bathroom and banged on the door. "Jesus, what are you doing in there?"

From the other side of the door: *"Jesus? Oh, right."* Coleman came out and smiled. "My children!"

"That's not Jesus," said Jansen.

"Yes, it is," said Serge.

"He's out of shape," said Roger.

"Give him some slack," said Serge. "It's been two thousand years. And if you don't believe it's really him, check out the shirt."

The pair looked in the middle of Coleman's chest, where something had been written in Magic Marker: WHAT WOULD I DO?

"I'm convinced," said Roger.

"Me, too," said Jansen.

"Then back to my main question," said Serge. "He's sure to win. I mean, even if you don't believe he's the son of God, you have to admit he's a people person. And if he wins for the other side, could you support his administration? Jansen, you go first."

"Wait a second." Roger interrupted from the other chair. "I have some issues to go over first before I can accept him as our candidate."

"Are you joking?" said Serge. "What's not to like about this guy?"

"The conservatives have been eroding separation of church and state for years."

"So?"

"Well, he's a little on the religious side."

"He's Christ!"

"Exactly. And politicians often visit schools. Since he's Jesus, anything he says will be the new gospel."

"I'm not following."

"Prayer in the classroom."

"You've got to be shitting me," said Serge.

"I agree it's a quibble," said Roger. "But we have to keep our base happy—"

"Shut up." Serge grabbed his head and turned to Jansen. "Don't tell me you also have a problem with him as a candidate."

"Actually, yes."

Serge's jaw fell open. "What?"

"Don't take this the wrong way, because we definitely respect all faiths. It's just that our polling data right now shows that the only viable candidate needs to be a Christian."

"Yeah?" said Serge. "Jesus, Christian, who better?"

Jansen shook his head. "He's Jewish."

"He's Christ!" said Serge.

"It's just that our pollsters—"

"Shut up." Serge massaged his temples and turned back to Roger. "Hypothetically, let's take the prayer thing off the table. Surely, he's acceptable in every other way."

"Not really."

Serge needed a chair. "I don't even want to ask."

"Remember that talk about telling his followers to render unto Caesar?" said Roger. "That they'd be rewarded in heaven?"

"Yeah?"

"I'm not sure he'd support shifting the tax burden to the rich."

"Incredible." Serge turned. "Jansen, can you help me here?"

"I'm afraid he scores very low on our Christian values test."

"He's Christ!"

"Associating with known prostitutes, creating a disturbance in a house of worship with that money-changers scene, the loaves and the fishes, which was a socialist food-redistribution program . . ."

"Stop talking."

". . . Mary was an unwed teen mom," said Roger. "We're concerned about his views on abortion . . ."

". . . And we're worried about His stance on capital punishment," said Jansen. "Because of that incident . . ."

"Both of you, shut the fuck up! I can't believe what I'm hearing!" Serge stood behind the drugged political operatives next to the fat Jesus, who was petting a lobster in a tank filled with iron pellets, and glanced over at the duct-taped hostage. "What's wrong with this picture?"

Chapter TWENTY-EIGHT

ALFONSO'S

Serge tucked Roger and Jansen snugly into their beds and made it back to the warehouse just as truck traffic cleared off the charcoal-black industrial road.

He moved the hostage outside, in back by the scrapyard, and made him change his clothes at gunpoint.

Now the captive was all shiny.

The tape remained over his mouth. In front of him, a giant aquarium with a lobster. The captive watched as Serge placed the lobster in a temporary bucket while he removed the iron pellets and replaced them with regular sea gravel "to establish the control element for my test results." Then Serge attached something to the side of the lobster with several wrappings of water-resistant tape.

The prisoner observed Serge walk backward with a giant spool, laying down wire like a demolition team, from the aquarium all the way out of sight around the corner and through the front door of the warehouse.

Serge ran back in joy. "Almost done. Barely any waiting left. Just one more thing . . ." He reached in a bag and hung a jumbo magnet over the far end of the aquarium. The hostage looked straight up and saw a much bigger magnet.

"And that's it!" said Serge. "Isn't this great? . . . Ah, you don't know what's going on?"

Coleman exhaled a cloud toward the moon. "I don't know either."

"This is one of my all-time favorites!" said Serge. "But to truly appreciate it, you must first understand a lobster's orientation mechanism . . ." And he laid out the whole scene, the internal sac and the little rock, blah, blah, blah. "You follow me? You have a grasp? Good! Then I taped this little gizmo to the side of Shelly. That's his name; you might need it later. The thing I taped is a ball-bearing tilt switch. The little ball stays at one end of the plastic tube unless it's tilted, and then it rolls to the other, where it simultaneously touches two metal contacts and completes the circuit. Very easy to come by, used in pinball machines and thermostats and car-trunk lids to turn the light off, and bombs—don't worry, this isn't a bomb—and some vending machines that now have alarms because people keep rocking them to get the bag of Cheez-Its hung up on the corkscrew." Serge walked over and patted the man on the shoulder. "Next, you're probably wondering about that spiffy new getup you're wearing. It's a shark suit, used to protect divers from nasty bites, and composed of a thin titanium mesh called chain mail. The only opening is the top part of the face where the scuba mask goes."

"Serge," said Coleman. "Can we get some Cheez-Its?"

"Not now." Serge crouched down in front of the chair like a baseball catcher. "Here's the deal: I always give my students a way out. So all you have to do is keep the lobster entertained and at your end of the aquarium until dawn, when Alfonso and the crew arrive and will set you free. Shelly likes music, so you might try humming. Or wiggling around. Any kind of motion, because it's probably pretty boring in the tank."

Coleman tossed a roach on the ground and snuffed it out with his shoe. "What if Shelly decides to explore?"

"That's what they call a game changer," said Serge. "If he reaches the spot under the magnet, it'll flip him over, tripping the ball-bearing switch . . ." His eyes followed the wire into the warehouse. "From there it's all computerized. Alfonso has an automated program to run the scrapyard."

"What's it do?" asked Coleman.

"Creates more irony." Serge pointed straight up. "The big magnet that lifts the junked vehicles will come down and grab him by the shark suit, and then it's a wacky ride over there, when the power to the electromagnet is cut off, dropping him into the car-crusher. Which, of course, turns on."

"What's the irony?"

Serge pointed up again. "See the big crane claws surrounding the magnet? It's like the reverse of the lobster game at the restaurant. This time the lobster captures the human."

"Cool."

Serge smiled a last time at his contestant. "I'll leave you and Shelly alone now so you can get to know each other."

The pair began walking away.

Coleman grabbed another joint from over his ear. "What kind of music do you think Shelly likes?"

"I'm guessing the B-52's."

The hostage watching in terror as Serge and Coleman climbed into the car on the other side of the yard, singing two-part harmony in the distance.

"It wasn't a rock . . ."

". . . It was a rock lobster!"

The Firebird drove out the gate. It was quiet again except for bull-frogs in a stagnant storm ditch.

The hostage looked at the lobster. The lobster looked back.

The lobster wasn't moving. Maybe it was asleep. So far, so good.

An hour went by. Since Shelly seemed quite inert at the moment, the hostage didn't dare move or make a peep, lest he disturb the status quo.

Another hour. Still an indolent lobster. This might be easier than he thought.

Suddenly his eyes flew open. The lobster's antennae began twitching more than usual. It backed up from the glass a couple of inches and stopped.

The man hummed as loud as he could.

The lobster began turning. The captive thrashed side to side to get its attention, but apparently the lobster had seen more interesting days. It completed the turn and began scooting through gravel toward the other end of the tank.

Humming went to max volume with no song in mind.

The lobster was almost under the magnet.

Now just hysterical screaming under the duct tape.

For some unexplained reason, the lobster simply stopped.

The man held his breath. Could he believe his eyes? The lobster began slowly turning around to face him again.

The burglar sagged with a huge sigh.

Then the lobster took a step backward . . .

. . . And flipped over.

"Mmmmmmmmmmmmmmmmmmmmmm!"

There was a loud *ker-chunk* sound followed by mechanical whizzing.

The captive looked up. This was no slow-motion, dramatic magnet. It came down with haste and was so powerful that the victim actually leaped off the ground with the magnet still a good foot away.

His face was mashed against it as the claw tongs closed underneath, carrying him into the night sky, legs wiggling like a detached lizard's tail.

Chapter TWENTY-NINE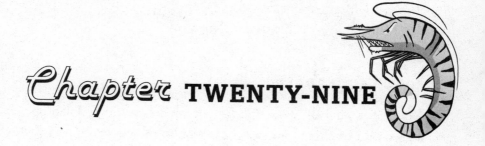

THE NEXT MORNING

Police cars with lights ablaze continued streaming through the entrance of Alfonso's Scrap Metal. More were already on the scene, taking notes and photos.

Alfonso had called them immediately to avoid an accessory charge. He played dumb. Not hard given the evidence.

The head detective sat on the other side of Alfonso's desk in the warehouse office. He crossed his legs and noticed something in the sole of his shoe. He picked out an iron pellet, looked at it a moment and flicked it over his shoulder. "You're telling me you have absolutely no idea who did this?"

"I don't even know *what* they did," said Alfonso.

"Our people just pulled a guy in a shark suit out of the crusher," said the investigator. "Was your lounge open last night?"

Alfonso shook his head. "And I made sure everything was turned off before I left."

"Our captain doesn't like headlines. If there's anything at all you can think of—"

A uniformed officer appeared panting in the doorway. "Sir, I just found something that might be important."

"What is it?"

"The lobster's upside down."

The detective quickly stood. "Not again."

FORT LAUDERDALE

Noon. The kitchen of an eighth-floor condo sat quiet. A laptop was logged on to a chat room, but the person in the kitchen wasn't paying attention to the online exchange.

Brook Campanella stood at the counter, pressing her left hand down firmly. Her right hand grabbed a molded rubber grip. The silence was broken by a rhythmic grinding noise.

Choco-holic: "What's the word from that private eye?"

Shitless in Seattle: "He's narrowed on the address."

Pirate Fan: "I've got my plane ticket."

Mets Fan: "Leaving in an hour."

Wasted in Margaritaville: "I'm already here."

The Fluffer: "Is Lucy going?"

Choco-holic: "See you all in Miami!"

The grinding noise stopped, followed by the sound of metal clanging on a terrazzo floor where nine inches of shotgun barrel had just landed.

Brook Campanella set down the hacksaw and picked up a file, smoothing out the new bore of the sawed-off twelve-gauge.

MEANWHILE . . .

A black Firebird pulled into the parking lot of a busy shopping center.

Coleman looked up from his hurricane glass. "We're stopping at Food King?"

"Supply run," said Serge, jumping down from the car. "You know what else pisses me off? People who say 'an' historic event. You don't say 'an' history book. The irony is it's usually only people who think they're smarter than you and also say 'incentive-*ize*.'"

"The pricks."

"And companies that say, 'Your satisfaction is our number one goal.'"

"If that's so, then give us the shit for free," said Coleman.

"Exactly," said Serge. "But instead they tell you they'll come to fix your cable between noon and five, and I say, okay, I'll pay my next bill between July and November, but they don't laugh."

They went through the automatic doors of the supermarket.

"Ooo! Ooo!" said Coleman. "I want to drive the cart! Can I drive the cart?"

"Go crazy."

Coleman got a running start down an aisle, jumped up on the bar between the back wheels, flipped backward and knocked himself out.

Serge sat his pal up and shook him back into the world.

Coleman stood and grabbed the cart. "What are we shopping for?"

"Required ingredients for my new inspiration," said Serge. "Things are starting to happen fast, so we'll also need super-high-energy food."

"What about Little Debbies?"

"Good thinking."

They turned up the aisle. "Serge, people are doing it again."

"Doing what?"

"Giving us looks. They see us with the single cart and think we're gay."

"Not that there's anything wrong with that."

"Of course not."

"But I see what you mean," said Serge. "Some are glances of abject disgust, while others over-sell their friendliness to compensate for the injustice of our struggle."

"Here are the Little Debbies." Coleman grabbed a box off the shelf and set it in the cart.

"Coleman, what do you think you're doing?"

"I'm putting it in the cart."

"You never just put it in the cart."

"Then what am I supposed to do?"

Serge shook his head. "Give me that." He took the box and walked backward several steps into three-point range and made an arcing jump shot. The treats crashed into the cart. "That's how you do it."

"But, Serge, I don't think I can shoot from that far away."

"Give me the box again." He paced to the other side of the aisle. "If you're not a good perimeter shooter, I can always hit you with a no-look, behind-the-back pass, and you slam-dunk it."

Serge slung the box to Coleman, who slammed it hard into the cart. "Like that?"

"You're a fast learner." Serge took the box again and began walking even farther than before. "The other options are the underhanded shortstop-to-second-baseman lob to begin a double play or, if the aisle is clear like this one, you can retreat as far as possible for a Hail Mary football chuck into the back of the end zone."

Serge went as far as possible, then slapped the side of the box in his right hand and unleashed a high spiral that almost reached the air ducts and could be seen from anywhere in the store.

The box crashed a few feet short of the cart.

Coleman picked it up and slam-dunked it hard again.

Serge returned. "Now, that's how you shop."

Coleman stared into the cart. "Serge, these Little Debbies are all fucked up."

"You're right," said Serge. "They should check those things before they put them on the shelf and hope we don't notice. Stick 'em back and grab another."

They continued, aisle after aisle, slinging and passing and tossing products, until the cart was half full. "Grab that cleaning product and look for giant ten-pound bags of sugar. It will become important later."

"Why? Another inspiration?"

"You think I bought all that food-storage stuff back at headquarters just to keep leftovers great? We're going to have the best Tupperware party ever!"

"Serge, I just noticed something." Coleman threw a tin of mixed nuts. "The people aren't giving us looks anymore. I mean not the gay looks. They've been replaced by these other looks."

"You're right," said Serge. "Now all the looks are bad except without a subtext of butt-fucking."

"What could possibly be the reason?" asked Coleman.

"You think maybe gay people don't shop this way?"

"Serge, I've been looking around, and I don't see anybody shopping like this."

"It's tourist season." Serge lobbed a grapefruit. "There are a lot of Europeans in town."

"They don't do this in Europe?"

Serge shook his head again. "The countries are much smaller, so they have very tiny carts and no elbow room in the aisles to go Michael Jordan on the store's ass."

A few minutes later, the cart was nearly full. "I'm tired of throwing things," said Serge. He grabbed an item off the shelf and set it on top.

A guy in a trucker's hat walked by and mumbled, "Faggots."

Serge turned around: "Hey, buddy, you should watch more *Glee*."

"That show's really growing on me," said Coleman. "Especially that one chick who's always plastered."

"I was particularly impressed by the Madonna episode," said Serge. " 'Express Yourself' was quite moving."

"Oh, definitely," said Coleman. "She's not just the Material Girl anymore."

"But you know what makes it the best show on television?" said Serge. "They teach the youth of America that it's cool to be tolerant."

"In real life, most of the kids on that show would get daily beatdowns if they broke into song and dance in the middle of the gymnasium during PE."

"But not on *Glee*," said Serge. "The coach always knows that jumping jacks must take a backseat if someone spontaneously feels a Broadway show tune coming on."

"Madonna would approve."

"But here's the most fascinating aspect of *Glee*. It proves that

Sean Hannity and the rest of the gang at Fox News are actually super nice."

"How's that?"

"*Glee* is on the Fox Network, run by the same corporation," said Serge. "And given the slant of Fox News talking points, you'd expect them to slam *Glee* for indoctrinating our youth with the San Francisco agenda. Yet they don't."

"What could possibly be the answer?"

"They're secretly in on the plan to help us all get along," said Serge. "Fox News creates a diversion of fake anger so *Glee* can slip through. Because the only other answer is that they're just hate farmers who don't want to bite the hand that feeds, which would make them the world's biggest hypocrites."

"And that can't be."

"I know." Serge reached for a shelf. "Hannity's my hero."

"Serge, why'd you put that in the cart? It looks yucky."

"We need to balance the Little Debbies with ultra-healthy stuff."

"How do you eat tofu?"

"Scoop it with Doritos," said Serge. "That's the last item. Time to check out . . ."

Chapter THIRTY

MIAMI INTERNATIONAL AIRPORT

Civilization was breaking down again at baggage claim.

Those higher up on the food chain pushed their way through to the carousels, flipping other people's bags over to check name tags and colored ribbons. The vegetarians hung back. A beeping cart went by carrying someone with two broken legs and a tropical drink. The PA system asked the public to report unattended luggage and weirdos. A heated conversation in Spanish was either about misplaced traveler's checks or the Havana regime.

A row of chauffeurs stood at the bottom of the escalators with a variety of white signs: Colson, Rockford, Mr. Fujitsu, Wilkes-Barre Wedding, and a blank sign for the psychic convention.

Off to the side, another person in a Mets jersey held another sign: Enemies of Rick Maddox.

They came dribbling in from the corners of the country. The first four arrived in a cluster of mid-morning flights, all wearing their team T-shirts: the initials *R.M.* surrounded by a red circle with a slash and a dagger. They pooled resources and got a rental car together. The next gathering came down the jetways and rented another vehicle. And now the last group was beginning to assemble around the Mets fan, who led them to the Hertz counter.

They took the Dolphin Expressway to Biscayne Boulevard and a row of high-rise resorts popular among conventioneers. In one of the hotels across from the basketball arena, the group had reserved the Flamingo conference room. They began filing in just before the first seminar was scheduled to start. There were rows of long tables with water carafes, notepads and pens with the name of the hotel.

The Mets fan tapped the microphone. "Good evening and thank you all for coming. A few housekeeping items first." He unfolded a page of notes and read matter-of-factly: "You probably already noticed, but on each of your chairs is the complimentary tote bag containing our official program, a local visitors' guide for restaurants and attractions and a plastic laminated badge attached to a lanyard. Please wear it at all times. Plus, everybody should have gotten two drink coupons. If you didn't, ask at the front desk. And I'd like to thank our sponsors. At our platinum level, Amalgamated Diodes, thanks to Silicon Valley Sally. Those are the little blinking rulers you got. Also, the Greater Miami-Dade Better Business Bureau, the New York Mets baseball organization and the National Rifle Association."

There was a polite round of quiet applause.

"And I have a positive update to report. Our private investigator just called me an hour ago with the confirmed home address of our esteemed pal, that fake DEA agent Rick Maddox . . . Now, if you'll refer to your official programs and agenda item number one: Let's kill this motherfucker."

FOOD KING

Serge wheeled the cart past checkout line after checkout line.

"There's a million people at every one," said Coleman.

Serge gnashed his teeth. "Let's try the express lane."

"But we've got like thirty items, and the sign says ten."

"We'll have to triage." Serge grabbed an empty cart from a customer who was wheeling it by. "Sorry, this is an official emergency."

The pair transferred the most essential items into the new cart and took off for the express lane.

They screeched to a halt at the back of a line that snaked out into the main aisle and curved around the magazine racks.

"Look at all the people at this register," said Coleman.

"Look at all the stuff they're buying," said Serge. "Son of a bitch! At least six of these miscreants ahead of us have more than ten items!"

"We're within the law."

"That's right," said Serge. "Even though we wanted more, we courteously winnowed it down to ten and stuck it in that cart we commandeered from that other guy."

Coleman looked over the top of the cashiers. "What's that place up front?"

"Good eye," said Serge. "The customer-service counter." Serge spun the cart out of the line. "They have a register, and there's only a few people. Let's hurry before the stampede."

The cart skidded around the last register and raced up to the counter.

They waited. Coleman looked at his fingernails, yawned and itched himself. Serge stared at the clock. Coleman thought about a traumatic incident he'd experienced when he was younger and got his head stuck between stair railings. He was twenty-eight at the time. Serge stared at the clock.

"Motherfu—!"

Coleman jumped. "What is it?"

"Now I know why we're waiting so long." He pointed with a shaking arm. "They've got one of those glass counters to see the scratch-off tickets. That woman can't decide between Gold Rush and Mega Slots." He emitted a piercing whine. "Now she's filling out a six-ticket Lotto form with her lucky family birthdays."

"Just hang in there."

"I'm trying," said Serge. "She'll eventually need food and water."

"Hey, I see another place. Those empty registers."

"Holy Jesus." Serge spun the cart again. "This store has automated self-serve checkout. There is a God."

The cart zipped back across the store, arriving at a total of eight do-it-yourself registers with only a few customers. They chose the one with a lighted number seven atop a pole next to a bar-code scanner.

"Wonder why there aren't more people over here," said Coleman.

"I don't care." Serge's head was down in the cart, unloading at battle speed. He swiped some chips over the glass plate that contained the laser. Nothing happened.

"Please scan again."

Coleman glanced around. "Who said that?"

"The *Clockwork Orange* machine." Serge wiped the bar code, turned it around and swiped it a second time.

"Please scan again."

"This one's fucked." Serge refilled the cart and moved to lighted pole number eight.

The chips swiped. A cheerful sound dinged a single time from inside the counter. "Excellent," said Serge. "This scanner works. The laser rang it up."

Coleman looked at the screen. "I think it rang up the wrong price."

Serge raised his head. "Dammit!" He turned around and looked toward a small, centrally located service stand where a woman was on duty to assist customers who were having trouble with the self in self-service.

Serge fleetly approached. "Yes, it rang up my chips wrong and I specifically checked the price on the shelf because I love sour cream and garlic, even though I know it's just flavor dust made from ground animal parts that are otherwise the least popular."

"I'll need to send someone to check the shelf price . . . *Jerry!*"

"I just told you I checked the price. And they're clear on the other side of the store. It'll take forever."

Jerry arrived and removed iPod earbuds. Serge heard faint Metallica.

She handed him the chips. "I need a price check."

"Where do we sell these?"

"Somewhere far away."

Jerry replaced the earbuds.

"No!" Serge's arms shot out. "I'll pay the extra. I can't wait! *Jerry!*"

Jerry disappeared into the aisles.

Serge gave the woman a punched-in-the-stomach look. "He took my sour cream and garlic."

Coleman had Little Debbie crumbs on the corners of his mouth when Serge returned to the service stand. "What happened to our sour cream and garlic?"

"No human will ever see that bag of chips again."

"Where'd he go?"

Serge watched Jerry emerge from an aisle, scratch his head and disappear down another aisle. "Teenage wasteland . . . Forget the chips. Life's too short."

Serge scanned another item.

"Please place item in bag."

"Serge," said Coleman. "It's already in the bag."

"I know." Serge lifted the item and set it down again.

"Unscanned item in bag. Please remove."

Serge removed it.

"Please place item in bag."

Coleman leaned toward the register's screen. "How does it know what's in the bag?"

"There's a magic scale inside the counter." Serge put the mixed nuts back in the bag.

"Item not in bag."

Serge stuck his hand into the bag and pressed down.

"Item weight does not match item purchased."

Serge removed the nuts.

"Try scanning something else," said Coleman.

Serge scanned something else. *Ding.*

"Item not in bag."

"There's an 'ignore' button on the touch screen," said Coleman. "It's if you don't want to place the item in the bag."

Serge pressed the button and placed the item in the bag.

"Unauthorized item in bag. Cannot proceed. Please see customer service."

Serge looked over at the service stand and a woman laughing on her cell phone.

"Screw it. I'm going on." He swiped another item.

"This is your first warning."

Serge ran over to the service stand. "Excuse me—"

The woman held up a finger. Into the phone: "You would not believe what I heard about Hector . . ."

"Hell with it." He ran back and scanned something else.

"This is your second warning."

"I'll just pay." Serge inserted a twenty. *Rurrrr.* He inserted it again. *Rurrr.*

"What's the matter?"

Serge flattened the corners of the bill. "It keeps spitting my money out." He stuck it in again. *Rurrr.*

"This is your third warning."

"Serge, the lighted number eight on the pole is now flashing red."

"Shit," said Serge. "Heat's coming down . . . but the woman's off the phone!"

He ran over again as she hoisted a purse strap over her shoulder.

"We're having a total collapse of your business model at number eight!"

"Sorry." The woman started walking away. "I'm on break."

"Is someone else going to replace you?"

"Oh, yeah. Linda."

Serge looked around. "Where is she?"

"On break."

Serge ran back as Coleman scanned a six-pack.

"Age-restricted item. Please show ID to service personnel."

Serge covered his eyes. "Not the age-restricted item!"

"Please show ID . . ."

"Serge, the flashing red light now has a bell going off with it." Coleman popped one of the beers.

"Please step away from the counter and cooperate."

"What do we do now?" said Coleman.

"Rage against the machine . . ."

The replacement clerk finished a smoke break and approached the store entrance as two men sprinted past her into the parking lot. She reached the service stand and stopped. A bunch of employees were standing around a pole with a now un-lighted number eight jammed down through the shattered glass of the product scanner.

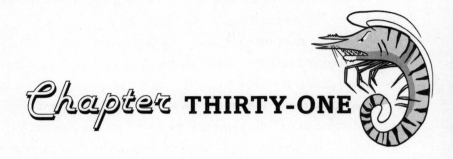

Chapter THIRTY-ONE

MEANWHILE . . .

The curtains were drawn tight on an upper-floor suite in a Biscayne Boulevard resort.

Enzo Tweel set a room-service tray down in the hall and returned to his suite's writing desk. He picked up an eight-by-ten zoom photo from the dossier, studying it while imagining permutations of how the target might appear with a beard and change of hair color.

Then he grabbed several pages of background workup. With the demise of Felicia, everyone thought a neat little bow had been tied on a quite messy mission at the hemispheric summit. It had been designed to take out an incorruptible undercover American agent who was getting too close to an arms pipeline from Miami to Latin America. And it worked. The agent was neutralized. But in the process, way too much collateral damage and an avalanche of unwanted media attention. Then it quieted down. Two years had passed without any blowback, and all the mistakes were considered ancient history.

Then a loose end.

Enzo had been hired by a South American junta from the tiny

nation of Costa Gorda. Actually a secret junta within the junta, who made their fortunes by allowing wholesale money laundering and letting all manner of contraband find safe harbor on the way to somewhere else. Oh, and open arms to any rogue CIA operation.

The junta's clandestine service had its own version of Big Dipper Data Management, but one that was far more effective. And the correlation of their data had just reached a tipping point beyond coincidence. They'd recently noticed a new spate of Web hits on the sites of several U.S. senators and congressmen, all with corresponding Freedom of Information Act requests. They came from a cluster of IP addresses in South Florida, and all the politicians had cozy, clandestine ties to the junta. They knew the secrets. Not big stuff like the assassinations of the agent and Felicia. They didn't want to know that. But they knew.

There could be only one conclusion: Someone, somehow, had begun snooping around about that two-year-old debacle in Miami. The junta's intelligence service dug some more . . .

Enzo set down the eight-by-ten photo of Serge. The target was far too mobile, but there was one known associate with a static address on the Miami River, and the wiretap on Mahoney's phone had yielded a mother lode. Enzo knew about all the clients, and about Serge picking off members of the gang, as well as the recently verified address of a fake DEA agent, and even about Sasha and South Philly Sal.

The junta never told Enzo how to accomplish his missions. Just get results. And Enzo now had sufficient information to rough out his plan on a legal pad. He picked up an untraceable cell phone and dialed.

"Hello? Is this Mahoney and Associates? . . . My name isn't important. This involves the safety of one of your employees named Serge Storms . . . Well, I'll tell you . . . I was discreetly working with him two years ago. Remember that sordid affair at the summit? Turns out they've sent someone back to Miami to tie up loose ends . . . Yes, I know who. His name is Enzo Tweel, but he's using the cover of a local scam artist named South Philly Sal." Enzo abruptly hung up.

Then he listened to the tap on Mahoney's phone and the outgoing call that he knew would be placed immediately to the consulate of Costa Gorda. The late Felicia still had friends there sympathetic to Serge's cause. They told Mahoney they would call him back, and when they did, they confirmed a bogus Bolivian passport issued in the name of Enzo Tweel and believed to be in the possession of an unknown gun for hire.

Enzo had heard enough. He packed a small leather satchel and tore a page off the legal pad with the address of the ersatz DEA agent.

Down on the hotel's ground floor, Enzo exited the elevator and walked with purpose past the open door of the Flamingo conference room, where a lively debate was in progress.

"But we need guns."

"No, absolutely no weapons."

"Why not?"

"Because we want to get our money back, not go to jail."

"We don't have to use them. Just scare him."

"We'll scare him instead with the power of our rhetoric."

"What if he tries something?"

"There's twenty of us. We'll hit him and stuff and then lay on top of him in several layers."

At the front of the room, the Mets jersey tapped the microphone to restore order. "We've heard enough from everyone now. Let's put it to a vote. How many for violence?"

It was a close tally, but the group narrowly opted for the weight of words.

A hand went up. "So what do we do now?"

"Wait until dark," said the Mets jersey. "Until then, there's free wings in the bar."

DARK

Serge and Coleman lay on their respective motel beds along the budget end of Biscayne Boulevard north of downtown.

A fully charged cell phone sat on the nightstand between them.

Because they were waiting for The Call.

Mahoney.

Coleman pointed at the old tube television with his beer. "It's the new *Beavis and Butt-Head*. I never could figure this show out."

"Me neither," said Serge. "And here's another music video they're making smart-ass comments about."

"Bono sure likes to lunge at the camera a lot."

"Then there's the other guy who has to be called the Edge," said Serge. "What's his deal? I mean how much attention do you need? *You're already in U2!*"

"It would be like if the president of the United States changed his name to the Edge."

"Actually, that would be cool."

"And what do the drummer and bass player think about all this?" said Coleman. "'Hey, how about us back here in the rhythm section? From now on, we'd like to be called the Pussy Magnets.'"

"And Bono goes, 'No, no, no, we've already discussed this thoroughly,'" said Serge. "'Only two obnoxious nicknames per band. That's the rule. There was going to be just one, but remember how the Edge made that big stink in Glasgow and started crying and wouldn't come out of the bathroom?'"

Coleman grabbed the remote control to change channels. "I'm bored watching *Beavis and Butt-Head*. Just a couple of losers watching TV and making lame remarks—"

The phone rang.

"That's the call!" Serge flipped open his cell. "Speak...I see...Uh-huh...Uh-huh...Right, just as planned...We're on it. Later—...What? One more thing?...But I don't know any Enzo. Who cares if he's going by South Philly Sal? What's that got to do with me?...Felicia?" Serge listened mutely and hung up without saying anything more.

"Serge, did I hear you say 'Felicia'?"

Serge remained a statue.

"Uh-oh," said Coleman. "I've seen that look before."

"We've got work to do." Serge went to the dresser with resilience. "Mahoney just gave us the green light, so suit up and stay focused. This could be a big one."

"You got it."

Serge diligently rechecked weapons and electronics a final time, then began strategically filling pockets for the assignment.

"Okay," said Coleman. "I got my joints and one-hitter, speed, Vicodin, a beverage . . ."

"Coleman!"

"What?"

"I said for you to get ready."

"I am." A miniature bourbon went into his hip pocket.

"Get ready *for work*!"

"This is how I always get ready for work."

Serge slapped himself in the forehead. "Just don't screw this up. Lives may hang in the balance."

Soon the Firebird crept along a dark residential street.

"Serge, you keep zoning out," said Coleman.

"I know. I just didn't expect Mahoney to bring up Felicia like that. But I'm good." He blinked hard a few times. "It's just that now I have a name and can't get it out of my head."

"Who?"

"Enzo Tweel, also known as South Philly Sal."

"The guy who runs the gang of scam artists?"

"And this fake DEA agent works for him. I plan to sweat him down good for where I can find this Enzo or Sal or whatever."

Coleman grinned and took a haughty sip. "Been meaning to ask: What's with your costume?"

"Element of surprise."

Coleman giggled over another sip. "I think it works."

They parked at the end of the block. Serge raised binoculars.

"What are you doing?"

Serge adjusted the focus. "Surveillance."

"But I thought we were going to—"

"We are," said Serge. "Just had to make an extra stop first."

"Why?"

"Because Mahoney was a little concerned about the latest scam victim who hired him to get her money back."

"Concerned how?"

"Just a hunch from her tone and emotional state. She might not wait for you and me to do the heavy lifting and instead take matters into her own hands." Serge rolled down his window for a better view. "That would put her in grave danger. She'd be out of her element and not thinking straight. She paid handsomely for the mark's home address, and Mahoney's going to hold up his end of the bargain. He's just building in a delay before he calls her to give us time to get in position and gauge her reaction."

"I don't understand," said Coleman. "If he's so concerned, why not forget the deal and don't call?"

"No good." Serge kept the binoculars glued. "People have been known to hire more than one private eye, and who knows what or when she'll find out. We definitely can't take the chance of a civilian like her walking in on the middle of our party. This way her reaction will no longer be an unknown variable. If she stays put at home in the condo for a reasonable period after Mahoney's call, we know it's a false alarm."

"What if she doesn't and goes after the guy?"

"Then we intercept before she's out of the neighborhood, and assure her we're on top of everything."

Coleman prepared another jumbo beverage from his portable bar designed specifically for stakeouts.

"Coleman," said Serge. "This is one time you must slow down on your drinking."

"I *have* slowed down," said Coleman. "Didn't you notice? I'm rationing my drinks to half as often."

"But the cup you're using is twice as large."

"How does that figure in?"

"Just stay sharp."

Coleman chugged and began pouring again. "So when's Mahoney supposed to make this call, anyway?"

Serge checked his glow-in-the-dark atomic wristwatch. "Two minutes ago."

A cell phone rang. Before Serge could answer, Coleman gestured at the house with a cocktail strainer. "The front door's opening."

"She's not staying put." Serge threw the car into gear. "Time to talk some sense into her."

"Wow," said Coleman. "She really looks pissed. Did you see how she whipped out of the driveway?"

"Just what I feared." Serge hit the accelerator. "This is going to be a hot intercept."

"Serge, look! She just blew through that stop sign at the end of the block."

"And took out a mailbox." The Firebird raced without stopping through the same intersection and scattered sparks bottoming out over a speed bump.

Coleman's eyes got big. "A station wagon's pulling out!"

Serge slammed on the brakes with both feet, throwing Coleman into the dashboard.

"Hey, I got a beverage here."

"Shut up! This other asshole's driving too slow and she's getting away . . ."

"Can't you get around him?"

"The street's too narrow and some other bozo who lives around here is having a party: Look at all these parallel-parked cars . . . Damn, and now I've lost sight of her. I need you to spot me through the gauntlet."

Coleman hung his head out the passenger window and looked down as they passed parked vehicles. "Three inches clearance . . . Still three inches . . . Alllllllmossst . . . *Now!*"

Serge worked the pedals with heel-toe precision, whipping around the station wagon and getting back over the line before rear-ending the next parked car.

"You did it," said Coleman.

"I haven't done anything until we catch up with her, and I don't see her taillights," said Serge. "She's going to get herself killed for sure, all because of me."

They started through another intersection. "There she is!" yelled Coleman. "I just saw her taillights when we were crossing that last street. She made a left turn."

Serge screeched in reverse and spun out across the intersection, leaving their car pointed in the desired direction. He floored it again, barreling down on the tiny Ford Focus four blocks ahead. Then three blocks, two, one . . . Now only car lengths, closing fast.

The Firebird was finally right up on her bumper.

"We did it!" yelled Coleman. "She's not going to die."

"All that's left now is a tactical traffic stop, which I've done a million times in my sleep." Serge stared down over the dash at Brook's taillights a few yards ahead. "Nothing can possibly go wrong now . . . Coleman, what are you drinking?"

"What?"

"That drink."

"Just a little Jack Daniel's."

"And?"

"And Coke."

"And?"

"That's it, just Jack and Coke."

"What's floating in it?" said Serge.

Coleman stared into the glass. "Huh?"

"Where'd you get those ice cubes—"

Bloooooooooosssssshhhhhhh!

Foam sprayed everywhere. On the windshield, in their eyes . . .

"Coleman, get that shit out of here!"

"I can't see!"

The Trans Am slalomed wildly back and forth across the road, threatening to go up on two wheels. Serge steered into the skid. "Coleman! It's still spraying!"

Coleman covered his face. "It stings!"

The Firebird whipped across the road a last time before jumping the curb, taking out a hedge and crashing head-on into a coconut palm.

Steam spraying from the radiator, but the foam had stopped.

Coleman looked over at the driver's seat. "Serge, didn't you see that tree?"

"You idiot."

Chapter THIRTY-TWO

MIAMI

An hour after dark, an oil-dripping Ford Focus cruised down a residential street a mile east of the turnpike.

Brook Campanella glanced in her rearview mirror again. She had grown suspicious of a Firebird that she could have sworn was following her, but now there was nothing back there. She'd heard the sound of a wreck and checked a side mirror to see the car a half block back, crashed into a tree.

Tough luck. Bigger things on her mind.

She headed south on I-95 and took an exit ramp six miles later. There was a hitchhiker heading to Key West, a homeless guy waving a cardboard sign and a broken-down Beemer with the hood up and someone bent over the engine.

Brook drove by. The man slammed the hood, jumped in the Beemer and hit the gas.

She found her way through a modest middle-class neighborhood outside Miramar. Brook cut the headlights and drove the last hundred yards in the dark before easing up to the curb. She unzipped a leather tactical bag in her lap and removed the sawed-off, pistol-grip shotgun. Then she grabbed the door handle. Headlights hit her car from behind. She took her hand off the handle and watched in the mirror.

At the end of the block, a Beemer rolled to a stop five homes back and cut its lights. The driver didn't get out of the car. Maybe he was waiting for someone to emerge from the house. Maybe he was getting a hummer. Who cared? The important thing was his lights were off her. She grabbed the door handle again.

Lights hit her again. This time a Camaro. Then a Datsun. "How busy is this street?"

Brook suddenly jumped as she heard gunfire. But it was just a loud TV across the street where the windows were open to save on A/C. The street may have been dark, but it was a noise fest on a Friday night. Multiple stereos, people laughing and yelling at a backyard pool party; other televisions were tuned to more networks that decided they needed even more weapon fire.

Every sound made Brook flinch. She reached in the glove compartment for an airline miniature of banana-flavored rum, her first drink of the day. She made a wicked face and began coughing as it went down like any non–call brand of well liquor.

She waited for the effect. Headlights appeared again at the end of the block, this time facing Brook and making her lie flat across the front seat. The lights passed, and she straightened up to reach for the door handle. And withdrew her hand again. She grabbed another miniature from the glove compartment and made another face.

Brook lowered her head with self-anger. "I just can't do it."

The car remained still while she flipped through photos in her wallet. Mostly of her parents. Emotion spiked in two directions, sorrow and rage. She nodded at a new idea. "But I can at least scare the shit out of him, just like he did to my father." She ejected the twelve-gauge's shells and opened the driver's door. "If he has a heart attack, it's fucking karma."

She reached the front steps with the shotgun slung under a light jacket. But now what? Did she ring the doorbell? Or find a darkened side door and bust out some jalousie glass. This clearly wasn't thought through.

For reasons known only to the rum company, something told Brook to try the knob. Unlocked. She gave the door a gentle push and poked her head inside. Lights blazed throughout the residence. Somewhere inside, a TV's volume was way up. That's where he must be. Brook silently slipped the door closed behind her, raised the shotgun from under her coat and followed the sound of a cop show where someone was being interrogated. She found herself in a hallway and concluded that the TV and fake Rick Maddox must be in the den.

Brook crept forward, chest pounding, sweat starting to trickle into her eyes, every inch forward an undertaking. She reached the edge of the den's door, and her legs began to buckle. She got mad at herself again, thought of her father and forced her muscles to steel themselves.

Brook told herself she was thinking too much: *Just do it.* She closed her eyes and counted to three, then jumped from around the corner into the den's open doorway with shotgun aimed high.

Sure enough, there he was, stretched out in a La-Z-Boy, watching TV with his back toward her. Just the top of his head showing. For some reason, she had pictured him with hair.

She took a forceful step forward. "Get up, motherfucker!"

The plan was for him to spring up from the chair in a freak-out. But he just continued lounging there smugly watching his cop show. What an asshole.

Brook began circling him in a wide arc, the aim of the twelve-gauge never leaving its target. She got halfway around to his profile and realized he wasn't ignoring her; he was asleep.

She picked up an ashtray—"Wake up!"—and hit him in the chest.

That's when . . .

Gasp.

Blood trickled out of the far side of his mouth. More blood in a circle on his shirt, just above the lung.

"He's . . . dead? . . . Oh God! Oh, Jesus!"

Thoughts pinwheeled, eyes shooting everywhere. She noticed something on the floor. Whoever killed him had been going through his stuff, scattering manila folders, computer disks and a disgorged wallet.

Brook slowly retreated in terror. "No! No! No! No! No! . . ."

Back down on the floor, the wallet had fallen open to display a silver badge.

"Dammit, they got the addresses mixed up!" Brook gulped air. "It's the real DEA agent! I couldn't be any more fucked!"

Not yet.

Then more perspiration, a slippery finger, and ignorance on how to properly clear a chamber.

Boom.

The shotgun exploded with a direct hit on the late Rick Maddox.

Brook had never fired a weapon in her life, and true to the gun dealer's word, it kicked like a stallion, flying backward right out of her hands before crashing through a window and landing somewhere out in the yard.

Now the pounding chest and unsteady legs were becoming a serious barrier to getting out of the house. Brook was going into shock. She hyperventilated and stumbled down the hall to the front of the house.

The doorbell rang.

Brook screamed.

The person at the door thought it was just another TV show. He rang the bell again.

Brook somehow managed to get to the peephole and look outside. What the hell? Just a bunch of feathers. It looked like some guy . . . in a chicken suit?

The bell rang again.

From the other side of the door: *"Cluck, cluck, cluck. Chicken-gram . . ."*

Brook severely fainted.

Outside on the porch, the man in the chicken suit grabbed a rubber mallet and turned to his assistant. "Coleman, apply force on the knob while I use the bump key."

"Serge, it's already open."

"Crap, still haven't gotten to use the bump key."

"And there's a babe on the floor," said Coleman. "Is she dead?"

Serge bent down for a pulse. "No, just passed out."

Brook woozily came around. She looked up. "The chicken!" And passed out again.

Serge removed the chicken head from his costume and scratched under his left wing. "She's acting really weird."

Coleman leaned in for a closer look. "Is she the one we were following?"

Serge nodded. "Pretty sure. Brook Campanella. Mahoney showed me a client photo he'd enlarged from her driver's license, but you know how those things look." Serge lightly tapped her on the cheek. "Where's the dude who lives here?"

No answer.

Serge pulled out the pistol tucked under his suit. "Stay here with her while I check the rest of the house."

"Roger."

A beer cracked open.

Serge crept down the hall toward the sound of a television . . .

O ut on the street, five houses away, a driver sat in a quiet Beemer and slipped on leather shooting gloves. A dead, straight line of a mouth as he stared ahead at a Firebird that had somehow limped across the city with a steaming radiator and was now parked behind Brook's Ford. On the Beemer's passenger seat sat the black-and-white photo of Serge that Enzo had positively matched to the driver who had exited the damaged vehicle moments earlier. As he unzipped a cushioned leather satchel and removed a silencer, memories drifted back to the last time he visited Miami. Enzo was a steady one, but it still stung that he had been assigned backup behind that ass who couldn't carry his water. What did he do to deserve cleanup duty? And it wasn't a small mess. First the clown with the rifle who couldn't get out of the way of his own dick. Then:

Felicia.

And now:

Serge.

At least he was the primary on this sanction. But what a pesky gnat that Serge was. Enzo could easily have taken him out with Felicia at that totally exposed sidewalk café on Ocean Drive. Except the only actionable target is the one you've got clearance for. That's the cardinal rule in a need-to-know business, or someone will be given clearance to take you out. Everything is compartmentalized, so for all Enzo knew, Felicia's lunch companion might have been someone on his own side who was helping set her up by drawing her into the open. You never knew.

And now here he was, sent back to Miami for more mop-up. One thing for sure, he wanted a raise . . .

. . . Back inside the house, Coleman sat on the floor drinking a Schlitz and cradling Brook's head in his arm. "Time to wake up, sleepy-head."

Serge came running back into the room. "Coleman, we've got serious problems. There's a dead guy in the den with his head blown completely off. I'm thinking Rick Maddox."

"Can I see?"

"Yes," said Serge. "I'm not doing this for your pleasure, but we need to sanitize the room for our client's sake."

"Cool!"

Brook had started coming around again, but Coleman got up and let her head hit the floor.

They went into the den and Serge turned down the volume on *Matlock,* which had resumed in its entirety following the game.

"So that's Rick Maddox, the fake DEA agent?" asked Coleman.

"Yes and no." Serge wiped down surfaces. "The scammer is using the name Maddox, which he lifted from a real agent in Miami."

"That's quite a coincidence."

"Not really." Serge picked a shotgun shell off the floor. "The grifter began his scheme somewhere else, but when victims and law enforcement started closing in, he migrated to Miami for cover."

"How's that cover?"

"Since the real Maddox had a legitimate address, the schemer was hoping his adversaries might be thrown off course by a false flame." Serge held up a wallet he'd found on the floor.

"Is that a real badge?"

"The cover worked: Mahoney got the two addresses scrambled."

"You're blaming Mahoney for the dead guy?"

"Not his fault," said Serge. "He doesn't know what his clients will do with the info—and he took extra precautions with this gal, even though the last thing she appears to be is a killer. But right now time's the new enemy."

He ran back into the foyer, tossed the badge on a table and shook Brook hard by the shoulders. "You have to wake up right now!"

"W-what?" Her eyes weakly opened.

"We work for Mahoney, so don't faint on us again." Serge propped her into a sitting position. "We're here to help you."

She looked around. "Dear God, I'm still here. It's not a dream."

"Or a novel," said Serge. "But right now you have to tell me as quickly as you can what happened here."

"Just scare him! I, he, TV on. Rum, badge, Dad, La-Z-Boy, shotgun, karma . . ."

"Okay, not that fast," said Serge. "Take deep breaths."

Outside, a Beemer started up, but the headlights remained dark. It rolled so slowly you could hear bits of broken beer-bottle glass from teenagers who had moved on to a vacant lot. The sedan stopped directly across the street from the Maddox place. The driver checked his ammo clip one last time and racked a hollow-point bullet into the chamber. He looked up and down the street a final time and opened the door of his car . . .

Inside the house, Brook caught her breath. "I swear he was already dead when I got here! You have to believe me!"

"We do," said Serge. "Someone blew his head off with a shotgun."

"I did that," said Brook.

"But I thought you told me—"

"He already had a gunshot wound in his chest. Then I got the shakes and my finger slipped."

"That's not good." Serge stood up. "But there's still time to get my arms around this. I've sanitized many a crime scene . . . Tell me, where's the gun?"

"I don't know."

"How can you not know?"

"It flew out the window. I think it went over the fence and landed in the neighbor's yard because I heard their dogs barking."

"That's also not good," said Serge. "But you didn't touch anything, did you?"

"Yeah, the whole wall down that hallway. I was having trouble standing up."

"So we've lost control of the weapon and left prints everywhere," said Serge. "But that's it, right? I mean you didn't leave any other evidence that might be helpful to police, like a DNA sample?"

Brook promptly jackknifed over and threw up.

"And that completes the hat trick."

"I don't think I can handle this," she said.

"You have to." Serge pointed at a table. "See that badge? You got the real agent mixed up with the fake one."

"But I didn't kill him."

"Right now that means less than nothing." Serge turned to Coleman. "Go out back and look for that gun in case it didn't clear the fence."

"How do I get there?"

"I don't know. Take a stab at that thing over there called a back door."

Halfway across the front yard, Enzo crept with a pistol pressed against his thigh. No ambiguity this time. The junta had given him total clearance for any eventuality, which meant two immediate taps to the chest of everyone found at the house, to drop them, followed by two more in the back of the head on the way out. Enzo reached the bottom porch step and eased his weight onto the wood.

Suddenly he was lit up and blinded in a blaze of high-beam head-lights from several vehicles that converged on the residence. "What the hell?" He sprinted back to the Beemer and sped away as more cars arrived. Tires screeched and braked to a stop at various angles on the lawn.

Inside, Brook leaped at the sound of squealing rubber. "The cops!"

Serge ran to the window. "No, not the police. They've got drinks. But who the hell *are* they?"

A swarm of almost twenty people in identical T-shirts spilled out of the vehicles and headed up the walkway with an unmistakable air of torches and pitchforks.

"This looks like trouble," said Serge. "Especially the guys wearing Pittsburgh and Mets jerseys. We better get ready." He put the chicken head back on.

Heavy pounding on the front door. *"Open up! . . . We know you're in there! . . . Give us our money back!"*

Serge opened the door. "How can I help you?"

The gang was prepared to unleash a merciless dialectic blitz on whoever answered. But the sight that greeted them created a confused pause.

"You're . . . a chicken?"

"Correct," said Serge. "Next question."

"Are you the guy going by the name Rick Maddox?"

"Not today."

"Do you know where he is?"

Feathers pointed. "In the den."

The Mets jersey pushed through the pack. "Well, if you're a friend of his and know what's good for you, you'll step out of the way."

The others: *"Yeah, don't try to stop us! . . ."*

"We're coming through! . . ."

"Stand clear! . . ."

Serge raised his wings. "I wouldn't go in there if I were you."

"Fuck you, chicken! . . ."

They shoved him aside and charged down the hall, running into the den, yelling profanities that even a sailor never heard.

The shouting unexpectedly halted. They slowly paraded out of the room with alabaster faces.

The shaken mob thought it couldn't get any worse than the horrific scene they had just discovered. Until one of them saw something on a table in the front room. "What's this?"

"What is it?" asked Silicon Valley Sally.

Wasted in Margaritaville held it up. "It's a DEA badge."

"But how is that possible?" said Lucy. "Unless . . ."

"The addresses got mixed up," said Mets Jersey.

"It's not the impostor," said Shitless in Seattle. "It's the real Rick Maddox."

"You!" The Pirates fan pointed at Serge and took a step back. "You killed him! You killed a real federal agent!"

"Now wait just a second," said Serge.

The gang looked around at one another. Nods and murmurs. *"The chicken killed him! . . ." "He'll fry for this! . . ."*

"Everyone needs to take it easy," said Serge. "I going to make myself a drink of rainwater, and the rest of you help yourself to whatever you like."

Panic only increased. They screamed more accusations as they backed up en masse toward the front door.

Coleman returned from the backyard with a big smile and a sawed-off. "I got it!"

Boom.

A chandelier fell.

The witnesses all raced out of the house and down the steps for their cars.

"You killed him! . . ."

"You blew his head off! . . ."

"We're telling! . . ."

Chapter THIRTY-THREE

BISCAYNE BOULEVARD

The number and condition of the budget motels along U.S. Highway 1 meant there would always be vacancy.

A black Firebird was parked in front of the one called the Coral Arms.

There were only two beds in room 17. So Serge assigned them to Coleman and Brook Campanella, while he slept on the floor.

The clock radio reached three A.M., and Brook still hadn't been able to nod off. Adrenaline from all the trauma. She just clutched the pillow and stared over the side of the bed at Serge, sleeping like a newborn with his own makeshift pillow of balled-up clothes.

Brook thought she had chosen the lesser evil by agreeing to leave with him. The only other options were to hang out at a murder scene with her fingerprints or drive herself back to the condo and wait for the cops to slap the cuffs. And those weren't options. So she got in the Firebird.

Brook was no babe in the woods. These guys were dangerous. Well, maybe Coleman was only a danger to himself, but definitely Serge. She totally expected to have to make a break for it at some point. Her mind reeled in terror of rape, or worse.

But there hadn't been any opportunity to get away. The Trans Am was a two-door, so there was no chance of escaping at a red light. And Serge didn't make any stops on the way to the motel.

Police cars were always going by on the boulevard. Brook could take off running in the parking lot and flag one of them down. And then say what? Okay, maybe try a cab or a Good Samaritan. But then she was suddenly at the point where they were at the motel. Decision time. Serge was already out of the car telling her to follow them into the room. Brook didn't know why she allowed herself to do it, but she went inside.

The first few minutes were the twin terrors of murder-scene memories and now being cornered in the room with Serge and Coleman.

It was an utter surprise when Serge made the bed assignments. It had to be a trick. She'd get all snug in bed, and then . . . She blocked off those thoughts.

But instead of taking advantage of her, Serge just grabbed some T-shirts from a duffel bag and slipped them under his head on the floor.

There was something about him, especially asleep. Some qualities like her father and brother had. She found herself unable to stop watching him curled in the corner.

He turned over in his sleep. Then Brook heard some mumbling. Couldn't make it out, even though it was steadily getting louder. He began rolling back and forth on the floor, slamming into the wall, over and over. Until finally:

"Felicia! Noooooo! . . ."

Brook sprang from bed and shook him. "Serge, wake up! You're having a nightmare!"

"Felicia! . . ." Now with tears.

She shook harder. "Wake up!"

Serge came around with slowly blinking eyes. "Felicia?"

"No, I'm Brook. Who's Felicia?"

"It's not important." Serge bunched up the clothes and wiggled his head into a comfy position. "I'm fine."

"No, you're not." She took him by the hand. "There's plenty of room in the bed. And you need a good night's sleep, so forget the floor."

Serge climbed into the sheets, staying as close to the opposite edge of the mattress from Brook as possible without falling off the side. Brook lay there watching him. Serge was on his back, staring wide-awake at the ceiling.

"Serge, who's Felicia?"

"Just somebody."

"Tell me. You were having a really bad nightmare."

Serge shook his head.

"I want you to tell me."

Serge shook his head again, but started talking anyway. Then the whole story gushed out, right up to the part about the fake DEA agent working for the person who was responsible for Felicia's murder. That's why he had hopes going to the house that night, but it didn't pan out.

Brook understood; she had lost someone, too. She reached under the covers to hold his hand. Serge let her but didn't grip back.

Brook wasn't interested in sex, but she knew she was at one of those vulnerable moments and wouldn't have objected if he made the overture. He didn't.

Serge had his reasons. They differed woman to woman. Like Sasha. Serge was on her in a heartbeat. But that was just a violent collision of dangerous people swapping fluids the way NASCAR drivers trade paint. Brook was pure.

Serge became silent again, studying the ceiling. Danger affects women differently. Sasha was drawn to it; Brook found a safe harbor from it.

She scooted over and snuggled into Serge's shoulder and felt secure. They dozed off together.

THE NEXT MORNING

All the lights were on before dawn in an upper-floor suite of a high-rise on Biscayne Boulevard.

Enzo Tweel sat at the writing desk. His demeanor never betrayed emotion, but inside he was a lava pit. All those stupid idiots in their matching T-shirts just had to show up last night at the worst possible moment. But Plan A hadn't been a total waste. The bright side was that Serge and his two companions would begin restricting their movements because of his ruse: After Enzo had shot the fake Rick Maddox, he dropped the DEA badge on the floor. And from the phone tap on Mahoney's line last night, he learned that they had fallen for it. They thought they were being hunted for killing a bona fide federal agent when it was the scammer all along.

It motivated Enzo. He put pen to legal pad. Time for Plan B. There had been a flurry of late-night calls to Mahoney, all from the same number. Enzo heard a woman tell the PI that she had been trying to get ahold of Serge but he wasn't answering his cell. Could Mahoney please ask him to call her? She wanted to meet with important information she couldn't divulge over the phone. Tell him it's Sasha.

Enzo looked up at the wall. The name rang a bell. He flipped back through his legal pad for notes from previously tapped conversations. Sure enough, there she was, in a phone call from Serge about cracking a dating bandit case.

An alert jingled on his smartphone. Another taped conversation coming in via satellite. Sasha again. The murder of her crime colleague Rick Maddox was too much. With the bloody winnowing of her gang, she wanted out. She wanted to meet Serge. Noon, the Fandango sidewalk café on Ocean Drive.

Another alert quickly followed. An outgoing call from Mahoney to Serge informing him of Sasha's request. This time Serge was eager: She was now his best and only lead to track down her boss, South Philly Sal or Enzo or whatever his name.

"I'll call her right after I get off the phone with you," said Serge.

This was good. Fit perfectly into Plan B.

Enzo packed his leather satchel again.

Wake up."

Brook's eyes fluttered open. "What time is it?"

"Time to go," said Serge.

"Go where?"

Serge was already dressed with duffel bag packed. "I need to get you someplace safe."

"But I'm safe with you."

Serge shook his head. "That was a federal agent last night. The heat's going to be unreal. There's all those witnesses, and by now the cops are looking for two men and a woman, so it's better we split up until I can sort some things out and get you in the clear."

Brook climbed into the Firebird again but without reservations. Serge drove a short distance to another roach motel and went in the office. He returned and led them to room 23.

Serge opened his wallet. "Okay, Brook, I've got you all set up. You're registered under an alias. Here's the room key . . ."

Brook Campanella took the magnetic card. "Why can't I stay with you guys?"

"I already explained. And I have an important meeting that just came up."

"Can I come along?" asked Brook.

"It's someplace you can't be," said Serge. "For your own good."

"But you will come back?"

"Right after the meeting," said Serge. "You have my word. But whatever you do, don't leave this room under any circumstances until I return."

She nodded.

"I'd like you to say it."

"I promise I won't leave the room."

"Good."

Brook gave Serge a tight hug, and he left the motel with Coleman. Brook picked up the phone. "Yes, I'd like a taxi . . ."

OCEAN DRIVE

The "it" address on Miami Beach. Trendy restaurants and hotels. Beautiful people walked around being beautiful. Rollerblades, champagne in ice buckets next to sidewalk tables, sprinting valets. Topless sunbathing was against the law but the law wasn't enforced.

Sasha arrived an hour early, sitting alone at her table in front of the Fandango. Six times already she'd had to fend off another male model who wanted to join her. She checked her watch. Fifteen minutes till Serge.

Another suitor made a play. But this one didn't ask before taking the seat across from her.

She made an exaggerated sigh and started off in annoyance. "Not interested."

"I'm a friend of Serge."

Her head swung and their eyes locked. "You are? What's the matter? Is he coming? How do you know him?"

"He's definitely coming, and I also work for Mahoney and Associates. The same case in fact. South Philly Sal."

"Serge told you about him?"

Enzo nodded. "But right now I need a favor. It's for Serge. Can you call Sal and vouch for me so I can talk to him?"

"What for?"

"It's Serge's idea. That's all he wants you to know, for your own safety."

"Sure, I guess." She reached in her purse and flipped a phone open. "Sal? It's me, Sasha . . . Oh, not much, but I have a friend here who wants to talk to you . . . I'm not sure what it's about. But he's definitely cool. I've known him since high school . . . Okay, here he is." She handed the cell across the table.

He got up from his chair and turned around for privacy.

"Is this Sal?"

"Who am I talking to?"

"My name is Enzo Tweel. Can we meet somewhere?"

"I don't know who the hell you are, and I don't care what Sasha says."

"We're in the same line of work."

"What are you, a fucking cop? It's not going to work."

"I know who's been picking off members of your crew. Gustave, Omar, the guy from the hotel heist with the toilet lids, the other one from the funeral burglary, and last night your so-called Rick Maddox."

"How do you know all this?"

"Because he's also been picking off my crew. Works for a private eye, except I don't think they did a proper psychological background check. The guy's totally out of control on some kind of vigilante crusade. His name's Serge. Serge Storms."

"Never heard of him."

"Neither had I, but frankly I'm starting not to feel too safe myself. And I'm guessing you've probably had the same thoughts. That's why I'd like to meet and see if you have any ideas. I don't really want to discuss this on the phone, and we can't exactly go to the police."

There was a pause. "Put Sasha back on."

She took the phone. "Hey, Sal . . . Yeah, I can swear for him . . . Whatever he says is absolutely on the level . . ." Sasha held up the phone. "Wants to talk to you again."

"Okay, let's meet."

"Seven o'clock, Tortugas Inn," said Enzo. "Room's registered under my name. If I'm not there yet, I'll leave a key at the desk for you." He hung up, set his leather satchel on the table and smiled.

"Hey!" Sasha pointed at the road. "There's Serge now!"

Across the street, Serge struggled to parallel-park his Firebird in a rare free space on Ocean Drive. "Dang it, these assholes didn't leave enough space." Reverse, forward, reverse, forward.

Coleman chugged a to-go cup. "This is like the final episode of *The Sopranos.*"

"I'm not amused." Reverse, forward. "There, finally!"

"Hey, Serge, that restaurant, the Fandango. Isn't that where Felicia—I mean, shit, why did I say that?"

"Let's just go."

They jogged across the road between a Jaguar and a Harley. Serge reached the sidewalk and looked around. There was Sasha under one of the tables with an umbrella. Someone screamed. Then another. With Sasha's platinum-blond hair, there was high contrast and no mistaking the matted blood on the back of her facedown head.

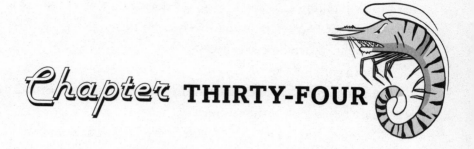

Chapter THIRTY-FOUR

The Firebird blew through traffic on the MacArthur Causeway back to the mainland from Miami Beach. It dodged and wove through slower-speeding sports cars screaming past celebrity homes on Palm and Star islands.

"Serge, you drive fast," said Coleman. "But not this fast. What if a cop spots us?"

"Then we'll be on live TV, because I'm not stopping."

"Righteous."

Serge flipped open his own cell and hit redial. "Brook? Serge. I'm sorry about this, but something's come up, and I swear to be back as soon as possible."

"What is it?" Brook asked from the back of a taxi.

"Once again, better you not know," said Serge. "But trust me that I won't let anything happen to you."

"Why? What can happen besides the police?" said Brook. "I've been thinking that a good lawyer can explain that."

"It's something else," said Serge. "Just give me your word you won't leave the room until I get back. You haven't left the room, have you?"

"Uh, no," said Brook, looking out the window at passing buildings. "Not for a second."

"Good girl," said Serge. "Now here's the hard part. I'm going to have to stop taking calls soon because I don't know what phones are tapped anymore. So you'll just have to hang in there."

"All right. When do you expect—"

"Got to go."

He hung up and the cell rang again before it reached his pocket. Serge didn't even look at the number.

"Mahoney, listen, I'm— . . . What? South Philly Sal is supposed to be where? The Tortugas Inn? Seven o'clock? . . . Who told you this? . . . They wouldn't say? . . . Okay, thanks." The phone clapped shut as Serge skidded over the line at minimum clearance between a Mitsubishi and a Pepsi truck, then whipped back into the fast lane.

Coleman made a rare check of his seat belt. "What was that about?"

"Mahoney got an anonymous tip. A room at the Tortugas Inn was registered to a customer named Enzo Tweel."

"What's that mean?"

"That Mahoney's phone is tapped."

"Just because someone called in a tip?"

"Enzo called in a tip on himself. Then listened when Mahoney forwarded it. He's baiting me." Serge nearly sideswiped a Gold Coast taxi skidding toward the exit ramp to Biscayne Boulevard. "What happened to Sasha back there. Same café, identical MO, even the same table. I'll never forget that table as long as I live. He's trying to provoke me into not thinking clearly."

Coleman's shaking hands prepared a drink. "What are you going to do?"

"Take the bait . . ."

Two miles south, a Cherokee was parked at a Citgo station. The driver had a telephoto camera aimed diagonally across the street at the Tortugas Inn. His other hand held a cell phone. "No, I don't trust him one bit," said South Philly Sal. "It's definitely a trap. I'd bet anything that this character who calls himself Enzo Tweel is actually

Serge . . . Because right now he has the edge since I have no idea what he looks like, and I mean to fix that. This Serge character is ruining our business."

Two blocks in the other direction, binoculars aimed out the driver's window of a parked Beemer. The Tortugas Inn filled the field of vision. Enzo was beginning to enjoy his role as puppet master in this demented marionette show. The binoculars swept the street, from the black-barreled barbecue stand three blocks north, then back to the Citgo station three streets the other way. All quiet on the western front.

A black Firebird turned off Biscayne a half mile south of the Tortugas Inn, and took a parallel road through a run-down neighborhood.

"Serge, if you know it's a trap, why are we going?"

"Because he expects my anger to rush me into the web." Serge checked all his mirrors during a prolonged pause at a stop sign. "Enzo is hanging back watching the motel for me to arrive. So, like a spider, we're going to drive in tightening concentric circles from the perimeter because someone on surveillance isn't looking backward . . ."

Over on the main drag, binoculars in the Beemer tightened again on the Tortugas Inn. A few hundred yards away, a telephoto lens snapped a rapid burst of room exterior photos from a Jeep Cherokee.

Serge explored the residential streets a block off U.S. 1 and turned into a trash pickup alley behind the storefronts facing Biscayne.

"I recognize that smell," said Coleman.

"Just watch for anything odd."

"Everything's odd." Coleman blazed a Thai stick. "Those chicks at the corner are dousing each other with spray paint."

"That's just huffing gone inaccurate." The Firebird rolled up behind a gas station. "Coleman, how often do you see a telephoto lens sticking out a car window at a Citgo station?"

"Let me count . . ." Coleman strained mentally. "Uh, zero."

"That's what I thought."

Serge parked out of sight behind the station's car wash. High-pressure water jets and giant spinning brushes created a cover of sound.

"Coleman, wait here and keep her running. He's no doubt armed but riveted on the room, so I have a good chance to outflank him."

Serge closed the driver's door but let it stay unlatched. He moved slowly along the back wall of the car wash, sliding his right hand into the waistband of his shorts and feeling a familiar grip. He peeked around the edge of the car wash, but his view was blocked by a wet, gleaming Audi that emerged from the building and dripped water as it drove back to the highway.

The view was clear. There was the Jeep, its driver still preoccupied with his camera and phone. Serge retreated a step behind the building and rested the back of his head against the wall. He closed his eyes, flicking the safety off his pistol. He had ached two whole years for this moment, and now closure sat across the parking lot a few yards away.

Serge crept from behind the car wash and worked his way around the edge of the property, passing the fifty-cent tire inflater and a blue pay phone stand with the phone removed. He stopped and studied the Jeep's mirrors and calculated the one, single straight line to the vehicle that would keep the mirrors blind to him. He began walking the asphalt tightrope.

The cell-phone conversation could be heard at a range of fifteen feet.

". . . Yeah, he hasn't shown yet. I think this is a big waste of time," said Sal. "But you have to consider the source that vouched for this. Sasha can really be out to lunch sometimes . . ."

The phone was snatched from his left hand and smashed to the ground. His head spun. "What the fuck?"

Serge cracked him quickly in the side of the head with his pistol butt.

"You're a dead man," said Sal.

"Just set the camera down slowly on the dash." Serge kept the .45 pressed to Sal's temple and opened the door with his other hand. "Now get out."

Sal eased himself from the driver's seat. "Are you Serge?"

"That's right, your new chauffeur."

Moments later, behind the car wash, Sal lay in the bed of the Firebird's trunk. Wrists and ankles bound with plastic ties. "You better make damn sure you kill me, or I'll leave you in a million pieces."

Serge tucked the gun behind his back and smiled. "I can work with that."

The hood slammed.

A couple blocks south, binoculars lowered in a Beemer. Enzo Tweel checked his Rolex. What could be taking so long? One of his areas of expertise was human behavior, and provoking Serge with that Sasha business back at the beach was a can't-miss.

And he was right.

The binoculars went to his eyes again just as a black Firebird sped south.

"Son of a bitch!"

The binoculars flew into the backseat as Enzo hit the gas to merge onto Biscayne.

And he merged T-bone-style into the side of a beer truck.

"You stupid fucking moron!" the beer-truck driver yelled down from his cab. "Look what you did to my truck!"

Enzo aimed a German pistol at the driver, who promptly raised his hands in silent surrender before diving across the front seat and scrambling out the passenger door.

The luxury sedan was crumpled to the side panels, and Enzo needed his shoulder to pop the door open. He crawled out of the car with a gash on his forehead and tiny pieces of windshield in his hair.

Enzo began limping away toward the camouflage of the adjoining neighborhood, looking up the highway as a southbound Firebird became a dot and disappeared.

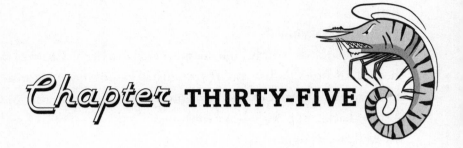

Chapter THIRTY-FIVE

BISCAYNE BOULEVARD

Lights glowed through the curtains of the second-floor motel room. Water ran in the sink.

Serge whipped a spatula around the mixing bowl. He had tremendously thick rubber gloves and a welder's apron. The gloves were orange.

"What'cha makin'?" asked Coleman.

"Don't get so close," said Serge. "You're not wearing protective goggles."

"Hey, that's some of the stuff we picked up at Food King."

"Right-o." Stirring continued. "People have no idea what's just sitting on grocery shelves if you know what you're looking for."

Serge decided the concoction needed more balance and grabbed another ten-pound sack off the counter.

"Sugar?" asked Coleman.

"Sugar leads a weird double life because of its unique molecular structure." Serge set the sack down and poured more water. "Most people think it's a benign and happy little compound because they free-associate it with candy, but there's a dark side."

"There is?" said Coleman. "I must know!"

"I'll tell you!" Serge grabbed the spatula again. "Mix it with certain other materials and you get a less confectious result. For example, potassium nitrate is one of the three ingredients of gunpowder. By itself, it's just saltpeter. But add some sugar—which has nothing to do with gunpowder—then toss a match and stand back. It doesn't explode but instead slowly burns through the pile like white-hot phosphorus. Torches right through metal. So of my four ingredients, sugar is the kick start, and water is obviously for the suspension. Now, this stuff is the primary—"

"I recognize that," said Coleman. "See it all the time at the store."

"So does everyone else, and they just walk right by." Serge tossed the can in the trash. "Homemakers use it every day without a second thought. But it's the bitch of the bunch. I don't want word getting out about what it is because everyone will start throwing this together. A lot of people don't have impulse control."

"The bunch?" asked Coleman. "You said four ingredients."

"That's correct." Serge nodded toward the garbage pail.

Coleman pulled out an empty box. "Cornstarch? What's that for?"

Serge pulled something from one of the shopping bags on the bed. "What else? The gelatin mold I got at Tupperware headquarters. I've been waiting to use this baby forever."

"You had this all planned way back when you bought that?"

"You think I just bounce around through life?" He placed the mold on the counter and carefully poured in the contents of the mixing bowl. "All the necessary ingredients are already present, but cornstarch gives it certain properties to use it in creative ways . . . Open the door of the mini-fridge."

Coleman pulled the handle, and Serge's orange gloves slid the mold onto the bottom shelf. "The mixture would otherwise just be a thick liquid, but cornstarch lets you turn it into Jell-O. But unlike normal Jell-O—and this is the crowning touch—it makes it incredibly adhesive." Serge stood back up. "And there you have it."

Coleman scratched his stomach. "Have what?"

"Homemade napalm."

"That Vietnam stuff that sticks and burns."

"It burns all right." Serge pulled off the gloves and threw them in the sink. "But not with fire, so it doesn't need an ignition source."

"Then how does it burn?"

"Chemical burn. Much, much worse than fire. Just keeps boring through the skin. I've been saving this project for when I needed serious closure."

Coleman pointed back at a bottle next to the sink. "I didn't notice that before. I thought I knew all the ingredients, but you didn't say anything about vinegar."

"It's not an ingredient," said Serge. "It's the antidote. Because of its pH, vinegar is one of the few substances that can neutralize a chemical burn. A lot of people use water, which only makes it worse."

"So what are you going to use it for?"

"What's the only thing missing?"

Coleman stared at the floor, then the ceiling. He tapped his chin and suddenly raised a finger. "The famous bonus round! You're holding another contest with that guy out in the trunk!" He clapped with good nature and took a seat on a bed. "Let's get it on!"

Serge held up his hands. "Not so fast. We finally must surmount the greatest challenge of all to prepare the game show."

"What's that?"

"Wait for the Jell-O to harden." Serge checked his wristwatch. "The stuff should take about four hours."

"*That's* the great challenge?"

"With your substance assistance, you have killing time down to an art form, but to me it's Chinese water torture."

Coleman shrugged. "Let's get rockin'." He grabbed a joint and a pint of vodka with a red-eyed crow on the label.

Serge grabbed a digital camera and notepad.

One hour went by. Coleman lay on a bed with a remote control, shot glass and bowl of chips on his stomach. Serge paced, ranting into a pocket recorder.

Two hours. Coleman slumped against a wall next to a broken lamp. Serge did a handstand in the corner.

Three hours. Coleman lay under the bed. Serge was down in the parking lot running high school suicide sprints.

Four hours. Serge ran in and urgently shook Coleman by the shoulder. "Wake up! Wake up! The gelatin's ready!"

Coleman raised his head and bonked it on the bottom of the toilet tank. "Ow. How'd that get there?"

"Stop fooling around and meet me at the mini-fridge."

Coleman employed his patented wedged-between-the-tub-and-toilet escape wiggle. "Wait for me! . . ."

Serge grabbed the door handle, then paused and looked over with a gleam in his eye. "This is going to be so excellent."

Coleman knelt next to him. "Do it already!"

Serge opened the door, and their smiles fell with their jaws.

"It melted clean through the Tupperware," said Coleman. "Only the ring around the edge is left."

Serge's eyes moved down. "And melted through the rack it was on. And through the bottom of the fridge . . ." He quickly pulled the appliance aside.

"And through the floor." Coleman stuck his face in the dark hole. "How far do you think it goes?"

Serge's face joined him. "The foundation of this second-floor room might have stopped it. Or they have the lights off in the room below."

"What'll we do?"

"Better call the front desk and tell them we don't like this room. Or the room under us."

A police commando unit tossed flash-bang grenades and boarded a Guatemalan fishing boat full of marijuana. They led four handcuffed crew members onto the bank of the Miami River.

"Mahoney stood in his office window, watched the raid go down like Linda Lovelace . . ."

He observed the drawbridge go up and wondered where Serge was. "Mahoney was nines to the Brook Campanella case tanking sour, and he'd gone a little soft for the dame."

It was unlike Serge not to call while on a case, but he didn't dare to do so since realizing Mahoney's line was tapped.

A rotary desk phone rang. Mahoney answered with uncharacteristic speed.

"Shaka-laka . . ."

"Yes, this is Wesley Chapel from Big Dipper Data Management. I'm calling because you asked me to keep an eye out for anything from an Enzo Tweel or a South Philly Sal. Couldn't really do anything with the latter because I only have a first name, but I thought you'd want to know that an Enzo Tweel checked out of a resort on Biscayne Boulevard a half hour ago. We got lucky. He apparently has some third-party credit card that isn't coming up, but he used a computer in the business center to print an airline boarding pass under his name, and I confirmed his departure with the front desk."

"Mojo Dingus."

"You're welcome."

Mahoney hung up and began dialing again. He listened to the rings, but Serge wasn't answering. He tried several more times with the same non-luck. Mahoney wanted to leave a voice-mail message, but the rotary phone didn't have any buttons for menu selection number two.

Mahoney got an idea. He reached in a case file and decided to try another number.

Elegant hands in long white gloves gestured confidently toward the product line on the table.

". . . This functionally attractive ensemble is from our new Fridge-smart collection, featuring modular design to maximize your valuable storage space and preserve flavor . . . Next, a colorful assortment of summer-cool pitchers to please the entire family and keep those beverages—"

"Serge, do I have to wear the white gloves?"

"Yes!" Serge lowered the microphone attached to a miniature karaoke amplifier and barked in whispers: "Stop it! You're ruining my presentation!" He raised the microphone and smiled again at the audience. "Sorry about that. Where were we? Oh, yes, and these Freezer Mate tubs are perfect for leftovers in a cost-conscious lifestyle . . ." Serge handed the microphone to Coleman.

". . . And the vacuum-fresh burp seals make them perfect to store your dope for a potent, more satisfying smoke . . ."

The audience was wide-eyed.

It was an audience of one, gagged and tied to a chair between the beds of a flimsy motel room just north of the Miami airport.

Serge finished the presentation and entered the next phase . . .

A half hour later, they were both lying on their stomachs on opposite beds, watching TV.

Coleman stuck something in his mouth. *Munch, munch, munch.* "I love this episode. It's the one with all Madonna songs."

Serge stuck something in his own mouth. *Munch, munch, munch.* "But it's not without a message. Take the song 'Express Yourself,' about self-empowerment in the world of men."

"The music's starting," said Coleman. *Munch, munch, munch.*

"I feel something coming on," said Serge. *Munch, munch, munch.*

"Me, too," said Coleman.

One minute later, both were dancing on their beds.

Serge: *"Express yourself! . . ."*

Coleman: *"Heyyyy, Heyyyy! . . ."*

The music ended. Coleman grabbed something off a platter. "I love *Glee.*"

"Me, too," said Serge. "Can I have a celery and cream cheese?"

"Trade you for a deviled egg."

"Deal." Two arms reached across the hostage's lap between the beds and exchanged finger food.

"This is the best Tupperware party ever!" said Coleman.

"And my neck doesn't itch!"

They high-fived in front of the captive's face.

"But it seems like we're forgetting something," said Coleman.

"I know what you're talking about," said Serge. "I just can't put my finger on it."

They stared quizzically at each other, then at their captive, then at each other again. Eyebrows shot up in unison: "The fridge!"

They hopped off their beds and collided in their haste.

"Good thing they let us get another room," said Coleman.

"It was only right," said Serge. "The floor in the other one was unsafe."

He opened the fridge and removed a ridiculously heavy cast-iron pot. "Lucky for us that they sold these more durable gelatin molds at the big-box store . . . You know what to do."

Coleman knocked all the plastic tubs off the display table and dragged it in front of the captive. Then he laid a baking tray on top. It was also made of cast iron.

Serge strained against the weight of the iron pot as he waddled across the room and flipped it over. *"Carefullllllll . . ."* He slowly lifted it, leaving a large, circular gelatin disk in the middle of the table.

"There!" Serge looked up at the guest and smiled. "Since you won all of our Tupperware parlor games—actually by forfeit since nobody else was here—you get the grand finale tribute celebration . . . That's right, a Jell-O cake . . ."

Serge stuck a single birthday candle in the middle.

Coleman reached with his lighter.

"Not yet." Serge's hand explored the bottom of his hip pocket. "Here we go!"

"An M-80?"

"These were mythical to me as a kid. Way beyond cherry bombs in strength, and totally waterproof." He squished it down into the center of the gelatin so that the only exposed part was the tip of the fuse, resting against the base of the candle. "Fire that fucker!"

Coleman flicked his Bic as Serge cut the room lights. The candle glowed in three faces.

Serge sat on the side of a bed. The hostage turned his head ninety degrees left to look at him. Serge grinned and leaned forward, crossing his arms on the guest's shoulder. He moved his mouth to within inches of the man's ear: "I know that South Philly Sal and Enzo are the same person, and have been searching for you for two long years. Well, now you're here, and now I need closure. And I know what you're thinking: You're wondering what *I'm* thinking. But that snake could eat its own tail forever, so I'll just tell you. That candle will burn down to the M-80, and then it's every kid's fantasy. Except yours. You'll be covered with chemically burning Jell-O that will stick like napalm and hurt worse than your most horrible nightmares. But on the bright side! . . ." Serge reached behind his back and thrust a bottle in the man's face. "You've entered the bonus round!" He slammed the bottle down next to the Jell-O cake with the ever-burning candle. "That vinegar is the platinum prize. It will stop the chemical reaction on your skin. As you've probably noticed, the chairs in this motel have arms, and your hands are tied to them instead of behind your back. But the ropes are nylon: normally strong but chemically cheesy. I did that as a favor to you. When the cake goes off, the nylon should melt away faster than your burns and allow you to reach the bottle. But remember, pain is an illusion: The first minute is insanely disorienting, but the wounds are still only superficial at that point. Later, it's a disaster. So my parlor-party-game advice to you is keep your head and focus on that bottle. Got it?" Serge stood and slapped his guest on the back. "Let me know how it turns out."

They headed for the door.

"*Express yourself!* . . ."

"*Heyyy! Heyyy!* . . ."

Chapter THIRTY-SIX

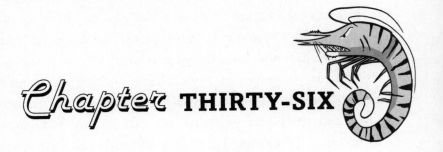

THE NEXT DAY

Ocean Drive.

Coleman held up a newspaper. "I see what you mean about the joy of reading. There's this story about a chemically scarred body found in a motel room."

"That's unusual."

"Says he was found lying in shattered glass with the label from a vinegar bottle in his hand."

"Ouch. Someone must have placed the vinegar bottle too close to the M-80," said Serge. "But I never shirk responsibility. My bad."

Coleman flipped over to the comics.

"Listen, I don't want you to take this the wrong way," said Serge. "But it's almost noon. Can you make yourself scarce?"

Coleman looked around the sidewalk café. "But I thought we were going to eat."

"When I said 'we,' that didn't mean us."

"Oh, I get it now. Brook's meeting you for lunch." Coleman stood and stuck the paper under his arm. "Say no more. I don't want to be a fifth wheel." He looked inside the restaurant. "There's the bar! . . ."

Serge watched Coleman depart with his trademark swerve. Then he looked back down Ocean Drive. The café was much like the Fandango, but there was no way he could ever digest food there again. For several blocks north of the Colony Hotel, the beach had no shortage of top-shelf alfresco diners. Many featured wooden stands strategically placed for passersby to be tempted by plates of lobster, filet mignon and iced-down stone crabs.

Serge stared at the empty seat on the other side of his intimate table. He checked his watch, then looked up again.

There she was, all smiles, waving to him a block away and carrying a designer shopping bag. So that's why she was late. Well, good for her, starting to bounce back from everything.

Serge was about to stand when an unexpected guest pulled up a chair.

"Excuse me," said Serge. "This table's taken."

"I know." The man smiled. "Just like the table was taken two years ago."

The words punched him in the gut. Serge whipped his hand behind his back.

The man continued smiling and pressed a pistol under the table against Serge's crotch. He shook his head. "You're not that fast. Now put your hands where I can see them."

Serge did as told.

"Remember I still have the gun pointed and it's a light trigger pull." The guest leaned back in his chair like he didn't have a concern. "So we finally meet."

"So South Philly Sal was a red herring." Serge shook his head. "You're the real Enzo Tweel."

"At least that's what my passport says this week."

"You've got me, okay?" said Serge. "Leave Brook out of it. She's an innocent bystander."

"That's an interesting idea," said Enzo. "Except I love sequels."

Serge scanned the surroundings with peripheral vision, trying not to allow his pupils to move and give him away as he sought possibilities.

"I know what you're doing," said Enzo. "There are no possibilities. Why don't you just accept your fate with dignity?"

Brook reached the edge of the café, smiling even more buoyantly with a cheerful hop in her step. At the other end of the dynamic, all the rage in Serge's life had just been eclipsed by what he felt now. He wanted to sound the warning, but correctly assumed Enzo's training. She could be taken out the second he tried anything.

Brook finally reached the table. "Hey, Serge, I didn't know you were bringing a friend." She took a seat on the other side and placed the shopping bag in her lap. "My name's Brook." She extended a hand.

"Enzo." He switched the pistol under the table to his left and shook. "Pleasure to meet."

Brook looked down and reached into her shopping bag. "Serge, I found these great new shoes that were on sale. Only two hundred dollars. Want to see them? . . . Serge? Is something the matter?"

Enzo put his free hand on hers. "It's nothing. We were just remembering a mutual friend who isn't with us anymore."

"Oh, that's sad." Brook turned to her new beau. "Were you close?"

"That was a long time ago," said Serge. "Enzo's right—it's nothing."

Enzo looked at each in turn. "How do we want to order? Serge, you want to order first? Or how about Brook?"

"But we don't have any menus yet," said Brook.

Serge was well aware of this. It was code.

"I think Serge should go first this time," said Enzo. "That way Brook can see what's on the menu for her."

Serge had made his decision. When the moment came, he would simply upend the table and dive into the gun. Of course Enzo was a pro and would be able to get several shots off; Serge would take the bullets but knock him down in the process, giving Brook a chance to escape.

"Okay, enough games," said Enzo. "You've been a thorn for far too long, and I have a plane to catch."

Brook looked around the table. "I don't understand what's going on."

The countdown clock reached zero.

Serge began to spring, but the shot was too fast.

Bang.

Serge jolted back in his chair.

The next second seemed an eternity. Serge's head fell toward his chest. Checking for blood that wasn't there. Then he noticed only two of them were left at the table. He looked toward the ground and saw Enzo on his back, eyes surprisingly wide, with a softball-size hole in his chest.

Patrons began to scream and stampede.

Serge turned with an open mouth toward Brook, who was holding a designer shopping bag. Smoke drifted out through a burn hole in the bottom of the bag, near the end of a concealed sawed-off shotgun.

Serge blinked hard. "Something tells me you didn't buy shoes."

She reached across the table and seized his hand. "We need to get the hell out of here. I'll fill you in . . ."

They took off running down Ocean Drive.

Epilogue

A cardboard sign hung from the doorknob of Mahoney's office on the Miami River:

GONE FISSING.

Fifty miles south, a black Firebird with a Florida-winged skull on the hood crossed the bridge from the mainland to Key Largo.

"That was some adventure, eh?" said Serge.

Brook was sitting up front with him. Her hand out the window, catching the wind like a kid. "Is this how you always live?"

"Most of the time."

One of the passengers in the backseat had a porkpie hat and the other a joint. Coleman turned to Mahoney and offered the doobie. "Wanna toke?"

"Hophead."

Coleman shrugged and took the hit himself.

They passed a fake conch shell, as tall as a building, where tourists were snapping photos. Then a giant lobster and a giant mermaid.

"It still hasn't sunk in," said Serge. "I've never had such a close one."

"You can thank Mahoney," said Brook.

Serge looked up in the rearview. A hand tipped the porkpie.

Brook cracked open a wine cooler and smiled as they crossed a bridge with emerald-and-turquoise water all around.

Serge smiled as well and stuck his own hand out into the wind. "I just can't believe how it all came together."

"The last piece was the call from Big Dipper that Enzo had printed his boarding pass at a resort," said Brook. "Which meant he wasn't at the Tortugas Inn."

"And wasn't South Philly Sal," said Serge.

"Except Mahoney couldn't get the word to you because you had stopped taking calls. So he tried my number from his client files. And used a different phone because of the tap on his."

"And after I thought I'd killed Enzo and started taking calls again . . ."

"You didn't know he was still alive," said Brook. "So I told Mahoney to call you and set up lunch. But we couldn't let you in on it because Enzo was still listening. We *planned* on him listening. There was no way he wouldn't show up at that café and expose himself."

"But your shotgun was empty," said Serge. "Personally checked it twice."

"I took a cab from the motel to get some ammo."

"You left the room after I told you not to?"

Brook opened another wine cooler. "We're still breathing, aren't we?"

"Can't argue with that . . ."

MIAMI REPUBLICAN HEADQUARTERS

Roger sat on the opposite side of the desk from Jansen.

"I know you'll think I'm crazy, but I had the weirdest dream a couple nights ago and haven't stopped freaking out. You were in it."

"Were we in a warehouse?" asked Jansen. "With Serge, Jesus, a hostage and a lobster?"

"How'd you know?"

"I've been freaking out, too." Jansen uncapped a prescription bottle. "Doctor has me on sedatives."

"I did some thinking," said Roger. "We've been bickering about the trivial, when there's a serious crime problem in South Florida."

"No kidding." Jansen chased his pill with a cup of water. "Chills me to the bone that there are people like Serge just walking around out there . . ."

And thus it was decided to form: Republicans and Democrats United for a Better Miami.

BIG DIPPER DATA MANAGEMENT

A small army of police officers hovered over the shoulder of Wesley Chapel.

The analyst pointed at a computer screen with his pen. "I plotted hits here, here and here. Three of them traveling together, possibly four."

"And they're heading down the Keys?" asked one of the cops.

"That would be my bet."

"Wonder where they are now?"

A Firebird crested the hump of the Seven Mile Bridge. Everyone euphoric from the palette of creation in all directions. It called for another round of tropical drinks, except bottled water for Serge. Off-key singing from the quartet drifted out the window.

" 'Waistin' away again in Margaritaville—' "

Blooooooosh.

"Coleman!"